10/18

SEEKING
Hyde

To the memory of my sister
Penelope Reed Doob
(1943–2017)
Spirit of play and soul of inspiration . . .

SEEKING

Hyde

A NOVEL

THOMAS REED

**BEAUFORT
BOOKS**

The following collections were quoted with permission:

Stevenson, Robert Louis, and Thea Kliros. *Childs Garden of Verses*. Dover Pubns., 1993.

Stevenson, Robert Louis, and Katherine Linehan. *Strange Case of Dr. Jekyll and Mr. Hyde: An Authoritative Text, Backgrounds and Contexts, Performance Adaptations, Criticism*. New York: Norton, 2003.

Stevenson, Robert Louis., and Ernest Mehew. *Selected Letters of Robert Louis Stevenson*. New Haven: Yale Univ. Press, 2001.

Stevenson, Robert Louis, and Janet Adam Smith. *Collected Poems (of) Robert Louis Stevenson Edited*, with an Introduction and Notes, by Janet Adam Smith. London: Hart Davis, 1971.

"Casebook: Jack the Ripper - Times (London)." Casebook: Jack the Ripper - Introduction to the Case. Accessed June 07, 2018. http://www.casebook.org/press_reports/times/.

Punch Magazine

Library of Congress Cataloging-in-Publication Data available upon request

For inquiries about orders, please contact:
Beaufort Books
27 West 20th Street, 11th Floor
New York, NY 10011

Published in the United States by Beaufort Books
www.beaufortbooks.com

Distributed by Midpoint Trade Books
www.midpointtrade.com

Printed in the United States of America

Reed, Thomas
Seeking Hyde

ISBN:
hardcover: 9780825308833
eBook: 9780825307713

Cover Design by Michael Short, cover image courtesy of Shutterstock
Interior Layout Design by Mark Karis

A Note to Readers

Much of what follows is fact—or could be.

Much of what follows is fiction—or could be.

Some disentangling of the one from the other may be found among the final pages.

Retrospective

(Stevenson to J. M. Barrie, 2 or 3 April, 1893)

Vailima

My dear Barrie.

Thank you for your most amusing self-portrait. Tit for tat. Now for your correspondent, holed up here in Samoa:

R.L.S.

The Tame Celebrity

Native name, Tusi Tala ("Tale-Teller")

Exceedingly lean, dark, rather ruddy—black eyes crow's-footed, beginning to be grizzled, general appearance of a blasted boy—or blighted youth—or to borrow Carlyle on De Quincey "Child that has been in hell." Past eccentric—obscure and O no we never mention it—presently industrious, respectable and fatuously contented. Used to be very fond of talking about Art, don't talk about it any more. Name in family, The Tame Celebrity. Cigarettes without intermission except when coughing or kissing. Hopelessly entangled in apron strings. Drinks plenty. Curses some. Temper unstable. Manners purple on an emergency, but liable to trances. Eternally the common old copybook gentleman of commerce: if accused of cheating at cards, would feel bound to blow out accuser's brains, little as he would like the job. Has been an invalid for ten years, but can boldly claim that you can't tell it on him. Given to explaining the universe. Scotch, sir, Scotch.

And now my dear fellow I want to thank you, encore un fois, for your last. I am quite sure that I know you and quite sure that you know me. People mayn't be like their books. They are their books.

Robert Louis Stevenson

Part One

FERRIER

1

I was born in the year 18— to a large fortune, endowed besides with excellent parts, inclined by nature to industry, fond of the respect of the wise and good among my fellow men, and thus, as might have been supposed, with every guarantee of an honourable and distinguished future. And indeed the worst of my faults was a certain impatient gaiety of disposition, such as has made the happiness of many, but such as I found it hard to reconcile with my imperious desire to carry my head high, and wear a more than commonly grave countenance towards the public. Hence it came about that I concealed my pleasures.
—HENRY JEKYLL, *STRANGE CASE OF DR. JEKYLL AND MR. HYDE* (1886)

LONDON, APRIL 1883

"Good morning, Mr. Stevenson. May I call you a hansom?"

The moderately well known author of *Treasure Island* was passing through the paneled foyer of the Savile Club towards the front door, leather traveling-case in hand. He paused in mid-stride, canting his head to catch up with what he had just heard. The ache in his right temple flared with the gesture into a stab of real pain, but he huffed it resolutely away.

"Beg pardon?" he asked, setting down the well-worn Gladstone and turning to the roundish attendant.

"A hansom, sir. May I call you a cab?"

"Ah! Yes, of course. A cab." He pinched at his chevron of a moustache, wondering distractedly if the man had exchanged any words with the night porter as he began his day—perhaps heard an embarrassing tale involving the past evening. The fellow's expression seemed stolid enough. "I'm afraid my mind was elsewhere," explained the writer. "I thought you'd asked, 'May I call you handsome?'"

"Oh my goodness, no."

It occurred to Stevenson that his flippant candor might have caused the man discomfort. It was something he might have called back, something that would not likely have escaped him in the first place had last night's indulgences not left his judgment somewhat compromised. He scanned the porter's face for a sign of his response. The ghost of a twinkle in his eye seemed the only possible rift in his professional composure. "Of course not. Much relieved, though, Dobbs. It would have been forward of you, don't you think?"

"Of course, sir," the man replied, with what was unmistakably a narrow smile. "Very forward indeed."

Stevenson nodded. What to say? "Now, Mrs. Stevenson, for some reason, frequently tells me I'm handsome."

"Of course she does, sir."

"Blinded by love, I expect." He managed a grin. "Are you a married man, Dobbs?" *And if so,* he wondered on the fly, *must your wife ever assist you to your bed of a drunken evening, as I was assisted only hours ago…sadly not by my spouse?*

"Why, yes, sir. Blessed to be, sir. Been dead and married, what, these thirty years?"

"'Dead and married,'" echoed Stevenson through a chuckle that approached a cough. "Excellent, Dobbs. Worth remembering." On a burdened morning such as this, an ounce of levity was worth hours of light opera on a sunnier day. Perhaps he could risk one more sally, if only to be sure his wits were truly restored. "Not to belabor a point, but

I do sometimes find it a wee bit confusing when anyone but my dear wife, you know, claims to find me…" Stevenson's hand fluttered to his unfashionably long brown locks.

"Of course, sir. Very sorry, sir."

"No need for apologies," declared the writer. "It was all in my damned head, wasn't it?" Damned head indeed! "No escaping it. We writers are constantly making things up."

"Yes, sir. And it does you credit, if you ask me."

"That's very good of you, Dobbs, I'm sure. Now, shall we put it all behind us? And, yes, thank you. Please do."

"Sir?"

"Do call me a hansom." He winked at the man, not without another twinge in his temple. "If you'd be so kind."

"Of course, sir. Right away." Dobbs snatched the bag from the lustrous tile and backed decorously towards the door. "Thank you, sir."

Waiting at the portico, taking in a reviving breath, Stevenson wondered how many London clubs boasted attendants as ready as this man to take such measured but refreshing liberties. Likely none. The Savile, though, had been specifically founded on "relaxed" principles. This, Stevenson assured himself, was the sole reason he hadn't laughed in Colvin's face nine years back when his friend and mentor offered to propose for membership an unknown scribbler such as himself. A quasi-Socialist Bohemian into the bargain, if Stevenson's *père*'s despairing estimate were to be trusted! As it happened, the Savile had proven an oasis of tempered ease amidst the arid respectability of Mayfair, especially since it had fled Savile Row and resettled just across Piccadilly from Green Park.

Today, of all days, it was cheering to witness that *soupçon* of wit flit across Dobbs's lips. The news in from Edinburgh with the most recent post weighed on him gravely, a fact he recalled trying to explain to Dobbs's fellow porter just the other side of a fitful sleep—as though sad tidings might excuse his humiliating condition. He tapped his stick, straightened his hat, felt vaguely for the letter in the breast pocket of his frock coat, and stepped as resolutely as he could manage down to the street.

"Thank you, Dobbs," he said, smiling as he joined the attendant at the curbside. "I am much obliged."

"Not at all, sir." The man extended his arm to help the lanky figure up into the cab, then handed up the bag. "Travel safely, Mr. Stevenson."

"Thank you, Dobbs. And thank you also for your flattering observations. Truly voiced or not. King's Cross, please, driver."

As the cab lurched away in a clatter of hooves, Stevenson craned back to spy Dobbs looking out after him, tautly erect in the morning sun. A full grin split the man's ruddy face. Heaven only knew what exactly for.

Settling himself on the tufted bench, Stevenson unbuttoned his coat and checked his watch. 8:43. The Flying Scotsman departed at ten sharp. That would put him into Waverley Station shortly after six in the evening, in time to drop his bag at his parents' house before joining Baxter in Old Town for dinner—assuming they bothered to eat. Well, eat they must, he quietly told himself. Surely, by then, he would be able to compass the thought of a meal.

He gazed idly at the minute engraving inside the cover of the turnip. *Robert Louis Stevenson, Attorney, 16 July, 1875. From an Admiring Father and Mother.* That legal career had lasted, what? A matter of weeks? Nothing more than an effective but disingenuous bridge between the engineering career he'd refused to pursue and the literary life to which Thomas Stevenson had sworn no son of his would ever stoop. He grinned, shook his head, closed the timepiece with a snap, and slipped it back into his vest pocket.

The hansom rattled through Piccadilly Circus and on up Shaftesbury Avenue, moving at a brisk trot despite the morning crush. Just short of Charing Cross Road, they slowed. There was some sort of disturbance ahead, and waves of curious pedestrians flowed across the thoroughfare and swelled into a mass on the left pavement.

Stevenson tapped on the hatch and the cabman opened up.

"What is it, do you know?" asked Stevenson.

"Can't rightly say, sir. P'raps we'll see in a moment."

"My train departs at ten."

"Naught to worry you, sir. There's a mess o' Metropolitans on the scene already. 'Ello there, constable! They'll see us through, certain."

The hansom edged forward until Stevenson could see through the shifting crowd. A slender, plainly dressed young man stood above the throng atop an imposing row of hogsheads stacked on a brewer's dray. His face was crimson, his veins distended, and he flourished his cloth cap right and left like a limp cattle switch. He was doing his best to shout over the buzzing crowd. Stevenson could pick up a phrase here, a word there—"Devil's cargo," "brothers," "every dram!" Some of the jockeying masses shook their fists and roared, "Aye!" Others scrambled to pull the lad from his perch, and he kicked vigorously at their grasping hands. "Fearful rocks," he bellowed on, struggling to maintain his balance. "Tear the bottom." Something "of life." Barque? "Barque of life?"

"Damme! It's them teetotalers again," sneered the driver, leaning his head into the cab. Stevenson caught a whiff of gin on the man's breath. Gin and onions. He bit back the urge to retch. "Lawson's mob. Can't abide a single drop, that lot. And can't abide no-one else 'avin' 'is." A belch might have added the perfect touch. Another pickled cabman. Everyman at Work. "I'd like to jump down and fix 'is wagon."

"I quite understand," remarked Stevenson, thinking that he himself would have done well to embrace Sir Wilfrid's abstemious principles the previous evening. "At the same time, there's a train to catch."

"Naught to worry about, guv'nor. Like I said." The hatch clapped shut, and the lean bay was soon back at a trot, wheeling them north towards the Great Eastern terminal.

Naught to worry about. That might be the case, for the short and the long term equally. It was hard to take too seriously any soul who could declaim in public about "the barque of life," if that is what the fellow had indeed said. Facile metaphors tried Stevenson sorely; at times, he thought, adversely affecting his digestion—especially on days when he had risen early and damaged. Still, disruptions like this one had become frequent throughout Britain as the multiple incarnations of the Temperance Movement grew ever bolder and more organized. Their nay-saying militancy had provoked an equally fervent and boisterous opposition, such that uniformed soldiers of the Salvation Army were now regularly challenged by rag-tag masses dubbing themselves a "Skeleton Army." Marching under a black flag emblazoned with skull and cross bones, Stevenson had been intrigued to learn, these real-life, gin-swilling mates of Long John Silver had taken to pelting their sanctimonious opponents with anything they could lay their drunken hands on: mud, stones, paint, hot coals—even, in one lurid incident, dead cats. Their increasingly violent clashes had left millenarian pundits at the *Times* declaring that the Drink Question had turned "one nation into two"—as indeed, thought Stevenson ruefully, drink itself so often turned a man against his own better judgment. Thinking selfishly, Stevenson doubted any new legislation would ever deny wine-lovers such as himself the pleasure of an evening glass or two.

In any event, any resolution to the fiery debate wouldn't matter much for Ferrier. The damage had long been done.

Goodge Street. Another ten minutes? Stevenson reached for the letter that had found him in Bournemouth the day before and called him away on the next express to London. He raised the flap of the envelope, removing and unfolding the single sheet of bond stationery. *Dearest Louis*, wrote his mother. *It pains me beyond words to let you know that we have heard again from Mrs. Ferrier. As we feared, poor Walter continues to decline, and his dear mother assures us that it must now be weeks and not months before he goes to his Eternal Rest.*

It struck Stevenson once again that Margaret Stevenson had not mentioned an "Eternal *Reward*." But would a good Scottish Calvinist ever use the term? Rewards presupposed a measure of control over one's doings on this earth—merit for deeds freely chosen, virtue freely embraced; an orange for the good boy, a wormy apple for the bad. Neither the watered-down catechisms of his nursery nor the interminable harangues of his boyhood kirk had ever spoken to him of "rewards"—scarcely ever about "choice," if truth were told. And by what Christian theology, even those based on some notion of the free and independent will, would Ferrier in particular "rest?" Would he not writhe interminably in deserved or undeserved perdition? Poor Walter! Had he ever been able to steer his "barque" at all?

Your father and I, he read on, *know how consuming your affairs have become these recent days and months. We are profoundly gratified to see the path upon which you have so promisingly ventured of late. Nevertheless, I know you realize that we are put on this earth to look after those who are dear to us. Walter, I know, yearns to see you one last time before he departs. Please, if ever you may, dear Louis, hasten home and dispatch this last obligation to one who has counted you among his most faithful friends. With the greatest hopes of seeing and embracing you very soon, I remain, as ever, your loving Mother.*

He lowered the sheet despondently to his lap. Could there have been any doubt he would come? He dearly hoped not. At the same time, he was pained to recall, his father had once declared that his sole child's godless antics had rendered his own life "an utter failure." The words of that particular missive had ever after stuck in Stevenson's head with the tenacity of a jagged splinter: *I would ten times sooner have seen you lying in your grave than that you should be shaking the faith of other young men and bringing such ruin on other houses as you have brought already upon this.* A father who could pen such words might easily think anything of him. Still, more nights than he could remember, Stevenson had staggered back to Ferrier's rooms under the weight of his nodding friend, lowering him into his bed and tossing a blanket over his crumpled frame before he lurched back to his own digs as first light began to glow over Arthur's Seat. One did not hold a man's head while he vomited or shield his eyes from a clawing whore and not speed to his deathbed when the call arrived.

The cab turned east on Euston Road and shortly pulled up at King's Cross. Modestly invigorated by all the fresh air, the writer leapt down from the cab, paying the driver and adding a generous tip. He glanced up at the station clock. Half past nine.

"You've made good time," he called up to the man. "Thank you."

"And thank you, sir, for making it worth my while." The fellow pocketed the coins with a grin.

"Well, good day, then." Stevenson expected he knew exactly where the fare and aptly named *pourboire* would go—most likely before the man took on his next passenger. There was a row of already-busy public houses just to the right, a half-dozen empty cabs pulled up in front of them.

"Your bag, sir?"

"Ah, yes," sighed Stevenson. It pained him to be this dull and distracted.

"G'day, sir."

Stevenson turned and raised his eyes to the terminal's façade, two huge glassed archways flanking an Italianate clock tower. With a half-dozen entrance doors from which he was free to choose—or so the anti-Calvinist within him presumed—Stevenson made for the centermost portal of the right-hand arch, aiming for Platform 10. He did not have the slightest notion how he missed seeing the little flower girl standing just inside the entrance. In a trice, she was down on the pavement in front of him, and it was all he could do to keep from treading on her. He extended his stride to avoid crushing a slender arm, but his heel landed squarely on a tangle of flower stems and skidded away in a slick green mash. Fortunately a stout man in a bowler, just to his right, caught his arm as he made to crash over backwards, holding him up as he got his feet back under himself.

"Oh my!" sputtered Stevenson, dropping his bag and reaching down to the blonde mite who lay there in a scattering of bright yellow daffodils. "Have I hurt you? Are you injured?"

"Just frightened, I expect," said the man with the bowler. "Isn't that right, little miss?"

Frozen at first, the girl soon nodded, though biting back tears. Stevenson helped her to her feet and brushed ineffectually at her threadbare frock. There was more bone than flesh to her. "Aye!" she replied.

"What a brave girl you are!" said Stevenson, gathering up the flowers. "And what a clumsy sod I am, running you down that way. I am so sorry. Can you ever forgive me?"

The girl stood and gazed uncertainly then slowly nodded. A single tear coursed down over pale skin the thinness of which Stevenson thought he had never seen. It was like a dusting of flour on glass.

"Here, I'll take them all," he said, stooping again to pick up the last of the flowers. "Will a shilling do? Two shillings?"

The girl's eyes widened and she nodded energetically.

"We'll make it three shillings then," he declared, dropping the coins one after the other into her dirty palm. "Will you forgive me, milady?" He went to one knee, taking both of her tiny hands into his own. "Will you accept a gentleman's sincere apology?"

"Oh, yes, sir," she piped, blushing as she grinned. "Bless you, sir."

"All's right, then?"

She nodded.

"Good. And bless you, too." He caught the bowler man's eye as she scampered away. "Would that all of our carelessness could be put right so easily."

"That's the gospel truth," said the other. "We'd all of us sleep better, would we not?"

Stevenson had dreaded the eight-hour journey north, alone with his thoughts. In the event, he found himself sharing a compartment with most agreeable company. Mostly agreeable, that is: a dour Scots barrister-type peered judgmentally over the top of his *Times* every time the writer lit a cigarette, which these days was increasingly often. Stevenson's wife berated him endlessly for what she histrionically referred to as his "addiction," claiming that a man with tender lungs could ill afford to fill them with tobacco smoke every time he had the chance. Often enough he simply nodded and allowed that it was a wretched habit. Now and again, though, he indulged the urge to reply that if her affection for him were as tender as she took his lungs to be, she might be less censorious. Then again, she and her son had willingly left the sun-drenched heaven of California and followed him back to a bleak insular climate about as salubrious as the inside of a drainpipe. They had cast in their lots entirely with his own, with no reservations he had been able to detect. It seemed only fair that he should try to keep himself alive—as long as he possibly could—for their collective welfare. If only Fanny worried less. Or stopped smoking herself.

The pretty young woman sitting across from him looked up and he suddenly realized he had been staring. She cast him a benign smile, easy enough to return. She was a governess, as he learned after a polite inquiry, on her way to York with one of her charges, the seven-year-old lad perched just to her left. The aesthenic scamp peered intently out the window as the landscape rushed by, his eyes wide with wonder.

Stevenson smiled. He had been a similar age when he took his first trip to Glasgow, along with his mother and father, but virtually glued to the side of his austere nursemaid. He remembered as though it were yesterday the dizzying thrill of the occasion, as the varied countryside hurtled past at an impossible pace. Ever since, whichever of his mental faculties it was that brought him his dreams had found an occasional but highly effective use for that vertiginous feeling of momentum, that enthralling sense of helpless acceleration.

Stevenson leaned towards the boy. "Is this your first journey by rail?" he asked.

The boy looked at him and shook his head, slightly apprehensive, it seemed, at being addressed by a perfect stranger.

"William has been to Edinburgh before," explained the young woman as she adjusted her trim figure in her seat. "And to Bath as well."

"Ah, Edinburgh," nodded Stevenson, leaning back on the plush bench. "That is where I am bound, in fact. All the way to Edinburgh. And do you enjoy riding on the train, then?"

The boy looked towards his custodian, who nodded her reassurance.

"Yes, indeed," he answered in a reedy little voice.

"And riding backwards? Are you happy enough to ride backwards?" Again the look for approval. Another nod.

"Very happy, thank you." The boy blinked at him uncertainly.

"Well if you tire of it," declared Stevenson, folding his hands neatly, "I would be more than happy to exchange seats with you. I am perfectly content riding along backwards. Seeing where I have been, you know. Surprised by where I'm arriving. It's most exciting!" He gazed over at the girl, who smiled in frank amusement. She was remarkably attractive: pale oval face, glowing chestnut locks, grey-blue eyes that sparkled with intelligence and wit. Where was she headed, he wondered? Beyond York. In life. Her finished manner spoke to good breeding, although the prospects for a young woman in her position were not particularly scintillating. He turned, with a sniff, back to the lad, who now studied him closely.

"If you were to ride a horse, shall we say, would you prefer to ride backwards or forwards?" asked Stevenson.

"Why, forwards, of course."

"And why is that?"

"So as not to ride under a tree branch...and clonk the back of my head," said the boy with a grin, "and tumble off into the dirt."

"No, we shouldn't like that, should we?" laughed Stevenson. "Dirt being so...dirty and all."

The boy giggled. "And heads not liking to be clonked and all."

"Not in the least," agreed the writer. He struck his brow lightly with the heel of his hand, crossing his eyes for effect. Again that giggle, liquid as a freshet bubbling off a heathered hill. There was such joy to be had in childhood, ready to burst out anywhere at all, on the instant, even in the least likely of places. His thoughts slid back to the little flower girl at King's Cross and he wondered if she had moments of joy. What might they entail? A minute or two resting in the sun? A sliver of warm pie?

"Can you read?" Stevenson asked the boy as he pulled his thoughts back to the speeding train.

"A bit. I'm just learning."

"He's a very good reader," the young lady affirmed, patting the boy's hand. "An extremely apt pupil." A blush warmed the lad's face.

"And are there things you especially like to read about?"

The boy nodded enthusiastically. "Of course there are! I like to read about knights who are heroes. And dragons. And fairies. And sometimes pirates."

"Ah, fairies and pirates. Are you frightened of pirates, then?" asked Stevenson. "I am. Constantly. Even on trains." He looked apprehensively from side to side, and then pointed slyly at the paper-reading gentleman, who took no notice.

"There's no pirates on trains," declared the boy sagely. "Are there, Miss Winton?" He looked at the young woman, who shook her head. "You see? You needn't be afraid of pirates here, sir."

"That's most reassuring. Thank you. And do you like poems?"

"Very much."

"And how might you like a poem about riding on a train? And perhaps fairies?"

"Do you know one?" the lad asked eagerly.

"Not yet. But perhaps I shall write one for you."

The boy peered at him quizzically, as though he had just suggested they all sprout wings and fly off together to the moon.

"You don't believe me?" Goodness! Why ever had he asked that? Now the little chap looked cornered, as though he were sensing all this chatter had been calculated to tease him rather than to woo him. Stevenson recalled his earliest days with Sammy, when Fanny's son had seemed as inaccessible to him as the North Pole. "Let's just see, then," said the writer, bending to extract a notebook from his bag and snatching a pen from his pocket. The cap flew off in his haste and skittered across the carpeting, coming to rest against the governess's buttoned shoe.

"How clumsy. May I?" Stevenson made to reach down to retrieve the item.

"Of course," said the young woman, moving her foot slightly to make room.

"There," said Stevenson, as he sat back up, fighting the vague dizziness that still haunted him. "I shall take this as a challenge." He adjusted his trouser legs and looked squarely at the boy. "I solemnly swear that, well before we reach York, I shall have written a poem about riding in a railway carriage—backwards or forwards—which I shall present to you in token of my esteem for the gifted young reader you are reported to be. And there shall be fairies in said poem. Whether they wish to be in it or not." He looked up and caught the young lady's eye before he turned to her beaming pupil. "Satisfactory?"

"Satisfactory," nodded the boy, with a wriggle of excitement.

By the time they had reached Sheffield it was done. Not perfect, perhaps, but passable enough for a quick and distracted draft. Stevenson realized, in passing, that he hadn't lit a cigarette the entire time.

"There. Ink barely blotted. May I read it to you?"

"Please do," said the boy, scooting up to the edge of his seat.

"Very well. Off we go."

Faster than fairies, faster than witches,
Bridges and houses, hedges and ditches;
And charging along like troops in a battle
All through the meadows the horses and cattle:
All of the sights of the hill and the plain
Fly as thick as driving rain;

(Oh my! I think we're missing a foot there!)

And ever again, in the wink of an eye,
Painted stations whistle by.

(And again. My goodness!)

Here is a child who clambers and scrambles,
All by himself and gathering brambles;
Here is a tramp who stands and gazes;
And here is the green for stringing the daisies!
Here is a cart runaway in the road
Lumping along with man and load;
And here is a mill, and there is a river:
Each a glimpse and gone forever!

Stevenson set the notebook down with a moderate flourish. "Well, do you like it?"

"Ever so much," replied the boy, beaming anew. The other man glowered at the three of them as though all this were the quintessence of uselessness. The girl, in contrast, looked positively charmed.

"Very well, then. Let me make a fair copy for you. I shall tear it out of my book and you shall have it forever and ever. The original I shall keep against future need—should I ever write a book of poems about, well, trains and fairies. One never knows, does one? Now, to whom shall I dedicate it? William…?"

The boy looked confused.

"To William Forbes, if you please," volunteered the governess, now in an unguardedly appreciative voice. Under the circumstances, Stevenson found it curiously unsettling.

"To the Honorable Master William Forbes then," trumpeted Stevenson, "from his most humble wandering bard, Robert Louis Stevenson."

The sullen man's head jerked up. Was he familiar with the name? The fellow shook his paper and looked back down with a snort. Perhaps it was only compounded disdain for a modestly renowned waster of words, the writer first of a vapid pirate story and now this stranger-wooing silliness. It was oddly satisfying, though—giving a little something to this wee sensitive soul as he hurtled northwards, his back to an unknown future. To pay a tribute to another boyhood, glimpsed and then gone forever from his ken. Was it better than the three shillings, Stevenson wondered, that he had given to a hungry London waif? It was certainly less likely to put a meal on a table. Either for the boy or, now that he thought of it, for himself.

2

Poor Harry Jekyll…, my mind misgives me he is in deep waters! He was wild when he was young; a long time ago to be sure; but in the law of God, there is no statute of limitations.

—GABRIEL JOHN UTTERSON, ATTORNEY TO HENRY JEKYLL

EDINBURGH, APRIL 1883

St. Giles tolled midnight as Stevenson and Baxter rounded into Advocate's Close. They had visited a good half-dozen old haunts before they wound their way up West Bow to the High, and both men were well into their cups. There were few nights now when Baxter was not, if truth were told. As for the oenophile writer, he was finding that an evening's forced resort to whisky, relieved only by the occasional ale, was leaving him a trifle wobbly. There was powerfully little drinkable claret to be had in Old Town Edinburgh, and had Stevenson even managed to find a decent bottle, Baxter would surely have savaged him for his newfound Froggish tastes.

As they trundled into the vaulted narrow at the head of the sloped alleyway, their laughter swelled up hollowly around them. The sound bore Stevenson back even more relentlessly to student days and student nights, more than a few of which had found the two of them just here and just so, stumbling down the slick steps and landings of the constricted way.

"And you remember Ferrier would lean his shoulder into the wall here, and slide along like…who was it in *Bleak House?* Bill? Old Bill?" Baxter slapped at the wet stone, drew his hand back with a sneer, and wiped it on Stevenson's sleeve.

"Phil!" laughed Stevenson, brushing disgustedly at his arm. "*Phil's* mark it was. But yes. I do. Ferrier's…um…what? Ferrier's smudge! Wearing down Auld Reekie, one drunken ramble at a time. Like rain on stone. Like…"

"Here's to 'im, Johnson!" erupted Baxter, raising his right arm with an extravagant flourish. He overbalanced and lurched heavily against his companion.

"Easy, Thomson! Ye havnae a drop in yer han'. Ye canna toast wi' nae glass."

"Nae technicalities, Johnson. Dinna pester me wi' nae technicalities."

Twenty yards further on, two undergraduates exploded from a low door, one of them missing the step and crashing to the cobbles in a muffled thump. He spat out an indistinguishable curse.

"What be these?" queried Stevenson. "Pickled Ghosts of Christmas Past?"

"Ach, mon!" exclaimed Baxter as he lurched to a querulous halt. "Are ye thinkin' nou yer Scrooge?"

"Scrooge?"

"Eleazer Scrooge!" Baxter sneezed violently and his hat tumbled from his head. "Must you always, Lou-ee? Must you *always* fancy you're livin' in a soddin' book?" He bent to retrieve the headgear and slapped it carelessly back onto his pate.

Stevenson grinned indulgently at his old friend. "Was it I, laddie, conjured up the venereal Dickens just now? 'Old Bill!' Trust a lawyer to bugger the facts." The writer turned and stooped to help the fallen stranger to his feet while the man's fellow stood back from the three of them, giggling insipidly. Once erect, the fallen student pawed at his trousers and coat, belched loudly, and staggered towards the head of the close.

"This way, ye daft catamite," yelled his companion, wobbling down towards the bend that emptied into Cockburn Street. "D'you mean to sleep in the High?"

"I'll sleep where I want," barked the youth, struggling mightily to reverse his direction. "And I'll drink what I want. And I'll fuck whomever I want. I'll fuck…"

"Not in your condition, you won't fuck anyone," shot Baxter, sidling recklessly up in front of the man. "Not with breath like"—he sniffed extravagantly at the air around the lad's head—"like a bilious fart."

The drunken youth took a long moment to register the insult and then squared up in an attempt at belligerence. Baxter smirked at Stevenson. He turned back to the lad and wagged his chin, whereupon the fellow cocked his arm and swung gamely. He missed his mark, twisting again to the cobblestones and toppling sideways off his rump with a pitiful "Ow!"

"Bravo, Thomson," chuckled Stevenson. "Worthy of Rabelais. 'Breath like a bilious fart.' I wish I'd penned that!"

"How's for a couplet, then? A veritable Capulet?" Baxter leaned over his target, pinching his nostrils. "Out of *fart,*" he keened nasally, "shall issue *art.* Thusly. 'Breath like a bilious fart—Da! Da! Da!—rude exhalation thou art!'"

The drunken man rolled up onto hands and knees, his head lolling like a clubbed dog's.

"Nobly coupled," declared Stevenson. "A master coupler thou art. Canst thou now copulate me this? As perchance, 'Primed for a vomitous sneeze?'"

"Sneeze, you say? Vomitous sneeze!" Baxter pulled languidly at his ear until his eyes bulged in merriment. "Prepare thyself." He cleared his throat and loosed a thunderous, "Bwaaahhhh!"

The fallen lad gawked in bewilderment, peering lamely down to see if he had actually been spewed upon.

"Primed for a vomitous sneeze," chanted Baxter, "sadly rained down on your knees."

"Bravo, Charlie!"

"Or perhaps on your arse. Your sorry bloody arse." Baxter kicked ineffectually at the fellow's rear, missed, and nearly toppled over himself.

Stevenson nearly choked with laughter. "*Arse* don't rhyme!" he cried, catching his breath.

"Of course it do. Rhymes with 'sparse.' Or 'farce.' And you bloody well call yourself a bloody poet?"

"Enough!" Stevenson yanked his companion towards the still-open door and the warm glow inside. "Exeunt. *Molto presto*. Methinks yon tumbled scholar may wax anon vexatious."

"Ach, aye. Vexatious he'd be," muttered Baxter as he stumbled through the entrance. "To be sure. My God, I've a thirst like to flay me, mon!"

The scent of Dunbar's hadn't changed an iota since Stevenson, cousin Bob, Baxter, and Ferrier had founded their legendary "LJR" in these very precincts what seemed a lifetime ago: the bracing smoke of tobacco, softly underscored by sulfur from the coal grate; roasted flesh and boiled cabbage; spilled ale and spirits; toasted cheddar and burnt bread; the dank redolence of seldom-washed clothing and bodies. The LJR Society—Liberty, Justice, Reverence—had sworn their eternal pledge to "disregard everything our parents have taught us." Stevenson cringed to recall his father's rage when the old man stumbled on a draft of their constitution among the papers in Louis's room. Sadly, the organization had not endured once the founding quadrumvirate had moved on from the university and, of necessity, turned from the prodigal consumption of wealth to its disappointingly sparse production—but other subliminally patricidal associations had doubtless risen from its ashes. Other over-educated wastrels had inevitably taken their places and, had those successors staggered just now under the low-beamed ceiling towards the bar, they would have been warmly hailed by the half-dozen bibulous youths who slouched there at the scarred and clothless tables.

At least the grizzled publican still recognized the older pair as they approached the massive oaken bar. He greeted them with gruff but unmistakable fondness.

"It's Johnson, damme, and Mr. Thomson too," he bellowed, making use of the venerable pseudonyms they had invented for themselves, most likely in this very spot. "In from the chill o' the night and the cruel rush o' years. Or is it Thomson and Johnson?"

"Small matter," answered Baxter, blowing into cupped hands. "But unco chilly indeed. Scrotum-clenching cold, you might say. Can you warm us with a wee dram then, Mr. Dunbar, sir?"

"Indeed I can," replied the burly fellow. His hand hovered over a half-empty bottle of spirits just in front of him before it dove beneath the counter and retrieved an earthen jug. "Better this mystic dew," he whispered behind his knuckles as he raised the crock and winked. "Fro' yon distant secret glen. Unparalleled tipple."

"If you please," said Baxter, licking his lips expectantly.

"To be sure," replied the publican. "I been expressly charged by the magistrate, I have, to attend to each and every need of Messrs. Baxter and Stevenson, Esquires."

"However can you remember me, Dunbar?" asked Stevenson, reaching for the tumbler extended in the man's meaty fist.

"How could I forget you, rather?" laughed the barkeep. "Baxter, here, misses nary a week wi' out dropping by to toast the success of his dear friend and fellow reprobate, R. L. Stevenson…esteemed author of *The Suicide Club,* is it? And who knows what other low yarns."

"I'm touched," said Stevenson. He turned to his friend and clinked his glass a mite over-hard, wincing at the spillage. "But, Baxter me boy, where do you get off peddling defamatory slander about a dear old friend such as meself?"

Baxter shrugged.

"You'll hear from my solicitor in the morning," Stevenson said.

"Your solicitor, you say?"

Stevenson nodded.

"*I* am your solicitor! Your solicitor would be me." Baxter tossed back a hearty gulp. "Would be I."

"Ah yes," replied Stevenson. "I recall. And, if I may say, no man ever had an advocate more likely to land his clients *in* the clink."

Baxter gestured obscenely.

"Well," quipped Dunbar. "It's good to see you two flighty toffs getting on so famous like. Take a seat by the fire there before you fall over. McNear's just given up the ghost an's all tucked in for the night. Sit down quickly, now, and you'll likely find his chair's still warm."

"McNear's given up the ghost again, has he?" quipped Baxter. "The sot has a thousand lives. Give him my regards when you see him next. In hell, I expcct that would be." He plunked himself down in a sturdy Windsor chair, which creaked dangerously under the sudden load. "And kindly inform him he owes me ten pounds."

"I will. And as to hell," grinned the publican, "I expect you'll be getting there first, yer honor."

"Here's hopin'!" Baxter raised his glass. "So, Stevenson," he said after a half-minute's silence.

"Aye?"

"The hoary patriarch and you. On civil terms again?" Baxter leaned back from the low table. He felt at the side of his chair, then jerked it awkwardly further from the fire. "Jesus! I'm like to combust here. The wifey would quarter me."

"So she would. And dinna breathe towards the flames, Charlie, lest both of us ignite."

"*Ignis fatuus,*" chanted Baxter.

"*Sic transit,*" responded Stevenson. "*Hocus pocus.* You were saying?"

"I was? Oh, yes. You and Old Tom."

"Old Tom and I."

"Still chums?"

"Ha!" snorted Stevenson. "If Zeus could be chums with Dionysus. But near enough, I ween. The coin comes in, Charles, in dribs and drabs.

But scribbling's yet to make my fortune. It's well Mother and Father haven't turned their backs on me entirely."

"An' ye dinna feel ye've sold yer soul for their few hunnert poonds nou an' again?" Baxter held up his glass and eyed it appreciatively, licking an errant drop of spirit off the side.

"Not hardly. And I think they've taken to Sam. I expect they're not wanting the closest thing they'll get to a grandson sleeping in a moor somewhere."

"Or an apple barrel!"

Stevenson chuckled. "So you've read it, then. My wee flight o' whimsy."

"Of course I've read it. Everyone has. What else is there to read these days? Burns is long dead, bless his pickled brain and poxy nose—"

"Blasphemy!"

"—and Scott gives me wind."

"Not the bilious sort, I hope."

"Not always. Only when the adjectives fly unco thick. Then I blasts like Vesuvius." Baxter extracted a handkerchief from his sleeve and loudly blew his nose, scrutinizing the issue in the cloth. "And do you think Fanny and you will ever have bairns of your own?"

Stevenson swept the back of his hand across his high brow, then he looked uncertainly at his nails. "I can't say. She may think two already are enough." He gave a little snort. "Three, if you count myself."

"You are a sickly youth, to be sure. And she's a good nurse, then? Fanny?"

"Aye, the best," replied Stevenson with a wistful nod. "Tender. Loving. Patient. Well, tender and loving."

Baxter guffawed. "Sounds much like my own dear love. How the likes of us, Stevenson, could ever expect anyone short of an angel to put up with our contrarieties is one of life's great mysteries. Well beyond me."

"And me," answered Stevenson. "The mistresses Thomson and Johnson will be well on the path to sainthood."

Baxter raised his forefinger and tutted with exaggerated fervor. "Wrong church, Louis. Pah! Look at what your bloody Froggy grape juice has done to you. Turned you into a bloody Papist!"

"Or worse," chuckled Stevenson, draining his tumbler and setting it with studious care on the table. "Talk to my father."

The door from the close flew open, admitting a gust of cold air and two ample ladies in calculated disarray. Shoulder to formidable shoulder, they surveyed the room like hungry she-cats appraising a colloquy of moles.

"Speaking of saints," whispered Baxter. "If it ain't Our Ladies o' the Cursory Tumble."

"Goodness," responded Stevenson behind his hand. "Perhaps they won't see us."

"Too late," sighed Baxter as he straightened himself in his chair. "Here she comes. Circe of the moonlit boulevard."

"Scarcely dressed for the night," laughed Stevenson. "Or perhaps I should say for the weather. Should we feel imperiled?"

Baxter clapped his hands over his crotch.

"Well, bless my soul and body!" crooned the taller of the women as she stormed up to the table in a flurry of skirts. "If it ain't the two most profligate laddies in the history of the 'Varsity."

"Oh, Mary," replied Baxter, tossing his hair with boyish affectation. "We're hardly that."

"Then I reckon you could tell me, quick like, whoever's been naughtier than the pair o' ye?" She looked from one to the other with a provocative flutter of her eyelashes.

"Oh, I expect I could," said Baxter. "Though every one of them, doubtless, woulda been set on the path to perdition by yourself. You or that lovable old flop-for-tuppence you travel with."

"Path to perdition, is it?" laughed the woman. "Path to manhood, more like. I'm thinkin' you'll have sat down to piss before you made my acquaintance." She winked knowingly at Stevenson.

"Ha! Now I do recall you did rather affect my urinary functions," replied Baxter. "But more along the lines of a wicked, nasty burning down there, if memory serves."

"Well," she scowled with a throaty titter, "if that remark's what passes for manners with your likes, Master Charlie, that'll be enough." She adjusted her disorganized bodice and turned to Stevenson. "And what a pleasant surprise to see you, Master S. I thought I heard you'd quit this fair burg for wholesomer climes."

"And what could be more wholesome than dear auld Edinburgh?" asked Stevenson. To have the woman standing over him like this made him strangely uncomfortable, he was surprised to realize. He entertained then resisted the urge to stand up, passing the reflex off as resettling himself in his hard chair.

"Let me see," she mused. "More wholesome than Edinburgh?" Crossing her arms, she fingered a yellowed tooth. "Maybe the privy in a Calcutta bawdy house."

"You've been?" asked Baxter.

"Not with what I garner from the likes of you, you tight bastard!"

"'Zounds!" exclaimed Baxter. "The lady's wicked dangerous!"

"Only the strong survive, Charlie. So," she said, turning back to Stevenson, "what've you gents been getting up to this fine evening?"

"Oh, revisiting old haunts is all. Renewing old acquaintances. Baxter here's just written a poem about breaking wind."

"Farts to you," added Baxter.

"Really?" The woman sneered at Stevenson's companion. "Charming! Don't hold it against me if I don't ask for a recitation. So, Louis, my love, do you see many changes, then?" She put her hands on her hips, thrusting them forward provocatively.

"Not in you," answered Stevenson. "You'd be timeless, Maire. Old Town's Cleopatra. Age canna wither ye."

"Nor," added Baxter, with an excited thump to the table, "custom stale your infinite variety."

The woman arched her eyebrow and ran her tongue across her lower lip. "And where *would* you look for 'infinite variety,' laddies? Surely not to your wives."

"Well," said Baxter, scratching his head, "there'd be the nuns. Am I right, Stevenson? The nuns?"

"Indeed you are, Baxter, lad. The nuns! Endlessly creative, those ladies!"

"But then one of those wretched Tudors threw 'em all off the island," Baxter lamented. "Although that will have been good for your business, Mary. Cutting down on the competition?"

"You forget the priests left right along with 'em," laughed the woman. "Our most faithful patrons, the priests. Them, at least, what didn't favor altar boys."

"Goodness," offered Stevenson. "I must confess a better man than I might find all this banter a wee bit unsavory."

"Have you gone all pious on us, now, Louis?" The woman eyed him thoughtfully. "I'm not sure I could abide a pious Louis."

"I think he could be joking," observed Baxter. "He's been known to joke before. But you know, Mary, Stevenson *is* clean off-limits now. No hunting on a private reserve!"

"What's this?"

"Married he is," affirmed the lawyer, tilting his head in pretended sorrow. "These three years. And to an American lady!"

The woman bent over Stevenson, eyes widened and mouth agape in theatrical surprise. "Can this be true?"

"I fear it is," admitted Stevenson, squirming in his seat. "So please to secure your charms a little there, m'dear, before I give way to temptation." He gestured awkwardly towards her abundant chest, which her pose and loose apparel had all but poured out upon him. She stood up straight and made a show of primness, winking at Baxter while she tucked herself back in place.

"And Mrs. Stevenson is ten years her husband's senior," added the lawyer, with mock sanctimony.

"Ten years?" asked the woman. "A whole ten years?"

Stevenson sighed and nodded.

"What, did you think you were marrying your mother?" She said it loud enough to turn heads at the neighboring tables, occasioning some snide titters.

"Good heavens!" protested Stevenson. "Are a gentleman's linens to be aired so publicly these days? Have the storied confidences of the Old Town come to this?" He glanced at Baxter and pointed emphatically at his empty tumbler.

"Here, Mary," said Baxter. "Let's not shame Louis any further than he has already shamed himself. Have a seat, while I fetch some whisky for the three of us."

"Much obliged, Charlie. Only make mine gin, if you would."

Baxter rose to his feet, bumping the table soundly as he did so. Mary stepped aside and, once he'd passed, sat down between Stevenson and the fire.

"So, Louis. We *have* missed you, the lassies 'n' me." She disencumbered a hand from her shawl and extended it halfway across the table. Before he knew it, Stevenson had reached out and grasped it. It was warm, despite the chill of the night. She gazed at him intently then leaned closer, squinting at his right brow. "And what's that over your eye?"

Stevenson reached up sheepishly, his fingertips dancing over the raised abrasion that still throbbed when his mind wasn't elsewhere. "Just a wee battle scar," he chuckled. "Comeuppance for my unbridled tongue."

"Ye havenae married a Harpy, have ye?"

Stevenson laughed again. "No. My wife can be a terror, but this wasn't her doing. I fear I became a little over-animated yester-eve. Owing to an excess of spirits. A little squabble over something I hardly recall."

"So you're still like to boil over, are ye? Oft and again?"

Stevenson pursed his lips then grinned. "I confess I am still known by some for my lively spirit. But how are you then, Maire?"

"Oh, you know," she replied with a cant of her head. Her auburn hair glowed in the lamplight—her best asset, she had often said. He blushed to recall that he had once had a lock of it, and hidden it so well it had never been seen again. Presumably it was still somewhere there under his father's roof, waiting to be uncovered at some uniquely inopportune moment. "Time rushes on."

"So it does," he agreed. "But you're well?"

"Well as I could hope. And you?"

"Passing well."

"They're saying you're a famous writer now."

"Who is?"

"Everyone, I'd think. Talk of the town."

"Well, a writer, anyhow," Stevenson replied with a weary nod. It was beginning to seem late, it surprised him to realize. Years back, the evening would still have felt young. All the younger for the presence of buxom and obliging female company.

"And it's good? Writing?"

"Better than being a barrister."

"Or keeping a lighthouse, was it? Your father wanted?"

"Yes. In essence. Better than that."

"So what would you be writing now? The story of a skin-and-bones 'Varsity lad who learned a passle more in the wynds of Old Town than in a draughty auld lecture hall?"

"Not exactly," chuckled Stevenson. "I own I've spun a low yarn or two along those lines. For the moment, though, I'm between projects."

"Lying fallow?"

"You might say." In truth, he was trying hard enough at something beyond the occasional poem—but fallow was most definitely the way it felt. Vacant, weedy soil he was struggling to till. He reached into his coat for his cigarette case, drew it out, and offered one.

"Thank you, no. Can't afford the habit."

"Hard times peddling?" queried Stevenson.

The woman shot him a filthy glance.

"I'm sorry, Mary," said Stevenson, piqued with himself for the thoughtless quip.

She eyed him skeptically.

"Truly I am."

"Well, you'd best be," said Mary, relaxing once again. "So, tell me about the lucky Mrs. S.," she said at length.

"My mother?" he grinned.

"No, the other. Yer missus."

"She's a bit older, it's true."

"And you met her…?"

"In France. Through Bob. My cousin Bob Stevenson."

"I remember Bob," exclaimed Mary. "Lord, Lou, give me some credit."

"I will. I do. It was at Fountainebleau, you know. The artists' colony. Bob was living there and he invited me to visit. Fanny was a student."

"Fanny? You've married a woman named Fanny?" Mary's face reddened with mirth. Stevenson nodded. "Well, damme! You always loved a good fanny, didn't you? So, are there any wee Stevensons then? Yours and your Fanny's?"

"Fanny—Frances—has two children, by a previous marriage. A girl and a boy. Twenty-two and twelve. There was a third."

"Was?"

"He died. Consumption."

"How terrible. To lose a bairn." She tilted her head in sympathy.

"It was shortly before I met her. She rarely speaks of it."

"All the more sign of her grief."

Stevenson nodded, snuffed his cigarette, and stared around the room. Baxter was still standing at the bar, with the other woman pressed up against him. She had her fingers on his watch chain and tugged at it playfully. "Baxter's married as well," he remarked, motioning towards his friend. "You know?"

"He doesn't act it. Do you?" It was difficult to know if her glance were an inquiry or an invitation.

He looked away. "It's the drink. Don't you think?"

She shrugged and looked back towards the bar. "It commonly is. The whore's best friend is drink. Ginny," she called out to her colleague, "take your talons off our Charlie, now. We're deadly parched over here, can't you see?" Her compatriot thumbed her nose, but she backed away from Baxter and traipsed gaily back to the table of youths, plumping herself languorously into the lap of the most inebriated of the lot. Baxter returned with the glasses and raised his own.

"To happy memories, friends. And to jollity."

"To jollity," echoed Mary, clinking with Stevenson and downing the gin in a trice. She inhaled deeply and, pulling back her shoulders, looked the writer squarely in the face. "Speakin' o' drink and bairns too soon gone, you know about Ferrier?"

"I do," replied Stevenson. "We do. Ferrier's why I've come up from London."

"I havena seen 'im in months. Word is, though…" She met his eye and nodded grimly.

"I know. I scarce know what to hope for."

"Well, it'll all be over soon, I ween." She leaned closer, her eyes cool but searching. "You've not seen him then?"

"Not yet. Likely tomorrow," answered Stevenson with a weary exhalation.

"It wilna be easy, I'm thinkin'. They say it's his liver. From all the whisky. I seen it before." She leaned back, reached into a sleeve, and pulled out a handkerchief to swipe at her nose. "They go all yellow. And bleed at the nose, often enough."

"Many thanks, Mary," interjected Baxter at volume. "We need a cheering up."

"Go bugger yourself, you nasty prick. He was your friend, too."

"Is, Mary," replied the lawyer. "*Is* my friend. Dinna bury the lad whilst he's still kickin'."

Mary ignored the remark, turning in her seat to gaze at the fire. "A sweeter man there never was. Most times, leastwise. There were nights," she chuckled, "when we'd hear singin' from afar up the street, Virginia and me…unmistakable. You knew it was him comin' along."

"La ci darem la mano," sang Stevenson. "Mozart."

"I wouldn't know. But he sung, he did, like his was the most beautiful soul ever created. The darkest December night turned summer gloamin' with it. But then…" She sighed and shook her head.

"Then what?" asked Baxter.

"Well, you know. There was other times—more of 'em later on in years—when he'd go all distant like. As though he didn't know you… as though he was looking for someone else. Or somethin' else." She folded her hands and looked down on them, pursing her painted lips.

For a moment, the three of them sat there, silent, in the hot glow of the grate.

"His tastes could run…well, no. Enough o' that!" She slapped her knee. "Least he wasn't never one o' them with a stick. Or a knife."

"Or a knife?" queried Stevenson.

"Takin' without payin', you know. They're all about these days, the bastards. Anyway, we're none of us saints, are we? Least of all me."

"Ach, you *are* a saint, Mary," countered Baxter, reaching out for her shoulder and shaking it roughly. "An angel of mercy. So proven many a time."

"Takes a lawyer to gild a common daisy," said the whore as she slapped his hand away. "Now off with ye both. Home to your wives and mothers. I've not the least interest in ye."

"But I may have some unfinished business here," protested Baxter. He peered over towards the bar, this side of which the other woman lay back against one of the young men, giggling as she held his hand tightly against a breast.

"No you don't," said Mary. "Not tonight. Take him home, Louis. And spank him if you get a chance."

"I fear he might relish a paddling," laughed Stevenson. "And then where would I be?"

"Possessed of a driving notion for your next unlikely fable?" suggested Baxter.

"I'm not sure my public is ready, Johnson…for such an unseemly narrative."

"Then you'll have to bring 'em along with you," offered Mary. "The public. Trust me, there's a market in this world for more than you can imagine."

Stevenson closed the front door of 17 Heriot Row as quietly as he could manage, one hand on the knob to keep the latch from clicking, the other pressed against both the door and the frame as the two met and settled firmly together.

He might have sobered some on the chilly walk from Old Town to the refined Georgian row where he had lived since he was seven. He pressed his cheek languidly against his fingers as they lingered on the wood, drinking in the cool of them, registering that strangeness when one part of the body is in a very different condition than another. Feeling more collected, he pulled back and turned his head to listen. No sound but his breathing broke the stillness of the entrance hall. He threw the deadbolt and slipped his key into his coat pocket. Stooping to remove his shoes, he went to place them quietly under the side table where, the last he knew, a pair of his childhood gloves still lay waiting for a winter that would never come again. No, he thought. Better not leave footwear down here to be found in the morning by parent or maid, mute testimony to the lateness and stealth of his return.

He shifted his shoes to his other hand, curling his fingers inside the still-warm heels, and slipped through the glass inner doors and across the wide flagstones to the staircase. Hand on the polished rail down which he had anciently slithered like a weasel, those times when no adult was present to see, he stepped up towards the moonlight that flooded in through the glazed cupola high above. He strove to tread weightlessly, fancying himself, for a daft moment, a Montgolfier balloon rising faster and faster until it burst in an apocalyptic clatter up through the skylight. Not a tread, in fact, creaked beneath his stockings, any more than they had creaked throughout his university years, when he had so often crept up past his parents' bedroom in far worse physical and moral condition than at present. Somehow it had escaped his recollection that the staircase was made of stone. He realized he had been holding his breath.

Halfway up to his room, he paused again, half expecting his parents to crash out through their bedroom door and ask if he had thought any further about the matter they had discussed that evening over a hasty tea. Instead, there issued from the room nothing but the cycling rasp of his father's breathing. The old man would be lying, as always, flat on his back in the stately four-poster, the one that had passed down through generation upon generation of successful Stevensons—carved walnut haven for engineers spawned by other engineers as each, in turn, commenced and concluded his narrow but remunerative life journey.

Beset by a sudden tickle in his nose, he fought the instinct to sneeze, tightening his throat and tucking his chin. He tiptoed through the moonlight pooling there on the carpet runner and climbed on up to his room, closing the door behind him as carefully as he had done below. Safely inside, he relaxed.

Damn! He had dropped his shoes without thinking, and one of them had tumbled off the carpet and fetched up against the baseboard with a resonant clunk. He imagined a company of mice inside the wall skittering along on tiny pink feet, towing behind them their obscenely naked tails. They would have frozen at the sound, peeping anxiously from side to side, nostrils twitching, whiskers as well.

He shuffled wearily towards his bed, shrugging off his coat and pulling half-heartedly at his cravat. Had he meant to stay out this late? He looked at his watch. Quarter til two. *"Merde!"* he hissed. He was expected for breakfast.

Fanny, counter to his every expectation, was unrelenting in her insistence that he hang or fold his clothing every evening. He remembered, in contrast, their first nights together, when some shaky dam of propriety had finally ruptured and they'd torn off each other's garments with the giddy abandon of children loosed on gifts at Christmas. They had awakened as in an arbor after a tornado, their copious fig leaves strewn hither and yon such that there was no disguising what they had done, no denial of what they had become; she the mother turned adulteress; he a wife-stealer, somehow evolved from the pious child who had so often lain awake, just here, trembling through the night's bleakest hours over the fate of his eternal soul. On more than one of those post-coital mornings he had found a button missing from his shirt, once even from the fly of his trousers. As soon, however, as that inaugural, all-mastering passion had waned—when Fanny in fact next welcomed her monthly "visitor"—it was ever and always folding before fondling. He grinned to think of her there at the hotel in Bournemouth, most likely with Sam in her bed, and he tossed his coat and cravat onto a chair.

He dropped his trousers to the floor and stepped out of them, shaking his leg to free a foot as he shuffled over to the basin. A candle stood on the washstand, matches in a box just to the side. Once the taper was alight—its apostrophe of flame barely quivering in the still air—he looked at the face in the mirror.

Lit from below and from the side, it scarcely seemed his own. Exceedingly lean, but a little ruddy from drink and the cold. Faint crows' feet, weren't they, just sprouting from the corners of those strangely plangent eyes. The eyes of a frightened hare, he sometimes cringed to think.

Alas, that encrusted welt above the right brow! He had almost forgotten it, feeling not a twinge for hours, washed away in spirits. Damn! Only an irascible fool would have taken on so over a singularly unimaginative insult, out and about as he was, completely on his own, in one of the West End's more questionable precincts. Tonight's lad outside Dunbar's had at least enjoyed the vigilance of a mate, sardonic as the other fellow had been. And while it was understandable that the prospect of an imminent meeting with Ferrier and his censorious mother had driven his own recklessness—the mindless folly of this goggling wraith in the mirror—it was fortunate there had been cool heads among the strangers at hand.

It taxed him to remember exactly how it had all transpired, but the rough outlines were still there. Some catty remark about his Edinburgh accent, thrown at him by a purse-mouthed Oxford type who brayed that Hadrian's Wall was the best thing the Romans had ever done for

England. How criminal it was, the fellow prattled, that "skirt-wearing savages" (it was "skirt-wearing savages," was it not?) had ever been allowed to venture south of the borders alive. An attractive young serving maid with whom Stevenson had shocked himself to be flirting called the man out, and when the nit turned his sozzled invective on her, an irresistible combination of gallantry and rage compelled Stevenson to mount a spirited assault.

The writer's sharp words had proved an unequal match for the man's blunt fists, at least in terms of tangible evidence of blows landed. Again, most luckily, the bulk of the crowd had proven more well disposed towards northern visitors than did the voluble cad. They counseled Stevenson amiably but very firmly to leave, escorted him to the door, and left him to find his way back to the Savile and its solicitous night porter. The crucial charge, for the present moment, was to keep it all a total secret from Fanny.

A wraith in the mirror. Mirror-wraith. What was it that Carlyle had said about blasted boys—or blighted youths, was it? "Children that have been in hell?" Well, no. Sod the self-romanticizing. He leaned closer. How could a man's eyes be set so far apart, eyes that were themselves too large, as though desperate to drink in the world while it was still there for the drinking? The lank hair parted over the right eye rendered him somewhat lopsided, as though his scalp had somehow slid off the strong median line of nose and moustache down towards his ear. How could Fanny want to kiss these lips? How could Old Town Mary have stood for this ferret face nuzzling under her skirts? How might today's trim rider on the train have stood for the same?

He sighed and splashed water onto his face, patting it away with a towel. Was his toothbrush ready at hand? Had he even brought it? Sod it. He picked up the candle and padded over to his bed, setting the light softly on the nightstand and drawing back the counterpane. His shadow suddenly huge on the wall in front of him, he climbed into bed, pulling the covers up over his bony frame.

Head on the pillow, bedclothes tugged up to his chin, he lay there and eyed the room in the flickering light. So little had changed, really. Gone, to be sure, were nearly all the ephemera of boyhood, the coveted fruits of birthdays and Christmases, props to endless lonely hours of play at war and piracy and polar exploration. This bed, though, had been his boat on a multitude of stupendous voyages, waking or sleeping or in the delirium of fever, when the seas were uncommonly mountainous and left him drenched and gasping till his mother's hand, or his nursemaid Cummy's, bore in the cooling cloth and stilled the waters like Jesus. *Why are you so afraid? Be still, my little smout. Morning's on the way, and the sun.* On the far side of the wardrobe, the black canvas of imagination still hung there tautly stretched, ready for the brush and the daub, ready to render whatever dread, half-founded or fully fanciful, might spring to mind.

Somewhere, within the sounding distance of a bell, Ferrier lay as well. Sleeping? Thinking? *La ci darem la mano!*

Stevenson blew out the candle and the night flooded in around him, swallowing him whole. What a comfort it would be to have Fanny curled up there next to him! He reached down and grasped his penis, stretching it out from its chilly, contracted state. He thought of the young governess standing over him, a riding crop now in her pale little hand. She faded uncooperatively into nothingness.

No matter. No life down there tonight. There was a touch of whirling in the room. He willed it away, smiling thinly, and slept.

3

All at once, I saw two figures: one a little man who was stumping along eastward at a good walk, and the other a girl of maybe eight or ten who was running as hard as she was able down a cross street. Well, sir, the two ran into one another naturally enough at the corner; and then came the horrible part of the thing; for the man trampled calmly over the child's body and left her screaming on the ground. It sounds nothing to hear, but it was hellish to see. It wasn't like a man; it was like some damned Juggernaut.

—MR. RICHARD ENFIELD

"Oh my! Have I hurt you?" He bends again to help the little one to her feet, but now with a distinct knot in his gorge. Has he been seen? Are there laws against this kind of carelessness? This kind of callousness?

"Of course you haven't hurt me," she says in a broken voice, as he raises her up and begins to turn her around. "Nothing happens to me that I don't want to happen. You of all people should know that." Fully erect now, she turns to face him with a giggle. Her hair is matted and it crawls with shiny, black beetles. Her face is not her face. It is Walter Ferrier's.

Stevenson shot up in bed, short of breath, feverishly reconstructing where he was. Edinburgh! In his own room. His temples throbbed. His mouth tasted like some vile sort of cheese. He groped for his watch on the bedside table.

"Damn!" he exclaimed. He had been expected for breakfast at eight; it was half-ten. He sprang from his bed, throwing on his trousers before he noticed that his bladder was full to bursting. He'd brought no robe. Was it worth the effort to dress more fully and walk down to the plumbed water closet his father had just had installed in the first-floor dressing room and bath? He gazed indecisively at the china pot under his bed and resolved to save the time. Holding the thing in one hand, he grasped himself in the other and loosed a torrent into the shiny container, nearly sending it steaming over the opposite rim. He surprised himself with vague recollections of some nursemaid or other, someone before Cummy, lavishly singing his praises when he managed to give adequate notice before something hot spurted out of one orifice or another. "Ach, but yui're a braw laddie nou! Kennin' about the pottie." How curious that one's sense of maturity and virtue should evolve so fundamentally from registering and then controlling the prime urges of the flesh. Surely there was a droll tale to be spun from that, or perhaps some gripping psychomachia of appetite and restraint. Then again, it might be that the more puritanical sects of Christianity had already exhausted the creative possibilities.

He washed his face and hands and then shaved, waking a little further with each splash, each clank of the razor against the laver. He pulled a fresh shirt from his bag and, studying himself in the mirror, buttoned it, fastened the collar with some difficulty, and tied his cravat. It was strangely pleasant to see Mary last night. Just as pleasant, finally, to have limited their intercourse to words. He sat down on the bed again and pulled on his stockings and shoes. He stood a bit too quickly; the blood rushed from his head, and he flailed for balance. He paused for a moment while his world steadied, then grabbed his coat, wriggled it on, and hastened into the hallway and down the stairs.

His father was in the library at the back of the house, lounging, legs crossed, in his favorite leather chair. He was reading the day's *Scotsman*.

"I am so sorry, Father," sighed Stevenson as he entered the room.

"We were to have breakfasted at eight."

The older man lowered the paper, eyeing his son over his spectacles. "Well, I didn't honestly expect you." He folded the broad sheets precisely and dropped them onto the small table just to his left. "You *were* with Baxter. And you haven't seen him for some time."

"Still—"

"We'll hear no more of it. You'll forgive me, I trust, for going ahead without you?" The question seemed sincere.

"Of course, Father. Of course."

"I fear my aging constitution is increasingly intolerant of irregular meal times. Come. Let's go through and get you something. I believe Isabelle's kept the kettle on." He smiled a crinkly smile and rose from the chair, stepping towards his son and extending his hand. Stevenson moved nearer and took it. The grip was almost painfully firm, uncustomarily so. Stevenson wondered if it had a meaning. If so, nothing in the level gaze under the stately brow revealed it.

"Good morning to you. And again, Father—"

"Wheesht! I won't hear of it. Come along."

They made their way through the hall and into the dining room, where a place remained set beside the head of the table. Thomas Stevenson took a seat in one of the two grand armchairs and his son settled to his left, sliding his napkin from the initialed silver ring he had used for as long as he could remember. He set the chilly thing soundlessly on the tablecloth. "So," he said, looking up, "I suppose I'm surprised to find that you're taking the *Scotsman*."

His father laughed. "And reading it too! One does well to stay abreast of the opposition's way of thinking. Would you mind pulling the bell? I seem to have neglected that little detail."

Stevenson rose, walked over to the fireplace, and gave a hearty tug on a brass handle just to the side. "I don't know that the Liberals are exactly your opponents," he replied. "I distinctly recall finding a few volumes of Hume tucked away in a corner of your upper shelves. Safe from prying eyes."

Thomas shook his head with a calculated snort. "Spy! Thankless child!"

"Time brings change, *pater*. Could there be a nascent Liberal lurking behind the respectable façade of Number 17?"

His father laughed again. "I am far too old for that. And how could I be a good father were I not resolutely and thoroughly Tory? Good heavens. Would you have me out carousing with you and Baxter? Making a fool of myself? Putting my eternal soul at risk?"

"Well—"

"I suppose you now expect me to add your worrisome Baudelaire to my Hume—perhaps even *The Descent of Man!*" He winked at his son as a prim, uniformed maid shuffled into the room.

"Sir? Oh, good morning, Master Louis."

"Good morning, Fiona. You've been well?"

"Very, sir. And you?"

"Wonderful, thank you."

"What do you fancy, Smout?" asked his father, slapping his hands on the tablecloth.

Stevenson looked sidelong at the maid, who blinked at the odd nickname his father continued to favor. *Wee fish.* "Oh, just a boiled egg, I think, and some toast. Perhaps a rasher or two of bacon, if there's any to be had."

"Of course, sir."

"Oh, and some tea as well. For two?" He glanced at his father, who nodded.

"Thank you, sir." The woman curtsied and left, and for a moment, the two men sat in silence.

"What's that over your eye?" asked the father.

"This?" Stevenson reached up to touch the mark.

"Yes. Were you and Baxter caught up in fisticuffs?" There had been times, some not in the terribly distant past, when the question might have been asked in earnest. It had often been difficult to know if Thomas Stevenson were more convinced of his son's deleterious influence on his various friends, or of theirs on him. The only certainty was that the old fellow had seen the whole lot of them as jointly, and inescapably, headed for perdition.

Stevenson laughed. "Hardly, Father. The train braked suddenly… coming into Waterloo. I struck my head on the doorframe. I'm surprised you didn't notice it last evening. You or mother."

"Well, the light was dim. And you were in a rush, were you not?"

"I was."

It distressed Stevenson, lying to his parents. Ever since he was nine, however—when they had been obliged to meet with his schoolmaster after he had lit the play yard bully's overcoat on fire—he had gone to considerable lengths to keep his volatile temper and its occasionally dire consequences from their ken. That he and his father had long seemed incapable of steering clear of heated exchanges over politics and religion made this all the more challenging. Fortunately, their testy male antipathies looked of late to have moderated.

"Mother wasn't down earlier, was she?"

"At eight? Heavens, no! We'll not see her for hours."

"Good."

"Good?" laughed his father.

"You know what I meant," Stevenson chuckled as well. "I suspect."

"Your suspicions are well founded. But, really, Lou—if you insist on being a writer, you know, you must learn to express yourself in ways that leave less room for misinterpretation."

Stevenson laughed again. "Do you really think that's what literature aspires to, Father? Uncontestably explicit communication?"

The reply was quick. "I am afraid I do. Everything must be as clear as a patent light…planted firmly on a rocky headland. Clear as Bunyan. Clear as the nose on my face." He flicked his substantial proboscis with a forefinger and winked again. Ever since *Treasure Island*—save for an occasional and always unpredictable resurfacing of his original dismay and outrage—Thomas had seemed grudgingly comfortable with his son's literary profligacy. It had not hurt that the old man himself had conjured up the crucial plot device of Jim Hawkins's nap in the apple barrel. That, and the suggestive contents of Billy Bones's sea chest: the unused suit of clothes that hinted at poignant hopes—perhaps of eventual marriage, perhaps of nothing more than a laying-out and burial on dry land rather than at the lonely bottom of the sea. And then there was the old pirate's little collection of exotic shells, unaccountably sentimental items to be found in an aged and battered trunk. Whether or not there lurked a Liberal inside him, his father could certainly compass nuance. He could craft it himself when no one was looking—although, for years, he had kept that capacity a total secret from his only child.

Fiona entered with the tea, setting the tray in front of the older man. "Shall I pour, sir?"

"I'll do," said Thomas Stevenson, sliding the cups and saucers slowly to the left of the squat Delft pot and filling them to within a half-inch of their rims.

Stevenson noted the tremor in the hand that passed his cup, and registered, in turn, a little catch in his own chest. It had once been fear that had complicated the love and grudging respect he felt for his father. Was pity now making a bid to do the same? Something in the situation moved him...to what? Surely it was beneath a decent son to feel betrayal or anger as his father made unavoidable concessions to the press of years—especially a father who had almost always come round to support his child in every important way. Eventually, at least.

"Thank you," said Stevenson, grasping the saucer.

"Of course." His father picked up his own cup and leaned slowly back. "Now, what do you have planned for your day?"

"Goodness, Father," replied Stevenson, setting down his tea. "I would have thought that was clear from yesterday's discussion."

The old man raised a reproving eyebrow.

"I'm sorry. You know how I dread all this."

"I quite understand, Smout. It is not easy, confronting the mortality of those we love. Dear friends."

"No."

"Your mother and I, naturally, have reached that point in life where we expect to lose friends and family. But to be scarcely thirty!" Thomas noted his son's silence and took a deep breath. "Perhaps we'll speak of other things."

"No. Really, Father—this is what it comes down to." Stevenson straightened his shoulders and smiled resolutely. "Best to face it bravely." And then, with a wink, "Manfully."

"There's a braw spirit! There's no opposing God's will."

"Perhaps." Stevenson's response was reflexive. But what, he wondered peevishly, was the use of saying that? It was difficult business, this. Writing one's self anew.

Any reaction from his father was forestalled as the door swung open and the maid bustled in with another tray, bearing a plate heaped high with egg cups and bacon, and a toast caddy similarly laden.

"Thank you, Fiona. And thank Isabelle as well."

"Of course, sir."

Stevenson eyed the plenty laid before him and shook his head in playful dismay. "Oh, 'Belle."

"Always trying to fatten you up," chuckled his father.

"The definition of a futile pursuit! Yet one in which she makes common cause with all of the other women in my life."

"And how *is* Fanny? I'm afraid your mother and I were very rude last evening not to ask after her."

"Not at all. There were other matters to hand. But she's well, thank you. And Sam also."

"A dear boy. And a very dear mother."

Stevenson set down his knife and fork and turned towards his tablemate. He paused for a moment to blink back an unexpected misting in his eyes. "Father," he began.

"Mmmm? Yes?" Thomas Stevenson looked indulgently over the brim of his cup.

"I must tell you how much it pleases me to hear you say that. To think that you and mother..." He was reduced to a nod and a shrug of his shoulders.

"My, we're being earnest now, are we not? And so early in the day."

Stevenson laughed, his father quickly joining in. "Well, you've heard me say it. I am grateful."

"Nonsense," exclaimed his father. "Fanny makes you happy?"

"She does. Mostly." Another shared chuckle.

"Well, there you are. 'Mostly happy.' As perfect a match as any earthly soul is likely to find."

"Verily."

"I must admit, Louis," said the older man as he rubbed the knuckles of one hand, "I do find your good wife surprisingly agreeable. Especially for a lady from the colonies."

"And there's the key," responded Stevenson with a grin.

"To what?"

"To your affection for her."

"Explain yourself."

"Fanny simply agrees with everything you have to say."

"She does not," sputtered his father with affected bluster.

"She most certainly does. Whether or not she is honestly of the same mind. Whether or not it's the daftest sentiment she's ever heard a man express."

The other reared back in feigned astonishment and outrage.

"She has told me so explicitly," declared his son.

"Well, there's no fool like an old fool. But I shall continue to love the lady and think the best of her. Despite her unfortunate choice of a husband."

Conversation yielded momentarily to the clinking of Stevenson's cutlery and a few busy noises from the kitchen below. A muted thundering outside announced a delivery of coal, sliding into a neighbor's cellar.

"Have you found anything in Bournemouth, then?" Thomas Stevenson asked.

"Not really."

"Have you looked? Truly looked?"

Stevenson again set down his knife and fork, raising his napkin to his mouth and moustache. He parted his lips to say something, but remained silent.

"I've offended you," muttered his father.

"Not exactly."

"What it is then? Your finances?"

"No. Not our finances. We're doing well enough. And you and mother have been extremely generous."

"What is it then?"

"I've been ordered south again, Father. *We* have been ordered south. For considerations of health."

Thomas Stevenson eyed his son warily. "The hemorrhages again? 'Bluidy Jack'?"

"Aye, Bluidy Jack."

His father's brow furrowed and his fists clenched on the tablecloth.

"Though really not so bad this time." Stevenson felt another unsettling bloom of pity for the old man. "Honestly."

His parents had been obliged to contend with the constant afflictions he had been prey to as a child—the lingering colds and bronchitis, the gastric and scarlet fevers, the chickenpox, whooping cough; all the endless nights of croup that left him gasping for air over a pot of boiling water. Nothing had quite prepared them, though, for that dreadful night three years back when he had wakened the household with the desperate, gurgling cough of a drowning man. He had sensed the blood immediately, flooding his mouth with its iron savor, dripping thickly from his lips and nostrils. It was only when a housemaid had entered with a candle that he had seen the entire front of his nightshirt, the whole of his pillow, and the better part of his bed sheet awash in the stuff. His eyesight had wavered as he spit and sucked for air. It had nonetheless remained sufficiently clear for him, looking up from his gory nest, to spy his poor parents standing in the doorway, unrobed and in their nightclothes, supporting each other in attitudes of helpless terror.

Of all the sights he had ever seen, that made a fair bid to be the one of which he would most gratefully have divested himself. Only witnessing the death of Fanny's little Hervey might have surpassed it.

"No?" His father's eyes were eloquent. "Not so bad? Truly?"

"They assure us, the doctors, that some months in Provence will work wonders. Just as before."

"Just as before." His father nodded. "And yet it's back again, is it not?"

"I shall be fine, Father. It's nothing, really. Merely a passing setback."

Thomas gathered himself with a deep breath. "Of course it is." He paused. "And where will you go, then?"

"Hyères, we think. Perhaps." Dropping his fork, Stevenson snatched a rasher of bacon in his fingers and nibbled at it guiltily.

"Barbarism!" fumed his father at the indelicacy. "You were too long in America. Your mother and I should disown you. But what of Hyères?"

"On the coast, you know. The Mediterranean." Stevenson licked his fingers, then reached sheepishly for his napkin. "It's a charming little *ville,* by all accounts."

"I don't suppose you could brook a visitor or two?"

"Of course we could!" Stevenson sat up straight and smiled broadly. "What a pleasure that would be! Honestly. Fanny would be delighted."

"And Sam?"

"Sam as well. Of course he would. We'll look for larger accommodations."

His father chuckled and shook his head. "I'll promise you nothing. Your mother and I aren't given to the inconveniences of travel. Your mother at least."

"And here I'd thought our grand tour had suited her well," countered Stevenson. "Lo, these many eons ago."

"Well…"

"It was Cummy, not she, who was like to have perished."

His father grinned in recollection. "Good heavens. The poor woman's dismay over their…their Carnival carrying-on? Lads dressed as lasses? Priests dressed as asses? She was nigh on apoplectic."

"Yui've brung us amang heathens, Mister Thomas," mimicked Stevenson. *"Canna we flee this cursed place? Canna we ga home?"*

"Aye," chuckled his father. "She was like to barricade herself in her room. But your nurse is a fine lady for all that. We lower ourselves to mock such ironclad righteousness. Am I right?"

"You are, Father. As always."

Again, the censorious brow. This time, though, an eye sparkled beneath.

"Cummy was like a second mother to me," said Stevenson.

"Aye, she was."

"Although she *has* scarred me for life."

"Scarred you?"

"I might as well have had John Knox minding me in my nursery! I can't swear she read me *The Justice of God in the Damnation of Sinners* before she read me *Jack and the Beanstalk*. But it was always 'irresistible Grace' this and 'total depravity' that. The dear lady left me feeling I had as much control over my soul's destiny as a goose feather in a hurricane."

"Off with you!" exclaimed the father. He waved his hand and made to rise from the table. "You are positively incorrigible." Then, as though suddenly remembering what lay in store for his son, he added, "We shall be in all day, your mother and I. What time do you go to see Walter?"

"At two."

"And your plans for luncheon?"

"At the North British Hotel. With Fleeming."

"Ah, the esteemed Professor Jenkin."

"Another, with Cummy, of my regrettably few salutary influences."

"Blessed soul," chortled his father. "I believe it is to him that we finally owe the completion of your baccalaureate?"

Stevenson grinned. "Quite plausibly."

"Please convey my regards. Together with my extreme gratitude." He extended his hand over the table, palm up. Stevenson grasped it and gave it a squeeze—precisely the way, it was odd to realize, he had taken the hand of a common prostitute just hours before. Folding and rolling his napkin, he slipped it into the silver ring and laid it softly back in its customary place.

Low cloud scudded over Edinburgh as Stevenson walked to the Ferrier house, a half-mile distant. Walter had evidently been back under his parents' roof for several months, since illness had rendered him unable to work or look after himself. As he walked, his collar turned up against an unseasonably biting wind, Stevenson found it distinctly more comfortable to revisit the conversation he had just left than to rehearse the one he was about to have.

He had hardly been joking about the way Fanny curried favor by agreeing with his father's every pronouncement. Like other women from her imperfectly-civilized continent, Fanny was possessed of some mannish traits and ways: she was outspoken and assertive in manner, constantly browned by the sun, and given, for heaven's sake, to rolling her own cigarettes and smoking them unabashedly in any and all company. She could be brutally honest, and all too often she was just that with her new husband. With Thomas, though, Fanny managed to be softness and graciousness personified. Damned if she hadn't all but wrapped the old fellow around her diminutive little finger—something Stevenson himself could never have managed. Was this hypocrisy in her, or was it simply sound strategy? She clearly knew that her own prospects and, in turn, her son's whole future, remained highly tenuous. The pair of them depended on Stevenson's pen and precious little else—and in turn, that pen depended on a body scarcely able to outlast a single damp Scots winter without ripping itself apart from the inside out.

Whatever its reasons, though, the uncontestable result of Fanny's demeanor was that, ever since the day Stevenson had first—and with such trepidation—brought his divorced colonial back with him to Heriot Row, his father had gradually softened from the stony patriarch into what he had revealed himself to be just that morning: jocular, affable, always quick enough to evince principle, but just as quick to posture in a playful way. For all that Fanny might put steel in her husband's spine, for his father she was the cup that fosters kindness. All told, Stevenson and his strange little ménage were worlds better for it.

A chilly drop exploded on his cheek as he approached the imposing façade of 28 Charlotte Square. As he climbed the granite steps, the spitting thickened to a full-bore shower. He stood for a moment before the deeply paneled door, rain pattering on the brim of his hat. Gathering himself, he reached for the heavy brass ring.

Tap! Tap! There was a long pause with no response.

Thunk! Thunk!

At last the door swung open and an older housemaid showed him into the ornate but welcoming entrance hall. Hat in hand, he extended his card and said that he had come to see Master Walter. The woman nodded, taking his hat and overcoat and ushering him into a drawing room just to the right.

"If you'll please to wait here, sir."

"Of course. Thank you."

The maid slipped out, closing the door behind her. Stevenson fussed with his shirt cuffs as he peered around the high-ceilinged room. The elegant furniture was of French manufacture, no doubt, but uncommonly clean in line. The walls were papered in a tasteful new Morris pattern. Over a fireplace of clear Italian marble hung a large mirror, framed in gold and flanked by two charming gold sconces sporting candles, not gas. As Stevenson stepped up to admire the skeleton clock ticking away in the center of the mantelpiece, he spied the reflection of Ferrier's sister sweeping into the room.

"Coggie," he exclaimed, turning to greet her. "How wonderful to see you! I—"

"And you, Louis." She approached with rustling skirts, extending her arms for a light embrace. As she stepped back, she retained his hands and squeezed them once, softly, before she let them drop. She had been a beautiful girl. She was now a beautiful woman, thought Stevenson, despite the creases that deepened on her brow as her smile fell away. He remembered Ferrier's frequent teasing about how his bosom companion must one day marry his lovely little sister. He recalled, as well, solitary moments when he himself had returned to thoughts of that match with no levity at all. Where would it have taken them, he wondered? Would he still be a barrister, wealthy but discontent? *Would* he be discontent? And where else might Walter now be as a consequence?

"You've come to see him," the young woman declared, whisking him back from his reverie.

"I have. If I may."

"Of course you may. Why ever not?"

"I don't know. It was a silly choice of words."

"It's so good of you, Louis. It will cheer him immeasurably." She smiled and crossed her arms over her slight chest. She stood there expectantly, her fingers fluttering over her elbows as though she were settling herself without thinking of it.

He rummaged for words, something finished and kind and consoling. Nothing came beyond the obvious.

"I am so sorry, Coggie." As, of course, was everyone.

"Thank you."

"I've heard that it may not be long now." And how thoughtful he was to remind her!

"Well," she replied, reaching up to push a stray wisp of hair off her ear, "we don't know, in truth. We'd thought he might not last the month. They've confirmed that it's consumption, you know. Walter is dying." Tears brimmed in her eyes, one of them dropping from a lash and tumbling down over her cheek. She swept it away with the back of a forefinger. "But the doctor thinks," she went on with a forced smile, "that he's had quite a good week, this past one."

"Really?" said Stevenson, gratefully buoyed. "That is wonderful."

"Wonderful indeed. He had barely had an appetite. But for several days now he's eaten like a horse. And I fancy his face is much fuller."

"Wonderful."

"It is. But you will find him changed, Lou." She reached again for her hair as her gaze shuttled back and forth between his eyes. Stevenson nodded. "Cruelly. Walter is jaundiced. They say it is his liver as well. From all of the drink, I suppose."

Stevenson nodded again.

"You knew that?" Her lips stiffened as she eyed him. "Well, there it is!"

"There it is," he echoed. "Shall we go up then?"

"Up?" For a moment she appeared confused. "Oh my, no! It's not come to that." She tittered nervously. "I fear I've let my anguish paint too grim a picture. Walter's not bedridden, you know. Most days, at least. He's in the library with mama. Here, let me take you to him."

She reached again for his hand and led him back through the entrance hall towards the rear of the house, past the wide staircase on which a second housemaid was busy with a broom and dustpan. They found Walter Ferrier reclining on a tufted chaise longue, fully dressed but with a light afghan tossed over his legs. His mother sat in a small chair just to one side, some needlework in her lap. Ferrier's collar was too big for his lean and corded neck, but he was dressed in a coat and tie, and he smiled brightly as Stevenson came into the room. His skin was a glossy ochre.

"Stevenson, my dear," he exclaimed, tossing back the afghan and dropping his feet to the floor.

"Don't get up!" said Stevenson and Mrs. Ferrier together in what might have been studied synchrony. Stevenson looked down at the woman, prepared to smile at their strangely orchestrated performance. He was met with a chilly stare.

"Mrs. Ferrier—"

"Mr. Stevenson."

"Of course I shall get up," insisted Ferrier, struggling to his feet as his sister rushed to steady him. He brushed her hand gently away and, with a strained but animated smile, extended his own to Stevenson. "Welcome to my new offices. You see I'm just…just putting the latest issue of *The University Magazine* to bed. It's only taken, what is it? Eleven years. My damn co-editor absconded, you see! Went off to write novels."

Stevenson chuckled. He took the proffered hand with caution, half-afraid the man's bones might crack in his grip. "A thousand apologies, Walter. Would that the old rag were still going. I believe it was the best writing we ever did." He was surprised to feel his friend's skin so warm, with so much meat in his grip. Ferrier's grin was lively and infectious, but the eyes that smiled above it were much the same disconcerting hue as his skin. It was hard to take in with equanimity.

"Ah," said Ferrier, with a penetrating gaze. "You have noticed that I am now *jaune*. *Tout jaune*. Like a Chinaman," he chuckled. "Head to toe. Every last appendage of me." He peered over at his mother, who shook her head in consternation and returned intently to her handiwork.

"Arresting," said Stevenson. "Artful, Walter. As always." What else could one say?

"Ha, 'artful!' Making myself my own best creation. If I were indeed a painting, though—I would say that my varnish had seriously discolored. No? Time to strip it off. Apply a new coat. Restore the bright undertints of youth!" Ferrier stared at his visitor, as though waiting for a nod or a smile. "Please, do have a seat, dear boy. Coggie, if you'd be so kind." He sat back suddenly onto the chaise as his sister fetched a side chair for Stevenson, then made to fetch another for herself.

"There's no need, Elizabeth," said their mother emphatically. "You may take mine. I have other business to attend to." She rose with the vigor of a woman years younger and, with a brusque "Sir!" moved quickly to the door and away.

Ferrier exchanged a vexed glance with his sister before he turned back to Stevenson. "You'll have to excuse my dear old mother, Lou. I fear my afflictions rather weigh on her."

"Of course they do. I take no offense." He felt, though, a sudden flush under his collar. "My welcome has otherwise been very cordial indeed." He glanced swiftly at Coggie, who met his eyes with an apologetic smile.

"So then, Stevenson," said Ferrier, resting his head on his propped arm. "You are well?"

"I am, Walter. Tolerably well."

"And your family?"

"They too, thank you."

Ferrier nodded. "Excellent. Excellent. So I have now read your pirate book!" He paused portentously.

"Yes? And?"

"I found it terrific fun. Coggie did, as well. Actually, it was she who read it to me."

"That so pleases me," beamed Stevenson. "It's not much, perhaps. For a juvenile audience. But it's a start."

"It's a pip, Lou. I wouldn't let her stop reading." He looked fondly at his sibling. "Words of genius—on the lips of an angel." She responded with a distinctly unladylike face, reminding Stevenson of the saucy young beauty she had been in Ferrier's university days—an intelligent girl who obviously yearned to burst from the domestic cloister out into the wider world. "It was the only thing that could take my mind off this infernal itch." Ferrier scratched in pantomime at his arm and then his torso. "Damn this affliction! Damn all afflictions! So has it sold well, Stevenson? Has *Treasure Island* brought treasure to *your* island?"

"It is selling tolerably well, thank you. But if there is a real fortune being amassed, I myself have yet to see it. Perhaps you should inquire at Cassell's."

"Ah, yes. Your esteemed publisher." Ferrier nodded and turned his free hand to examine his nails. "Honestly though, Lou, I kept looking for some kind of love interest. Knowing your weakness for the ladies— them, and the devotions they inspire." He looked puckishly at his friend and then at his sister. "Or should I say the deviations?"

"Really, dear brother. There are ladies *present.*"

"Well, none of them in Stevenson's damned book! Unless you count the mum. Jim's avaricious mum. Fumbling for her due through a pile of coins whilst the killers rush their way. Marvelous suspense, that! I was cursing her, Lou!"

Stevenson smiled. "The poverty of ladies was Sam's requirement.

Not that I do them very well. Ladies."

"I have heard others say as much." Ferrier peered over his fist as he nibbled at a nail. "And ladies can be so very difficult…to *do.*"

"And Sam?" queried Coggie, clearly determined to ignore her brother's provocations.

"My stepson. He was ten when we hatched the story, the two of us." Coggie nodded sweetly.

"All full of Captain Maryatt and Mungo Park. And pirates. He insisted there be no women. No significant ones, at least."

"But Coggie, you know," blurted Ferrier, "Coggie contends that all women are significant. Ain't that so? Vital 'cogs,' every one, in our galloping social engine."

"Oh my goodness," exclaimed his sister theatrically. "Walter's made a joke! A wee pun. You see what a wit I have for a brother, Louis. A veritable Mercutio."

"Mercutio indeed," sighed Ferrier. "Thou speaketh wiselier than thou knoweth. 'Ask for me tomorrow, and you shall find me a grave man.'" He eyed her intently then turned back to Stevenson. "But look now. I've gone and dampened our levity. Self-indulgence is such a bother in the terminally ill. Don't you find?"

Stevenson scrabbled again for something to say. "There's hardly anything you could offer up, Ferrier, that I wouldn't be delighted and privileged to hear."

Ferrier fixed him with narrowed eyes. "Hmmm! I struggle to assess the sincerity with which you speak, dear friend." He paused again, then added sunnily, "Yet I shall take it for the best."

"As it was meant," said Stevenson. "Although, as always, Ferrier, I do treasure your infinite capacity for skepticism."

"There's my old Lou," cried Ferrier, clapping his hands. "Splendid. Now, where were we? I find it so hard lately…"

"Louis's book, I believe."

"Oh yes. That's right. From Cassell's, as he reminds us. How apt, really, that it should be Cassell's."

"Apt in what sense?" asked Coggie.

"They've a strong Temperance leaning, have they not?"

"They do indeed," replied the writer, feeling now a vague disquiet at the trend in conversation. "Temperance, along with every other righteous cause one might conceive of. We took their *Family Paper* when I was a child, so I am particularly well versed."

"So did we!" exclaimed Coggie. "It *was* always full of admonitory stories. And pictures."

Stevenson gazed at her and smiled. "Personally, I much preferred *Punch*."

"Indeed," declared Ferrier. "*Punch* the magazine and punch the beverage, both. Ha! So I'm driven to wonder, Lou, if the Cassell family's position on drink weren't instrumental in their decision to present your genius to the world."

"Whatever do you mean?" asked Coggie.

"I fear your dear brother is suggesting that Cassell's decision was based on something other than literary merit."

Ferrier grinned but shook his head.

Coggie looked at him insistently. "It is simply an excellent book, Walter. Nothing more and nothing less. Anyone could have seen that it deserved an audience. I've heard that even Mr. Gladstone found it admirable."

"Q.E.D., then!" exclaimed Ferrier, with a slap at his thigh. "The Temperance conspiracy confirmed. A teetotaling publishing house and a teetotaling Prime Minister—who, as we all know, is hell-bent on turning this into a completely dry island. It's, it's…"

Stevenson's budding unease gave way to concern as the sick man winced with surprise and started to cough, more and more rapidly and violently. His face flushed with the strain, turning a gruesome reddish-brown.

"Walter," cried Coggie, rushing to his side. She laid her arm across his back and took his hand in her own. "Can I fetch you some water?" The man nodded, his eyes extruded, more than a hint of fear in them as he struggled to check the spasms. Stevenson felt his own muscles tense, knowing all too well what Ferrier was going through—waiting for the blood to come with its gagging taste of iron. He could only sit and watch, as impotent in the moment as in the larger sweep of Ferrier's life.

Coggie hurried back with a glass, steadying her brother as he sipped and swallowed. Soon enough his shoulders relaxed and he settled back with a sigh. "Not so bad," he whispered once he had glanced down to inspect his palm. "No gore at all. Perhaps there's none left in me." He looked at Stevenson with a softer expression than he had shown the whole while. The look recalled the Walter of old. "Quite the conversation stopper, that. My apologies."

"Not at all. Are you all right?" As though he could ever be right again.

"Better. For the present. I am indeed." Ferrier paused for a moment, gazing back and forth between his two companions. "You are both so dear to me. I fear, Louis, I can play the tyrant at times. Interrogating you the way I seem to have been doing."

"You were merely showing interest in my work, dear Walter. As always, your interest flatters me."

"I am glad." Ferrier smiled graciously. *"Will* you, though, indulge mc in a serious question?"

Stevenson laughed a mite uneasily and shook his head. "I'm not sure I'm quite prepared for a serious question from you, Walter. It might be the very first you have ever addressed to me."

Stevenson looked for some witty repartee, but his old friend regarded him with earnestness. "All this playful talk of your publisher emerges from a powerful reaction I had to the story from the very start. Which led to a curiosity about its author's intent."

"Please go on."

"You once declared yourself, Lou, 'Literature is a mirror held up to life.'"

Stevenson grinned. "That was Dr. Johnson, Walter. Not humble I. A mirror up to nature and life, he spoke of. And poetry in specific."

"Damn!" swore Ferrier, chuckling. "Of course. You're quite right.

But then," he added with a twinkle, "perhaps I have always thought of you as the nearest thing to the learned Doctor that Auld Reekie has managed to spawn."

"I assure you I have neither the wit nor the talent," responded Stevenson. "Nor the Boswell. Though perhaps, being a good Edinburghian, you might care for the job."

"I fear I am destined to other tasks," answered Ferrier. "Still, it is a corking good observation, whoever made it. To the point, though. This book for boys? Your charming adventure? Some grown men may be moved to look deeply into the mirror you hold up there, Lou. To real life!"

"And see…?" The writer glanced over at Coggie, who peered at her brother attentively.

"'Fifteen men on a dead man's chest'?" Ferrier leaned towards his old friend, studying him under gathered brows. "'Drink and the devil have done with the rest?'"

Stevenson might have found such close scrutiny unsettling in and of itself. Given the line their conversation seemed to be taking, it was all the more so.

It was Coggie who broke several seconds of awkward silence. "Walter! What are you on about?"

Ferrier leaned back and sniffed. "It's not lost on me, Lou, that your tale is primarily a broadside against the follies of avarice. Wise men and fools alike seduced by the lure of immeasurable wealth." He waved a hand as though to include the richly appointed room itself among the vain treasuries of the world.

Stevenson shifted restlessly in his chair.

"Jim vowing, in the end, never to go back to Treasure Island. Jim haunted all his days by the horror of what he has witnessed—that, and the awful echo of Silver's parrot—and how apt the man's name, no? Silver!—'Pieces of eight! Pieces of eight!'" The sick man screeched in perfect imitation of a bird.

"I expect I should again be flattered. You've evidently studied my little entertainment with some care."

"Aye. And drunk deep of it, laddie. And, as I say, caught a strong whiff of your notoriously imminent socialism."

"Oh, Walter!" exclaimed Stevenson. "My dark secret is a secret no more. Promise me this will never get back to my father." He winked nervously at Coggie, who grinned her reassurance.

"Nonetheless," Ferrier continued more earnestly, "you seem to have written at least as strong an indictment of drink. Have you not?"

Well, hell and damnation! thought Stevenson, as the grimmest potential of his visit was somehow coming to fruition. The conversation had run hard up against exactly what made the present moment so very dreadful. "Walter," he protested, looking assertively at his friend. "It's a boys' entertainment, the silly book. Not a polemic."

Ferrier leaned forward once more. "Don't you know what I'm saying?"

"You think my book is a Temperance tract?" Stevenson thought back to the wet and dreary week in Braemar when he and Sam, cottage-bound, had drawn the treasure map and hatched the plot, and his father had joined them in the giddy excitement of invention. Any of them would have sworn under oath that it had been undertaken as pure amusement.

"I do. In its way. Should I not?"

In an instant, it was as though the morning's colloquy with his father had been a calculated prelude to all of this. *Uncontestably explicit communication.* Somehow, he now found himself precisely in his father's position, naively assuming that writing ought to be "clear as a patent light," that he had written a tale whose motive and effect were irrevocably linked to one another. Perhaps they seldom were.

"Well," he responded, "I don't know. I can't honestly say I thought of all the drinking as anything more than a way to color character." He looked at Coggie as though to muster her support. "Rum for pirates, wine for gentlemen, you know. Muskets for the pirates and a fowling gun for the Squire. I don't think of myself as a writer of allegories."

Ferrier sat up and turned to his sister. "Am I daft? You read it. Look at all the men dead from drink. The fifteen on the chest ain't the half of 'em."

"I don't know, Walter," replied Coggie. "I've not had the privilege of attending university. It is not for the likes of me to judge complicated matters of textual understanding."

"For God's sake, Coggie," sputtered Ferrier. "When did you turn into the New Woman? I might as well have Nora Helmer for my nursemaid." Despite his animation, he managed to smile at her before he turned back to Stevenson. "Far be it from me to point it out to their creator, Lou—but, thick as I may be, I could hardly help noticing that the wisest of your characters demonize drink. Silver and the doctor both. The survivors. 'The fittest.' I don't know if it's a case of moral justice or of Darwinian science, but that's surely one of the lessons that emerge from your little adventure. No?"

Stevenson waited for a moment before he spoke, guiltily wishing he were somewhere else entirely. Playing at tin soldiers with Sam. Resisting Mary's proffered charms. Even arguing theology with his father. "Remember, Walter; Silver and Livesey are drinkers, too. Both of them. And *I* am hardly one to demonize drink. How long is it that I have been sober now? Six hours?"

"You're right," conceded Ferrier, guffawing at that. "I phrased it poorly. But neither of *them* drinks to excess, Lou."

Excess, of course, was the thing. Read it that way and the tale might well constitute a sermon decrying the extravagance of the Walters of the world. Or, perhaps more kindly, as some kind of warning *to* the Walters of the world—late as it may have been delivered.

For a moment, none of them spoke. Finally, Stevenson found it in himself to concede to the inevitable, uncomfortable as it might be. "I suppose, Walter, you might justly see the narrative as warning against… the kinds of indulgence you cite. Also against the mindless pursuit of wealth."

Coggie nodded.

"And you intended that first?" asked Ferrier pointedly.

"Perhaps I did. Indirectly. I fancy I was writing to please my father. At least in part I was. He was there, you see, with Sam and the rest when it was written. He always frowned on my carryings-on, you know. On our collective carryings-on." He grinned at the irony of it all: to have defied one's father by becoming a writer, only to write just what a father would want one to have written! The goose feather in the hurricane.

"Thank you, Louis. For indulging me." Ferrier settled back on the chaise. "I am relieved to think that I'm not utterly mad. Now, let us put this to rest, this latter-day Inquisition."

"I am so very relieved," sighed Coggie. "I do like to think a university education makes for an improved life, not a more fractious one."

"Behold the idealism of the uninitiated!" pronounced Ferrier. "Matriculate, my dear girl, and you will quickly see what a complete waste it all is, this baccalaureate nonsense. By the by, Lou, I won't for a second say that your rummy book didn't sometimes make me as thirsty as it made me fear the thirst."

"Alas! I seem to have scribbled shoddy propaganda."

"Rather like those sermons," Ferrier chuckled, "where the sins we are meant to eschew are described in such alluring detail that they become far more appealing than their remedies?"

Stevenson grinned and was about to respond when there came a loud knock at the door.

"Yes?" called Coggie.

The maid who had shown Stevenson into the house reentered the room. "Mrs. Ferrier would like to see you in the drawing room, Miss Elizabeth."

"Thank you, Annie," said Coggie, rising to her feet. "Tell her, please, I shall be there presently." She turned to Stevenson. "I don't know how long I shall be gone. Perhaps I should bid you adieu."

"*À bientôt*, rather," said Stevenson, standing to take her hand. "It has been lovely to see you."

"And you. You are so good to have visited."

"I shall come as often as I can."

"We shall count on it, Walter and I." With a smile at her brother, she turned to slip quietly out the door.

"You should have married the lass," declared Ferrier with a shake of the head. "I always said so. Nothing against…against…?"

"Fanny."

"Of course. Fanny. Damn my shriveling brain! Now, fetch me a glass!"

"Pardon me? A glass?"

Ferrier pointed to a small decanter across the room.

"Walter!" Stevenson looked askance at his ailing friend. "I thought we had just determined—"

"For God's sake, Louis! That was all amusing chatter. A renewal of our entertaining debates at the Speculative Society. But I'm past saving, don't you know? You can plainly see I am past any cure. No matter how many compelling morals I may draw from my literary diversions." He looked imploringly at his friend, who stood immobilized. "Damn it, Stevenson! Even my sanctimonious mother knows I can't live without a drop. That's the only reason there's any of it in the house! Besides, it's not as though I can drown myself in the stuff. Look at the size of that bottle. It's a bloody thimble, Lou. Please!"

Still Stevenson hesitated.

"For the love of God, man!"

The writer rose and slowly crossed the room, sensing his friend stewing with impatience behind him. He poured a glass half-full of spirits and started back.

"Fill it!" barked Ferrier. Then, more softly, "Fill it, if you would. And one for yourself." His look was, in equal measure, imperious and imploring. "Don't stand there like a statue, man. Surely you'll drink with me. Who knows when you'll have another chance?"

There was obviously no cure for Ferrier's ailment. It could well be that a further dose of his curse was the man's only palliative. Stevenson recalled his own Jim Hawkins finally breaking down and fetching Billy Bones his forbidden rum at the Admiral Benbow. Perhaps, in this, his creature was his better.

"Of course I will," he sighed. "Even if this is not the last time. Which I hope and trust it will not be."

"There!" exclaimed Ferrier as he savored a deep swallow. He composed himself almost instantaneously. "Here's to friendship!"

"To friendship."

Their glasses clinked. In the silence that followed, Stevenson felt the inevitable wave building in his chest until he knew it must break. "I fear, though," he offered up in a voice almost too soft to be heard, "I have not always been much of a friend."

"Nonsense. You have been as loyal as Damon to Pythias. Or is it Pythias to Damon? I'll be damned if I can ever remember which of the buggers went off to prison for the other." He guffawed yet again and held out his empty tumbler.

"Should you?"

"No. But there's scarce an alternative, Lou. You can see it's my only solace. Excepting the ministrations of my dear sister. And, of course, your coming back to see me." He took the refilled glass from Stevenson's hand and raised it anew. "To Pythias. And Orpheus. And Jesus Christ. Would-be rescuers all."

"I fear I've come too late," sighed the writer.

"You've come."

"I was with you too seldom when you…while…"

"While what?" asked Ferrier, with a slight cough and slap at his chest. "When what? Do you think you could have made a difference for me, Lou?"

"I don't know, Walter. I suppose I should like to have tried."

"I believe you did try. Well before you even wrote your book—if that was truly a little admonitory salvo." He smiled kindly. "When and as you could. I think you told me more than once that I was living with no regard…well, recklessly, I suppose. I honestly recall cursing you for some of the things you said to me, so you must have said some forceful things, and said them more than once." Ferrier chuckled. "And the way you would sometimes look at me! My God! *It has all been great fun, Walter,"* he intoned, mimicking Stevenson's soft tenor voice. *"But we have serious lives to get on with."*

"So let us embrace the wisdom of our fathers?" Stevenson smiled at the poignant recollection. "As opposed to disregarding everything they ever said?"

"Exactly!"

"It wasn't the kind of advice a wastrel could readily take to heart, was it? Any of us."

"Not precisely."

"Well, I should like to have done better. I should like, at least, to have spent more time with you."

"You had other things to attend to. Things that were more important to you."

"Walter!"

"No, Louis. I am perfectly serious. We all have our own lives to live. I have found my own way, and you have found yours. I wish you every happiness pursuing it."

Stevenson remained silent. Here and now, there was painfully little to be said, unless it were to offer some insipid hope for Walter's fate at Judgment—that, or the simple wish for a painless end.

"Besides," Ferrier continued, "I would have been poor company far too much of the time. Even distasteful company, I suppose. Certain days and nights." He looked at Stevenson piercingly. "I don't wish to be immodest, Lou, but I could write a book, a life, to shock the respectable world. I abhor the man I have sometimes become."

"Walter!"

"No. Abhorrence is not too strong a word. For his endless indulgences. For his damnable disregard for others. And mostly, you know… mostly…" He paused, nodding to himself.

"For what?"

"For the way his indulgences continued to beckon. Night and day. As inescapable as the skin on my bones." Ferrier flinched visibly. "He called me back like a fucking siren every time I resolved to take back the helm and steer another course. To live to some end, for God's sake, other than myself. This wretched self."

It was a moment before Stevenson could speak. "We've all of us been selfish, Walter. At one time or another. It can never have been worse than some of the silly jinkings we used to get up to."

Ferrier smiled but shook his head. "You wouldn't have known me, Lou. Honestly. I quailed to know myself."

Stevenson labored to whisper. "Is it too late?"

Ferrier held up both of his hands, as though to frame his face. *"Ecce homo*. Behold what I have done to myself."

4

I had learned to dwell with pleasure, as of a beloved daydream, on the separation of these elements. If each, I told myself, could but be housed in separate identities, life would be relieved of all that was unbearable; the unjust might go his way, delivered from the aspirations and remorse of his more upright twin; and the just could walk steadfastly and securely on his upward path; doing the good things in which he found his pleasure, and no longer exposed to disgrace and penitence by the hands of this extraneous evil. It was the curse of mankind that these incongruous faggots were thus bound together—that in the agonized womb of consciousness, these polar twins should be continuously struggling. How, then, were they dissociated?
—DR. HENRY JEKYLL

The weather had begun to clear by the time Stevenson left the Ferrier house. Despite a mounting wind, he resolved not to return directly to Heriot Row. As he often did when grappling with a challenge of a personal or literary sort, he took to his feet, ambling south in the dying sunlight. Beyond the Castle, Arthur's Seat glowed stunningly against a retreating bank of cloud, and he struck out in that direction, nudged along by the freshening gale. To make his way home, he would be obliged to walk straight into the teeth of it. For now, though, it was easy to sail straight before the wind, heedless of futurity, collar turned up, hands thrust deeply into his overcoat pockets.

Thank goodness Coggie had been there. He had gone with no distinct sense of what it was he wanted to say to Walter, and with her in attendance, he could at least hope that his dreadful incapacities were less glaring. Still, his virtual bankruptcy of any significant or consoling words to offer the dying man surprised and bewildered him. And he affected to be a writer! It reminded him of those wretched days when, try as he might, as energized as he might be by tea and tobacco, he festered over a blank sheet of paper with a skull as void as a vacuum bottle. It occurred to him, by way of self-consolation, that little in his past had prepared him for the demands of the moment. The death of a beloved cat—even of a beloved grandparent—had hardly set him up for the challenges of the day. He had also been thrown off balance by Ferrier's tart manner, not to mention his mother's singularly abrupt departure. In Ferrier's position, of course, he too might have been determined to show an old friend that his wit was still in the finest order. Nonetheless, the sweet playfulness of Walter's wonted humor had been strongly tempered by something more acerbic. Perhaps his rather abrasive jocularity was a gift of sorts, perhaps even a double gift—both lightening the somberness of the moment and also, given its sharp edge, sparing one the awkwardness of feeling too much pity for the man.

By the time Stevenson passed the hotel where he had lunched what seemed like eons ago, the sun had dropped to within a few degrees of the Pentland Hills. He reached the long series of steps leading up to Calton Hill just as the lamplighters began their rounds in the streets below. Climbing steadily towards the prospect he had long considered Edinburgh's best, he recalled countless nights when, as a child, he had perched in a dining room window at dusk, waiting for the man called Leerie who, regular as clockwork, hastened through their terrace, setting each lamp aglow. The mysterious functionary had seemed to young Louis like a nocturnal honeybee—or better, perhaps, like an angular moth—settling for a perfectly motionless instant at each gaslight before he flitted off to the next, leaving behind him a magical trail of brilliance.

Stevenson often wondered if he himself could be seen from the street, silhouetted in the tall window, and if Leerie might ever notice him waiting there and wonder about him in anything like the same way he wondered about Leerie. Where did the man live? Did another little son wait patiently for him in another snug home? Did the man sleep all day long so that he could wake all night, linking each Edinburgh street and wynd in a twinkling net of tiny yellow stars?

As the western sky deepened through crimson into violet, Stevenson halted and took a seat on a bench overlooking the great city. The evening's high wind had cleared most of the smoke that so often dulled the grand prospect, but the acrid scent of a thousand coal fires still found its way to him. On a clement day, even at this hour, scores of people would have been there to share this choice vista. Now he was the only soul in sight. It was almost certainly rash to be here on his own, a ripe mark for anyone wanting a quick and unearned coin. Just a week back, he had read, a drunken railway navvy had been beaten and robbed right there at the base of the Nelson Monument, left for dead—and would have died, had a constable not stumbled upon him. On a day such as this, though, caution be damned!

Below him, beyond a stand of trees that tossed darkly in the wind, sprawled the meandering, medieval by-ways of Old Town, its tall lands packed with the destitute and hungry: society's oft-decried "residuum." Above and beyond them loomed the Castle, perched unassailably on its mighty rock, bastion of the transcendent, tyrannical might of ages past. To the right of that lay the scrupulously regular patterns of New Town, founded on trade and commerce and all of the less baldly brutal engines of modern dominance, a stylish yet deadening precinct of respectability and good taste. Just past there would be Ferrier's house, final venue for a life of which all too much had unfolded in the dark and weathered haunts that lay, just now, much closer to hand, side sinister.

Stevenson could surely chart his own days and moral condition alike by placing them on an imaginary line between Old Town and New. If, after the fancy of St. Paul, there were a great schism between the law of one's members and the law of one's mind, that schism lay materially embodied before Stevenson, disposed in physical space, crafted in stone and mortar, steel and cement. The one city was two, the New always in peril of tumbling, like the boulder in the myth, back into the Old— of being drawn to it, of hearing its call and reverting to it, through a damning act of will. Or would even such a backsliding be scripted in advance by a divine hand, for whom no chapter of the earthly narrative could be anything other than predetermined? Stevenson no longer really prayed; but there, with the harsh wind whipping his long hair and darting its chilly way into his tightly gathered clothing, he could have prayed for Walter Ferrier.

His thoughts coursed back to the little lad on the train—only yesterday, was it?—so very much in the inaugural miles of his own life's journey. It had been so easy, so gratifying, to scrawl a few amusing lines for him as he sped into his un-limned future. Perhaps something for Ferrier, as well, had already sprung from Stevenson's pen; so Walter had alleged. If so, however, what possible good had it done him? And what could he possibly do for his old friend now? The whole auctorial enterprise seemed at times so pointlessly indulgent. It might well have been wiser to follow docilely in the family footsteps—to design and build lighthouses and incontestably save a man's life now again. Even the practice of law would surely have yielded more patently useful results.

He rose from the bench with a sigh and set off down the hill into the teeth of a formidable gale.

As Fiona cleared the pudding plates, Thomas Stevenson pushed back from the table and turned to his son. "Port?"

"If you please." Stevenson wiped his moustache and laid his napkin off to the side.

"Maggie?" asked the older man as he rose to his feet.

"No, thank you, dearest."

Stevenson senior walked over to the claw-foot sideboard, clearly battling stiffness in his hips.

"Too much on my feet today," he declared, raising two crystal glasses to the gas lamp for inspection.

"I told him to take the barouche," said Stevenson's mother. "But when does your father ever listen to me?"

Stevenson smiled and brushed distractedly at a few breadcrumbs on the tablecloth as his father poured two full measures from the flared decanter. He hobbled back to the dining table and extended a glass.

"Thank you, Father."

"You are most welcome." The older man made his way to his own seat, patting his wife on the shoulder as he passed. "I do listen, you know, Maggie. At least once a day, I listen." She gazed up at him adoringly. "I think, Lou, you'll find it a pleasant vintage."

"Thank heavens this is not a teetotal house," exclaimed Stevenson. He took a good swallow of the ruby draught, relishing its syrupy warmth as it rolled back over his tongue.

"Moderation in all things," responded the father. "How readily we seem to forget the wisdom of the ancients."

"How true," agreed the son. "How true." He sipped again and set the little glass down, rotating it slowly by the base with his long fingers. "This is very nice indeed."

"You know, Lou," said his father, in a softer tone, "reflecting on it, I don't know that I could have managed the conversation with Walter any better than you did."

"It was so dispiriting, Father. I was so little up to the task."

"The important thing is that you were there," observed his mother, reaching out to press his hand.

"Of course I was there," sighed Stevenson. "And I am grateful to you for your letter, Mother. I expect I had simply been putting it all out of my head."

"You can thank Mrs. Ferrier for the notice. It was she, you know, who wrote to me. To us." Maggie Stevenson looked quickly at her husband, then back at her son.

"I suppose," allowed Stevenson, "but Walter, as I said, is hardly as close to the grave as she might have led us to expect. And I confess I wasn't much moved by the reception she gave me."

"What do you mean?"

"She was extremely chilly to me, Mother. Called me 'Mr. Stevenson' and 'sir.' Left me with Walter and Coggie with no ceremony whatsoever. One might almost say she stormed out of the room mere minutes after I arrived."

"Of course she will be devastated by the sad turn of events," observed his father.

"Of course. But I fear she holds me responsible. Somehow."

"Holds you responsible, Smout?" asked Thomas Stevenson. "However so?"

"I was his friend…"

"And?"

"And I suppose I neither set a very good example," confessed Stevenson, pointing towards his glass, "nor truly took him aside when it was plain that he was doing himself in."

"We have been through all of that most thoroughly, you and I," declared the elder Stevenson with some force. "The old business of influences and the like. I own I was far too hard on you in some of the things I said. In the end, however, Walter chose for himself the path that he has walked down. There is little use in pointing fingers—either at others or at ourselves."

"Surely we can point a finger at the drink trade, can we not?" asked his wife. "To some degree, at least? I think Mr. Gladstone surely has a vision of a better way."

"Maggie," sputtered her husband in feigned amazement. "Honestly, should we look for you to start clamoring for every other Liberal cause as well?"

"I expect we should," quipped Stevenson. "Mother's like to join the battle for women's suffrage! Our gray-haired resident Amazon." A sudden and unwelcome image of his mother swam into his ken, naked to the waist with a bow drawn over a surgically removed breast. He blinked it into oblivion.

"Well, gentlemen," exclaimed his mother, twitching in a show of indignation. "I believe this may be the moment for me to retire for the evening. It is perfectly clear that I enjoy no respect in my present company."

"We shall move on, dearest," said Thomas Stevenson, checking to make sure that was indeed a smile poised on his wife's lips. "I still maintain, however, as I always have, that there is nothing either demonic or angelic about alcohol. It is a neutral commodity. It merely makes a good man more engaged and jovial. And, as it seems from the depredations of this Skeleton Army about which we hear more and more, an evil man more remote and cruel."

Stevenson struggled to hold his tongue—to no avail. "And if drink is a neutral commodity, Father, and it is the nature of the man that determines its effect, what then determines the nature of the man?"

"The nature of man is to be mired in sinfulness…to one degree or another. We were speaking of that just this morning, if I'm not mistaken. When you so fondly recalled Cummy's daily pronouncements on 'total depravity.'" Thomas Stevenson smiled in a playful manner.

"But some of those depraved ones are ultimately saved," his son responded flatly. "Through no particular virtue of their own."

"There are indeed the recipients of Grace—God's Chosen. And then there are the others."

"The others," repeated Stevenson coldly. "The doomed. How I should like to know if Walter is doomed. Has always been doomed."

"Has Walter been evil?" asked Margaret Stevenson with evident concern. "What has he done, Louis, aside from squandering his life the way he has?"

"I don't think I can definitively say, Mother. I have not been with him so much of late."

"I expect," said Stevenson senior, "we will not in truth know how your friend is to be judged until we all stand before the Great White Throne and all things hidden are revealed. He may have *done* evil things.

Unseemly things." He paused and looked solicitously at his wife.

"I should like to know a bit sooner than that," said his son. "And to know if Walter's fate was determined, in essence, before he ever took his first step. And, selfishly, if anything I have done or said could really have made any difference to him at all."

"Louis!" exclaimed his mother.

"No, Mother. I should also like to know why we must always wrestle, endlessly it seems, with what is unruly in our nature. What so many deem illicit—Paul and the rest. Is it truly *illicit,* I wonder? Or is it merely *implicit,* that part of us? Perhaps even *important?*"

"Of course it is important," exclaimed Thomas Stevenson, warming in the face of his wife's mounting distress. "It is our essential means of enacting virtue on this earth. We demonstrate our virtue by eschewing vice."

"Yes, of course. I know. *I cannot praise a fugitive and cloistered virtue,*" recited Stevenson dismissively. "But how unconscionably cruel it is, Father, that the urgings of our nature, of our very being, should be voices we must endlessly struggle to silence! I sometimes think that Ferrier drank so much precisely because he drank so much."

"Oh my!" exclaimed his mother. "I am thoroughly confused."

Stevenson reined in a snort of annoyance. Far too many postprandial discussions had, in past years, ended in outbursts of temper and tears; he was newly determined to amend that. "Walter merely had a young man's inborn thirst for amusement, Mother," he explained. "But when he committed a few more solecisms than he ought, the raised eyebrows of respectability ultimately drove him to destruction." A quick look at his father revealed to Stevenson that his self-restraint had come a trifle too late.

"Enough!" cried the latter. "We'll have no more of this! Especially in front of your mother. Is this what comes of reading your wretched Spencer? All of that godless balderdash about...I don't know what?"

Stevenson blinked momentarily, then loosed a nervous laugh. "Apparently it is." He looked at his mother, who fanned herself busily with one hand. "I am sorry, Mother."

"I should think you are," declared his father. "I can barely tolerate that you've become a writer, Louis; I won't have you becoming a theologian as well. Least of all an heretical one."

"Again, I apologize for that. It has been a difficult day." Stevenson looked once more at his mother, whose air of confusion resolved itself into an understanding nod.

"And this from a lad whose first literary undertaking was nothing less than *A History of Moses*," observed Thomas, beginning to regain his equanimity.

"Indeed," said Stevenson, with a wry chuckle. "Such a start! I seem to have wandered from the path. In the future, I shall endeavor to do better."

"Excellent," said his father. "We shall count upon it. Will you join me, then, in another splash of port?"

Dear Pig, wrote Stevenson, settled into the library after his mother and father had labored up the stairs to their bedroom. Twin gaslights sighed on the wall, and the oil lamp on the table in front of him filled the room with a distinctly antique odor as it cast its warm glow on his paper. Now and again, behind the drawn draperies, gusts rattled the frames of the high windows.

> *How I miss you—and miss your dear head on the pillow beside me. Almost certainly you will have embraced me myself—in all of my spindly glory— well before your sweet and plump little fingers caress these pages. I return to London and Bournemouth on the morrow, while the post will hardly travel as fast as I. Well before you receive this, wheedling soul that you are, you will doubtless have extracted from me every detail that may follow, rendering this epistle nothing more than an empty…well, the metaphor eludes me. And it is not the first time today that the flighty presumption that I am a man of words has been exposed for the fantasy that it is. You needn't fear, sweet Goose, that I shall abandon my struggle to become the famed scribbler you would have me be. But as for all verbal pretentions, I went to see Ferrier today and was as dumb, in the end, as the Sphinx.*

What a wreck poor Walter has made of himself! And how easily I say that, as though he were the product of his own choosing and nothing more. But, dearest Fanny, when (as I sat there) I wasn't clawing my way out from under the old conviction that we control where we are bound no more than we can stifle a sneeze, I was ransacking a thousand memories for times when Baxter or Bob or, most of all, I could have picked him up by the scruff of the neck and shaken him powerful good and shouted in his pickled face, "Walter, cease this sotted buffoonery and become a Man!" Then again, when I might have done so, you had yet to make a Man of ME!

More on this later, no doubt, but how little of use I had to say to the poor lad. To him or to his most wonderful sister, whom I believe you have met. His mother, however…remind me to recount her behavior, and what I take to be its cause.

Last night Charles and I did waste a few hours in bibulous foolery, but none that ran us afoul of the Law, much to Mother Maggie's relief. He remains such an entertaining fellow—as indeed does Ferrier, despite the grave decline. The poor lad's good humour and wit are a wonder, although there is a roughness to it now. Sweet Walter peeks out now and again from behind that awful yellow mask he is wearing, but the poor fellow may have seen too much ever to be the dear old boy he was. I had such an inescapable sense of a man turned against himself. When he spoke of the depths to which he had descended, he spoke of himself in the third person, as though he were decrying an other fellow altogether for "his indulgences," or "his damnable selfishness." I cannot begin to know the whole of it, although he did allude sadly to a "Life" he could write that might "shock the world." While I am certain he will not pick up the pen, invalided as he is under the roof of his censorious mother, I must confess to a certain morbid curiosity about what he might offer up. The sins of others are so enticing, especially when one has the courage to admit to oneself that "there but for fortune…" How much more engaging and worthy would something from Walter be than this farcical Bohemian three-decker fable to which you have me bound. O Otto, Otto, feckless Otto! Another Meredith I shall never be.

Mother and Father are well and ask after you fondly—and after Sam. I believe I shall have a last cigarette and retreat to my little bed in the attic to dream of you. Tomorrow I shall race back to you, leaving these limp and lifeless words to trail in my wake like dry and rustling leaves—if dry leaves can be limp. You see? O, but my muse has fled!!!

I remain, as ever and for all time, your devoted and doting slave,

Uxorious Billy

5

The pleasures which I made haste to seek in my disguise were, as I have said, undignified; I would scarce use a harder term. But in the hands of Edward Hyde, they soon began to turn towards the monstrous. When I would come back from these excursions, I was often plunged into a kind of wonder at my vicarious depravity.

—DR. HENRY JEKYLL

HYÈRES, MAY 1883

Stevenson lay sprawled on a Persian carpet, his legs jutting out from beneath a green paisley robe. The long, pajama-shrouded calves were tense with excitement, but they were scarcely stouter than chair legs.

Since he and Fanny and Sam had come to Hyères, his health had unquestionably improved. There had been little coughing now for weeks, and no hemorrhages for much longer than that. Still, his weight hung at the lowest level of his adult life, seven stone eleven, and this had sent Fanny into the latest of her intermittent panics. Despite their slender means—imprudently depleted during an extravagant pre-departure stay at the Grosvenor Hotel when they had entertained scores of Stevenson's London literary friends—she had insisted that they hire a cook-cum-general domestic in order to enhance their cuisine. Henceforth, the unmarried daughter of the local baker had laid on a groaning table of fresh meats, fish, and fowl; many of them bathed in the rich sauces of the region and accompanied by exquisite golden baguettes and croissants from her father's shop. From time to time, Stevenson joked that he needed a diving suit to reach the bottom of Valentine's soup bowls. It remained, nonetheless, a moustachioed scarecrow that greeted him each morning in the shaving glass.

"Sound the charge!" cried Sam, squatting across the carpet from his stepfather. He held his fist to his mouth in a commendable imitation of a bugle rousing men to battle.

"Pickett's battle-hardened companies surge out from the trees along Seminary Ridge," intoned Stevenson as he watched Sam advance a dozen lead soldiers from a fold in the carpet that was Longstreet's position outside the small provincial town of Gettysburg, Pennsylvania. "Grey and lean as starving wolves, brazen to a man, they stride out into the hot July sun."

Eyes wide with excitement, trumpeting on in ever-higher keys, Sam pushed his troops forward, towards General Meade's Union position— the fold that lay six feet away, just under Stevenson's chin.

"Secure behind their advantageous stone wall," the writer droned on, "Meade's men hold their fire as the gray masses venture out onto the killing ground." He chuckled demonically as he adjusted several of his own troops behind a small woolen kink he had dubbed the "Bloody Angle."

Sam grinned at the dark narrative and inched his men bravely on. "Pickett's loyal hundreds cross the Emmitsburg Road," he chanted in turn, advancing a half-dozen men over the silk belt that had been stripped from Stevenson's robe and laid diagonally across the carpet. "They hook north towards the Bloody Angle. Trimble, too, advances from the west."

"Prepare to meet your maker, rebel scoundrels!" taunted Stevenson, reaching for the spring pistol that lay by his side. Aiming it at Sam's troops, he growled, "Hold your fire, men. Hold! Hold! Now!" He pulled the trigger and a pellet shot forth, taking one of Sam's men full in the face. "Smile at that, you slave-whipping scoundrel. Smile if you can, without your *head!*"

Sam snarled his defiance and again sounded the rebel charge.

"Ye gods! Still they come," sighed Stevenson. "'Tis a pity such brave men must die. But," he cackled as he reached into his robe pocket, "it is time for the heavy artillery." He extracted a half-dozen sleeve-links and shook them maniacally.

"Steady, men, steady. We're gaining ground."

"Fire!" yelled Stevenson, his voice cracking with excitement. Fighting back the urge to cough, he launched one of the sleeve-links at Sam's troops, knocking two over outright and tumbling the thing viciously into two more. "Load again. You there! Ninny! Sponge out before you recharge. You'll blow us all to smithereens." He looked anxiously at Sam. "Where are these damn recruits coming from? Bedlam?"

"Bedlam's in London," laughed his stepson, back in his boy's voice. "This isn't England's Civil War, Lulu. It's America's!"

"Well, yes. Perhaps. But they're all the same, these civil wars." Stevenson's eyes widened with playful frenzy. "It's madness. Utter madness. Brother against brother. Father killing son."

"Son killing father," laughed Sam as he thrust a metal marauder over the Bloody Angle and gored one of Stevenson's men with his bayonet.

"Son killing father?" The new voice was high and heavily accented. The warriors looked up to see the baker's daughter, Valentine Roch, standing above them with a tray in her hands. She loomed over the battlefield like a colossus in a black dress, white apron, and cap. "Is this what you English do to—how do you say?—to occupy your time on a quiet *après-midi?*"

"*Bien sûr,*" answered Sam. "Oops. Is that right?" He peered at Stevenson, who nodded. "Of course, we're not English. Either of us. You know?"

"Of course," answered the woman with a tiny smile. "I forget. And what battle is this, please?"

"Gettysburg," Sam answered proudly. "From the American Civil

War. It's the fateful third day!"

"Oh my," said Valentine. "Fateful! Excuse me that I have spoiled your fateful small war. But do you wish some coffee?"

Sam looked at his stepfather, who nodded. "Yes, please. Thank you, Valentine."

The maid crossed to the table, careful not to stumble over the low Pennsylvania hills, and set the tray down with a graceful stoop. She was nearing thirty, but she retained a girlish figure—somewhat in contrast to Fanny, it had occurred to Stevenson, who was far shorter and inclined to plumpness. Stevenson's doctor had recently outraged his spouse, in fact, by telling her she was substantially overweight and should be eating half of what her husband consumed. Only a few inches shorter than Stevenson, Valentine was slim but not slight. There was something mildly feline about her face—intense green eyes and strongly arched brows that swept down into a strong length of nose, and a small mouth that was slightly pinched unless she laughed. She had not married, it seemed, but not for want of physical appeal. At the same time, there was a collected aloofness about her that left Fanny feeling relatively comfortable about sharing her house and household with an attractive young woman—as inimical to deferential service as aloofness may have been.

"I should pour?" she asked, looking back over her shoulder at Stevenson.

"If you would, please."

"And will you…mmmm…sit? Raise yourself from the floor?"

"No, you may serve us here," smiled Stevenson. "Al fresco. We don't want to disturb the battlefield. Or let the cannons cool."

Valentine returned the friendly expression as she leaned over to hand a cup to Sam, then to his adversary. "Your *ceinture?* Your belt?" she asked, pointing to the center of the carpet.

"Oh, that," laughed Stevenson. "That is the Emmitsburg Road."

"Comment?"

"It's a road," Sam interjected. "A road on the battlefield." The woman nodded as he took a sip from the steaming cup. "Yum. But very hot! Be careful, Lulu."

Valentine adjusted her apron and stood back from them. "Now, please. Can you tell me who wins?"

"The battle or the war?" asked the boy.

"Either. Both."

Sam turned to his stepfather in mild disbelief.

"The Union won," explained Stevenson, looking obligingly at their questioner. "The Northern states. The rebels—the Southerners—were defeated at Gettysburg. And went on to lose the war."

"So this revolution fails!" concluded Valentine, clasping her hands neatly in front of her apron.

"Yes," answered Sam.

"*Quel dommage!* Such a pity! Here in France, we embrace revolution." She turned to the writer. "Sometimes."

"Some revolutions are indeed a good thing," observed Stevenson, sipping at his cup. The coffee was very strong, very much to his taste.

"Our revolution against the English was a good one," said Sam, looking up smartly at the maid. "You French helped us with that one, you know. Lafayette and all."

"I am content," replied Valentine. "It is good to help others. There is honor in helping."

"Indeed," said Stevenson. "And we are grateful for your help here, Valentine. And for your coffee." He raised his cup in a small salute.

"*De rien.*" She dipped a shallow curtsy and looked back and forth between them with a bemused smile, struck perhaps by the oddity of employers who spoke to her from the floor. She began to leave, but then turned suddenly back. "Do you have French battles? Fight French battles? Or will you perhaps some day?"

"I don't know." Sam looked quizzically at his stepfather. "Will we, Lou?"

"If you'd like. But I should think it would have to be Wellington at Waterloo. Don't you agree?"

"I guess so," answered Sam. "And," he added, with a grin at the woman, "I'm afraid that wouldn't work out very well for you, Valentine."

"Waterloo?" she asked.

"Yes," answered Sam. "Lord Wellington defeated Boney, you know. Bonaparte. Completely."

"I know this," replied the maid. "I think, though, there are other battles of France you can do. Marengo? Austerlitz?" She studied them both again. "Balaclava? We French, we triumph in all."

"Goodness!" said Sam. "That's…that's…" He turned to Stevenson. "Valentine knows a lot!"

"Of course she does. Which is why your mother hired her." Stevenson eyed the maid kindly. It was hard to tell if the compliments brought out a slight blush, so composed was the young woman.

"Do your battles always end just as they happen?" she inquired a moment later.

"What do you mean?" asked Sam.

"I think she means," offered Stevenson, "do we always go by the book—the history book? Or do we ever change history? The outcomes?"

Sam laughed. "How silly. Change history! History is history."

Valentine eyed him intently. "We change some things, if we wish, no? Imagine things different? Different*ly?*"

"You sound just like Lou," laughed the boy. "He's a writer. He makes things up."

Valentine nodded, adjusting her apron once again as she looked coolly at Stevenson.

"But that's just writing," Sam continued. "Stories and things. History is actual *fact*. What people really do." He picked up an officer, poked his sword lightly into his own finger, and set him back down. "History really happened. Why would we want to do a battle that didn't really happen that way?"

"Oh, I don't know," replied the maid, raising her eyebrows in what struck Stevenson as classically Gallic fashion. "Because it would be pleasant?"

For a moment, Sam simply stared at her. Then he looked at his stepfather. "Well, that's not the way we play, is it?"

"No," answered Stevenson. "At least not how we have been playing up to this point."

"How haven't you been playing?" queried a second woman, as she burst unannounced into the room.

Fanny Vandegrift Osbourne Stevenson pulled a scarlet scarf off her tangled locks and settled it snugly around her shoulders, looking attentively about. A strong and earnest brow, coupled with the slight natural downturn to her mouth, lent her an air of perpetual concern, even melancholy, but her dark eyes sparkled with wit and curiosity. She stood there waiting for an answer, very much the deeply tanned Gypsy Inquisitor.

"Inventing your own ending to battles, Mama," answered Sam. "Valentine was saying we might change history."

"Was she?" responded Fanny, with a smile of polite interest. "How quaint of her. Will she be joining your wars, then? Another Joan of Arc?"

"No war for me, madame," replied the maid, with a breezy laugh. "It is not for women, these things."

"Really?" Fanny turned to face the younger woman. "Then I believe I may have wasted all those hours I spent practicing with my pistols."

"Surely no," declared Stevenson as he struggled to his feet and gathered his robe about him. "You shall be our security, love. When next we cross the Russian steppes. Or...*goodness*, I am stiff. Sam, would you mind if I take back the Emmitsburg Pike? I must secure my nakedness."

"Louis!" Fanny glanced in exaggerated alarm at both Valentine and the boy. "Sometimes your company is an embarrassment."

"Then there is life in me yet," laughed Stevenson. "All dire medical predictions to the contrary."

Fanny slapped him playfully on the arm and walked over to Sam, her richly patterned skirt swinging jauntily behind her. She patted him on the head, then trailed her hand down to the nape of his neck. The boy squirmed, seeking Stevenson's gaze.

"Does madame wish coffee?" asked Valentine.

"Not just now, thank you. Perhaps later. I will let you know."

"*Très bien, madame.*" The maid left them, descending once again to the kitchen.

"So," said Fanny, planting her hands on her hips. "You've both been enjoying yourselves?"

"We certainly have," replied her husband. "Killing thousands. This has been the single most lethal day in the history of warfare," he explained—adding, as Fanny shook her head with amusement, "to date."

"To date," agreed Sam. "The slaughter will likely get worse." He grinned at his stepfather with affected savagery.

"Honestly," sighed Fanny, as she walked back across the room to her wonted chair. "Of all the things you could be playing at." She settled on the edge of the seat, knees tightly together with her small hands folded on top.

"Well," said Stevenson, rising to the game. "I suppose we could be playing Noah's Ark."

"With thousands of animals dying," added Sam. "And plenty of people, too. Evil ones."

"Or we could be playing Henry the Eighth."

"With dead wives lying all over the place." Sam dissolved into giggles.

"Enough," cried Fanny, slapping her knees imperiously. Still, she beamed at the sight of her two men, so obviously happy in each other's company. "So, Louis, have you written today?" she asked at length.

"Not yet," shrugged Stevenson. He sniffed and reached for a box of cigarettes.

"Louis!"

"Damn it, Fanny!" He looked abashedly at the boy.

"You've been so much better, love," urged his wife. "Every cigarette you don't smoke is a hundred coughs un-coughed."

"And a hundred words unwritten," sighed the writer. "More likely a thousand. Tobacco is fuel, Pig. Tobacco and wine."

"Sammy," Fanny said softly, turning to her son. "Perhaps you could give Louis and myself a few moments of privacy. Then maybe we'll take a stroll down to town. To get our blood flowing."

"But Mama. It's no secret that Lulu—"

"Samuel Osbourne!" Fanny said sternly. Then more gently, "Please."

"Oh, all right." The boy reached towards his toy soldiers, starting to pick them up.

"You can do that later. We'll pick up together."

"That was hardly necessary," declared Stevenson, once the boy had left the room.

"No? It's bad enough he should see you ill. I don't want him to see you claiming your talents depend on...depend on anything but your fine parts."

"My fine parts!" scoffed Stevenson. He kicked at the soldiers lying closest to him. "Honestly, this damned shapeless behemoth you have enslaved me to is sucking the life right out of me." He grabbed his pajama legs and held them out to either side, kicking his slipper-clad feet in comical fashion. "I am a mere husk here, Fanny. The lees of the grape. A scraped-out potato skin."

Fanny took a deep breath before responding. "Look at all you've written so far, Louis. How many pages? How many chapters?"

"How many utterly lifeless scenes, you mean? How many stilted, stupid, brainless characters? Prince Otto?" He threw his hands in the air and sputtered. "I don't know. He's one part Hamlet, only less decisive; and...and one part some foppish baboon from a Gilbert farce."

"You're far too hard on yourself." Fanny reached mindlessly for the cigarette box, caught herself, and sat back with a guilty smirk. "You are! For example, finally—*finally*—you have some strong women in the making. Wonderful women." She adjusted her scarf and smiled encouragement.

"Unlike *Treasure Island.*"

"It was good of you to oblige Sammy with *Treasure Island,*" she said soothingly. "It meant so much to him. And so to me, too. But," she went on, folding her arms more assertively, "everyone, I'm sure, has been waiting for someone like Seraphina. Your 'woman of affairs'?" She eyed him for some kind of response.

Stevenson snorted. It had been fortunate that Sam had banned any significant female characters from his pirate story. He was certain he had no talent for them.

"A princess who's beautiful, like in any romantic fable. But she has, what did you say? 'Manlike ambitions,' too!" Fanny's eyes sparkled. "She's brilliant, Louis. A Rosalind for today. I'm so eager to see what she gets up to."

Stevenson squinted at his wife, then loosed an exhausted grin. "Don't try to commend me, dearest. Not when I'm in the pits. It's perverse of you."

"But honestly!" Fanny persisted. "What a welcome novelty to come across a woman who's got the gumption, when her man dithers off into dreamland, just to take charge! Damn it, she's good." She smacked a fist into the palm of her hand. "No feckless mooning for Seraphina. No Elizabeth Bennett pride and…" She shook her head and scanned the ceiling for a word. "Prissiness!"

Stevenson jerked up straight as a fencing foil. "What a deplorable mischaracterization that is, Frances!" How much better, he thought, to have been continuing on with Gettysburg! Easier, at least. "I refuse to stand by and let you to call Elizabeth Bennett a feckless mooner."

"Well, that's what she is. To me she is. Why, she wouldn't last a minute in this day and age. Can you imagine her or any of those silly sisters of hers trying to survive in a town like Virginia City?"

There was an especially fine image, thought Stevenson. Something for a drawing in *Punch* decrying the rise of American power. "Maintaining their bourgeois virtue, I suppose you mean, in a town full of bars and bordellos?"

"Precisely."

"As you yourself are alleged to have done?"

Fanny shot him a scathing glance. Spying his tired but affectionate grin, she went ahead and plucked a cigarette from the small ormolu box.

"Aha!" laughed Stevenson. "I see it was only a matter of time."

"I am weak. I should be strong." She lit the cigarette and inhaled robustly. Stevenson drew in his breath along with hers and held it in a moment of vicarious indulgence. When she exhaled, he watched wistfully as the thin jet of smoke diffused in the air between them.

"Was it weakness, dear," he asked at last, "that led you to cross the Isthmus of Panama unaccompanied by a single white soul? On a mule? And heavily armed?"

Fanny's eyes twinkled at the memory. "I was younger then."

"Ah, yes. And remind me…had I, at that date, even been born?"

Fanny kicked a shoe at him, but it fell short of its mark. "I have not had an easy time of it, Mr. R. L. Stevenson. And you are not making it any easier right now."

"Do I detect a smile behind that calculated petulance?" He craned his neck to inspect her more closely. The hint of a blush suffused her dark skin.

"If there is, then it's very much against my will," she replied. "Setting my own experience to the side, though, the challenges any woman faces today require strength and a bold character. So it behooves any serious artist to represent them that way."

Stevenson studied her impassively. "I am inclined to think," he said deliberately, setting his chin on his fist, "that the challenges women face have remained rather similar through the ages. As have their capacities and means for survival."

His wife looked at him with surprise. "Look at you! You've gone and turned into a philosopher of the sexes! How thoughtless of you to have left me completely in the dark about such an important new development."

Stevenson waved his hand and chuckled. "My dear Fanny…once women here have earned the vote—and perhaps when your own country elects a woman president—then the terrain will be substantially altered." He eyed his wife playfully. "You are now in your second marriage, if I am not mistaken. Is your need for a husband any less than that of any of the Bennett girls? And has your skill with a pistol proven to be an avenue to financial independence?" Her eyes opened wide, wresting from her husband an unlooked-for surge of compassion. "Damn it, Fanny! You didn't deserve that," he said quickly, making as if to rise and go to her.

"No!" Fanny raised her hand to stop him. "I do. I do deserve that. It's perfectly true that I have been married twice—and that I can't conceive of a life without a man in it. A husband."

Again, Stevenson started to rise.

"But," she quickly added, fending him off yet again, "that is quite probably because I do have one thing in common with your far-too-highly-esteemed Jane Austen heroines."

"And what would that be?"

She leaned forward, glancing mischievously to the side before she looked him straight in the eye. "A longing for balls!"

For a moment Stevenson was honestly stunned. Then an irresolute grin crept over his lips.

For all of her shrewd social calculation, Fanny's occasional knack for indelicacy both appalled and delighted him. She would doubtless have guarded her matrimonial virtue in Virginia City, even while married to the philandering Samuel Osbourne, Sr. But some of her language and humor she could well have learned from Nevada's most brazen ladies of pleasure—along with a few other things. Even after years of marriage, there were nights when her volatility in the bedroom literally took his breath away.

As he hovered between laughter, intimidation, and the first twinges of arousal, she abruptly changed the subject.

"Why don't you take up the law again, Louis?" She lay back in her chair, crossing her legs primly at the ankles. "You always fancy yourself so damn logical and precise."

"Or perhaps I should return to engineering?" said Stevenson, spun around by this chaste coda to what had come before.

"Perhaps." Fanny snuffed her cigarette in the nearby ashtray, staring at him with a just-detectable smugness. "It would make your father happy." She reached up and plucked a stray bit of tobacco from her lip and wiped it slowly on her sleeve, holding him fixed in her gaze while she inscribed a few languid circles in the air with her diminutive, shoeless foot.

"Mmmm," cooed Stevenson. Their exchange had indeed brought up her blood, and she glowed in that mysterious way she had glowed when he had first met her in Grez—when she'd eyed him with a room-stilling intensity, as though she were sighting one of her oft-touted pistols. "So you long for balls," he purred, sliding to the front of his chair.

"Louis!" giggled Fanny, sitting bolt upright and straightening her skirts. "Sammy might come back." It was not the least of her tricks, this turning of the tables.

"Or Valentine," he suggested, pulling softly at his moustache. "Then where would we be? *Touts les trois ensemble?"*

"You're a lost soul," tittered Fanny, shaking her head. "Your father was right about you, all those years ago."

"And you, my dear," winked Stevenson, "are far less my model for Princess Seraphina…than you are for the most dangerous…Countess… von Rosen."

"You mean…?" She eyed him with giddy delight.

"Yes, my dear! For the jolly, elderly—how shall I say?—*fucktress."*

With a tiny squeal, Fanny leapt from her seat. She skittered across the room and threw herself upon him, upsetting his chair and throwing them both to the floor, where they lay, giggling hysterically, amidst the carnage of the Gettysburg battlefield.

The walk from La Solitude to the center of town was not particularly arduous, the bulk of it being downhill. It took Stevenson, Fanny, and Sam through a maze of meandering streets, all of them lined with venerable old houses that crowded the cobbled pavement with their wrought-iron grillwork and their cracked plaster walls. Stevenson strolled arm-in-arm with his wife—tall with short, angular with blocky, as though a European mantis and an American ladybug had made common cause and set off together down the road of life. Sam trailed happily behind, scrabbling after the lightning-quick lizards that seemed to fleck every still-warm façade, peeking into dark doorways, lingering at enticing shop fronts before he scampered along to catch up.

It had not been a particularly good afternoon for Stevenson, and he was eager to tip back a glass or two of some engaging vintage. The day's post had brought a letter from *Blackwood's Magazine* declining to publish a story he had sent to them a month or so back. "The Travelling Companion" was, in the end, a scurvy little piece, dashed off in a bid to net some quick capital to help offset the costs of the move to France. It was the kind of thing, in fact, that Stevenson might have been tempted to send out under a pseudonym, had the budding name of its author not been its most saleable aspect. Yet the editor's rationale, that the tale was "a work of genius and indecent," had pitched Stevenson into a vortex of annoyance.

The subject was a youth of privilege embarked on the grand European tour, visiting palaces and galleries by day, low drinking places and houses of carnal pleasure by night. There was an ingenious disguise involved, one requiring the offices of an unscrupulous servant who assisted—nay, encouraged—the principal as each of his unseemly tastes dulled from usage and the need for novelty drove him on to diversions ever more vivid and depraved. In the end, the servant was revealed to have kept scrupulous records of each folly and crime, and he parlayed the damning information into a modest fortune in blackmail—which, at tale's end, he was seen enjoying with a song on his unrepentant, and unpunished, lips.

The thing had shown some initial promise as a compelling treatment of a theme that, Fanny's reservations notwithstanding, Stevenson had been of an increasing mind to explore: that unsettling sort of imminent, other self that threatens to destabilize, often at the least predictable times, the psychic status quo. The story's principal might have been named Johnson or Thomson, or even more plausibly of late, Ferrier. The effort soon devolved, however, into irredeemably shoddy stuff—the low spawn of truant moments he had stolen from the more weighty projects he felt obliged to pursue. Even in the writing, Stevenson had been disappointed to watch the scheming servant become much the most interesting character, rendering the piece more a study in social exploitation than in psychological exploration. What galled him after the fact, however, was that an editor could recognize the story's genius yet still decide not to publish. Fanny had simply rolled her eyes, advising him not to fritter away his days and talents on worthless diversions.

The afternoon had been exceptionally hot, and the evening remained warm. By the time the trio reached Le Désire, the tiny restaurant touted by an Anglican cleric who served the gaggle of Britons come south for their constitutions, Stevenson's thirst was definitely elevated.

"Perhaps we should start with a drink," he suggested once Fanny and Sam had seated themselves beneath the striped canvas awning shading the outdoor dining area. There were three other tables outside, two of them occupied. At one, a young and evidently English couple leaned towards each other over their small table with a rapt intensity that could only mean they were newlyweds. Fanny surveyed them with amusement and, as she looked back his way, Stevenson winked knowingly. At another table sat what must have been a local family, a stout father who had somehow failed to remove his flat cap, an equally stout but more florid mother, and two stout daughters who appeared to be twins, dressed in identical white pinafores. They were close to Sam's age, and the boy eyed them uneasily, as though they might momentarily leap up, dash over to his table, and mount an inquisition in their strange tongue.

"Yes, please," said the boy, turning back with relief to his immediate company. "I'm parched. But we probably can't have water, can we?"

"No," replied Fanny. "Unless they've boiled it."

"Ginger ale?"

"Alas, they're unlikely to have ginger ale here," sighed Stevenson. "I am afraid *les citoyens de Provence* put scant stock in Temperance beverages."

"Gosh," sighed Sam. "Then I guess it's wine again for me. *Hic!*"

"Or cider," offered Fanny, frowning at the feigned inebriation.

"You've liked the cider pretty well."

"Sure. Except it gives me an awful headache."

"Let's try some wine," suggested Stevenson, waving away the first of the evening's marauding moths. "If you find you don't like it, we can always order coffee."

"Oh, Louis!" Fanny laid her hand on her husband's arm. "Sam's so sensitive to coffee. He'll never get to sleep if he drinks coffee this late."

"Then wine it is," declared Stevenson with a smile. "The poor lad's liver be damned!" He craned his neck to look around. "Hmmm." Various kitchen noises echoed from inside, and a delicious mélange of scents wafted out on the light breeze: hot oil, garlic, onion, the maritime tang of seafood. "Has anyone taken note that we're here, have you seen?"

"Well, those girls keep staring at me," answered Sam. "The fat ones."

"I believe Louis meant someone who works at the restaurant," said Fanny quietly. "And it's not polite to call anyone fat."

"Really?" asked Sam, looking squarely at his mother. "Then why does Louis call you 'The Fat One' in his letters? That and 'Pig?'"

"Dearest!" exclaimed Stevenson, with a playful scowl at his wife. "Have our epistolary confidences been breached, then? Is my loving correspondence open for the world to see?"

Fanny blushed uncharacteristically. "Well!" She drew a handkerchief from her clutch and dabbed busily at temple and brow. "Sammy. You know I never left letters out for you to look at."

"And you didn't hide them very well, either. Did you?" Again the boy peered uneasily towards the French twins.

"I think I can say," offered Stevenson, in a conciliatory tone, "first of all, that your mother is not fat." He dipped his head towards Fanny, a gesture she returned in kind. "And, second of all, that these are terms of *endearment*. Like 'butterball.' Or 'Dear Mother Hen.'"

"All of which he calls me when he is being especially sweet," confessed Fanny. "And he calls himself, of course, 'The Skinny One.'" She studied her son for his response.

The boy looked intensely at his stepfather. "Well…he is skinny! But very loveable. And he is my own and only Lulu."

"Thank you, Sam," said Stevenson, resuming his scan of the estab-lishment. "Hello! *Allo!* Anyone home?"

The English pair looked up from their enraptured mutual contem-plation and smiled amiably. "They are very slow," observed the young man in a stage whisper. "But such delicious *bouillabaisse.*"

"So we've heard," Stevenson whispered back, with a little wave. "Thank you." He turned back to his tablemates. "Good enough, perhaps, to make this particular one slightly less skinny. If we are ever to be served."

Girlish titters from across the way drew a headshake from Sam. The Stevenson trio sat on in silence as a trill of gay laughter burst from the young woman in the romantic couple. Stevenson looked at his watch and sighed.

"Louis! Let's just enjoy ourselves."

"Let's just—! You're right. Of course."

A mule-drawn cart rumbled by, laden with crude baskets over-flowing with turnips and potatoes. Stevenson waved away the dust and coughed shallowly as a tall man in shirtsleeves finally emerged from the doorway and slouched over to their table.

"Monsieur."

Stevenson stared at Fanny, and then back at the man. *"Et madame?"*

The waiter tossed his head in affirmation and pursed his lips.

"Bon soir," said Stevenson.

The man simply nodded.

Stevenson inhaled deeply. "We…are very thirsty. We should like to start with some wine. Might you have some Bandol?"

"Bien sûr," said the man, nodding phlegmatically.

"Then could you bring us a bottle, please? And three glasses?"

"Three?"

"Yes. Three."

"Of course." The man turned slowly to leave.

"Tout de suite," added Stevenson with a rap on the table. *"S'il vous plaît."*

The man turned back with a raised brow, huffed, and then trundled back into the building.

"Was that really necessary?" asked Fanny.

"The man was rude. But you're right, dear heart. Apologies." He looked at Sam and stuck out his tongue. Sam crossed his eyes and giggled. "Well, we know the *bouillabaise* is excellent. I believe they are known here for their *fruits de mer*—and veal as well."

"I'm starving," exclaimed Sam. He snatched his napkin from the table and tucked it in at his neck, spreading it out like a nun's collar. Grinning at them both, he crossed himself ostentatiously. "Look. I've converted!" he exclaimed.

"Sam," scolded Fanny. She pulled the cloth away and dropped it into her son's lap. "Don't be a Philistine."

"I know all about Philistines," chirped the boy. "That's what you called the men in Antwerp who wouldn't let you and Belle take art classes because you're women."

Fanny looked at Stevenson and shook her head.

"Momma would have loved to crush them all. Just like Samson."

"Here's to mannish women," chuckled Stevenson, raising an imaginary glass.

"I think I'd rather be called fat," muttered Fanny, laughing nonetheless.

The waiter emerged once again, making his way slowly back towards the table. He halted briefly, scuffed a cigarette stub off to the side, sniffed, and carried on.

"I expect he's paid by the hour," whispered Stevenson to Sam. Fanny kicked his shin under the table.

"Monsieur," said the man, presenting the bottle for inspection.

Stevenson had a quick look and nodded. *Bandol '75.* The man retreated to a stand just inside the door and pulled a corkscrew from his apron. The ensuing pop set Stevenson's mouth to watering.

"This should be pleasant. '75 was an excellent year." The writer leaned back in his chair and placed his hands on what passed for his belly. Sam shrugged while his mother looked contentedly about.

The man returned to the table and extended the bottle once again. Stevenson nodded, pushing his glass forward. The waiter poured a finger of wine and stood back with a look of almost complete disinterest.

Stevenson raised the glass to his nose, swirling it elegantly before he inhaled. He winked at Fanny, then took a sip.

"What's this?" He lowered the glass briskly to the table, grimacing at the taste, and reached for his mouth. There—a small but distinct shard of cork. He turned to the man. "This wine is corked. We'll have another."

"*Comment?*" The waiter looked mildly perturbed.

"There is cork in the glass." Stevenson held his finger under the man's nose then grabbed the bottle from him. "And look!" He pointed down into the neck. "You can see it there as well, can't you? The wine has gone off. Another bottle. *S'il vous plaît.*"

The man frowned but turned away, remembering only then to come back and remove Stevenson's glass. He swept it away with an impertinent flourish.

"What's wrong?" asked Sam.

"The wine is spoiled," sneered Stevenson. "There's cork in it." He peered at Fanny. Her head was canted in the cautionary way he knew only too well.

"So?" responded Sam. "Isn't cork how they keep the wine in the bottle in the first place?"

Fanny turned to her son. "If it falls apart," she explained, "the air gets in. The wine goes bad, and the cork gets in the glass and all. It's not right. It spoils the taste." She looked intently back at her husband.

"Oh." The boy resumed the challenging task of balancing his knife on his forefinger.

Stevenson could see just inside the door as the man placed the offending bottle back on the serving stand. He vanished for a moment, returning with a glass decanter. Picking up the bottle, he poured the wine carefully into the new container until the liquid rose up into the neck. He waited a moment, eyed the thing carefully, then stuck his finger down into the wine. Pulling it slowly back out, he peered intently at his fingertip before wiping it on his apron. He took another glass from the rack on the wall and shuffled back outside.

"Voilà," he said, presenting the decanter.

Stevenson looked at Fanny and rolled his eyes. "It's the same wine," he said softly, turning back to the man.

"Monsieur?"

"Look. It's not even in a bottle. You poured the old wine in here, into the decanter, from the first one. I saw you."

"Monsieur?"

"I *saw* you!"

"This is a nice Bandol. From the cask. Taste." He looked over his shoulder towards the English couple and shrugged.

"I will not taste," exclaimed Stevenson. "This is the very same god-damned wine that was corked…and now you're trying to pass it off as something different."

The occupants of the other tables stared over at their party as Fanny reached for Stevenson's arm, keeping him from rising.

Stevenson cast her an angry glance and swept her hand away. He looked quickly at Sam, who peered at him with his eyes wide as saucers. Settling himself back into his chair, Stevenson breathed deeply and turned once again to the waiter.

"Why would you do this? You poured the first bottle into the decanter," he said, with exaggerated slowness and enunciation. "Then you stuck your f—" He swallowed hard. "Then you stuck your finger into the neck of the damned thing and pulled the damn cork out."

"Non, monsieur."

"Yes, you did. I damn well saw you, and you know it perfectly well." He glanced at his two companions, who were poised on the edge of their seats. "Just," he said in a barely audible voice, "just bring me a new bottle of Bandol—please."

"Monsieur," said the man, pulling himself up to his full height. "It

may be that you do not understand the wines of France. You come from—?"

"You miserable bastard!" yelled Stevenson, springing to his feet with such force that his chair tumbled over backward and spun off into the street. As the man reeled away from him, he grabbed the decanter and hurled it with all his might against the wall, where it smashed into a thousand pieces.

Silence ruled the eatery as the wine dripped slowly down the plaster onto the cobblestones. Stevenson looked at Fanny, who was reaching across to embrace her son. The boy's eyes brimmed, and he started to sob. The young Englishman had risen to his feet and was only now beginning to sit down again, slowly and warily, across from his wife, who was pale with shock. The French man sat there with jaws agape, mirroring his wife and daughters. The waiter had dropped into a simian crouch and edged himself away, only half-erect, towards the door.

"Goodness," whispered Stevenson. "My goodness," he said a bit louder. "I am sorry. So sorry. But you see—"

"Come, Louis," said Fanny, gathering her things and helping Sam to his feet. The boy's cheeks were tracked with tears, and he stared up at his stepfather with a mixture of incredulity and fear. "Let's just go home."

"Home," repeated Stevenson vacantly. He reached down to pick up his chair and slid it back under the table. "Yes. We should. Certainly."

"Pay the man, and let's go home."

Stevenson took a handful of coins from his purse and walked over to the cringing waiter. "Here," he said softly. "This is more than I owe you." The man stared at him blankly, a fist held up to his lips. "It is more than I owe. Take it."

The man opened his hand cautiously, and Stevenson dropped the coins into his palm, remembering suddenly and rather unaccountably the little girl he had trampled at King's Cross.

"With a little *pourboire* for your trouble." He turned to the others present. "I am so sorry. It was beastly of me. I know. I was upset, you see."

The Englishman nodded weakly. "Of course."

"Of course," echoed his wife.

"I'm sorry," said Stevenson once more as he edged away. *"Je suis désolé."* He turned, then, to follow his distraught little family back to La Solitude, catching up with them well before he had any notion of what he might say.

Fanny found Stevenson on the narrow first-floor balcony overlooking the street. He was facing away, gazing out towards the distant water, on which the lights of a few ships glimmered intermittently like foundering stars. One of his hands rested on the wooden rail. The other, cocked tightly next to his right shoulder, held a cigarette.

She stepped quietly up beside him. "You shouldn't be smoking."

He looked at her, expressionless, then turned back outward. "I needed something to settle myself."

"You certainly did." Silence reigned for a moment, broken only by the click and whir of invisible insects. "Sam is finally asleep."

"That's good," sighed Stevenson. He expelled a jet of smoke into the still night air and cleared his throat.

"He was extremely upset."

"His first real sighting of Old Man Virulent, I suppose."

"Yes. And don't be flip."

"I am devastated. I don't know what came over me."

"I certainly don't, either. Ever. And I don't like it one bit."

"You think I do?" asked Stevenson, louder than was called for. He took another long draught on his cigarette, the flaring glow of the tip illuminating his somber features.

"I'm not saying that, Louis. I am saying Sam was extremely upset. So was I."

"I shall do my best to make it up to him."

"More playing at war?" She said it pointedly. "Teaching your stepson to be violent too?"

"Do I deserve that?" He looked himself like an injured boy.

"I'm sorry." She paused. "Moderately."

Stevenson sighed, then shook his head and sniffed. "We both love our play at soldiers. Those hours together, I expect he feels as close to me as I feel to him. I hope so. It reminds me of my childhood. With all of my cousins. Stevensons. Balfours. Boys and girls. A palliative for loneliness." He took a deep breath. "They are such gifts to me, Fanny. Sam and his sense of fun."

His wife made to say something, then simply nodded in the darkness beside him. When she put her arm around his waist, he took his hand off the rail and covered hers, leaning closer to her as he squeezed.

"Well," sighed Fanny. "At least we know it wasn't the alcohol."

"No," laughed Stevenson, "not this time. I hadn't managed to down a single drop." Again he cleared his throat. "But then *that* became the problem, no? Not too much, but too little."

He turned to look at her. In this light, the gray in her hair was all but invisible. She could have been her own daughter Belle, so young did she look. He turned and put his hands on her shoulders, and she pressed her cheek and ear down onto one of them.

"You could always leave me," he said.

"I have left one husband already. A far worse husband than you. I don't mean to leave another."

"I'm reassured," he said, with a melancholy grin. "You won't re-embark for California even if I abandon this wretched *Prince Otto* I seem to be chained to?"

"Do we have to go through that again?" Fanny stepped back into a vaguely confrontational stance. Just how sincere it was meant to be Stevenson found it difficult to judge. "Finish the book," she said. "I know you don't believe in it, but just finish it. And then you can go on to something that's more to your liking."

"You are to my liking," cooed Stevenson as he reached out to stroke her cheek.

"So it's Young Master Playful now, is it? Rearing *his* ugly head?"

"Ugly?"

"Unruly, then."

"Perhaps."

"My God, you're changeable! I sometimes think you could be a woman, the way you change."

"Perhaps you'd like that," he remarked with a grin.

She shook her head and turned back out towards the sea. "I won't be distracted, Louis. If you were half as devoted to your work as you are to reliving martial glories of the past with Sam, we wouldn't be living hand-to-mouth."

"I would have thought we were living quite well," observed Stevenson. "Here on the very skirts of paradise." He gestured to the prospect in front of them.

"You owe it to me to be serious. Especially after tonight."

"I've always been given to rages, Fanny." The weariness in his voice was unmistakable. "Someone once said that my emotions are my reasons."

"Who would that have been? Your father?"

"That would be the height of irony," huffed Stevenson. "If Old Man Virulent comes from anywhere, he comes from Old Tom Stevenson. Talk to my mother one day about father's explosions. Or talk to Baxter." He waved at a mosquito buzzing tinnily at his ear. "He makes himself out to be the paragon of rationality, but foil him one too many times, and he is a holy terror."

"Well, he's a man," quipped Fanny, turning back to face him. "I hardly know a man who doesn't have a holy terror in him."

"You sound like Ferrier. And women don't have the same?"

Fanny eyed him warily. "They may. But they rarely get away with expressing it."

"Oh, you have your ways," countered Stevenson, suddenly keen to see how she would respond.

Fanny glowered for a moment, then her face relaxed into a tolerant smile. "I was saying earlier a woman has to be able to seize the reins. But the ones who survive are the ones that do it subtly. Men, you know," and she gazed out again at the water, "men can just rage away and everyone just says, 'Mind you, he's a bit irascible. But he has strong convictions, you know, and he is such an energetic fellow.' It's not survival of the fittest with men. It's survival of the feistiest."

"Does my father know you have been reading Herbert Spencer?" joked Stevenson. "Because, until now, he has been very fond of you."

Fanny slapped his arm and, for a long moment, they stared in silence at the twinkling horizon.

"I am truly sorry about tonight," offered Stevenson in good time. He could feel Fanny squeeze his arm. "I think if I were not so thoroughly enervated by *Otto*, so utterly stymied—"

"Finish and move on," Fanny whispered insistently in his ear.

"Once…" confessed Stevenson dreamily. "Once I so desperately wanted to write a big, three-decker novel." He tilted his face up towards the stars. "Some Walter Scott sort of thing, you know. Something massive about the Covenanters. Or about ancient chieftains splitting each other's skulls on top of Hadrian's Wall."

"More of that, is it?"

Stevenson shook his head. "Now, here I am in the thick of something pitched at the epic scale, the grand scale, and—I haven't kept it a secret, have I?—it feels so labored and false! So utterly calculated. God, Fanny! Let me just throw off everything that's old and ponderous and windy and spin a tight little yarn about something visceral."

"Visceral like the *Blackwood's* piece?"

Stevenson snorted into the dark. For minutes they were still, listening to the sounds of the night, then Stevenson spoke again.

"I don't mean to excuse myself, but I expect the *Blackwood's* affair played a role in this evening's eruption."

"It didn't seem to leave you feeling very chipper."

Stevenson chuckled softly. "There's another irony for you. The fate of a story of duplicity setting the scene for my own unruly 'other fellow' crashing out onto the stage."

"I'll admit it occurred to me."

"What peeved me the most, I think, was the man's choice of conjunctions," Stevenson continued. 'A work of genius *and* indecent.' Not 'but,' but 'and!'"

"And that peeved you because…?"

"Because it suggests that he acknowledges some kind of tie, some link, between genius and indecency, no? The amoral. What your Mr. Spencer would call the 'natural.'"

"*My* Mr. Spencer?" responded Fanny. "Honestly, Louis. I think Spencer and those other ones are more intoxicating for you than alcohol."

Stevenson laughed. "I know. But I am honestly coming to think, Fanny, that one of a writer's most needful charges is to portray the very same primitive urges and responses that this damn thing, respectability, this damn universal demigod, does everything it can to stamp out. To portray them and exercise them in the reader."

"That's a bit radical, don't you think? You want us to read novels so we learn how to throttle highwaymen?"

"It *could* just be, my arch little skeptic, that we do in fact grow in strength and resourcefulness when we run up against the rough and arousing—even the 'indecent'—in the things we read."

Fanny shook her head, but she smiled all the same.

"At the very least," Stevenson forged on, "it tests our moral mettle."

"I know what your father would say. And I know what the *Blackwood's* man did say." Fanny's expression sobered. "We depend on you, Louis. Sammy and I. I can't encourage you to fly in the face of propriety just because you have some kind of primordial taste for the wild and wooly."

Stevenson chuckled indulgently. "For all of my love for Jane Austen, dear heart, I may increasingly need convincing it's more salutary to read about characters negotiating social niceties over a teacup than about buccaneers fighting for their lives over a bottle of rum."

"Buccaneers are amusing, Louis. They aren't the stuff of real art."

"Better pride and prissiness then? This from the woman who just said she so admires Seraphina and the Fucktress?"

"I just think it's better to write things that can be published than things that can't."

Stevenson sighed loudly, turning back out to the sea. He suddenly stiffened and rose excitedly on his toes. In the middle distance, from the terraced garden that was one of the little chalet's most paradisiacal features, a liquid, chirruping trill rolled out into the still evening.

"That's a nightingale!" he exclaimed.

"I think so. What else could it be?"

"Charming!" He took a deep breath of the cool, scented air. "You know, Pig, perhaps I am meant for a new Keats. Instead of scribbling decadent trash in a vain bid to toss off the stultifying bonds of respectability. I want my own *annus mirabilis*. Instead of this *annus terribilis* you have me muddling through."

"So I suppose, then, you want to die young just like him? And leave me a grieving and penniless widow?"

"You would cut such a fine, romantic figure, dear heart. You and your darling son. Begging for a ride to the poorhouse. Ouch!" Fanny had grabbed his right forefinger and was bending it over backwards. "Ouch! What a demon you are."

"I am," hissed Fanny, leaning close to his ear. "Tell me now what will make you a rich and famous writer or I'll dismantle you limb by limb."

"I shall write a new Coleridgean rime. About a castrating hag who aspires to become the first female pope."

Fanny pulled back further.

"Oww! I shall write a new *Commedia*. I shall lavish the bulk of my efforts on a grim depiction of the Circle of Mannish Women. I shall—" He suddenly felt Fanny's hand shoot down the front of his trousers. She gripped the whole of him and squeezed threateningly.

"Tell me what you will write," she whispered, taking his earlobe in her teeth.

"Goodness," replied Stevenson, struggling for breath. "Perhaps something about the things we do when no one is looking."

"But I am always looking," whispered Fanny. "Come to my bed and I shall show you."

6

Presently after, he sat on one side of his own hearth, with Mr. Guest, his head clerk,
upon the other, and midway between, at a nicely calculated distance from the fire,
a bottle of a particular old wine that had long dwelt unsunned in the foundations
of his house... In the bottle the acids were long ago resolved; the imperial dye had
softened with time, as the color grows richer in stained windows; and the glow of
hot autumn afternoons was ready to be set free and to disperse the fogs of London.
— THE NARRATOR

Stevenson sat alone at the dark trestle table that dominated the dining
end of the main room at La Solitude. He had crossed his slipper-clad
feet on the table top, next to his breakfast dishes, and he slouched in
the straight-backed chair with a bowl of café au lait cradled in his hands.
He was only moderately comfortable—a state that nicely tempered the
vexing self-indulgence he seemed to be giving way to at the moment.

He was conducting a scientific experiment. Perhaps an essay in
augury. Perhaps even in destiny. If the sunlight that was just touching
the wick of the candle at the center of the table were to descend and
hit the candlestick itself before it moved off the taper altogether, he
would spend the day writing. If it did not, today would be the day for
the family to bottle the barrel of Grenache he had just purchased in his

bid to economize without compromising the quality of their evenings' wine. He hoped the sun left the candle soon, as he was lately finding it much easier to tipple than to create.

A light breeze wafted through the open casement, heavy with floral and earthen scents from the garden. A black redstart must have been perched nearby, for a familiar tweet and chuck kept pace with the morning's crescendo of cicadas. He knew redstarts migrated from the British Isles. Had this one followed them from Bournemouth?

He heard the creak of a stair tread and turned to see Valentine coming up from the kitchen below.

"Will there be something more?" She wiped her hands on a cotton cloth as she stepped nearer with a polite smile.

"I don't believe so. The eggs were excellent."

"Merci, monsieur." The woman gave a small curtsy, more appropriate somehow for a dancer than for a cook. It was another of her charming foibles. "I take these?"

"Of course." Stevenson made to remove his feet from the table but, before he could manage, she had snatched up the dishes and stood back.

"Non! Restez! Stay. Please."

"As you wish," chuckled the writer, settling back into his calculated semi-comfort.

"Not as *I* wish. I am here only to be useful."

He gazed at her in mild amusement. Somehow she always managed to affirm her domestic subservience in a way that bordered on self-assertion. "Well, that you are, Valentine. Useful. *Très utile.* Mrs. Stevenson and I are very happy to have secured your services. And Master Sam as well."

"Merci, monsieur. Is there anything more?"

"Nothing short of luncheon, Valentine. Unless we bottle wine today." He glanced at the candle. Their fate was still at issue. "In which case I shall let you know."

"Très bien, monsieur. Merci." She curtsied again and turned to descend the stairs.

Life here was indeed gratifying, thought Stevenson as he watched her trim white cap drop from sight. It would be totally so, if only he could scratch out something worthwhile by way of real work. How different from his and Fanny's first days together as husband and wife, roughing it in the arid old mining camp at Silverado—mounding up straw for mattresses, hanging blankets for doors, boiling potatoes for supper on a tiny alcohol stove or over a smoky fire. Now there was the faux-Swiss but comfortable La Solitude, its effulgent garden, and Valentine's cornucopial cuisine—blessings almost beyond measure. It was curious how accustomed he had once been to having servants. In Edinburgh, it had seemed a birthright. Actually, it had not *seemed* like anything, as he had never known anything else. From his earliest memories onward, a maid had been like an arm or a leg. One had one, or two, or four—to carry one about, to hand one things.

He studied the candle once again. It was going to be a near thing. If he were meant to write this day, would it suffice to pen a jocular verse about a maid who was his right arm? Who made his bed? Who rubbed his temples? Who wiped his bum? Diverting alternatives all of them, and progressively inappropriate, to be sure. A bed-making-maid poem might turn either on innocent nostalgia or on something subtly erotic— along the lines of Robert Herrick, perhaps. Rabelais had really already done the bum-wiping. Surely he could find something new. A maid who peeled grapes for him as he bathed in the fountains of Versailles? Bather and fruiterer both naked, perchance? A maid who walked him about the garden on a leash, airily chastising her *chien mauvais écossais*.

He shook his head and giggled. Would he even be dallying with such mores-testing fantasies if it were not for last night's dream?

A door creaked on its hinges and Fanny entered the room, her robe tied loosely about her, her bare feet shuffling with studied daintiness across the carpet. On her way to the window, she kissed him on the forehead, scarcely needing to bend.

"What of the night?" asked Stevenson, turning to watch her as she leaned out into the morning light.

"The perfect sleep of perfect satisfaction." She took in a great breath before she turned towards him, leaning back against the sill. She smiled sleepily and crossed both ankles and arms.

"*Moi aussi,*" winked Stevenson. "Any dreams?"

Fanny laughed. "Not after I fell asleep. That was truly delicious, though, Louis. Being on French soil has clearly pumped iron into your veins." She gave a little shiver of delight.

Stevenson felt himself on the brink of a blush. "Man of iron, am I? No wonder my feet feel so heavy this morning." He thumped his heels on the tabletop. "And chilly."

"Do you want me to warm them?" She opened her robe and began to walk his way. But for the robe, she was naked.

Stevenson pulled his eyes up to her grinning face. "Pray, leave me an ounce or two of my vital fluids, woman. You'll drain me dry."

"I shall," laughed Fanny, re-belting her robe and shaking out her unbound hair. "In time, I shall have all of you there is to have." She tapped him lovingly on the hand, then pulled out the chair opposite him and sat.

"*I* dreamed," offered Stevenson. "It was quite a remarkable little drama that my brownies produced last night."

"Your wee sleepy Ibsens? Was it something inspiring?" She leaned forward over the table, resting her chin on her fists. It was a distinctly girlish gesture, one that Stevenson never failed to respond to without a surge of complicated emotion—as she knew perfectly well.

"I'd thought it might be. And then I thought perhaps not." He smiled enigmatically. "I'd be curious to know what you think."

"Do tell." Fanny leaned further forward, her eyes wide with interest.

He set down the coffee bowl and cleared his throat. "I was the son, you see, of a very rich and wicked man. Possessed of a huge estate and a most damnable temper. I'd lived abroad, and when I returned to England, I found him married again. To a very handsome young wife."

"What happened to your mother? Wife number one?"

He smiled. "The brownies didn't attend to that."

"I suppose they have no interest in the fate of older women."

"It was a rather long and involved dream, Pig."

She leaned back and folded her hands, the emblem of patience.

"For some reason, then, I went to meet with the old man in some desolate country by the sea—waves crashing, wind howling, and all that. And we somehow fell to quarreling and, when the old bastard stung me with some intolerable insult or other—I don't remember what—I took my walking stick and struck him down."

"Dead?"

"Dead!"

"Goodness! Had he corked your wine or something?"

Stevenson laughed. "He was assuredly the type, had we been drinking. In any case, his corpse is subsequently discovered and buried and I inherit the whole of his estate. Everything. And there I am, finally, living under the same roof with my father's beautiful young widow. Widowed *par moi.*"

"Goodness, Louis. This is rather Greek."

"It is. I suspect my brownies have been reading Sophocles." He gave a shallow cough and again cleared his throat. "So she and I dine together, and share the long evenings quite amiably, until we become very good friends."

"'Good friends!' Oh my, Louis. I'm not sure you should go on."

"No?"

"I'm joking. I haven't felt this excited for several hours."

"Fanny, please. As I said, we live together quite happily until, one day, unaccountably, she suddenly takes to asking me the most searching questions. Where was I on the day of the murder? Have the police had any success with their investigations? Suddenly it seems perfectly clear to me that she suspects it was I that did the foul deed."

"Perfectly clear. She seems quite smart, this beautiful young woman. Despite her youth."

Stevenson sighed, but went on. "The following morning, I see her slip from the house in a veil. I follow her to the station and onto a train, you know, that carries us to the same seaside country where the thing happened, and I follow her out over the sandy hills to the very place where I had murdered the old coot." He paused for a moment to take a breath, shifting to sit more upright. "And there she begins to grope among the rushes, with me watching her, lying there flat on my face in the sand. And suddenly she has something in her hand—something I can't see at first. And then I realize with horror that she is holding part of my stick, the one that I had used to kill the old bastard. It now turns out, of course, that it had broken in half as I'd clubbed him and I had neglected to carry away both pieces."

"Oh my," sighed Fanny.

"Indeed."

"Go on."

"Well, I follow her home at a distance, and that night, she seems somehow even kinder to me than she had been before."

"Kinder, you say?"

Stevenson nodded. "So very kind, in fact, that I was convinced that it was a ruse. That she now knew me for a murderer, and was frightened that I would somehow do her in as well. So I, of course, am driven increasingly mad with suspense and fear. I am sure that, the very next day, she will go to the police with her damning evidence and consign me to the gallows. But she doesn't. So I am certain it will be the next day. But it isn't. And so the burden grows more unbearable by the day, and I waste away like a man with a disease. Strange, isn't it, how our real lives creep into our dreams?"

"You are not wasting away from a disease, Louis. You simply need caring for. That's why Valentine and I are going to such lengths to fatten you up."

Stevenson laughed, leaning forward to extend his slender forefinger in her direction. "Feel."

She slapped his hand away. "Get back to your dream."

"Mind you, I am quite sure there is no future for this little tale I am recounting. It is nothing destined for *Blackwood's,* damn their souls.

Or *London.*"

"It's gripping enough," laughed Fanny. "At least for early-morning entertainment."

"Damn!" blurted Stevenson, looking down at the candle. The sunlight was inches from the base of the candlestick, and well off to the left. He had missed the moment of truth.

"What?" Fanny looked truly alarmed.

"I'm sorry. It's nothing. I've just lost track of the time."

"Does it matter?"

"Not really."

"So go on." She settled herself and leaned towards him again with a keen expression.

"So, as I recall, she's left the house for some reason or other and I ransack her room and, at last, I find the damning evidence. It's hidden away in a drawer among her jewels. My broken stick, engraved with my initials! So there I stand, holding this thing in the hollow of my hand. And I marvel at her unaccountable behavior—that she should seek the thing, and keep it, and yet not use it. And then the door opens. And behold, herself!" He paused and stared hard at his auditor.

"Yes?"

"I don't want to bore you."

"I don't want to wring your neck, you perfect goose. Now go on."

"All right. So we stand eye to eye, with the evidence there between us. I look for her either to denounce me or to run screaming from the room. But she looks at me with a face brimming with some sort of vital communication, and she is about to speak when I raise a hand and cut her off. But before I leave the room, which in my search I had turned positively upside down, I lay my death warrant back in the drawer where I had found it. And at that, strangely, her face lights up."

"Hmmm."

"Precisely. And the next thing I know, she is explaining the disorder of her things to her maid, coming up with one ingenious lie after another. Why this should be, I have absolutely no notion, and that uncertainty combines with all the others until I absolutely reach the end of my rope. We were breakfasting together in one corner of a great, parqueted, sparely furnished room of many windows. Very Renoir. Curious those details should stick."

"Yes. And insignificant, I'd think. Go on."

"Perhaps. But throughout, she has tortured me with these probing looks and the hint of questions unasked. And no sooner are the servants gone, and we two are alone together, than I leap to my feet. And she too springs up, with a ghostly pale face, and she stands there as I rage and rave: 'Why do you torment me so? You know everything. Why do you not denounce me? Why on earth do you torture me?'"

He paused and Fanny gazed at him in the silence, transfixed.

"And when I have done," Stevenson continued, "she falls down on her knees. And with her hands outstretched to me, just like this, she cries, 'Do you not understand? I love you!'"

"Oh my!" sighed Fanny. She shivered visibly and tightened her robe around her.

"Indeed," replied Stevenson. "And I awoke, as I said, with a sort of pang of wonder and mercantile delight." He raised his eyebrows and nodded with the thought. "But the mercantile delight was not of long endurance. Owing to there being certain unmarketable elements in the thing."

Fanny erupted in laughter. "You might say. Patricide, I think it's called. Added to unquenchable lust for your stepmother. I can just imagine the impression it would make at Heriot Row. Or at Cassell's, for that matter."

Stevenson chuckled. "So…I gather you would have me wait patiently for further inspiration?"

"I would. If you insist on turning to a new subject."

"As I thought."

For a moment they sat in silence, the redstart chirping busily away. The wind had picked up, and it soughed through the trees just outside the window.

"It was certainly an artful little reverie, though," said the writer. "I must confess that I had no idea whatever as to the motive of the woman. Throughout. Right up until the instant of her dramatic declaration. My artful little Land of Nodders kept me completely in the dark."

"Remarkable."

"It is remarkable. And what's more remarkable is that I'm sure there is more life in this un-publishable little vignette than in the whole of… you-know-what."

"Enough!" declared Fanny, with an impatient toss of her mane. "God, Louis! Enough of that."

Stevenson rose and walked over to the window, where he leaned against the wall, looking out. He crossed his arms tightly over his meager chest. "So you really won't allow me to walk away from this stillborn monstrosity."

"I will not have you writing stories about killing fathers and bedding mothers, if that's what you're suggesting."

"Not at all. But weren't you somewhat titillated—even just a trifle— by my little fable of forbidden love?" He raised his eyebrows suggestively.

Fanny laughed again. "A naughty yarn between husband and wife is one thing. The next *oeuvre* of a noteworthy author is another."

"A respectable author, you mean."

"Of course."

"You'd unman me, then?"

"Louis! Really!"

"Would you unman me?"

Fanny paused for a moment, then replied in a slow and deliberate cadence. "As an author and celebrity, I would have you virtuously tame. Although a wild man in my boudoir."

"That smacks of hypocrisy."

"It smacks of good sense. Now what, pray tell, are you planning for the day?"

"May I offer you another glass?" asked Stevenson, holding up a bottle in the candlelight. He and Fanny sat again at the dining table that evening, the window still open as the air cooled. The deafening whir of midday cicadas had long since given way to the chirp of crickets, but the volume of their chorus bore further witness to the explosive fecundity of the Provençal clime. England and Scotland knew nothing like it.

"I don't think so," replied his wife, pushing her glass to the side. She held her fist up to her mouth as though to check some mild digestive ruction. "I've seen enough of the grape for now."

Stevenson had not written a single word the whole day, unless one counted the labels they had pasted onto the scores of bottles they had filled from their barrel of Grenache. The enterprise had taken them close to six hours, sitting in the warm sun in front of the house while natives passed by, wondering at the strange industry of these foreigners.

Valentine and Fanny had managed the bottles. Fanny had taken them from the wooden boxes they'd come in and placed them on the worktable next to Stevenson, who'd inserted a small funnel into each and held the assemblage under the wooden tap, working the sticky valve with his other hand. At the start, it had been challenging to calculate the level of fill, leaving room for the cork and the requisite finger's width below. Soon, though, he fell into a comfortable, mindless rhythm, absurdly gratifying after his recent attempts to write. Once the bottles were filled, Valentine had passed them along to Sam, who insisted on manning the corking machine. The boy kept careful count of the first forty or fifty corks that he levered down into the necks. Eventually, though, he lost track, humming odd bits of song in what seemed to be total contentment. The only real breaks in the exhausting procedure, save for the occasional call of nature and a mid-day meal of cheese and crusty bread, involved times when the cork-pot needed refilling with warm water, and one other, when Stevenson caught his sleeve on the tap and yanked it hard enough in the bunghole that the liquid spurted out explosively, soaking his white cotton trousers. While Valentine scurried away for a mallet to pound the thing back into place, Fanny and Sam fell all over themselves laughing—which had inspired Stevenson to leap up and perform a few dripping pirouettes. *La valse erotique du vin*, he'd waggishly dubbed it, threatening to take the performance to Paris.

"So Symonds wrote you?" asked Fanny that evening, waving at a big moth that flitted perilously near the candle flame.

"He did."

"And what did he have to say? Is he well?"

"He seems to be. He says that Davos continues to agree with him. And that he is close to being done with his Renaissance book."

"I don't know why it takes you men so long to finish things," quipped Fanny. "Women manage to make babies in only nine months' time."

"So I have heard. I only hope that your career in that regard is now complete."

Fanny cast him a disapproving glance.

"Oh, and he *is* hoping to visit," Stevenson added.

"Visit here?"

"Where else?"

"He's coming to steal you away from me," laughed Fanny. "After everything I've done to nurse you back to health."

"Symonds is a married man, Pig. He has four daughters."

"And that means something more definitive here than in America? Wasn't he always reading Walt Whitman? I distinctly remember him going on and on about Walt Whitman. *Ad nauseam.* And I have to say, you seemed to encourage him." She eyed her husband with an overwrought air of suspicion.

Stevenson laughed and poured himself another half-glass. Half-glasses always felt more innocuous, two halves seeming much more abstemious than one whole. "If you must know, *Leaves of Grass* tumbled the world upside down for me," he declaimed, affecting the tone and posture of an orator addressing an audience of hundreds. "I am perfectly happy to admit it. It blew into space a thousand cobwebs of genteel and ethical illusion. But it is only a book for those who have the gift of reading."

Fanny bridled visibly. "And by that you mean…?"

Stevenson laughed again. "I am toying with you, Pig. But Whitman is your man if you want to see life afresh. If you want a world in which women are afforded the same rights as men—to carry firearms, roll their own cigarettes, and curse in public."

"Perhaps I'll give him another chance."

"As for Symonds," Stevenson continued, "he is the best of talkers. He sings the praises of the earth and the arts, flowers and jewels, wine and music." He held his glass high in front of him, sweeping it grandly from side to side. "In a moonlight, serenading manner, as to the light guitar."

"Just listen to yourself! Are you describing Symonds, or writing a poem about the man?"

"I'm sure it is the wine speaking," replied Stevenson. "It loosens the tongue." He grinned mischievously. "And the tail!"

"You never speak about me that way. 'Serenading with a light guitar.'"

"How do you know how I speak about you when you're not there? For all that you know, I routinely surpass Dante on the storied Beatrice."

"Well then, prove it."

"How?"

"Talk about me that way when I am around you."

"Impossible!" declared Stevenson, setting his empty glass so close to the edge of the table that it almost tumbled off. He flinched sheepishly.

"Impossible?"

"When I am in your presence, love, your ethereal radiance positively stills my tongue with rapt bedazzlement."

"Why are your eyes closed? Are you falling asleep, Louis?"

"Not at all. I am merely shielding myself from your beauty."

7

*All the time…we were keeping the women off him as best we could, for they were
as wild as harpies. I never saw a circle of such hateful faces.*
—MR. RICHARD ENFIELD, COUSIN TO UTTERSON

Fanny had spent much of the afternoon outdoors, first at the market
with Valentine shopping for the evening's meal, then in the garden
attending to some much-needed weeding and pruning. The day was
unseasonably warm, and for the last half-hour she had been sustained
by the thought of a cool bath followed by a glass of wine with Louis on
the balcony overlooking the street.

She climbed up to the sitting room with a vase of freshly-cut lav-
ender, something to grace the dining table in what she thought would
be a rather Claude Monet fashion. Her eyes were still adjusted to the
bright sunlight, and at first it was difficult to tell that the long room
was empty. Pulling off her broad-brimmed hat, she tossed it onto the
table and set the vase down beside it.

"Louis!" she called. "Sammy!" She wiped her sleeve across her brow.
"Is anybody here?"

Stevenson had told her before she went out into the garden that he
and Sam might wander down to the center of town for a bit, should the

spirit move them. He had spent the morning hard at work on *Otto* and, although he continued to profess little taste for the project, he also confessed to feeling mildly inspired by Symonds's recent visit. He and his erstwhile fellow patient had enjoyed close to an hour reminiscing over their winters in Davos with the infamous Dr. Ruedi when Symonds had pulled a small volume from his bag and handed it to Stevenson. A just-published collection of medieval students' songs translated by Symonds and entitled *Wine, Women, and Song,* it was dedicated to "Dear Louis" in memory of their many alpine evenings of witty conversation. When Stevenson read the dedication aloud, Fanny had darted a quick but assertive look in his direction. Symonds was so effusive, though, about her husband's talents—deeming his *New Arabian Nights* to be among the most engaging pieces he had read in years—that when she thanked him at the door for visiting, she had been unqualifiedly sincere. True, she had afterwards teased Stevenson yet again about the precise nature of Symonds's affection for her man—but seeing Stevenson so patently energized by Symonds's praise had powerfully warmed her heart. That Symonds had also brought Sammy a lavish supply of Swiss chocolate had sealed the bargain.

Stepping away from the table, Fanny heard a rustle and a cough from Stevenson's study. Venturing in, she found her husband slumped in his chair. One arm drooped towards the floor and the other covered several sheets of stationery that lay on his chest. There was a half-empty bottle of wine on the desk. No glass. The air was heavy with tobacco smoke. As she parted her lips to remark on his indulgence, something in his aspect took her past admonition to concern.

"What's the matter, Louis? You're not feeling ill, are you?"

"Mmmm? What's that?" He turned his head in her direction, not quite meeting her eye.

"You don't look very chipper. Are you all right?"

"I don't know." He turned back towards the wall in front of him.

"What do you mean, you don't know?"

Stevenson grasped the papers in both hands and, folding them over in a wad, held them up over his shoulder, his gaze still averted.

"Bad news?" asked Fanny, walking closer.

Stevenson heaved a loud sigh and nodded.

"What is it, then? Who's it from?" Fanny pushed a nest of other papers aside and half-sat on the desk.

"From mother. Margaret."

"And?"

"The family business, to start with. It's evidently in a bad way."

"Your father's? He's retired." She slid herself closer to him. "You told me he'd stepped down."

"He has. But he maintains a substantial stake. And Uncle David is apparently running it all into the ground."

"It can't be that bad."

He eyed her challengingly. "No?"

"What have you heard?"

"I've heard that, last month, meeting with a very important client, my dear uncle evidently had a strange visitation."

"A visitation?"

"He claimed to see Grandfather Stevenson standing there in the office, right beside him."

"Oh my!" sighed Fanny. "Your long-dead grandfather?"

"The very one. And standing there, it was claimed, with a switch in his hand. And angry."

"Oh my goodness!"

"Uncle David swore, later on, that grandfather's ghost had ordered him to drop his breeches. On the spot. For a flogging. Mother doesn't say, but I wager he told the old bugger to stick the switch up his arse."

"Louis!"

"They always had their differences. And better defiance, I suppose, than to have dutifully bared his bum while the client watched."

Fanny suppressed a titter. "Well, yes."

"It *would* be comical, you know. It would. But evidently it cost the firm a five-thousand-pound contract. Of which father's share would have been considerable."

"Oh my!"

"I don't know if that puts our thousand a year from Father in jeopardy. I shouldn't be surprised, though. I suppose I shall have to pander to the masses in deadly earnest now if we're to keep our myriad creditors at bay."

Fanny leaned towards him to stroke his cheek. "I'm sure we'll be fine. I can always take in washing." She smiled in reassurance.

"And Sam can black boots at the railway station?"

"Precisely. There's honor in manual labor."

"So say manual laborers." He smiled grimly. She could see there was more.

"There's something else?"

Stevenson pinched his lips and nodded. His eyes looked large and liquid as a cornered hare's.

"What is it, Louis?"

He lifted the letter off his chest and unfolded it. He looked at the topmost sheet, then shuffled to the one behind it, holding it out and pointing with his finger at the middle of the page.

Fanny quickly scanned the sheet. "She's heard from Ferrier's mother!"

Stevenson nodded again. "Walter's near the end. Read it aloud. Read what that woman wrote."

"Oh my!" exclaimed Fanny. "*My son now exists among the number of those degraded ones—degraded* ones, she says!—*whose society on earth is shunned by the moral and virtuous among mankind.* My God, Louis. And she blames you. She blames it all on *you?*"

"Enough of it, she does. So it seems." The writer coughed again and reached for the bottle. He took a long swallow and held it up to Fanny. She waved it angrily away.

"That old bitch! That perfect old bitch! I've a mind to go up to Edinburgh on the next express and strangle her."

"Her son is dying," sighed Stevenson, his voice as sympathetic as it was anguished. Then very softly, "You of all people know how that is."

Fanny's look bordered on fury. "It's not the same, Louis. It's inhuman. I never blamed anyone for taking him. I never..." Springing from the desk, she stormed over to the window.

Stevenson rose wearily and followed after her, pressing up behind her and laying his hands on her shoulders. She was very warm from her work outside and, now, from her mounting ire. A strong and not unpleasant animal scent rose from her scalp, and he found himself nuzzling her head distractedly. "No one *was* to blame for Hervey. It was God's will. Ferrier? That might be a different matter."

Fanny turned to face him, fire in her eyes. "Don't you go feeling responsible, Louis! Don't! You're not. We've been through all this. That's her lunacy, and it's vile."

"Fanny—"

"It's *vile!*" She stood there with her hands on her hips, her jaw thrust out like a pugilist's.

For a moment he weathered her fiery gaze. Then he turned quietly and walked back to his chair. He sank slowly down, leaning forward with his head in his hands. As his long fingers snaked back through his hair, Fanny could hear him breathe in deeply, expelling each breath through his nose as he tried to settle himself. He coughed once or twice, tentatively, and then she realized he was weeping. She was reluctant to soften her stance, but within the minute, she crossed to him and rested her hand gently on his shoulder.

"Louis, I love you so terribly much. And I know you so well. These other people don't. You mustn't heed what others think or say about you."

"No?" he asked almost inaudibly.

She was relieved to think she might be prevailing. "No."

"Then our only worry, Pig, is what I think of myself."

Dear Belle, wrote Sam to his sister in California. *How frightened I was last night. I woke up after midnight to hear Mama calling out for Valentine.*

*"Valentine go and fetch the doctor! Go and fetch the doctor!" I didn't like
at all the way she sounded and I thought it must be Lulu again. I got up
and ran into Mama's room and Lulu was sitting in the bed coughing most
awfully. He was holding his pillow up to his mouth as he coughed and it
was all covered with blood. I think he saw me standing there but his eyes
were so frightened looking and he was so pale in the candlelight especially
compared to that awful pillow. He just couldn't stop coughing. I thought he
would choke to death on the blood that just poured out of him. Oh Belle. I
have never been so scared in my life. Mama told me to go back to my room
but I just couldn't. She sat next to Lulu on the bed hugging him and so she
got all covered with his blood too. Finally the doctor came with Valentine
and gave Lulu some medicine from a little bottle. He told Lulu to sit very
very still and not to move at all. He listened to his chest and when Lulu
started to be sleepy from the medicine the doctor tied his right arm close to
his chest and told Mama he must stay just that way for a good long while.
It wouldn't be good for him to move at all. He also said that there could
be no smoking and no drinking wine either. I know Lulu won't like that
especially the no wine part but the doctor says it is very important. Oh, he
is also not supposed to talk. At all. You know how he'll feel about that. I
will write again soon I hope with news that he is better. The doctor says
he should get better if he listens. By the way I am doing well at my lessons
Mama tells me. I am even learning French. Please say hello to Joe. I may
send you a poem soon. I miss you. Sam.*

Stevenson sat in bed in the darkened room, trussed up like a Christmas
goose. More than anything, he simply wanted to free his arm from the
mummifying bandages and swing it wildly in the air…or throw something…or just stretch it out straight and flex his fingers. He felt like a
genie in a bottle, and he did not like the feeling at all. By his left hand
lay a notebook and a pencil. Forbidden as he was to speak, it was his
sole means of communication, and it bore witness to the anguish and
frustration of recent days. The block letters were like a child's, ill formed
and uneven, necessarily written with his left hand. *Lift me straighter…*

Don't be frightened. If this is death, it is an easy one. … What I want is for you to do what you want and to go about your own affairs, and you won't understand me. … Why did you come? I can now never ring again. … Will you read to me? … What is the fat one up to? … You are tired.

On the bedside table, under a carved jade paperweight, lay a single sheet that had been torn out and carefully set aside. Fanny had found it when she awoke there on the third morning, and she read the lines aloud as he watched her, tears swelling in his eyes.

When I am grown to man's estate
I shall be very proud and great,
And tell the other girls and boys
Not to meddle with my toys.

And just below:

A child should always say what's true
And speak when he is spoken to,
And behave mannerly at table;
At least as far as he is able.

When she had done reading, he picked up his pencil and wrote: *Must we always be dutiful?*

Fanny spent almost every waking hour with him, and most nights she sat in the chair at his bedside. At every hint of a cough, she shot from her seat and leaned over him, searching his features manically as though his fate were written there in runes that only she could read. He longed to embrace her then, to comfort her, but all he could do was reach over with his left hand and touch her lightly on the cheek. At times, the closeness of death gave him a shocking sense of calm, and he tried to share that feeling with her, struggling to fill his eyes with it and pour it straight into her soul.

When Fanny tired to the point of illness, Valentine took her place, sometimes watching through the long hours of the night until she dozed in her chair. One morning, she awoke to find him smiling at her. As she stretched to shake off the slumber, he handed her the notebook. Written on the open page was this:

Come up here, O dusty feet!
Here is fairy bread to eat.
Here in my retiring room,
Children, you may dine
On the golden smell of broom
And the shade of pine;
And when you have eaten well,
Fairy stories hear and tell.

And below it, *We must, after all, eat if we are to tell our tales. Merci V.* She bent impulsively to kiss his forehead, and when his eyes widened in feigned shock and a smile cracked his wan features, she knew he was on the mend.

"I am so glad to see you are better," cried Sam, bouncing with excitement. For the first time in weeks, the window of the sick room was thrown open wide and the sun poured through with the morning zephyr, driving out the musty closeness that had bound it for a fortnight.

"Be careful of the bed," warned Fanny. "You mustn't jostle it. Lulu's not out of the woods yet."

"Sorry," said the boy, struggling to contain himself. "I really am glad, though. I was awfully worried, you know."

Stevenson nodded sadly. "I am sorry to have put you through that. It's not being a very good father, is it?"

"It's nothing you can help. Being sick. It's not as though you're trying."

"No," the writer answered. "It's not as though I'm trying."

"Will you be up and about soon?" asked the boy. "I think it would be loads of fun to go sailing. That wouldn't be too much of a strain for you, would it?"

"I'm afraid the doctor says it will be a good deal more bed rest," observed his mother. "But look. At least Lulu has two arms now."

Stevenson lifted his right forearm off the bed, rotating his hand to inspect both sides. "Hallelujah!" he said with a grin.

"I have an idea!" cried Sam. "Let's reopen the Davos Press. You can write some more poems, like you've been doing. And maybe I'll write a few, too. And then we can sell them in town!"

"We'll need to find another letterpress," laughed Stevenson. "Remember, we gave our old one to the Symondses when we left Switzerland. To Katherine."

"Oh, damn! I forgot."

Stevenson looked quickly at Fanny, fully expecting her to admonish Sam for cursing. She merely smiled at them both. "That's a wonderful idea," she said. "Perfect."

"Perfect," echoed the writer. "We shall produce a new *Lyrical Ballads*. You shall be Wordsworth and I shall be Coleridge. Most of what I try to write ends up like 'Kubla Khan' anyway."

"What's 'Kubla Khan?'" asked the boy.

"Oh, what was the start of a very great poem, but it never got finished."

"Why not?"

"The author, Samuel Taylor Coleridge, you know, had a dream and he woke up with the whole poem forming in his head. But as he sat down to write it, a man came and knocked on the door and—poof!— the poem was gone. Except for what he had already gotten down."

Sam gazed at him quizzically, then shook his head. "Well, we'll lock the bedroom door, then. And tell Valentine there will be no visitors. And *you* won't get to eat unless you write one hundred lines a day." He eyed his stepfather sternly.

Stevenson laughed hard enough that Fanny leapt to her feet and rushed over to him. Raising his hand, he coughed experimentally, then cleared his throat. The look of concentration left his eyes, and once again he smiled. "You sound as though you've been talking to your dear mother." He cocked an eyebrow at Fanny. "You both want this poor goose to lay more quickly than she can."

"This is serious business," said Sam. "We depend on you."

The following afternoon, Stevenson timorously offered for Sam's approval a little poem about "The Land of Counterpane," in which the narrator fancied himself "a great giant and still, that sits upon the pillow hill," who "sometimes for an hour or so watched his leaden soldiers go, with different uniforms and drills, among the bed-clothes, through the hills." Sam instantly and generously deemed it a work of genius, so vividly did it evoke their pastimes on the sitting room floor.

"I'm so glad you liked the soldiers," said Stevenson, once he had finished. Reading aloud had tired his voice more than he expected, but it was a great pleasure to look up from the page and see Sam beaming at him dreamily, hanging on every word—and, in turn, to see Fanny watching her son with a look of perfect contentment.

"A very good effort, Lulu. But you've got more, don't you?" He grinned at his mother like Puck.

"What a taskmaster!" complained Stevenson. "What a cruel, unmerciful audience I slave for. Would you crush art? Would you insist on the letter of your law when…when the muse is such a delicate soul? When she skitters away, frightened, from any commanding voice?" He winked at Fanny, who shook her head.

Sam giggled and bobbed his head emphatically. "Of course I would. You must do as we say. Now recite your next one, or you go to bed hungry."

"Goodness. I've only this." Stevenson opened with exaggerated weariness to another page. "And I am positively drained. Could I prevail upon you to read this one yourself?"

"Well," said Sam, pinching his chin dramatically.

"There's another soldier in it!"

"I suppose," said the boy, continuing to stroke his imaginary goatee. "Just this once." He cleared his throat and read in a high, dramatic voice, exaggerating every stress and rhyme.

When the grass was closely mown,
Walking on the lawn alone,
In the turf a hole I found,
And hid a soldier underground.
Under grass alone he lies,
Looking up with leaden eyes,
Scarlet coat and pointed gun,
To the stars and to the sun.
When the grass is ripe like grain,
When the scythe is stoned again,
When the lawn is shaven clear,
Then my hole shall reappear.

"Wait a minute," said Sam, lowering the page. "'When the lawn is *shaven* clear'? Do lawns get *shaven*, Lulu? Like with a razor?"

"Poetic license," smiled Stevenson.

"Shhh, Sammy!" said Fanny. "Go on."

Sam raised an eyebrow but he continued energetically.

I shall find him, never fear,
I shall find my grenadier;
But for all that's gone and come,
I shall find my soldier dumb.
He has lived, a little thing,
In the grassy woods of spring;
Done, if he could tell me true,
Just as I should like to do.
He has seen the starry hours
And the springing of the flowers;

And the fairy things that pass
In the forests of the grass.
Not a word will he disclose,
Not a word of all he knows.
I must lay him on the shelf,
And make up the tale myself.

When Sam had finished, Fanny applauded, stood up, and applauded some more. Sam bowed, extending his hand theatrically towards Stevenson, who dipped his head in turn.

"It's very good," said Sam. "Except maybe for the razor bit. I guess you've earned your supper."

"I am so relieved."

"And he's just like you've been, Lulu," his stepson continued. "The little grenadier. For the longest time, he couldn't speak a word."

"Nor can he yet," nodded the writer. "We have to speak for him."

He was gazing at Sam with great pleasure when the thought of Ferrier swept darkly back over him. Very soon Walter's lips, as well, would be sealed forever.

Stevenson lay in bed on his back, his left arm around Fanny, who nestled up against him with her head on his shoulder and her leg draped over his knee. He was perhaps a little warm, but it felt like a moment to relish, so he lay still. The moonlight promised to glide into their room at any moment. Already, its silver sheen etched the window frame sharply against the jet darkness of the interior wall. Crickets chittered thickly near and far, and the neighborhood nightingale added its liquid trill, now and again, to the whole inebriating chorale.

"Should I tell you how completely happy I have felt here?" he whispered. "With you?"

Fanny raised her head to look at him, her backlit features almost indistinguishable—save for her eyes, which were open wide with attentiveness. "Oh, Louis." She craned up to kiss him, then settled back onto his shoulder.

"I feel almost guilty about it, given what is unfolding in Edinburgh." He paused, half expecting a response, then added, "I do feel guilty."

Fanny looked at him again. "We can control only what we can control. What is it that you say yourself about the duty of being happy? That, in being happy, we sow anonymous benefits upon the world?"

Stevenson laughed. "How gratifying it is that someone is listening. Even if only to turn my own words back against me."

"I am your most devoted reader," cooed his wife, nestling in once again.

He tightened his arm around her. "How I longed as a younger man to be where I am right now—at least in terms of my matrimonial circumstances."

Fanny tittered, adjusting herself on his shoulder. "'Matrimonial circumstances.' You make marriage sound like part of a lawsuit. Or a murder investigation."

"You did marry a barrister," chuckled Stevenson. "It's too late to rue his lexicon."

She knocked his leg with her knee, then rested it once again over his.

"I recall lying under the stars in the Cévennes all those years back on my great Gallic walkabout—my only companion little Celestine. Celestine the estrual donkey—"

"Louis!" Again her head rose.

"—and thinking how right it is for a man to have a woman. And, indeed, how wonderful it would be to repeat a journey such as that with you. To cook over an open fire. To share a bottle of the local *plonk*. And crawl into a marital sleeping sack under the wide and starry sky."

"Mmmm!"

"With your pistols under our pillow. In case of highwaymen."

"Or boy donkeys in rut."

"Or boy donkeys in rut!"

For a moment they lay still.

"Would you mind, love? I'm a little warm."

Fanny groaned softly and pulled back from him.

"Thank you. We could both of us be dumb soldiers. Tucked up in the same hole."

"Ah, so that one was about you, too."

The writer laughed. "Everyone says I'm a damned egoist."

"And you're sure you wouldn't rather be alone out there? Like your little lead grenadier? What was it? 'Doing as you would like to do'? Gratifying all your secret cravings?"

He tilted his head to kiss her forehead. "You are my secret craving. And I have never needed you more."

"You're working again," chirped Sam. He stood in the doorway of Stevenson's study, arms akimbo. "I guess you're feeling better."

"I am," answered Stevenson. "Writing and feeling more like my old self."

"You're not old, Lulu. Not nearly as old as Mama." The boy grinned like an imp.

"Shhh! Your mother has the ears of an owl."

"Do you have a poem for me today?"

Stevenson laughed. "I thought I had fulfilled that contract."

"Technically, I suppose. But I do miss them."

"So do I."

Sam walked over to the desk and looked at the notebook his step-father had been writing in. *"Otto,* still?"

Stevenson sighed.

"Why don't you write about something interesting? Like the deacon."

For almost as long as Stevenson had known him, Sam had been entranced by the story of Deacon Brodie, the infamous Edinburgh cabinet maker—by day, deacon of the carpenters' guild and city councilor; by night, burglar and profligate gambler. Brodie had been hired to install locks in the houses of Edinburgh's wealthiest citizens, and then pressed the keys into wax to make duplicates for his midnight larcenies. Most gripping to the lad, it seemed, was the legendary claim that, when

Brodie and his accomplice were hanged from a gibbet that the deacon himself had designed, Brodie had devised a steel collar to protect his neck, and then bribed the hangman to remove his supposed corpse posthaste from the gallows and whisk him off to France and another life. Stevenson had always punctiliously withheld the fact that, beyond his partiality for the risks of burglary and games of chance, Brodie was thoroughly given to carnal pleasures. He had fathered five illegitimate children on two mistresses, each of them unknown to the other.

Stevenson chuckled.

"Why are you laughing?"

"My friend Henley has been begging me for years to write a play about Brodie. He claims it would make us rich."

"Well it could, couldn't it?"

"I don't think your mother would approve," replied Stevenson. "In fact, I'm certain she wouldn't."

"You may be right," agreed the boy. "But even after you've finished *Otto?*"

"Or *Otto* has finished me?"

Sam giggled.

"No," Stevenson said wistfully. "Someday, perhaps. When I've earned a little latitude through more commendable efforts."

"Well, I'm glad you're at it again," said Sam. "So is Mother."

"I expect she is. Can you tell her I shall be out soon? I've promised her a glass of burgundy before the sun is down."

"Sure," said Sam, smiling as he turned and left the room.

Deacon Brodie, thought Sevenson to himself as he took up his pen once again. Many were the glasses that the LJR Society had raised to Brodie's checkered memory—the bulk of them proposed by poor Walter himself. It was curious, though, that Sam had suggested he write something about the Edinburgh guildsman with the two lives. As far as Stevenson knew, the boy could have known nothing about his previous attempt in that vein, the piece at which *Blackwood's* had turned up their noses.

On the day, Fanny offered to come out with him, but he said that, above all else, he needed to be alone. The post had arrived at about two in the afternoon, and when he saw the envelope bearing Coggie's writing, he knew the news it must contain. At first he had just stood there with the thing in his hand, his heart racing. It was only when the straight edge of the paper and the regular beauty of her script began to waver with his building tears that he ripped the missive open and forced himself through the contents.

The very end had been blessedly easy. There had been a week when the swelling of Walter's liver and spleen had been very painful, and he had required large doses of laudanum to manage. One morning, upon waking, he had refused the usual draught until his family could be summoned. It was, Coggie said, as though he knew the end was upon him. He made his farewells, apologizing for having caused his loved ones such endless trouble, and then he drank his laudanum and slept. He never regained consciousness, lapsing into a coma and dying the next day but one. The doctor explained that the fluids in his abdomen, fluids resulting from the total failure of his liver and the subsequent packing-in of his kidneys as well, had put such pressure on his heart and lungs that he had died of cardiac arrest. In Walter's comatose state, the doctor assured them, the end would have been painless.

Stevenson left La Solitude with no notion of where he was headed, except that he was drawn to the sea. He reeled through the busy town, subliminally registering the scores of milling citizens and the frenetic activity of midday trade but feeling utterly, irrevocably cut off from it all. It was as though he were, once again, stuffed inside the diving suit he had donned all those years ago in Wick Harbour, and were trudging along the sea-bottom through silent schools of fish. It was only when he had left the town completely and made his way up and over the pine-covered hill of Costebelle that he found a spot that felt attuned to his mood. He settled in a tiny clearing with a view of the snaking Giens peninsula, threw himself onto the carpet of soft, auburn needles, and wept.

How long he gave way to the all-consuming grief, he had no way of knowing, for he had ultimately fallen asleep. By the time he awoke, the sun had sunk low in the western sky and its rays slanted in baroque majesty through the trunks of the graceful trees. Beyond the far tip of the peninsula, some sort of passenger ship crept slowly across his line of vision, leaving a blur of smoke above its creamy wake. Stevenson imagined finely dressed passengers gathering in a comfortable lounge for a late afternoon tea or aperitif, serenaded by a string quartet playing light airs from Strauss. He smiled briefly at the fancy that a nineteenth-century Charon might well pilot a boat such as this, and might have welcomed Walter personally to the convivial bevy of passengers as they steamed across the Styx to the underworld. Then he felt guilty for smiling, rose to his feet, and made his way back to the town.

He must have wandered every street and square of Hyères, winding in and out, boxing the compass once, twice, and then boxing it again. Bits and pieces of what he saw and heard, he took in: a raven-haired girl of six, perhaps, sitting on a window sill facing inwards and laughing with an intoxicating, bubbly beauty at something that someone was saying or doing; a man beating a dog that cringed, tail between its legs, but evidently too frightened to run for fear of augmented reprisal; two young men, no doubt intoxicated, weaving through the cathedral square with their arms slung over each other's shoulders, singing out of tune with one another—singing, perhaps, two entirely different melodies. A pretty young woman passed in front of them with a market bag in her hand. She shook her head in a mixture of amusement and disdain. She became Coggie, of course, and the two dithering youths became…

He bought a bottle of some indeterminate red at a dusty and foul-smelling shop near the railway station and, fortified by its cloying sugars, continued his aimless odyssey. Twice, when darkness had fallen, he was accosted by prostitutes, one of them baring a thigh to him under a flickering streetlamp. Once a beggar asked him for a coin, and he reached into his pocket for a handful, dropping them onto the cobblestones with a callousness he quickly regretted. He passed Le Désire, the restaurant of his humiliating undoing, concealing his face so as not to be recognized, although there was no sign of either the diners or the waiter of that troubling evening. He settled for a half-hour at a similar establishment in the same section of the town, but, after picking at an indifferent plate of trout, he purchased another bottle of red and rambled on.

It was well past eleven when he found his way back to the Rue de la Pierre Glissante. As he opened the ground-floor entrance, he was surprised to see Valentine sitting at the kitchen table, leaning over a book. She rose as he entered, straightening her apron and quickly adjusting her cap.

"Monsieur is home," she said in a soft voice.

"Yes."

"I am so sad about your friend. Madame has told me."

"Thank you, Valentine."

She seemed almost to lose her balance, shuffling back quickly before she steadied herself. In the candlelight, he could see color rising to her cheeks. "I am sorry. How clumsy."

"No," said Stevenson, stepping instinctively towards her. Unaccountably, he felt a flush in his own cheeks. He dropped his hands to his side and gazed at her.

"We were worried for you. Madame was worried for you. And little Sam." Again, she adjusted her apron.

"I am sorry to have given you concern. It was thoughtless of me."

"It is not often that one loses a best friend. May God send you a good rest this night."

"Thank you, Valentine."

"Madame is waiting upstairs." She lowered her eyes and reached over to close her book.

Dear Baxter.

Poor Ferrier. It bust me horrid. He was, after Bob and you, the oldest of my friends. This has been a strange awakening. Last night, with the window open on the lovely, still night, I could have sworn he was in the room with me. I heard his rich laughter as, even now, I see his coral waistcoat studs that he wore the first time he dined in my house. I see his attitude, leaning back a little, already with something of a portly air. How I admired him! And now in the West Kirk!

I am trying to write out this haunting bodily sense of absence, besides which what else should I write of? Looking back, I think of him as one who was good, though sometimes clouded. He was the only gentleman of all my friends, certainly the only modest man among the lot. He never gave himself away; he kept back his secret. Dear, dear, what a wreck! And yet how pleasant in the retrospect!

When I come to think of it, I do not know what I said to his sister when I learned the news, and I fear to try again. Could you send her this? It would let her know how entirely, in the mind of (I suppose) his oldest friend, the good, true Ferrier obliterates the memory of the other, who was only his "lunatic brother." This came upon me, overall, with terrible suddenness. I was surprised, in the end, by this death; and it is fifteen years since I first saw the handsome face in the Spec. I expected to have died first.

Love to you, your wife, and her sisters. Ever yours, dear boy.

R.L.S.

8

"I have had what is far more to the purpose," returned the doctor solemnly: "I have had a lesson—O God, Utterson, what a lesson I have had!"

—DR. HENRY JEKYLL

EDINBURGH, APRIL 1884

"We do believe we've turned up a comfortable house in Bournemouth. A wee bit dear, I would say. But thoroughly respectable." Stevenson grinned at his father. "Even Fanny seems to have taken a fancy to this one."

"She's given up her mad notion, then? Of returning to America? California?" Thomas Stevenson reached slowly to his right. Lifting the decanter from his desk, he held it up towards his son with an inquiring glance.

"Thank you, Father." Stevenson rose from his seat and padded across the oriental carpet to where the older man sat, bespectacled and draped in a crimson lap robe. "Just half." He held out his glass, cringing slightly when the flanged top of the decanter struck hard against the rim. He lowered it a jot to make it easier for his father to pour.

"Will that do?"

"Perfect." Stevenson raised his glass perfunctorily, then returned to his seat while his father poured himself another measure. Stevenson eyed his glass to make sure it had not been chipped. "I believe I've persuaded her that Sam will have a better education here than there. I am afraid, though, that she continues to find the English stuffy and overbearing. Especially my London literary friends. Perhaps to a man."

"Well," laughed Thomas Stevenson. "Fanny is a perceptive lassie. Not fond of the Sassenachs. Why don't you come north?"

Stevenson smiled and shook his head. "Our dear Dr. Mennell. I fear he claims the Edinburgh winds would finish me unco hasty. He deems the Hampshire coast a sufficiently risky proposition."

"You could always go back to France," huffed the old man, with what appeared to be a touch of resentment. "For all your mother and I see of you. Any of you."

"No, Father. We really do wish to be closer to you and Mother. Besides, we've brought the best of France here with us."

"This Valentine of yours?"

"Valentine."

"I must meet this wondrous woman. But tell me about the house."

"Well," said Stevenson, setting down his glass, "it has a name. 'Seaview.' And it is perhaps a mile's walk from the coast. A comely yellow brick villa on an acre or so of land. Scores of pine trees for the lungs. Disused stable and coach house—"

"A coach house!" his father exclaimed. "Then we shall have to get you a coach!"

Stevenson smiled. "A pigeon house—"

"And pigeons!" The old man chuckled. "How big?"

"Big enough for the three of us, when Sam's not at school. And Valentine. Perhaps some other help. And guests, of course. If any can be enticed to visit."

"How much?"

"Seventeen hundred, I'm afraid." He looked at his father guiltily.

"Fanny likes it?"

The writer nodded. "There is a wonderful spot for a garden. She claims she could grow tomatoes."

"Done!"

"Pardon?"

"Done. Buy it. Your mother and I will make up what you can't manage. And we shall come visit. God willing, we shall eat Fanny's tomatoes—prepared by this much-vaunted Valentine." The old man raised his glass as a pledge. "Not that you will ever be able to grow good tomatoes on this godforsaken island."

Stevenson found himself with his mouth agape. "You amaze me, Father," he was able to declare after a moment. "Your generosity is… What can I say? It's simply overwhelming."

"Don't be daft. You need a place to live. This sounds like a place to live."

"Well, it assuredly is." Stevenson gave a nervous giggle. "You're certain you can afford it?"

"Of course we can't afford it. Not since my damned brother ruined us. But, if it keeps you from running off to America, then we'd be fools not to make the investment, would we not? I'll just call it an investment. Tell your solicitor to be in touch with me."

Stevenson laughed. "You do remember that Baxter is my solicitor?"

"Well, tell him to be in touch with me nonetheless. I shall try my damnedest to be civil to the wretch."

Stevenson rose again and walked across the room. He placed his hand on his father's shoulder and gave it a gentle squeeze, struck in the act at how strangely paternal it felt. "Again, I don't know what to say."

His father set his glass carefully on the desk and reached up, clapping his hand on top of his son's. "Just be happy in it, Smout. That's all I ask."

For a moment, Stevenson could do no more than nod. Then "We will," he just managed to say, as he walked back to his chair.

They sat for a full minute in silence, save for a slight rasp in the older man's breathing. A chunk of coal popped in the grate, followed by the sigh of slumping ash.

"Shall I tend to the fire?"

"Mmmm? No. I shall be retiring soon."

"As will I." Stevenson had thought about going out for a walk to clear his head in the cool evening air. The urge, though, seemed to have left him, washed away by the third glass of port. What seemed urgent now was to see his father safely upstairs and then to collapse into his childhood bed, giving himself up to the darkness.

"So you called on Elizabeth?"

"I did."

"And Mrs. Ferrier?"

"Wouldn't see me."

"Shame. What a shame."

"Indeed. But at least she spared me the torture of the conversation."

His father eyed him censoriously. "That remark is beneath you, Lou." He tucked the lap robe more closely about his legs and noisily cleared his throat.

"I know it is, Father. This is not a situation I relish. In the least."

"No. And how is Elizabeth?"

"Struggling to be strong, I would say. It is a bitter charge for her to bear, as well—her dear mother claiming that Walter died because those of us who loved him just stood by and let it happen. Or, in my case, encouraged it."

Thomas Stevenson shook his head. "May the good Lord grant them understanding and mercy. Both of them."

The waning fire crackled and sighed.

"I showed her a piece I had written," said Stevenson.

"Oh?"

"A piece about mortality. A silly little thing inspired by *Hamlet*. But about Walter, really. I'd wanted to say something for a long time, you know." He gazed over at his father, whose head was tilted back on his chair.

"And the gist of it?" The old man's eyes were closed.

"I've brought it back with me. It's quite short. Perhaps you'd like to read it."

"I would. But not tonight." He raised his head and smiled wearily at his son.

Stevenson returned the smile. "Tomorrow, then."

"Tomorrow. Leave it in the dining room, if you would. I shall read it over my breakfast."

"I shall run up and fetch it. After I have seen you to bed."

"No need. I can still haul this old carcass up the stairs on my own."

"Please. I insist."

"Thank you," said his father. "You have always been a most satisfactory son."

It occurred to Stevenson that, at this particular moment, the words might be entirely devoid of irony.

The wind came up during the night, barreling off the Firth to rouse Stevenson from his slumber. Somewhere nearby, a shutter must have come unlatched, and it banged away in the gale with a maddening regularity, like a giant clock ticking at quarter speed. He willed the owner to wake, to register the racket, to rise and throw the sash open to secure the damn thing—but to no avail. He rolled from his side onto his back, lying there stiffly with his arms tight against his body. The tucked-in covers pulled uncomfortably on his toes, so he kicked them free, rearranging his feet to feel less constricted. He knew he could never sleep in this position, but he often found that if he could coax himself close enough to the edge of slumber while he was lying supine, then a simple turn onto his side could plunge him quickly into oblivion.

As the shutter clattered on, he ventured in his mind's eye out into the windy streets, passing from one pool of lamplight to the next like a boy hopping, rock-to-rock, down a tumbling stream. He passed Ferrier's house, peering up to see Coggie weeping in a window while, at the door, her mother belabored a cowed magistrate over arrests he was failing to make. He passed Dunbar's, where Baxter sat laughing in front of the crackling fire, one hand cradling a huge tankard of ale while the other fiddled briskly inside the bodice of a fiery-haired lass. He found his way back to the valley that cleaved the city, New from Old, and to the Waverley Station where, that very day, in the hiss and steam of a brace of idling engines, the feral little man who peddled Parisian photographs had flashed his wares with a conspiratorial grin. *Next best thing to being there,* he whispered again, his breath scalding and rank. *Looking's almost touching.* There now, shockingly, was an image of Coggie, resting her bare breasts on Walter's coffin while she stared boldly and coldly into the prying camera lens. There, as well, was Fanny, also naked to the waist, fondling the stiffened member of a youth masked as Death. And there, too, was Valentine, waiting at the door of a room in which hideous old men were being ministered to by nubile girls of every race and stature. *Take all three,* hissed the man. *Never know when you'll have another chance.*

The day dawned clear, with a few clouds gliding off to the southwest as the night's gale eased. Stevenson shuffled in his robe and slippers down to the dining room to find his mother and father sharing a pot of tea.

"Goodness, Mother," he said, sidling around to her chair. "What a surprise to find you up so bright and early. A pleasant one, to be sure. And good morning, Father."

"Good morning, Louis," said his mother, offering her cheek for a kiss.

Thomas Stevenson gazed neutrally at his son's attire, then bobbed his own greeting. His hand rested on the manuscript Stevenson had left on the table the night before.

"Have you read it, then?" asked the son.

"I have, indeed. 'Old Mortality.'" His father smiled wistfully. "Let us all have a bite, and then perhaps we shall discuss it."

Once the table had been had been cleared of all but the tea things, Thomas Stevenson turned to his son and patted the manuscript that lay next to him. "I say again, Louis, it's a poignant day when a man sees his own son, his only son, tendering thoughts on the fragility of human life. Such wise and sober thoughts into the bargain."

"I gather you approve, then?"

"I do approve. It is a truly moving tale of error and redemption. And so often aptly phrased, Lou. You do write masterfully, I must admit." He turned a number of the pages, evidently looking for something in particular. "This, for example, which I read to your mother earlier." He adjusted his spectacles and read. *"From this disaster, like a spent swimmer, he came desperately ashore, bankrupt of money and consideration; creeping to the family he had deserted; with broken wing, never more to rise. But in his face there was a light of knowledge that was new to it."*

He looked pointedly at his wife, who nodded in appreciation. "The spent swimmer is so nicely drawn," she averred. "I can just see him dripping. And so very cold and weary."

His father turned another page and tapped a passage with his fore-finger. "Or this: *The tale of this great failure is, to those who remained true to him, the tale of a success. In his youth he took thought for no one but himself; when he came ashore again, his whole armada lost, he seemed to think of none but others.* These are noble perceptions, Lou. Nobly expressed. A life all but lost—but manfully brought back into balance. All by the Grace of God."

Stevenson could not honestly recall having written divine agency into the tale's resolution, but he thought better of saying as much. "Thank you, Father."

"Now tell me this. Is it all true?"

The question took Stevenson aback. His mind coursed, in a reflex of unguarded frankness, back to that last afternoon with Ferrier and to the desperate craving for drink that had followed so hard on the heels of the demonstrations of self-knowledge and courageous good cheer. "I believe so," he answered. "Though one never knows."

"No," his father agreed. "One doesn't. But we shall hope so, for the sake of poor Ferrier's soul. Elizabeth has seen this, then?"

"She has. She very much wants me to send it out into the world."

"I should think she would," said his mother. "From what your father says, you manage to show Walter in such a good light. In the end, at least."

"Only the good light he put himself into," responded Stevenson, smiling soothingly at his mother. But his father's bald query continued to give him pause. Had Walter indeed placed himself in any positive light at all? Or was that only the self-indulgent illusion of sentimental portraiture? Was it even self-*exonerating* for the portraitist, to the extent that it was all made to come around right in the end, at least in regards to the man's soul?

"How satisfying it must be to write as well as you do," cooed his mother, setting her cup and saucer off to the side. "And think of all the young men whose lives you can help with an edifying tale such as this."

"One can always hope," answered Stevenson.

"Why should you doubt the efficacy of what you've written?" asked his father.

"Well, I suppose I suspect that, whatever good my little piece may do for Walter's dear sister and friends, it's tricked out in such a laudatory and abstract and allegorical way that the common man is unlikely to take the moral to heart. If he even extracts one."

"Whatever do you mean?" asked his mother.

"Walter's downfall was drink, as you and I and everyone who was close to him knew very well. But I hardly felt as though I could make that explicit, for fear the particulars would bring more shame than consolation to his family. So while the narrative speaks in one way to a reader in the know—to us, for example—its effect upon someone who has simply pulled the thing out of a pile of random papers is likely to be altogether different—and quite possibly boring into the bargain, stripped as it is of vivid particularities."

"What else could you have done?" asked the older man.

"As Hardy has done, perhaps. In his latest."

"And that is…?"

"The story of a man who, drunk almost senseless on some highly adulterated beverage, sells his wife and daughter to a sailor."

Thomas Stevenson bellowed with laughter. "The outcome seems as implausible as its purported cause is commonplace." He looked jovially at his wife, who now appeared vaguely mystified.

"True enough," allowed Stevenson. "Yet the moral is crushingly clear: partake of doctored spirits and you'll end up peddling your entire family for tuppence. What's more, the selling has an alluring touch of prurience to it, no? It's not far to search why a sailor might wish to possess himself of two females at once in some remote inland town."

"I am not sure I like the line this conversation is taking," remarked Margaret Stevenson, looking to her husband for support. Stevenson's father eyed him with a raised brow.

"I don't like to cram my opinions, willy-nilly, you know, down anyone's throat," Stevenson continued. "At least I don't think I do. But I don't mind thinking that the yarns I spin might somehow contribute to someone's prosperity and happiness. And I should damn well like to make some money at it." He slapped his hands on the tablecloth on either side of his plate.

"Now there's a commendable goal," laughed his father, "for all of this vanity and vexation of spirit."

"Hardy will make a bundle, of that you can be sure." Stevenson drummed his long fingers on the damask. "The days of Mr. Mudie's prune-dry pieties are long behind us, and the writer who knows that is the writer who sells. Give me real heroes and villains. Real flesh and blood. Happily married and virtuous one day, whoring the next."

"Louis!" exclaimed his mother. "I'm speechless!" She looked indignantly at her husband, whose air of jocularity hardened again into mute admonition.

"Of course I don't mean that," averred the writer. "Nor does Hardy, in the end, provide it. Tease us he may, but when it comes to matters of the flesh, it's all implication and assumption and surmise with him. The spice without the honest truth." He shook his head and sighed. "And yet it sells."

"Still, you've done rather well of late, have you not?" asked his father, clearly interested in redirecting the conversation.

Stevenson grinned at him. "Have you seen anything that's been written about *Otto?*"

"Your friend Henley was kind enough to send his piece from *The Athenaeum,*" replied the older man.

Stevenson chuckled. "Friendly it was to send, and friendly to write."

"He said such lovely things," offered his mother.

"He would," replied Stevenson. "Being, as I said, a friend. And a collaborator."

"What do the others say?" asked his father.

"Well, *The Saturday Review* was wonderfully flattering. Something about how painful it is to have no words of praise whatsoever to lavish on a book by Mr. Stevenson. Then Meredith wrote to say that my prince was 'morally limp.'"

"Perhaps you intended him to be morally limp," offered the elder Stevenson. "Perhaps it was a commendation."

"Perhaps. He didn't make himself abundantly clear. Yet there was little beside that observation in his letter. I can hardly take it as a staunch endorsement."

"My, but it's a brutal world out there," sighed his mother, rolling her napkin and sliding it back into the ring. "Thank goodness mothers aren't subject to such fierce public appraisals as authors are. Or wives." She looked appealingly at both of her men.

"You would fare magnificently, dear," declared her husband. "There would be hell to pay for any naysayer."

"Our revenge would be swift and terrible," added Stevenson. "And hideously just."

Part Two

JEKYLL

9

It chanced that the direction of my scientific studies, which led wholly towards the mystic and the transcendental, reacted and shed a strong light on this consciousness of the perennial war among my members. With every day, and from both sides of my intelligence, the moral and the intellectual, I thus drew steadily nearer to that truth, by whose partial discovery I have been doomed to such a dreadful shipwreck; that man is not truly one, but truly two.

—DR. HENRY JEKYLL

BOURNEMOUTH, AUGUST 1885

"I thought we might have some tea a bit later on," said Stevenson. "Anything for now, James? Sherry? Whisky?"

"Whisky, please. A small one. As long as you will join me."

"If I must," laughed Stevenson. "Love?"

"If I must." Fanny adjusted a striking new Kashmiri shawl about her shoulders and gazed cheerfully at their visitor.

Fanny's fellow expatriate took his place in the squat blue chair by the drawing-room door. Henry James's first visit to Skerryvore, as the Bournemouth house had been renamed in honor of Uncle Alan Stevenson's most celebrated light, had been an unexpected delight for

Stevenson and Fanny. Both of them had invited the celebrated American author to call as often as he might. Now James was in town for an extended stay, keeping his sister daily company as she took treatment for a longstanding but ill-defined emotional affliction. The two writers had already exchanged respectful but contentious essays in the pages of *Longman's Magazine,* but Stevenson now relished every chance to debate, *viva voce,* with one of the only men he had met who seemed inclined to think as seriously about the craft of fiction as the lighthouse-building Stevensons thought about the science of refracted light. Fanny had dubbed Thomas Hardy a "frightened little man" when she had met him months back, and her attitudes towards the rest of the Anglophone literary elite were even more dismissive. Nevertheless, despite James's owlish physique and his equally owlish tendency to sit in one's presence with uncannily observant stillness, she found him to be a man of considerable warmth and charm. It didn't weaken her endorsement that James clearly adored her husband—or that the only James story she had read straight through touched on the stoic grace of a dying child in ways that mirrored, with wrenching perfection, the last days of her own little Hervey.

Stevenson went to a side table and, righting three tumblers on the lacquered tray, poured two inches into each and carried them back to his companions. He settled himself in a straight-backed chair opposite James and raised his glass.

"They speak o' my drinkin'," he intoned, "but ne'er think o' my thirst."

"Open confession is good for the soul," countered their visitor.

Fanny joined the toast, took a small sip, and lay back in her chair, draping one arm over the side. "So. How is Alice?"

"It is exceedingly difficult to say," sighed James. "Her doctor seems sanguine; a sort of mesmeric procedure devised by Charcot, he claims, may be of some use. Some days she seems perfectly lucid and content. Others…"

"I'm so sorry," said Fanny. "I'm sure everyone is doing everything they can."

"I am sure they are, thank you." James smiled genially, looking down into his glass before he turned to Stevenson. "Have you had any more news on the Deacon?"

The two writers might well have met months earlier than they managed, when James attended the London opening of the drama that Stevenson's blustery friend Henley had finally coerced him into co-writing: *Deacon Brodie, or the Double Life*. Fanny, as Stevenson had anticipated, had been exceedingly reluctant to approve of the project, but when Henley assured her that the stage was the quickest way to literary fortune, she ultimately conceded. Sam was naturally delighted to see his favorite tale take dramatic life. As for Stevenson himself, despite the financial attractions, he worried even before the play had debuted that it might well checker his reputation. When he had taken ill the day before the first curtain, he in fact wondered whether his body weren't rebelling against his mind's questionable calculations. In any event, he and James had been obliged to wait for Alice James's indisposition to bring them face-to-face.

Stevenson laughed. "I don't know. Henley is a bulldog. I expect before long he'll have Irving himself involved. And a lavish new production on at the Lyceum."

James smiled, fixing Stevenson in that gaze that always seemed capable of penetrating several feet of stout English oak. "You do know, do you not," he asked as he swirled the liquid in his glass, "how much I admire you as a writer of *narrative* prose?" The stress on the penultimate word was unmistakable.

"Point taken," chuckled Stevenson. "Not that I would be opposed to obscene degrees of personal wealth."

"Few would."

"No. Especially given the way our butcher seems to have taken to lurking about the premises—account book in one hand, bloody cleaver in the other."

Fanny grimaced at her husband, but then turned towards James with buoyant cheer. "Did Louis tell you he had one of Brodie's hand-crafted chests in his room growing up?"

"I don't believe he did. How remarkable! And you were aware of what it was?"

"Of course I was," replied Stevenson. "Every Scotsman knows, from birth, everything there is to know about duality." Again he raised his glass. "You've read Hogg, I trust."

James nodded. "I have. Although you can hardly claim duality as a Scottish distinction. Over on our side we have Poe, for example. *William Wilson*. You know it?"

"I do."

"And the French have Gautier. *Le Chevalier Double.*"

"That I don't. Should I?"

James shrugged and took another sip.

"Well," offered Fanny, pulling her chair closer to the two men, "do you really think you need to invoke books—anyone's books—to make a point about the double self? I can't imagine how any soul with an iota of self-knowledge could think we aren't, all of us, impossibly jumbled bundles of dreams and desires. Men and women equally."

Stevenson looked at his wife in amusement. "Fanny likes so much to feel included. As to her authority in the matter at hand, I do sometimes call her my 'violent friend.' My 'weird woman.'"

James turned to gauge Fanny's response. She smiled at her husband with clear affection. "I would venture to say," he remarked, "that, on this particular score, there is indeed little to distinguish between the sons of Adam and the daughters of Eve. For years, you know, poor Alice has spoken about the fight between her body and her will." He sniffed and looked again into his glass.

"The fight," repeated Stevenson.

James nodded. "You might say it is a constant of her sad odyssey." He tugged at the sharp crease in his trousers. "But enough of that. Your son is well? Sam, is it?"

"Yes. He is," replied Fanny. "Thank you."

"Adjusted to school? The British variety can of course be challenging."

"His letters paint quite a rosy picture. We couldn't be more encouraged."

For a good quarter of an hour, the trio spoke about the ways Americans and the British schooled their various sexes and social classes, with Fanny touting what she took to be the virtues of the general American practice of educating boys and girls in each other's company. She confessed to an initial reluctance to send Sam to an English public school, having heard that bringing boys of disparate ages together without the largely civilizing presence of girls might lead to all kinds of questionable relationships and practices. Once she had conducted a lengthy probationary interview with Sam's prospective headmaster, she nonetheless declared, she had been convinced that her son might find the man's institution at least survivable, and perhaps even beneficial.

"So, Louis," said James, repositioning himself in his chair after Fanny's final pronouncement. "To return, with dear Mrs. Stevenson's permission of course, to our wonted line…I have been meaning to ask you how you felt about Archer's recent assault."

"Calling me a 'jaunty writer with no moral sense?'" chuckled Stevenson, with a coy glance towards his wife.

"Louis claims William Archer is a friend," Fanny sneered. "Friends like that we don't need."

Stevenson turned to James. "This one is remarkably solicitous of my literary reputation, you see.'"

James smiled at Fanny before he turned back to Stevenson. "What *do* you say to Archer, though? Honestly. In an age of insistent literary proprieties such as our own, the matter truly interests me."

Stevenson leaned back in his chair and crossed his ankles. "I suppose being called 'jaunty' seems more appropriate for a drum major than a writer. That, or a polo player."

James smiled. "Although the term might suit some of your *Child's Garden* poems, don't you think?" Grateful for Stevenson's agreeing to collaborate on *Deacon Brodie*, Henley had taken it upon himself to arrange for the publication of the series of little poems Stevenson had tossed off over the years. It was a touching gesture, to be sure, but not one that either Stevenson or his wife considered important to his literary ascendancy.

"Amusing trifles!" spat Stevenson.

"On one level, yes," allowed James. "But to sell them short would, I think, show a serious misappraisal. I don't know that I have ever encountered anyone who has managed to capture, as you most undeniably do, the pure joy of children at play. I don't know that anyone has. You may have invented an entirely new genre."

"You embarrass me, James," responded Stevenson after a moment's pause. "I confess, however, that it is rather dispiriting to think that I may ultimately be remembered for penning cheery fancies for the nursery and schoolroom. Provided, that is, that I'm remembered at all."

"Let me hasten to reassure you as to your prospects," replied James earnestly. "Your promise is as unlimited as your accomplishments are undeniable." He looked over to see Fanny nodding her approval. "And *jaunty* may indeed be the wrong word. One might do better to say that your virtue as a writer has a great deal to do with a kind of imaginative abandon."

"Imaginative abandon!" snorted Stevenson. "Now I sound like an acrobat who goes about flinging himself off of tall buildings."

"Precisely!" replied James, through a widening grin. "Precisely. Without a care for whatever might lie below. And by that I mean without a care for whatever anyone may have told you in advance about the dire consequences of writing a fiction that is as free in its invention as a child at play."

"There are those, of course, who look for me to put away childish things." Stevenson peered at his wife.

James inhaled deeply and shook his head. "I am simply talking about the power of imagination. Its focus needn't be, you know, on fabulous polar voyages or quests for pirate treasure or balloon flights to the moon. Those subjects may do for the childish reader. Yet what the mature reader is so charmed to find in you, Louis—what *I* find—is the freedom to pursue the question, 'What if?' without all the deadening ballast of that other question, 'But would it?' In a setting, all the while, of some realism and sophistication."

"You are entirely too kind. I think."

"No, truly. Your untrammeled inventiveness is a rare tonic to those of us who bemoan the trajectory of modern literary endeavor." He flicked at a speck on his trouser leg. "It occurs to me that the idea of making believe appeals to you more than the idea of making love."

Stevenson convulsed in laughter. "Good God!" he half-choked. "Where did you get that? You must be in secret correspondence with my wife!"

James blushed deeply. "That is not what I meant."

"Mark this, Fanny. The most perceptive, the most studious, the most exact Henry James caught out in something that he did not mean to say."

"It may just be that you have me there," James allowed. "What I meant to say, of course, was that rather than depending on the ladies, if you will, to achieve your romantic effects—in your *fiction,* I hasten to add—you rather impertinently manage to achieve your *frissons* with pure, untrammeled invention. Make believe."

"And I should feel flattered?"

"You should." James smiled.

"I am much relieved."

"As, then, am I," said James.

"And as for Archer's charge that I want moral gravity?"

Steps echoed in the hall, and Valentine appeared in the doorway, carrying a tray of tea and cakes. "I may?"

"Of course," replied Fanny. "Right over here." She motioned to the table to her left. The maid crossed the room and set the tray down, turning back to the three of them with a tiny curtsy.

"Thank you," said Fanny. "By the way, James, I hope Valentine didn't send you around to the back again today." She laughed with a careless exuberance, looking for Stevenson to join in. On the American's first visit, their cook had in fact mistaken the eminent writer for a tradesman and had directed him to the kitchen door. It was only Stevenson's coming to see who had rung that had set the situation straight. Fanny, the proud mistress of Skerryvore who at long last felt respectably established in the world, had been utterly humiliated by the gaffe.

The American waved his hand and grinned uncomfortably. "Not at all."

Stevenson peered at his wife with annoyance. Since their household had moved to Bournemouth, he had felt rather like a weevil in a biscuit, locked in a provincial English town chock-full of invalids and all of the numbingly respectable professionals who catered to them—too far from London but even farther from the ever-dependable invigoration of the Continent. Fanny, on the other hand, seemed delighted to be the doyenne of her own villa, and she marshaled the services of their three domestics and part-time gardener like a Bonaparte in skirts. Stevenson was finding her quasi-imperiousness increasingly bothersome, although he had thus far been hesitant to address the topic with her.

"Tea?" asked Fanny, with exaggerated cheer. "Or will it be more whisky for the menfolk?"

With the turn in conversation, Valentine stepped quietly from the room, her face impassive, looking neither left nor right. If she had taken any offense, it was impossible to say.

"I will have a little tea, if you would," said James, setting down his tumbler. He caught Stevenson's eye and raised his brow, following that with a gentle smile. "Archer, was it?"

"That…?"

"That we were talking about."

"Ah, yes," replied Stevenson, collecting himself. "I was about to ask if my lack of moral gravity went hand in hand with my esteemed childish abandon."

James shook his head dismissively. "You know perfectly well my own feelings on the so-called 'moral obligations of art.' All that silliness Besant goes on about."

"And what is it Besant goes on about?" Fanny asked.

Stevenson paused and pulled at his collar to release some of the heat that he could feel building up in his neck. "He contends that writers should have a conscious moral purpose. Above all else."

"Well, shouldn't they?" she asked, turning to James. "In the main, I mean?"

"So some believe," replied the American. "Myself excluded."

Fanny looked vaguely incredulous. "You don't mean to tell me your work, your characters, pay no heed to morality?"

"Not at all. Just that what I mean by writing—the stories I write—should undertake to trace the implications of things, far more than the imperatives."

"What exactly do you mean by implications?" asked Fanny, bemused.

"I mean," explained James, "that the novel should deal with *all life.*" He indulged himself in an uncharacteristically expansive gesture, one incorporating both of his arms at once. Stevenson looked for tea to slosh from the man's now-elevated cup, but James executed the maneuver with the practiced grace of a priest raising the chalice. "With *all* feeling, *all* observation, *all* vision." He looked with intensity back and forth between the two of them and then gathered his hands back into his lap, with nary a drop spilled. "I should say writers should indulge in the freedom to see life whole, not parse it into sterile and rigid categories of right or wrong. That is for the law, surely. Or religion. Not for art."

"Can you say, truly," Fanny asked, "that you are not at all interested in the moral impact of art? Of your art?"

"Of course I am interested," replied James. "How could I fail to be? We live in a world of legal and ethical obligation." He returned Fanny's stare, as she eyed him now with overt skepticism. "It is simply that I am far more interested in the possibility and indeterminacy of that impact than I am in saying—presumptuously, I might add—that this is a right or this is a wrong thing for us to represent in our imaginative world. Or that this is the precise effect that a work of art will undoubtedly have, for better or for worse, on the delicate and thirsty young souls who partake of it."

"I'm afraid I can't agree with you, at all," said Fanny, after a substantial pause. "Perhaps it comes of being a mother."

"Well," responded James, "motherhood is a window onto life through which I have not yet had the privilege to look."

Stevenson fingered the end of his moustache as Fanny and James shared a cathartic laugh. After a moment, he remarked very quietly, "I once lost a friend whom I believe I might have helped…had I been more forceful in my ministrations. Both personal and literary."

"I am very sorry," said James.

"In fact," Stevenson continued, "I have since written of him—if rather indirectly. And I have wondered about the value of his story—of his life—for others of his sort."

"Of course." James set down his tea and clasped his hands together over his knee, looking on attentively.

"I must also admit," said Stevenson, leaning forward in his chair, "that I have wondered about how any exemplary quality of his life might or might not correspond to its reality."

"Whatever do you mean?" asked Fanny.

Stevenson looked at her coolly. "Just that in order to point a moral one is sometimes tempted to exaggerate. To distort. To represent as a thorough penitent, for example, a poor wretch who remained desperate to the end for the very thing that had ruined him."

Fanny eyed her husband with a chill gravity.

"Perhaps you find, as I do," offered James, "that what seems most verisimilar in your imaginings—the most faithful, that is, to the experience of life as it is lived in the moment—is infinitely more interesting than what might perhaps be the most instructive?"

Stevenson managed a smile. "Perhaps that comes of all of those dreary and crippling years we spend with sententious schoolmasters. And sanctimonious clerics. I must admit, in any case, that my quirky little midnight muses—my brownies, you know—they have never had the least rudiment of a conscience."

"And so they are free to create art."

"Oh, good heavens!" sighed Fanny.

"Indeed they are," Stevenson continued. "If there's to be anything by way of the ethical in what I do, I am obliged to add it after the fact. Sometimes with the most pointed encouragement."

"Heavens!" Fanny repeated after a moment's pause. "Have we determined, then, that neither of you esteemed men of letters has, in the end, anything to tell us about how we ought to behave ourselves in life?"

Stevenson looked at James, and then back at Fanny. "Why turn for guidance to any men at all, love? If you are ever in need of moral edification, merely take counsel with yourself. You never seem to be at a loss for what it is that you or anyone else should do or say."

Fanny turned to James, her mouth agape. James extracted his watch and peered at it with a theatrical precision.

"Well, then," declared the American. He slid his cup and saucer further onto the table and softly tapped on his knees. "This has been delightful. Thank you both, as always."

"Must you leave?" asked Stevenson.

"Regretfully."

"Well. Perhaps we can take this up again another time. Once we have all of us achieved the moral omniscience of motherhood." Stevenson rose and walked over to his friend. "Do come again, James. We'll promise to behave. Won't we, love?"

Once they had seen James to the door, Stevenson returned to the drawing room, hotly pursued by his wife. He walked to the window and stood there peering out at the garden, his arms folded, one hand cradling his jaw.

"What in God's name was all that about?" asked Fanny, bending towards him like a diminutive prizefighter.

"What do you mean?"

"Your cynical and demeaning treatment of me just now. In front of our dear friend James."

"I'm not sure I know what you're talking about."

"Like hell you don't."

Stevenson swallowed hard. "I'm sorry if you somehow found my remarks demeaning. I was merely caught up in a stimulating conversation."

"I find that hard to believe." She straightened up, her hunched shoulders settling. "But I shall endeavor to forgive you."

"Ever so grateful."

Fanny resumed her seat and took up her knitting with a modicum of residual intensity. For a full minute the only thing breaking the silence in the room was the clack of her needles. "James is a sweet man," she observed at length, "and an author of undoubted note. But how disappointing, that 'trace the implications of things' nonsense of his. What's the point of being as wise as he is, and then just 'tracing implications?' If I had the public's ear, the way he does, I wouldn't waste it that way. Just being '*interesting*,'" she said with a sneer. "In fact, I don't know many women who would."

"Never fear," Stevenson responded. "I expect he is already well on his way to revising his entire sense of literary purpose." Fanny opened her mouth to speak, but he forged on. "Or perhaps he is crying his eyes out at the pub. Across from his sister's madhouse."

"Well there's something, isn't it?" Fanny sat up especially straight. "Did he bring poor Alice down here just to 'trace the implications of things?' Or is he trying to make a difference for her?"

"Perhaps you should have brought that up with himself."

Fanny laid down her knitting and turned to face him squarely. "Really, Louis. Who put the damn burr under your saddle today? You've been fuming now for hours. What is it? Do you think I was rude?"

"Not to James."

"What do you mean, 'not to James?'"

Stevenson ran his finger along his lower lip and stepped closer to the window. Perhaps it wasn't worth taking the plunge. Perhaps it was. He eyed a luminous bluebottle crashing intermittently against the glass.

"Well, then, was I rude to you?"

Stevenson took a deep breath and, spinning on his heel, stared directly at her. If anything, her grizzled hair had lost even more color in the months since they had come to Bournemouth. Why should life here be aging her so?

"No," he murmured.

"Who else was there? I have no idea why you're carrying on this way."

He had kept the die pocketed up as long as he could manage. Willy-nilly, he cast it.

"You didn't need to embarrass Valentine. Yet again."

"What?" Fanny exclaimed. "Embarrass Valentine! What in heaven's name are you talking about?"

"*I hope she didn't send you around to the kitchen door again, James,*" he intoned, in a slightly over-Southern American twang.

Fanny was silent for a moment, then burst into a girlish giggle. "You sound like Jefferson Davis," she declared. She sprang up and skittered over to him, grabbing him around his ears and pulling his head towards her for a kiss. "Don't you think you're being overly protective? I didn't see any sign she was offended."

He wrested his head away from her, sharply reminded of his indignity as a boy whenever he was manhandled by doting aunts. "Valentine is a proud woman."

"Well, if she is," huffed Fanny as she returned to her chair and resumed her handiwork, "it doesn't become her as a maid. Or as a cook. Besides," she added, needles clacking once again, "it was all in fun."

"Fun for you, perhaps. If I were Valentine, I would have been embarrassed by your dredging up—once again—what was a simple mistake."

Stevenson could see his wife's jaws working strongly as she knit on. Something ill-defined, but not at all unfamiliar, drove him forward. "And I believe James was embarrassed for her as well."

"For God's sake!" cried Fanny, making a show of throwing down her knitting. It landed unsatisfyingly back on her lap, and she flailed it away in a growing fury. "Now you have James taking sides with you against me. I won't have it, Louis. Especially not for *her.*" She shot him a glance that made him miss a breath. It was suddenly as though he were staring into a mirror at his own most irascible self.

Stevenson paused as he groped for a calm he did not in the least feel. "Look at what she has given up for us," he said quietly. "Hundreds of miles from her home. No family. No one to speak her language."

"You speak her language with her all the time. I don't know what you say, but you do. *Parlez-vous* this and that. *Qu'est-ce que c'est?*"

"You know perfectly well what we say. You've lived in France for almost as long as I."

"It's what you say to her when I'm not there to hear you that I worry about. Your proud French maid. All tall and slender and young."

Stevenson was both stung and shamed by the insinuation. Throughout Valentine's tenure, nothing remotely improprietous had passed between them. At the same time, it was undeniable that his daydreams, now and again, swept him enticingly into her orbit. He had sometimes imagined her being as available to him as he had often imagined the young domestics of Heriot Row to be. There was a certain poem he had written...

"You say, look at what she's given up for us," Fanny was near to shouting. "Well, look at what we've given up for her." She held her small hands out wide, tears suddenly tumbling down her cheeks. "I don't know, Louis. I don't know how I can go on, worrying every day that you will die the next. Watching you struggle to write, dished up who knows what kind of nonsense by your damned brownies. And then struggling, tooth and nail, against every bit of good counsel I try to give you." She wiped her tears away with clenched fists, whipping her head from side to side. "And now you take a friendly joke as some kind of attack on her—on our goddamned fucking cook."

Stevenson's sigh could have come from the marrow of his bones. "I don't know how you do this to me, Fanny."

"Do what?"

"I know how hard life with me has been for you."

"No, you don't."

He took a deep breath. "How hard for you and Sam. And there is not a day that passes that I don't marvel at the love and care that you have lavished on me, little as I might deserve it."

"But all of those sacrifices don't make up for the fact that something is wrong," Fanny asserted. "Am I right? That I'm too old. Or too fat. That I don't want to lose you to someone else." Though her face was wet and reddened under her tangled mop of gray, she still managed to look like a helpless child. "What is it, Louis? What is it that I can't give you?"

He had been about to say that suspiciousness was beneath her, that it might actually be the only thing she could indulge in that might indeed drive him away. As satisfying as that would have been in the moment, however, it compassed the possibility of a dismemberment that he knew he could never endure.

"I'm sorry, Pig," he said at last. "You give me absolutely everything I need. And yearn for. I am a fool to doubt you."

"You are a fool," replied Fanny, wiping away the last of her tears. "That's why you'd be lost without me."

10

As he lay and tossed in the gross darkness of the night and the curtained room, Mr. Enfield's tale went by before his mind in a scroll of lighted pictures. He would be aware of the great field of lamps of a nocturnal city; then the figure of a man walking swiftly; then of a child running from the doctor's; and then these met, and that human Juggernaut trod the child down and passed on regardless of her screams. Or else he would see a room in a rich house, where his friend lay asleep, dreaming and smiling at his dreams; and then the door of that room would be opened, the curtains of the bed plucked apart, the sleeper recalled, and lo! There would stand by his side a figure to whom power was given, and even at that dead hour, he must rise and do its bidding.

—THE NARRATOR

Dear Henley,

I wish I felt better about the Deacon. I am daily more certain, though, that we ain't delivered ourselves of a real, knock-'em-dead treatment of that "other fellow," you know—that lurking, bridling, recidivist self I've gone on about for these last hunnert years. You tried mightily, you did, but I fear I sadly missed the mark. Brodie is so damn calculating and controlled, don't you know? "Goodness, Smith. See how we have ignored the clock! I do say it is very much time to be out a-burgling." What truly haunts us, if we're honest about it, are urges that bust out of nowhere with no notice at all—that or those insidious whisperings, equally unannounced, that we can't for the life of us resist. But merely burgling like the man? Copping coin to gamble away? Hardly the designings and the doings that are the real dark stuff! No, I truly hope we do well enough with the old dodger, but he ain't the last word, not in the least he ain't!

For now, I must tackle Kidnapped *seriously, or be content to have no bread, which you would scarcely recommend.*

Sorry for this.

Post.

R. L. S.

My dear Father,

Many thanks for a letter quite like yourself. I quite agree with you and had already planned a scene of religion in D. Balfour; *the Society for the Propagation of Christian Knowledge furnishes me with a catechist whom I shall try to make the man. I have another catechist, the blind, pistol-carrying highway robber, whom I have transferred from the Long Island to Mull. I find it a most picturesque period, and wonder Scott let it escape. The* Covenant *is lost on one of the Torrans, and David is cast on Earrid, where (being from inland) he is nearly starved before he finds out the island is tidal. Then he crosses Mull to Torosay, meeting the blind catechist on the way; then crosses Morven from Kinlochaline to Kingairloch, where he stays the night with the good catechist; that is where I am; next day he is to be put ashore in Appin, and be present at Colin Campbell's death.*

Today I rest, being a little run down. Strange how liable we are to brain fag in this scooty family. But as far as I have got, I think David is on his feet, and (to my mind) a far better story and sounder than Treasure Island.

I do trust Bath may do the trick for you; but I suspect the great thing is rest. Mind your allowance; stick to that; if you are too tired, go to bed; don't call in the aid of the enemy, strong spirit, for as long as you are in this state, an enemy it is and a dangerous one. Believe me,

Ever your most affectionate son,

Robert Louis Stevenson

Stevenson sealed the second of the two envelopes, flipped it over, and inscribed the so-familiar address on the front side. Halfway through "Edinburgh," the nib of the pen caught and snapped a tiny constellation of ink across the paper. "Damn!" Was it worth putting right? Had it been the letter to Henley, he would never have bothered. This was to his father, though, in a time when not much was going right for the old fellow. A stoic all his life, the old man had been persuaded to spend a fortnight in Bath taking the waters and seeing medical specialists of one sort or another. Why send him a "black spot" when Stevenson might easily avoid it?

He tore the envelope open, slipped the letter into another, addressed it without blemish, and slid the pair of missives into his coat pocket. Fanny was away, visiting Sam at school and then on to London to spend a few nights with Colvin's Fanny, shopping for furniture to help make Skerryvore look, she said, a little less like a Hampshire Silverado. He told no one he was going out, expecting to be back by tea. Donning his hat and snatching his stick from the Chinese vase in the entrance hall, he bounded out the front door and down the front steps, as relieved to be escaping from his work as he was eager to take the fresh sea air.

He walked briskly down Alum Chine Road, past other houses of Skerryvore's general stature and vintage, wondering offhandedly what intriguing tales each of their decorous façades might conceal. Was this one, august red brick with the rather secretive entrance, the bolthole of a pack of Fenian bombers? Was this one, looking vaguely Dutch with its narrow profile and scrolled pediment, a bordello catering to Church of England prelates on recuperative holiday? Was this one, with a froth of Japanese cedar gracing its stately walk, the secret lair of Mahdist villains, plotting to whisk Queen Victoria off to Sudan as the Sultan's consummate concubine? And would he be prey to any of these mad fancies, he wondered, if he had stuck with the practice of law—or, even more dryly, to engineering?

He himself might have declared this day a day of rest, but his brownies had evidently not gotten the word, and they labored on inside his skull with unbridled lunacy. He voiced a mad cackle and threw a skip into his next stride—to the evident confusion of an aged couple hobbling past him with their liver-spotted spaniel. He ambled through a swelling crowd of fellow strollers into the town center, past the elegant new Mont Dore Hotel with its vaguely Parisian lineaments, and around to the Post Office, where he dispatched the letters to Henley and his father.

As he stepped back out into the pale sunlight, Stevenson's eye caught the immense gray finger of St. Peter's spire, and he turned his steps in that direction. A tiny voice inside his head suggested he might duck inside the expansive sanctuary and offer a prayer for his ailing father. Feeling sure, however, that his mother and especially Cummy had that particular matter well in hand, he contented himself with a walk around the outside of the building. Halfway through his circuit, he spied the low profile of Mary Shelley's grave, a substantial gray sarcophagus capped with a massive, hipped stone lid. Frequently enough, on walks through town, he stopped for a moment to visit with the long-suffering author of *Frankenstein*.

Mary Wollstonecraft Shelley, he read as he stood over the grave. *Daughter of William and Mary Wollstonecraft Godwin and Widow of the Late Percy Bysshe Shelley. Born August 30th 1797, Died February 1st 1851.* She had been only nineteen, half his age, when she had taken up the pen and written as profound and chilling a tale of misdirected aspiration and desire as he knew. He was particularly fond of the tale of Mary's inspiration—of the tempestuous night near Geneva when she and her husband and Byron had each undertaken to write ghost stories, the core ideas of her own narrative coming to her afterwards in a dream.

She had never been specific, as far as he knew, about which images and motifs had been delivered to her whole. He would have laid his money on the poignant scene in which the Wretch seeks out his creator in the doctor's bedroom, only to have the man recoil, revolted, from the very creature he had been so intent on bringing to life. It was, he believed, one of the most affecting scenes in all of fiction: the simple quest for understanding and love; the crushing disappointment of an ideal envisioned but not attained; and all of it vested in that arresting image of the curtains of a bed being drawn back and revealing to both actors, in the starkest and most brutal of ways, the impossibility of anything other than a tragic resolution.

Mary's eminent parents lay there together, hard by their daughter. Where might he himself finally rest, Stevenson wondered? And in whose company? He had once been all but certain he would predecease his own father, but if that did not turn out to be the case, as recent developments suggested, would either he or those left behind to dispose of his willowy remains plant him in Thomas Stevenson's vicinity? The thought of dissolving into the soil of Auld Reekie was, he smiled to acknowledge, substantially more appealing than the thought of living there.

He strolled on to a newsagent to purchase a copy of the *Times* and, rolling it tightly and tucking it under his arm, headed towards the Lower Gardens and its row upon row of shaded benches. Halfway there, he spied a gangly boy in a navy-blue jacket and breeches bursting from a confectioner's shop with a bag of sweets clenched happily in his fist. The sudden thought of tart lemon drops sparked a strong reaction back at the base of his tongue and a yen he found impossible to resist. Walking into the tiny establishment, he was greeted by a pert young woman with old-fashioned blonde ringlets. Learning his pleasure, she pointed him to a glass jar charmingly labeled "Grandma's Acids."

"And Grandma has tasty acids, does she?" he asked, a mite flirtatiously.

"My little brother loves 'em."

"Ah, but they would be for me."

The girl blushed. "Oh. I'm sorry, sir."

"No need," replied Stevenson. "I fear I've never outgrown certain boyish cravings. A quarter of a pound, please."

He paid the tariff and left the shop, turning south towards the Lower Gardens, beyond which the long stretch of Poole Bay sparkled under a pewter sun. Four hundred yards on, he turned into Invalid's Walk. The freshly raked gravel of the path crunched pleasingly beneath his boots. Hard upon his stop at St. Peter's, the long rows of pine suggested the aisles of a vast, airy cathedral, and a breeze susurrating through the countless needles above might have passed for the whispered supplications of those unfortunate souls for whom the walk had been named. As it was, there were few of the infirm and suffering present to meet the eye. Dozens of well-dressed men and women walked at various paces along the sun-dappled track, quietly conversing or breathing deeply of the salutary, resinous air.

Stevenson was struck anew by the deadening uniformity of class in the town. Here were lawyers and their spouses, children of bankers, wives of civil servants, parents of doctors, all of them more than amply heeled by the salaries of the professions, seeking the favored new cures of modern medicine and, supplementing or failing those, the solace of being seen by others as arrived and respectable Britons. "Am I one of them?" he asked himself, cringing at the possible answer. Not so those early times in Edinburgh, and even later on in London, when he had donned the clothes of a rag-and-bone man and wandered about whichever city he was in, taking careful note of how he was—or was not—seen by the respectable folk he encountered along his way.

Stevenson sighed and took a seat on a vacant bench. Extracting the *Times* from under his arm, he unrolled it and smoothed it flat on his lap. "Salford Explosion Kills Hundreds," read the first headline to take his eye; "Disaster at Clifton Colliery." His initial instinct was to be glad it had not been an act of Fenian terrorism. Not that it would make an ounce of difference to the families of the lost men and boys. "Queen's List Names John Everett Millais First Artist to Be Granted Baronetcy." He smiled to think how his mother and father would feel if he were ever similarly honored. Small chance of that!

He suddenly remembered his cache of acid drops and reached into his pocket for the bag. He opened it and popped one into his mouth, relishing the tartness of lemon as it cut through the sweet sugar dusting. *Had his palate been this refined as a boy?* he wondered with a smile. Or had decades of vinolence taught him things about the complexities of taste that he would never otherwise have known? He heard a scuffling in the carpet of ochre needles near his feet, and looked down to see a red squirrel staring up at him, whiskers a-twitter. What would the creature do with a lemon drop, he wondered, half tempted to find out. "Children's Poet Chokes Helpless Rodent," penned his Fleet Street brownies.

A gust of wind caught the paper and nearly tore it from his hands. Damn! A mite of dust must have landed in his left eye, and he grimaced as he reached up and tried to wipe it away. How annoying it was in a public place to have something interfering with one's vision. There was a sort of nakedness about it, as though one could not see but could still be seen. A passing gentleman caught his eye.

"Breezy, i'n'it?"

Gentleman? Well, the fellow had certainly looked the part before his speech gave him away. Then again, it occurred to Stevenson, the man may somehow have taken *him* for the working-class interloper, and condescended to a low parlance either in a companionable or in a mocking way. He ultimately decided that this bothersome spate of self-consciousness called for a measure of compensatory self-indulgence, and he broke his normal sweets rule and bit into the lemon drop well before it had completely dissolved.

"Hyde Park Rally Cites 'Immorality' of High Officials," he read. In the wake of the previous week's Criminal Law Amendment Act and the attached Labouchère Amendment, public outcry in London over the "gross indecency" of various men in high places had spilled out into the traditional open-air forum of the park for heated public exchange. Stevenson imagined the bowlered and top-hatted crowd just below Marble Arch, gathered around this particular day's jeremiad. How many of them milling about there had attended public school? How many of them would, as a result, have known far more than they cared to admit about "gross indecency"—either as an unwelcome violation of their boyish innocence or as the natural consequence of affections and instincts that could enjoy, in their exclusively male environment, no other avenue for expression?

He searched his own emotional and sexual inventory. There were men he had loved, and still loved: Cousin Bob and Ferrier, Baxter, and perhaps now James, despite their brief acquaintance. Had he lived with any of them, he might well have found their foibles and particular forms of willfulness just as bothersome as he sometimes found Fanny's. Yet one could perhaps say that his love of men—for example, of Walter—had been purer and finer than his love for his wife, even than his love for his Platonic Madonna, the London Fanny—Fanny Sitwell, now and apparently forever waiting to marry Colvin. Of physical longing, though, there was nothing he could identify, unless one counted the tipsy joy of carousing, arm-in-arm, through the midnight streets with Bob—or the almost unmanning tenderness of tucking Ferrier, drunk to insensibility, into his bed before he himself floundered home alone. Of course he coveted attention and affection, as he found it easy enough to admit to himself and to select friends. But he had never gone beyond the usual schoolboy explorations, either *at* school itself or with his venturesome cousins at Colinton. He never expected that he would, despite his three-quarters-in-whimsy, one-quarter-in-earnest jokes about Fanny's mannish pistol-shooting and cigarette-smoking being precisely what kept her interesting to him. He remembered what Fanny had said about Symonds, and felt neither threatened by it nor inclined to explore what James would call the "implications." He wondered, truthfully, about James himself—but that was neither here nor there.

"Indecency" might indeed be "gross," in which case it had no place in civilized society. The old adage, though, about the first stone being cast only by him who is without sin struck him as never more valid than now. Curiously content with his interior exchange with the Hyde Park finger-pointers, he folded the paper and set out for home.

Stevenson sat alone in the half-furnished dining room, staring at the remains of as good a brandied flan as he could ever recall tasting. Valentine had clearly outdone herself, wanting him to know, as she said rather coyly when he came in from his walk, that Madame Stevenson's absence must not prove to be a time of too great distress.

He gazed at his wife's empty chair, surprised by a twinge of melancholy. It was not necessarily that she was gone for a week. He had prepared himself for that and was frankly grateful to have some time to work on a number of projects that called for concentrated effort, his new tale of a kidnapped youth being foremost among them. Perhaps it was that very relief, however, that lay at the heart of his malaise. His mind returned to their most recent conversation with James, and the way Fanny had asserted herself in matters about which she honestly knew so very little. Of course she was a woman of intelligence and worldly experience, and of course her total dependence on him and on his literary output justified her driving concern for how he fared in the literary marketplace. Yet the fact that she felt herself to be, somehow and in some regards, on an equal footing with a writer of James's brilliance smacked either of presumption or of an inadequate grasp of certain realties.

He loved Fanny's forwardness, but at the same time resented

it. Perhaps it was the womanly change of life that accounted for her mounting assertiveness and unpredictability. Perhaps it was Sam's departure for school, and Belle's being so far away, all compounded by Hervey being so long now in his grave. Or perhaps he was making far too much of it. Had she been there, sitting now across from him, he would have flattered or teased her into a charming little display of Fanny-ness. If James's assessment was accurate, and he was indeed uniquely gifted in his knack for remembering, as a grown man, the essence of the boy within, Fanny too was always within a wink and a titter of the girl she must long ago have been. Nothing about her was more alluring. But she wasn't here for him to evoke that frivolous charm, and Stevenson worried that another side of his wife might day-by-day, week-by-week, be gaining some kind of embittered ascendancy. He refilled his glass with port and stared over into the fire.

A slight commotion at the door to the kitchen brought him back to the here and now. One of the new maids, a mousy girl with red hair and a wealth of freckles, stood on the edge of the carpet, her hands working anxiously against her apron.

"Yes, Millie?"

"Will that be all, sir?" she asked in a tiny voice.

"Pardon?" He had heard her perfectly well, but, without thinking, here he was requiring her to say it again, louder. It was something Fanny would have been apt to do, as it peeved him to realize.

"Will that be all?"

He restrained himself from requiring a second "sir." "Yes, Millie. Thank you very much. It was all delicious." He smiled encouragingly as the wee thing came around and removed his pudding plate and fork. "Please tell Valentine how pleased I was with her supper. Better yet," he added, folding his napkin and tossing it onto the table, "please ask her to come in."

"Yes, sir. Thank you, sir." She edged shyly away, facing him all the while and nearly backing into the sideboard. Here she was in his employ, and it was all he could do not to scrunch his shoulders and wave at her

171

and say, "Bye-bye, then" as she crept back into the kitchen.

In a moment, Valentine entered the room, a perfect study in contrasts. She wiped her hands on a towel as she strode directly to the table, stopping there with her eyebrows raised in anticipation of his having something to say.

"That was wonderful, Valentine. *Magnifique!*"

"Thank you, monsieur." She bobbed her head once in acknowledgment, the slightest smile blooming on her lips.

"The lamb was exquisite. And the flan divine."

"Divine," she echoed, drawing the word out just perceptibly in a way that suggested, frankly, that she was amused by the adjective he had chosen. She stood there silently, perhaps a tiny bit closer than she would have had they not been alone. How did one determine such things? Suddenly, totally unexpectedly, something tightened in Stevenson's chest and he found himself a hair's breadth away from telling her he loved her. No, not that he loved her, for she would have laughed at that, but that he craved her with every ounce of his being.

What was it? The reserve, surely, that had never been broken. The austerity of the uniform. He had never seen her in anything else. The way, a thousand times it seemed, she had observed such perfect decorum, yet managed to suggest, through an infinite variety of gestures and intonations, that it was all an act that she continued to find it amusing to play but of which she might, at any moment, tire. *"I will pretend to serve you, cher monsieur, but we know who truly desires to serve."* It was only when he felt reasonably certain he would do or say nothing daft that he allowed himself a thought: if she were a lemon drop, she might already be in his mouth. He smiled and shook his head.

"Monsieur Stevenson is troubled?" Again the raised brow, this time above what he swore was halfway to a calculated moue. If so, it was her least subtle manipulation of all of their time together. And Fanny was away.

"Not at all," he managed to reply. "I was just reminded of something amusing. But I did want to thank you for taking such good care of me in Mrs. Stevenson's absence."

Valentine nodded. "You miss Mrs. Stevenson?"

"I do. And Sam."

"She will be home again soon, no?" She crossed her arms and looked abstractly around the room, and then straight at him. "Is there anything else for me tonight?"

"No," answered, Stevenson. "I don't think so. Thank you very much, Valentine."

"Thank you, monsieur. Have a good night."

"And you as well."

Lying in bed, his candle still flickering on the nightstand, Stevenson resisted as long as he possibly could. "Is there anything else for me tonight?" he whispered to himself, doing his best to catch every detail of her intonation. "Oh God, yes," he sighed, throwing back his covers to expose himself. A few quick strokes and he gushed ecstatically over the sheets, covering the spot where, a few short hours ago, his wife had lain snugly up against him.

As the last contraction died away, he sat up in bed, wondering what to do. It would be hellish to clean up. Surely it could wait until the morning. He blew out the candle and curled up onto his side, facing away from Fanny's half of the mattress. In a spasm of guilt, he reached back to touch where she customarily lay, only to draw his hand back from the already chilly mess.

"It doesn't mean a thing," he assured himself. "Not a thing."

11

The steps drew swiftly nearer, and swelled out suddenly louder as they turned the end of the street. The lawyer, looking forth from the entry, could soon see what manner of man he had to deal with.

—THE NARRATOR

BOURNEMOUTH, OCTOBER 1885

The man dashes along, his coattails flying, footfalls clattering between darkened façades that lean in, like huge stone spectators, over the twisting thoroughfare. Lamplight glints off the damp cobblestones as he sprints on, his breath coming in sharp gasps. It is a racecourse to break an ankle, but his pace never slackens as he whips his head from side to side, looking desperately for a gap in the endless ranks of buildings that line his flight from his pursuers. At last, all but breathless, he spies the dark doorway of a public house slightly ajar and he bursts through the opening into a low-ceilinged room. He finds himself utterly alone, the only presence and movement a fire that lies dying in the grate. As he approaches it, stealthily on his toes, its glow unaccountably mounts until it lights his face like a footlight on the stage. His complexion is swarthy, his features coarse, and as his breathing slows in the silent room, he wipes a bead of sweat from his low brow. Dropping to a seat at a table by the fire, he reaches into a pocket and, pulling out a folded packet of paper, lays it out before him and peels back the layers. At the very center of it sits a clot of white powder, still compressed by its wrapping. Grinning with satisfaction and relief, the man lowers his head and laps at the pile with his tongue, noisily, like a hound. He licks every crease and fold, then holds the paper up to the fire to be sure nothing remains. Evidently satisfied, he throws the paper onto the table and leans back in his chair. For a moment he is still. Then, with a sudden grunt, he thrusts his legs out straight before him, sending the table flying across the scarred floor. His arms straighten rigidly as well, and his head arches back, the cords in his neck straining as though they will snap. Side to side his head flails, in quickening rhythm, and his dark features swell like a child's balloon. His cheeks surge out to swallow his nose, his brow bulging out above until his eyes all but disappear into the dark crease between the two mounting waves of flesh. A gurgle and then a scream break from his distended lips, and his hands fly to his face, pulling and clawing as though they belong to another creature altogether. Staggering to his feet, he stumbles towards the bar and towards the mirrored wall behind the serried bottles. Sweeping them aside, he reaches into his pocket for a box of lights and, striking one with difficulty in his shaking hands, he holds it up to his face. Even as he watches, the grisly swelling begins to subside and, as his skin settles back into patterns of human order, a new set of features emerges. A high and pale brow. Eyes wide-set and sensitive on a narrow, even delicate, face. A chevron of moustache where, before, there had been none. He holds the match more tightly, and leans closer to the mirror to be sure. Yes. Yes indeed. The powder has done its work. Standing back in the litter of smashed glass, he throws his head skyward and laughs, a deep howl that shakes his very bones, shakes him again, shakes his shoulder, pulls at him like someone wresting a drowning man from a cold river, calls to him with a voice of dread.

"Louis! Louis! For God's sake, what is it? Louis!"

He raised his head from a sweat-drenched pillow, struggling to orient himself. Fanny shook his shoulder again and leaned closer, her breath hot in his ear. "You were screaming in your sleep, dearest. What was it? Are you all right?"

Stevenson rolled onto his back, then sat up in the darkened room. The house was utterly silent. "Damn it, Fanny? Why did you wake me? I was dreaming a fine bogey tale."

"My God." Fanny laughed with relief, sitting up beside him. "You were screaming bloody murder. What was I supposed to do? Just lie here and let the neighbors think...I don't know what the neighbors would think."

Stevenson rubbed his eyes, then wiped a drop of something from the tip of his nose. "Damn! I don't know. Perhaps that I was reviewing our finances."

"Louis!"

"Or," he turned to her, "that my savage American wife was molesting me once again."

"Molesting you?"

"Fulfilling her wifely duties, then."

"Is it that awful?" laughed Fanny. "What I do for you?" She reached over beneath the counterpane and slid her hand down to his crotch.

"Well. Not exactly awful." He could feel himself hardening to her touch.

"Oooh. I think I sense some interest down there."

"Perhaps." He adjusted his hips to make himself more accessible.

"You're not about to scream again, are you?"

"I don't think so, no." He lay back in bed, banging his head on the headboard. "Ouch."

"Does it hurt?" Stevenson chuckled. "Let momma kiss it."

When it was done, Fanny curled up next to him. "There. That should help you get back to your dreaming."

"Thank you."

"Mind you, no more crying out."

"Of course, ma'am. Thank you, ma'am."

He felt a slight blow to his shoulder, and then her arm crept across his chest as she nuzzled closer. Darkness welled back.

Fanny awoke to find herself alone.

"Louis?" she called. She sat up and looked about the room. "Louis?" There was no reply.

She rose, donning her robe and slippers before she hurried downstairs. She found him in the dining room, bent over a sheaf of papers with pen in hand, a cup of tea off to the side. "Here you are."

He peered up at her distractedly.

"I woke to an empty bed," announced Fanny.

"What? Oh! I'm sorry, Pig."

"You couldn't sleep?"

"Oh, I did," he replied with a smile. He laid down the pen and pushed the papers away. "I did. Your ministrations were marvelously soporific."

"I'm not sure how I should take that."

"Well, I hope. But I'm afraid I was too excited to linger this morning, as adorable as you looked just lying there. Softly snoring."

"Louis!"

"I was far too aroused."

"Still?"

Stevenson waved his hand. "The dream you so rudely interrupted?"

"Like the man from Porlock?"

"In the interrupting, perhaps. Hardly in what followed."

Fanny grinned and rearranged her robe.

"I've been jotting things down. Playing the sedulous ape to my brownies." He gestured towards the papers and pen. "I think they have provided me with my missing link."

"Your missing link?"

"The body for the story I've been after, you know…it seems like forever. About that sense of one man being two that I am always dithering on about."

"You mean we'll finally be able to put all that to rest?"

"I should get it all down today. I must."

"Weren't you saying you couldn't wait to get back to David Balfour?"

"Did I?"

"Haven't you left him and his companion starving out there on the moor somewhere?"

Stevenson snorted. "Let them eat rabbits." He reached for a cigarette.

Fanny frowned.

"It fuels the muses," he explained.

"Then at least give me one."

He pushed the box over to her, then struck a match and lit for both of them.

"Do you think you could meet Sam's train?" he asked, exhaling with obvious relish.

"He'll be expecting you to be there, too."

"I know he will. I'm simply too energized by what my little midnight artisans have tossed my way. I must play about with them before they flit away."

Fanny sighed. "What do you have, then? Tell me."

"Yes, ma'am."

She glanced at him impatiently. "This could get tiresome, you know? All this newfound ma'aming."

Stevenson eyed her from beneath an arched brow. "Yes, dearest."

He detailed excitedly the flight through the darkened streets, the powder, and the transformation—judiciously omitting the curious but intriguing portrait in the public house mirror of the dreamer himself. "There was that," he said, "and before that there was a very vivid scene of the man in the mirror, the transformed man, but this time he was sitting at a window high up on a wall. A particularly filthy wall. It was inside a narrow courtyard of some sort, and the evening sky was fading higher up above. And as he sits there, disconsolately, two acquaintances walk into the musty court—perhaps I myself was one of them, I don't recall—and they see him sitting there. And as they speak with him, just pleasantries you know, this look of fright creeps over the poor soul's face. And, even as he reaches out to lower the sash, a dreadful change sweeps over his features and this poor old gent turns into…well, a horror."

"Fascinating." Fanny tapped the ash of her cigarette into his saucer. "And may I ask…?"

"Of course."

"Was this horror he turned into anything like your runner in the streets?"

Stevenson laughed. "You are acute, Pig!"

"Goodness! I'm getting a bit of a chill."

"And I as well," cried Stevenson. "The wretched man just…reverts under the cool eyes of friends. There's no stopping the transformation!"

"No," responded Fanny. "I can't wait to see how you flesh it all out."

"Nor can I, to be honest. Thus my appeal to you."

Fanny reached across the table to clutch his hand. "I'll be happy to fetch Sammy, then. And you can devote your whole day to cavorting with your brownies."

"Yes, ma'am."

Fanny reached for his teacup, pretending to toss it at her husband. She failed to notice it was still half-full, and a good measure of tea spilled out onto her robe and the tablecloth below. "Fuck and piss!" she exclaimed, reaching up to cover her mouth in embarrassment.

"'Oh, is that you, Millie?'" sang Stevenson, cupping his hand dramatically behind his ear. "'Yes, indeed. That *was* Mrs. Stevenson calling out for you.'"

Home for a brief vacation and filled with tales of arrogant sixth-formers, Latin grammar, and wretched food, Sam had taken up rugby football and had both a swollen nose and a blackened eye to prove it.

They shared a late luncheon together, after which Stevenson excused himself and retreated to the bedroom, where he had been writing the

entire morning. Fanny had been surprised to find him sequestered there
when she returned from the railway station, propped as he was against
a huge bank of pillows in a cloud of tobacco smoke, oblivious to Sam's
racket as he barreled into the house and up the stairs with his luggage.
When she had questioned his location, he mumbled something about
the best place to recapture the dream being the same place he had had it.

So it went, remarkably, for three full days, two of them marked
by as nasty a tempest as Bournemouth had experienced in decades.
Never had Fanny seen Stevenson so consumed by a project. He left
strict instructions with the maids not to be disturbed, and the few
times when Fanny, in daylight hours, deigned to come into the room,
she found him hunched intently over his manuscript, heedless of the
torrents of rain lashing at the windowpanes three feet from his head.
Only twice could she prevail upon him to come down to the dining
room—for lunch the second day and a late breakfast the third. Once,
when Valentine knocked at the door with a light supper on a tray, he
sent her away with a snarl.

After a full day of this, Sam, as unaccustomed as Fanny to seeing
his stepfather so totally consumed by his writing, swung between filial
concern and clear disappointment at being ignored, such that Fanny felt
she had to say something. "It's for Sam that I am doing this," Stevenson
shot back at her. "Sam and the rest of you." Each of the nights, Fanny
fell asleep amidst the flicker of candlelight and the scratching of the nib,
and two of the mornings she awoke to the same sound.

"Did you sleep at all, Louis?"

"Enough."

On the third morning, Fanny woke to the gentle whistling of her
husband's breath. She raised her head from the pillow and looked over
to see him lying on his back, his mouth slightly open and one arm
tossed back over his head. The counterpane lay halfway down his chest
and, since the room was chilly, she pulled the cover gently up to his
unshaven chin. She sat up slowly so as not to disturb him and, looking
at the table to his side, noted a pile of paper stacked neatly beneath the

extinguished candle. Next to it lay Stevenson's pen and an uncapped bottle of ink.

She slipped her legs out from under the covers and, dropping her feet to the floor, slid them into her slippers. She cringed at the creaking bedstead as she rose from the mattress, but Stevenson whistled on as she donned her robe and tiptoed around the bed to stand there next to him.

The tempest had abated. Outside the window, the nearly naked branches of an oak tree scarcely moved against the brightening sky. Somewhere in the middle distance, a rook or two cawed away. She screwed the cap onto the inkbottle and gazed down at her sleeping spouse, wishing he would close his mouth. How many marriages would ever be solemnized, she wondered, if everyone who intended to marry were required to see a future spouse lying asleep before the banns could be proclaimed? How often might Louis have wondered the same thing while he peered at her dozing? She clenched her jaw tightly and looked down at the stack of papers. There was a look of finality about it. Should she slip the manuscript out from under the candle stand and begin reading it at once? She decided against it, adjusted the covers once more around him, and slipped quietly out of the room.

Valentine must have heard her descending the stairs, and she came into the drawing room to find her mistress standing in front of the fire, warming her hands.

"Are you wanting breakfast now, madame?"

"I don't think so, Valentine. I believe I'll wait for Sam."

The maid nodded. "And Monsieur Stevenson? Will we be seeing him today, do you think?"

Fanny stared at the young woman, vaguely galled by the secure smile on her lips. She was tempted to reply that it was hardly any business of hers. "I don't know, Valentine. We'll just have to see, won't we? I wouldn't be surprised."

"The master is finished with his writing, then?"

"I don't know. I expect he might be. But you know him almost as well as I do," she added, regretting it as soon as she said it.

"Not at all," Valentine replied. "But I do know he is not always content with what he writes."

Her smile seemed completely open and sincere. In place of her doubts, Fanny felt a sudden and unlooked-for kinship with this woman, as far removed as she herself was from her native home and all things familiar.

"So," said Valentine. "I will be in the kitchen. Tell me, or send Millie, when the young master has come down. Or monsieur himself."

She turned and left the room without a curtsy—leaving Fanny to wonder what, if anything, that might mean.

Sam tramped down the stairs shortly past nine, calling out loudly for his mother.

"Shhhh," hissed Fanny, rushing out into the hall to quiet him. "Your father is asleep."

"Oooh, sorry," said the lad, hunching his shoulders. "You're still in your robe?"

"I didn't want to wake Louis by dressing." She looked askance at his jacket and tie. "And look at you! I keep telling you you don't need to dress for breakfast here."

Sam looked down at himself and laughed. "I promise to be more slovenly tomorrow. So has Louis finished writing whatever it is he's been writing? Or are we going to spend yet another day in collective banishment?"

"I know," sighed Fanny. "But the signs are promising. I found papers stacked neatly by his bedside. I didn't dare touch them, of course. We'll just have to see. Breakfast?"

"Hell, yes! I'm bloody well starving."

Fanny cringed theatrically. "I'm glad to see your fellow scholars are having such a positive effect on your language. Or is it the masters?"

"Oh, Mother. I am learning so much," exclaimed Sam as they passed into the dining room. "I can conjugate the verb 'bugger' in Latin."

"Samuel Lloyd Osbourne," cried Fanny, turning and shaking him by the shoulders. "That's awful."

"I'm joking, Mother. All we've been doing is *amo, amas, amat. Cogito, cogitas, cogitat.*"

"Well, I'm relieved to hear that. Just don't let your father hear you talking that way."

"Six thousand miles away? I doubt he will."

"You know what I mean."

Sam and Fanny were just finishing their breakfast when they heard a creak on the stairs. Moments later, Stevenson stepped into the doorway in his striped pajamas and hastily donned robe. He raised a packet of papers in his hand, beaming.

"Good morning, beloved family."

"Good morning, Lou," replied Sam. "I *can* call you Lou, can't I?"

Stevenson felt a curious stab of emotion. "I suppose we have out-grown 'Lulu,' haven't we?"

"Well…"

"You may call me anything you like. Lou. Lulu. Velvet Coat. Writer of Genius."

Fanny motioned briskly to her husband, fumbling at her waist.

Stevenson looked down and, throwing the papers onto the side-board, belted his robe. "Thank you, dearest."

"Writer of genius," repeated Sam. "Are we talking about something recent?"

"My goodness!" exclaimed Stevenson, picking up the manuscript and walking over to the table. "Am I to assume from your phrasing that nothing I have penned in the past decade is worth a goat's bleat?"

Sam laughed and shook his head. "Lou! Lulu! Really! Have you finished, then?"

"I have!" He threw the lot of paper onto the table, halfway between his wife and stepson. "At least a solid draft."

"And?" asked Fanny.

"And…" He reached up to stroke his moustache. "I do believe it may be the best thing I've written. Ever!"

"Honestly? The best?"

"It came like a tidal wave. I could barely stop writing." He held up his right hand like a withered claw, then shook it energetically.

"So we noticed," grinned Sam. "What's it about?"

Stevenson looked at Fanny. She tipped her head briefly from side to side, weighing the situation, then nodded.

"A rather bad man, I would say. Who makes a show of being good."

"Oh, like Brodie," observed Sam. "Not another cabinet maker, though?"

Stevenson chuckled. "No, not another cabinet maker. A doctor."

Sam reached over and laid his hand on the papers. "Can I read it?"

"I'm not sure it's quite ready for such an important eye. Perhaps your mother will oblige me by being the first to subject herself to my immodest scribblings."

"So they're immodest, are they?" asked Fanny.

"I shall leave that for you to judge."

"Very well, then. Perhaps I can find a few moments for a quick look-through. You're sure it will be worth my while?" Her grin was especially impish.

"If you would indulge me, dear heart, I would be ever so grateful." Stevenson held the manuscript out to her. "Remember, it's the fruit of only three days' labor." He smiled cautiously as she snatched it from his hand.

After Sam's time away at school, Stevenson was prepared for his stepson to have outgrown forever their war games of yore, especially given his new preference in names. Nonetheless, once the lad had run upstairs to brush his teeth and tromped down again to the drawing room, it was Sam himself who proposed the idea.

"I don't suppose you have any old soldiers lying around, do you?" the boy asked as he idly picked up the latest copy of *Punch*.

"Of course I do. I must tell you, though, that their pensions are costing me a fortune."

Sam laughed and closed the paper. "Do you suppose you could dig them out? Perhaps we could fight a battle or two…for old times' sake?"

The expression hit Stevenson, for the second time that morning, with unlooked-for poignancy. Could Sam the growing boy already be mourning a vanishing age of innocence and play? Or was Sam the young man revealing a maturing solicitousness for him, Stevenson, for whom games of war had so long been the surest means of rapport between them? He thought back to his own most recent visit to Heriot Row, when he had found his father standing alone in the old day nursery, a toy boat in his hand. Thomas Stevenson claimed he had felt a draft flowing down into the hall below; he was just checking, he'd protested, to be sure all the windows were latched.

"Nothing would please me more. Let me just go fetch a pair of armies. Who shall it be?"

"Oh, I don't know. Napoleon and the Russians? Borodino?"

"Very well. And I suppose you'll want to be the French," sighed Stevenson in mock resignation. On his way to the stairs, he stole a glance into the dining room. Fanny sat at the table, her chin propped on a fist as she pored intently over his work. Hearing him pass, she looked up and smiled. She seemed, from the relative size of the piles, to be a fair way into it. As he turned again to climb to his room, Stevenson registered, for reasons that were hard to ascertain, more concern than he was used to feeling over the customary spousal review.

They had fought the battle of Borodino more than once before, and it unfolded with reasonable speed. Stevenson's roundly beaten Cossacks were already retreating from the field when Fanny stepped quietly into the room.

"Borodino," he explained in response to her puzzled look. "Sam is Napoleon. I am Kutuzov. I am in full retreat."

"Oh my!"

"And look at Sam, if you would. You can tell how much he wants to break the rules."

"I do not," laughed the youth.

"Yes, you do. Do you see those troops over there?" he asked Fanny, pointing to a clutch of lead horsemen massed around Sam's left knee. "That's the Imperial Guard."

"I see. They do look imperious."

"And if Sam—Napoleon—if Napoleon were to send them after me right now"—he looked up at her with an air of helplessness—"it would result in a terrible, crushing defeat. Cataclysmic."

"Oh my! But he can't?"

"Well, he could. But that's not the way it happened."

"Napoleon wouldn't risk them," explained Sam. "So I won't risk them either."

"So the battle's over?" asked Fanny.

"Nothing to do but bury the dead," replied her son.

"And dash home for some vodka," added Stevenson. "A great deal of vodka, I should think."

They shared a happy laugh.

"So," said Stevenson, climbing up from the floor and walking over to lean on the mantle, "have you finished as well, love?" He pointed to the papers in Fanny's hand. "Am I now to be crushed on this front as well?"

"Not at all." Fanny stepped carefully over the battlefield and seated herself in James's chair. She laid the papers in her lap and patted them gently, an uncharacteristically prim smile on her face.

"What do you think?" asked Stevenson. Again he felt a curious surge of anxiety.

"I can certainly see why it consumed you totally. For days."

"And by that you mean…?"

"I mean it is remarkable, Louis. It is remarkable."

"You like it?"

"I do."

Stevenson's knees nearly buckled with relief. A part of him bridled, as always, at depending on Fanny for approval, but at least this insistent little fable seemed to pass muster. "What do you like about it, then?"

"Well, the plot is ingenious. Brilliant, even. Your resolution took me completely unawares."

"Goodness," said Sam. "Now you really have to let me read it."

Stevenson smiled at him. "We shall see."

"It is so, so suspenseful, Louis. And the language all through is perfect. Powerful. There were times when I felt I was right there in the streets of London—caught up in all of the city's tumult, swept along by the rush of the crowd. Even choking on the fog." She made a little gesture towards her mouth. "I declare, when I finished the last page, I felt as though I might have to jump in the bath to wash away all the filth."

"It sounds just delightful," quipped Sam. "Maybe Pear's Soap will decide to publish it, Lulu. To further their sales, you know."

"Then I shall have truly arrived," chuckled Stevenson. "What a consummation, to have penned the first shilling shocker destined to improve its readers' hygiene." He looked at Fanny, who laughed more guardedly than he might have expected.

"It *is* a shilling shocker," she remarked.

"I know it is," replied Stevenson. "A perfect book-end for 'The Body Snatcher.' Or worse. But I expect it will help us buy our Christmas goose."

For a moment, Fanny sat there silently. "You know, Louis," she said at last, "it could be a masterpiece."

"You are too kind." Stevenson reached up to adjust the watercolor over the mantle. "Unless by 'could be' you mean that it's not." He turned and looked at her uncertainly. "Quite. Yet."

Fanny slid forward in her chair and restraightened the papers in her lap. "You said you thought it might be the best thing you'd ever written."

Stevenson wagged his head equivocally.

"Well, I really think it could be."

"But?"

Fanny glanced at her men. Both were staring at her expectantly.

"Out with it!" exclaimed Stevenson. "You're not helping me with insinuations."

She sighed and drew her shoulders back. "You've made a story of it. And a fine story, Louis. It's extremely exciting."

Stevenson nodded.

"But it should be an allegory, don't you see? And I'm afraid…"

"What? You're afraid of what?"

"I'm afraid you've totally missed the point."

Stevenson took his elbow off the mantle, crossing his arms and standing squarely on both feet. He inhaled deeply and evenly. "An allegory. Explain what you mean."

"Your man is bad all through," Fanny declared. She spoke softly, as though she knew she was venturing onto perilous ground. "The transformation is only to escape detection and blame."

"Yes?" With his neck raked forward, Stevenson looked vaguely like a brooding crane.

"So it really *is* only *Brodie* with a twist. In prose."

"It isn't at all like *Brodie,"* Stevenson shot back. "Brodie was a petty thief, not a…"

"Voluptuary?"

Stevenson paused briefly and then nodded. "And, what is more, Brodie was always in complete control of himself. This man…" There was a spell of total silence. When Stevenson spoke again, his voice was as soft as his wife's, but there was clearly something mounting underneath. "What, then, do you propose that I do?"

For a moment Fanny was still. "It's the tale of a criminal, Louis. A clever criminal. But it could become the tale of anyone. Everyone. An allegory of all humanity, don't you see?" She waited for a response, but nothing came from him. Sam sat perfectly still on the floor, looking back and forth between the two of them. "You could make him a good man, Louis. You should. A normal man, struggling with his appetites. Urges of the flesh. You remember we talked about all that with James."

She looked up at Stevenson, who was breathing ever more deeply, his arms folded tightly across his chest.

"You wanted to write something about Walter Ferrier? Or someone like him? Something good and strong that might make a difference? That's what this ought to be, love. Really. That would be your masterpiece. Instead of, like Sammy said, another *Deacon Brodie.*"

"Another *Brodie,*" Stevenson repeated flatly after a long and awkward silence. "Another...*fucking*...*Brodie.*"

Fanny turned towards Sam. His eyes were wide in surprise. When she looked back at her husband, it was as though he were holding his breath before a plunge into deep water. At length, his lips began moving, shaping what seemed to be words, although he didn't utter a sound. Slowly he turned to the mantle and, with an eerie languor, reached for one of the crystal glasses that rested there. He hefted it briefly, looking around the room, and then jerked the tumbler up to his chest with both hands. Fanny watched, transfixed, as his forearms began to tremble.

"Louis!" she exclaimed. "What on earth are you doing?"

There was a sharp snap and her husband's hands flew apart, the remains of the tumbler falling to the hearth. He looked down as blood oozed then rushed from his left palm.

"Oh my God," cried Sam, leaping to his feet. He ran into the dining room and fetched a napkin, which he brought back and pressed into his stepfather's open hand.

"No, there's glass," said Stevenson. With his other hand, he pulled a long sliver from his flesh and turned to place it on the mantle. Looking vacantly at the boy, he wrapped the napkin tightly around the ugly wound and walked across the room to where his wife sat frozen in dismay. He held out his uninjured hand, palm up. She stared at him, uncomprehending. He extended his hand again, and she realized what he wanted. She doubled the manuscript over on itself and handed it to him, looking down as he walked quietly out of the room. A single drop of his blood trembled like mercury on the pale blue bombazine of her skirt and then, as she watched, it sank dully into the fabric.

The afternoon was almost gone when Valentine stepped into the drawing room.

Fanny and Sam had taken luncheon alone and then retreated to the fire, where they sat for hours, neither of them speaking of what they had earlier witnessed in the room. Fanny knitted, jumping up every now and again to straighten something on the wall or move a piece of furniture ever so slightly. Sam worked his way through the old numbers of *Punch* that Stevenson kept stacked in the bottom of the Dutch cupboard. Occasionally he chuckled quietly to himself, and when Fanny asked him what he found amusing, he explained or came over to her chair to show her a clever drawing. One of them, curiously a propos both of Sam's Pear's Soap remark and Stevenson's unbroken three-day sequestration, was entitled "A Good Advertisement." It showed an ill-groomed, unshaved, and obviously odiferous man stooped over his desk. "I used your soap two years ago," read the motto; "since then I have used no other." The only real cheer in the room, though, came from the fireplace and the ironwork cage in which the two family canaries trilled in ignorant bliss.

"Monsieur Stevenson would like to see you," Valentine announced.

"Me?" asked Fanny, looking up from her knitting.

The maid nodded.

"Thank you." Fanny set her wool and needles aside and gazed over at Sam. The boy shrugged and went back to his reading.

Fanny rose and made her way to the stairs. She stole with real trepidation to the bedroom door, peering in to see Stevenson sitting once again in the bed, his head thrown back on the bank of pillows. He had unbuttoned his shirt, and his long neck and concave chest looked grotesquely wasted and pale. He heard her approach and turned to her with a look of strained resignation.

"There," he said, pointing a long finger towards the fire. "There it lies."

"My God, Louis," shouted Fanny as she rushed over to the grate. Trembling on the glowing coals sat layer upon layer of feathery ash. Only at the very center did any paper remain, a round the size of a communion wafer bearing a tracery of familiar script. Fanny turned to her husband, her mouth agape. No words came.

"You were right," he said softly, his voice hoarse and broken.

"My God, Louis. Is that the whole thing?"

He nodded silently.

"Why? What on earth were you thinking? Why?"

"I would have been tempted."

"Tempted how? To use it after all?"

"This was the only way. To start over."

There was a rustle at the door, and the two looked over to see Sam standing there, leaning against the doorjamb with an expression of grave concern. "I heard you call out, Mother. Is everything all right?"

Fanny choked back a curious urge to laugh. "Everything is fine, dear. Lulu is just saying he's sorry for frightening us."

Sam looked at his stepfather, who stared straight ahead.

"Everything is under control here," said Fanny. "We're fine. Why don't you run along downstairs?"

Sam looked doubtful, but he took his hands off the doorjamb and made to leave. "If you need me, let me know."

Once her son had left, Fanny walked over to the bed and began to sit. Stevenson moved slightly to the side to make way for her.

"Oh, Louis. I'm so sorry. Look what you've done to yourself."

"I was so angry."

Fanny reached out to touch his arm.

"I think I was about to hurl that glass, Pig. God help me, but I was." He paused for a moment. "But I knew that you were absolutely right. It was nothing more than the deacon again, back from the dead. And, naturally, that enraged me even more!"

Fanny sighed and nodded.

"I suppose I took my anger out upon myself." He held up his bandaged hand. "And on that!" Again he pointed at the fire.

"Oh, Louis!"

Stevenson turned to her with a guarded smile. He held up an open notebook that had been resting on the counterpane to his left. "Look."

Fanny could see two short passages on the recto sheet, separated by a tracery of doodles.

"What is it?"

"I have started over."

"Oh my!"

"May I?"

"Of course," replied Fanny, feeling something between giddy relief and genuine excitement.

"The solicitor was a man of a rugged countenance, never lighted by a smile," he read. *"Cold, scanty and embarrassed in discourse; backward in sentiment; lean, long, dusty, dreary and yet somehow lovable.* I'm afraid I don't have his name yet, but the fellow will be our eyes and ears. What do you think?"

"Well, it's hard to tell." She giggled nervously. "There's not much of it, is there?"

"There will be more. It will be better."

"Louis!"

"It will. I shall end up thanking you."

She looked at him uncertainly.

"Of course I have not quite reached that point. Not just yet. But I will, I expect." Incredibly, there was a grin on his haggard face.

She reached out and touched his cheek with the backs of her fingers.

"So," he said, holding up the notebook. *"Lean, long, dusty, dreary."* He stared at her with those vulnerable eyes, the cornered hare's. "Am I, too, in any way lovable? Still?"

Fanny shook her head and laughed outright. "You are not lovable. You are impossible."

"Impossibly lovable?"

"Let's just stick with impossible," she said through a widening smile.

"Fanny."

"Yes?"

"This is important."

"What is it, Louis?"

"About this." He shook the notebook. "I have a notion how to develop the allegory, as you so bravely envisioned it. And you were right about Ferrier, as well. I feel poor Walter can breathe real life into this. Not that it should be about him in any literal way, you know…but as the tale of a good man plagued by a damnable addiction." In the incalculably dark moments that had come on the heels of the manuscript's going into the fire, Stevenson's departed friend had indeed found his way back into the writer's creative mind. Watching grimly from the bed as the flames subsided, Stevenson had recalled with arresting vividness that confessional moment when Ferrier had resorted to another set of pronouns to describe his addictive self—his depraved "other" self, if his testimony were to be trusted. Stevenson could almost instantaneously imagine a scene in which, in the renewed fiction's own confessional interlude, his protagonist would similarly distance himself from a concealed and now condemned side of his nature, seeking in that way to escape all responsibility for his deeds: *It was he*, the man might insist. *He, I say. I cannot say I!*

Stevenson gazed intently at his wife. "Walter is my dumb grenadier. I must speak for him. You do remember that poem?"

"Of course I remember it."

"Let me read you the other bit. From what I imagine will be a kind of denouement from the man himself: *I was born to a large fortune, endowed besides with a lively mind, by nature inclined to industry, fond of the respect of the wise and good among my fellow men, and thus with every guarantee of an honourable and distinguished future. And indeed the worst of my faults was a certain impatient gaiety of disposition, such as makes the happiness of many, but such as I found it hard to reconcile with my imperious desire to carry my head high, and wear a more than commonly grave countenance before the public. Hence it came about that I concealed my pleasures.*"

Fanny shook her head and tittered.

"What? What is it?"

"That's not Ferrier. Or not just Ferrier."

"What do you mean?"

"I'm just remembering our little exchange after your patricidal dream. The one you had in Hyères. About respectability driving you to hypocrisy."

Stevenson smiled through a moderate blush. "One writes what one knows. But, Fanny…"

His wife nodded.

"If there is anything else I need to know, please…" There was perhaps the hint of a tear in his eye.

"Tell you now?"

"Tell me now."

She wiped at his cheek. "Well…goodness. This suddenly feels awfully momentous. It makes me so nervous."

"My God," sighed Stevenson over-loudly. "You have broadsides in reserve? I thought perhaps another swipe or two from your cutlass, but there are broadsides?"

Fanny shook her head and laughed softly. "No, Louis. Just two things, I suppose."

The writer pulled his head back and squinted at her.

She plunged ahead. "There was too much sex."

Stevenson's eyes opened wide, then he slowly nodded. "I thought you might say that. You can't shake yourself loose of Mrs. Grundy, can you?"

Fanny shook her head. "Why should I? Louis, you simply cannot write about a gentleman using prostitutes."

"But gentlemen do."

"Of course they do. But this story will never see the light of day as is. As *was*," she corrected herself, with a wistful glance at the fire. "And you must get rid of that bit about your 'disgraceful pleasures.' Jekyll's 'disgraceful pleasures.' What were they, 'indulged from an early age?'"

"Why?" asked Stevenson. "That seems innocuous enough to me. Ambiguous enough."

"Oh, please," objected Fanny.

"All right. What did you make of them, then?"

"What else? Self-abuse."

Stevenson chuckled. "Self-abuse?"

"Of course. What else could it be?"

"I don't know. Anything. A childish taste for sweets. Dressing like a woman?"

Fanny slapped him on the arm. "I mean it."

Stevenson studied her closely then sighed. "Done, love. No masturbating from an early age. And?"

"And?"

"You said there were two things."

"Yes. And the powders."

"What about the powders?"

She looked at him uncertainly. "They are too fanciful. Don't you think? Really!"

"They were part of the dream," Stevenson replied, with more than a touch of impatience. "Right at the core of it. They are where the whole idea came from."

"Couldn't you make them something else, though? Something closer to what a man might really use to endow a night self."

"Such as what?"

"I don't know," answered Fanny. "Opium. Strong spirits."

"This needn't be Ferrier's actual life, you know, Pig. In fact, it shouldn't be. He has a family."

"Still."

Stevenson sighed. "Then what about the physical change?"

"I don't know, Louis. There could be a disguise."

"It's not a story about what a man wears," responded Stevenson with some animation. "Or about make-up. It's about what a man *is*. And you'll recall," he added, "I tried a disguise in 'The Travelling Companion.' It was tripe!"

"You could do it here, too," Fanny persisted. "Honestly. This is just so very much better than 'The Travelling Companion.' Besides, you never had any takers for that."

"Thank you for reminding me."

"I feel quite strongly about this," Fanny went on. "Perhaps you should talk with James."

Stevenson laughed. "I know what James would say. Precisely what he would say." He looked up at the ceiling and grinned. "My man should begin by taking insufficient sugar in his tea—and then move on to taking far too much lemon—which would leave him, to begin with, a sour companion—and ultimately a murderous blight on the gentlemen's club."

"I can see I'll be making no more headway here."

"Don't you think you've already made enough headway?"

She studied him closely, very much aware of the fire that still burned off to the side. "I'm sorry, Louis."

"Let us just see where we end up. The brownies and we. I have made mistakes in the past by not trusting them sufficiently."

"And by trusting me too much?"

"Never," replied the writer. "You are my unfailing bulwark against artistic disaster. Not to mention self-abuse."

His eyes dropped reflexively to Fanny's side of the mattress. It was distressing to stretch truths with his wife, even in the smallest ways. Already, though, the two extant seeds of the tale were germinating at pace in his fecund imagination. Perhaps he could be forgiven if he were to ask Fanny to step away, just for a bit, so he could get on with it.

12

"Well," said Enfield, "That story's at an end at least. We shall never see more of Mr. Hyde."
"I hope not," said Utterson.

—*STRANGE CASE OF DR. JEKYLL AND MR. HYDE*

BOURNEMOUTH, JANUARY 1886

"You're certain that you won't come out with me?" Stevenson shouted from the entrance hall as he donned and buttoned his overcoat. "It's a bonnie day. For January."

"I don't think so. I still don't feel very lively."

"Would you prefer that I stayed here with you?"

"Not at all. Honestly, you go out. I'll be fine."

Stevenson walked to the door of the drawing room and looked in at his wife. She lay on the chaise longue, half-covered by a thick woolen lap robe. She was reading through what now seemed as though they might be the final chapters of *Kidnapped,* the title Stevenson had settled on despite James's marked distaste for it. Fanny had been suffering for two days from a marked female indisposition, troublesome enough to be sure, but in fact a considerable relief after several long weeks of worry that the Stevenson ménage might inadvertently be growing by one member. Stevenson had had more than one nightmare about changing diapers, something he suspected Fanny might well require him to do.

"Can I bring anything back for you? Chocolates? Champagne? A wee dog?"

"Ooh, a puppy would be lovely."

"What color?"

"You choose."

"I shall see what I can do."

The day's post had brought a letter from Andrew Lang mentioning that his review of the newly published *Strange Case of Dr. Jekyll and Mr. Hyde* would be appearing in the *Saturday Review*. Stevenson expected it would be positive, although not revealingly so: the Scots man of letters was a close friend. At the same time, Lang's would be the first appraisal to appear, and Stevenson was eager to see it.

It was in truth an exceedingly pleasant day, for the dead of winter, and Stevenson grew warm as he sauntered along. By the time he reached the town center, he had loosened his cravat and doffed his broad-brimmed hat, earning him a stare or two from the more staid among his passers-by. He knew he could find the *Review* at his regular newsagent's, but he resolved to check at a bookshop nearer to hand, west of the central square.

As he approached the broad, copiously-mullioned windows of the establishment, he smiled to remember long-ago days when he and Cummy would peer into similar windows at Wilson's in Leith Walk, scanning the covers of the penny-papers on display for any indications of their contents. Once a hopeless devotee of cheap periodicals, his deeply pious nursemaid had become increasingly concerned that they might harbor some kind of subtly sordid matter that could blotch the soul of her innocent charge, perhaps even blotch her own. She had consequently and abruptly called a halt to all suspect acquisitions. At the same time, readerly curiosity lived on in her undiminished, and time and again the two of them would stand, their noses to the glass, scouring the woodcuts and their legends for hints of the fates of various characters they had once so avidly followed. "The Baronet Unmasked." Who could have discovered his secret identity, and would the revelation foil all of his hopes for a happy marriage? "Dr. Vargas Removing the Senseless Body of Fair Lilias." "Senseless" did not necessarily mean "dead," but just what, then, had rendered her unconscious, and what were the doctor's intentions? Stevenson cringed to think what Cummy would make of his own latest literary production, and was still shaking his head as he walked through the door and set the little sprung entrance bell a-tinkling.

There was something about a well-stocked bookshop that pleased Stevenson to his bones. A well-provisioned wine merchant's had a similar effect; and in France or Italy, such a place might even hold a slight advantage in its promise of imminent delight. Still, as he entered, Stevenson rejoiced to inhale the delicate pungency of fine leather bindings and to spy a half-dozen refined readers poring happily over prospective purchases. He strode over to where periodicals were kept and, spying *The Saturday Review,* picked up a copy. *23 January 1886.* He thumbed through and found Lang's piece—unsigned, but recognizably in the Scotsman's style. *"Mr. Stevenson's 'Prince Otto' was, no doubt, somewhat disappointing to many of his readers. They will be hard to please if they are disappointed in his* 'Strange Case of Dr. Jekyll and Mr. Hyde.'"

Hmmm. Well. It went on at some length, and he resolved to save the rest for later. He carried the magazine over to the bookseller's desk, smiled a greeting, and asked if he might leave it there while he continued to look around the establishment.

"Of course, sir," said the bespectacled man. "It will be right here when you're ready."

Between the high shelves at the rear of the shop there was a table with canted bookstands, back to back, bearing new arrivals. Moving down one side, Stevenson bent to see the title of a rather large buckram tome. *Capital, Volume II.* He chuckled. Perhaps he should buy Engels' latest and send it up to his father. That would surely precipitate the old fellow's demise. He spied the new Howells, *The Rise of Silas Lapham.*

Stevenson had enjoyed *A Modern Instance.* Despite its sterile realism, he had found its honest treatment of divorce both bold and refreshing—although he had gone to some lengths to keep the exact contents a secret from Fanny.

Goodness, there was his justly maligned *Otto* and, right next to it, *A Child's Garden of Verses.* Lang's review would obviously do nothing to move the former out of the rack, and he doubted the prime audience for the latter would be tall enough to see over the edge of the table.

Now here was a new novel by that young lad who had written him to praise *Treasure Island,* Rider Haggard. *King Solomon's Mines.* He pulled this one out with his forefinger, picked it up, and opened to the first page. *"There are many things connected with our journey into Kukuanaland that I should have liked to dwell upon at length, which, as it is, have been scarcely alluded to. Amongst these are the curious legends which I collected about the chain armour that saved us from destruction in the great battle of Loo, and also about the 'Silent Ones' or Colossi at the mouth of the stalactite cave."* The great battle of Loo! No need to worry, it was clear, about sterile realism here. Perhaps they could read it aloud when Sam was at home. Stevenson tucked the volume under his arm.

The bell over the door tinkled again, and a tiny woman well along in years toddled into the shop and over to the bookseller's desk.

"Good morning," she piped, in high, fluting voice.

Stevenson looked at the clock behind the desk. It was just past two in the afternoon.

"Good morning, madam," replied the shopkeeper, removing his spectacles with an indulgent smile. "May I help you?"

"You may, thank you," said the woman. "I am hoping to find a book."

"Yes?" The man waited patiently, rubbing his hands together. "And… the title?"

"Goodness. I'm afraid I don't remember."

"Perhaps the author?"

She held a gloved hand to her mouth and tittered. "I can tell you what it is about!" A twinkle in her eye hinted at a vein of mischief that might have made her an intriguing companion in years past. That might still. "I am looking for that novel about the doctor here in Bournemouth, you know…who took something. And came to a bad end." She raised her eyebrows and nodded with obvious excitement.

"Ah, you must mean *Dr. Jekyll.* It's just in. I haven't even had the chance to put it out. Let me just fetch you a copy." He bustled past Stevenson towards a door at the back of the shop and, a moment later, emerged with a slender volume in paper covers. "Here it is. *The Strange Case of Dr. Jekyll and Mr. Hyde.*"

That's "Strange Case," Stevenson observed to himself. *No definite pronoun.* He had rather thought the title might appropriately sound like the call of a newsboy hawking papers on the street. So much for attentive readings.

"R. L. Stevenson," said the man as he handed her the volume.

"That's the one!" exclaimed the old lady, grasping it in both hands. "Stevenson. Our vicar at St. Peter's, Mr. Ram, you know. He gave a positively gripping sermon on Sunday. About the poor doctor and whatever it was he was taking. I have been positively dying to read it ever since."

"Well then," said the bookseller, "I am very glad we had a copy for you."

"I hope it won't be injurious to my health." The woman tittered once again. She turned the book to look at the back cover. "I am told it is extremely exciting."

"Well, you can always set it down if you must," suggested the man, smiling once more.

"Of course I can. Thank you for reminding me. I wish I had known that when I read *Udolpho* as a girl." Again the twinkle. "That one was nearly the death of me. I do so like a good chill now and again, though. Especially if it all works out in an edifying manner." She jabbed at the cover with her gloved forefinger. "It says one shilling. Is it really only one shilling?"

"It is, madam."

"Excellent." The woman reached into her purse and extracted a single coin, handing it to the man with a bob of her head.

"Read it in good health," he said, quickly wrapping the volume in brown paper and handing it to the woman.

"Thank you, I will. Good morning."

"And good morning to you, ma'am."

Once the old soul had left, Stevenson moved to the desk and laid Haggard's book on top of the *Review*. "Both of these, if you would."

"Very good, sir."

"A charming lady."

"She was, sir. Charming."

"She very much knew what she wanted."

"More or less, sir," the man grinned.

"Do you expect to sell many copies of, what is it, *The Strange Case?*"

"Oh, it's hard to say, sir. One never knows with these little paper-covered shockers. Our clientele are quite refined." He gave Stevenson a conspiratorial wink.

"How remarkable that it should already have found its way into a sermon, of all things."

"It is, sir. It is."

"I'm curious. Do you think the notice by the clerics is likely to help with its circulation? Here in Bournemouth?"

"Oh, yes, sir. Yes, indeed. For my money, if a crawler can pass muster with the pulpit, there will be no stopping it."

"There's nothing like titillation buffered by moral justification, I suppose. This Stevenson fellow must know what he's doing."

"Well, he does," exclaimed the man. "Don't you know him? He's the one who wrote *Treasure Island.*"

"Ah, yes," said Stevenson. "I believe I've heard of that one."

"Of course I'm not sure that his next-to-latest is very good," said the fellow, lowering his voice. *"Prince Otto.* We have it over there." He pointed to the table Stevenson had browsed. "I believe he writes mainly for boys."

"Really? Is *Jekyll and Hyde* for boys, then?"

"Oh, I don't know, sir." The man grasped his chin in contemplation. "You may have a point there. Perhaps not."

"Well, perhaps I shall pick it up later and see for myself."

"Of course, sir. We'll make sure to have copies on hand."

"Thank you very much. I would appreciate that."

When Stevenson arrived back at Skerryvore, Fanny was resting. Valentine said she had gone upstairs shortly after he had left and, aside from ringing down at one point for a glass of warm milk, she had been quiet all afternoon. He considered going up to see how she was doing, but when he learned about the milk, he assumed that she was napping. He decided to wait for a bit.

"May I bring you some tea?" asked Valentine, as she took his overcoat and hat.

"If you would, dearest. That would be very nice."

The woman laughed gaily, putting her wrist to her mouth just as Stevenson realized what he had said.

"Oh, good heavens," sputtered Stevenson. "I am so sorry, Valentine. I don't know what—"

"No, no," she replied. "I am not upset. It is just funny, is it not?"

"It is." He saw she was blushing. Was this the first time? "It is funny. But, again, please excuse me."

"There is no need." She regained her full composure even as he looked. "You will be in the drawing room?"

"I will. Thank you."

Stevenson walked through to his favorite armchair, hard by the fire. Unwrapping Haggard's novel, he tossed the paper into the flames, then laid the book on his reading table. He sat down, chuckling at himself, and turned to *The Saturday Review*.

He had long finished with his tea by the time Fanny came down. She walked through the door, stretched extravagantly, and walked over to kiss him full on the mouth.

"What was that for?"

"I feel so much better. I took a little nap. Life seems like it's worth living again."

"I am so glad. I was quite unprepared to be a widower."

"Well, that's good to know. Marrying younger men does come with certain risks," she offered with a wink.

Did British ladies have the capacity to wink? Stevenson wondered in a flash. Were they even born with the musculature?

"Well, did you find Lang's review?"

"I did." Stevenson pointed to the paper lying on the table. He had been reading Haggard when she walked in, having found himself immediately captured by the adventurous tale. It was something Sam would love, as indeed would Stevenson's own father. If the rest of it were half as gripping as the start, he would have to send a copy up to Edinburgh.

"What did he say? Tell me!"

"Would you like to read it?"

"You read it to me."

"All of it, or just the good bits?"

"There were bad bits?"

"Well, he did say that I should have thrown in a sprinkling of prostitutes."

"You great goose," snorted Fanny. "You need a good spanking."

"All in good time."

"I believe I shall make you wait until you beg me." She leered at him imperiously.

"Well, in the meantime," said Stevenson, reaching for the paper, "attend." He turned to the relevant page, making a show of flattening the sheet. *"Mr. Stevenson's* Prince Otto *was, no doubt, somewhat disappointing to many of his readers. They will be hard to please if they are disappointed in his* Strange Case of Dr. Jekyll and Mr. Hyde. How is that for starters?"

"I hardly like the first observation, but he's moving in the right direction. So go on."

"*To adopt a recent definition of some of Mr. Stevenson's tales, this little shilling work is like 'Poe with the addition of a moral sense.'*"

"Aha," cried Fanny.

"I thought you might cotton to that. *Mr. Stevenson's idea, his secret (but a very open secret) is that of the double personality in every man.*"

"Damn him. Now he's gone and given the whole story away before anyone's even bought it."

"True enough. But attend: *It is proof of Mr. Stevenson's skill that he has chosen the scene for his wild 'Tragedy of a Body and a Soul,' as it might have been called, in the most ordinary and respectable quarters of London. His heroes are all successful middle-aged professional men. No women appear in the tale (as in* Treasure Island*) and we incline to think that Mr. Stevenson always does himself most justice in novels without a heroine.*"

"But there *are* women in it. Did he even read it?"

"Shhh! *It may be regarded by some critics as a drawback to the tale that it inevitably disengages a powerful lesson in conduct. It is not a moral allegory, of course, but you cannot help reading a moral into it—*"

"Goodness. He cuts it rather fine there, don't you think?"

"He goes on: *You cannot help reading a moral into it, and recognizing that, just as every one of us, according to Mr. Stevenson, travels through life with a donkey (as he himself did in the Cévennes), so every Jekyll among us is haunted by his own Hyde. But it would be most unfair to insist on this, as there is nothing a novel-reader hates more than to be done good to unawares.*" He looked at Fanny pointedly. "*Nor has Mr. Stevenson, obviously, any didactic purpose.*" He looked at her again. "*His moral of the tale is its natural soul, and no more separable from it than, in ordinary life, Hyde is separable from Jekyll.* Blather, blether, blather. *In the end, in this excellent and horrific and captivating romance, Mr. Stevenson gives us of his very best and increases that debt of gratitude which we all owe him for so many and rare pleasures.*" Stevenson laid the paper down and stared noncommittally at his wife.

Fanny paused a moment, then broke into an unguarded grin. "That's a wonderful review, Louis. Anybody who reads that will certainly rush out to buy it!"

Stevenson shrugged. "I confess I'm not at all displeased with what he had to say."

"Of course, he *has* given it all away." Fanny picked in annoyance at some bits of lint on her skirt. "How can anyone now have the full, unfolding experience of it all? The way I did."

"I know. Dear old Lang."

"Then," she added with a little huff, "there was that silly bit about your having no didactic purpose but, at the same time, a clear moral emerging."

"He did seem a little muddled."

"I am sure most readers will easily take a moral away."

"Well, I know that at least one reader has." Stevenson shared with her his story of the little old woman at the bookshop.

"So they're talking about my husband's latest book in church!" marveled Fanny, after a hearty laugh. "My goodness, but we have arrived."

"So it would seem. And I clearly owe it all to you. If you hadn't made me consign the original to the flames…"

"Stop it!" Fanny glowered briefly, then she fiddled anew with her skirt and grinned. "I would love to have heard the parson's final summation for his flock."

"As would I. That, and know what hymns he chose that morning. 'How Firm a Foundation?' 'Amazing Grace?'"

Fanny shook her head in amusement. "But if you were a man of the cloth, Louis, how would you wrap up a sermon on the thing?" Her eyes sparkled mischievously.

"You should tell me, Pig. You are the one who asked for an allegory."

"Ha! Which Lang said it wasn't. Even though he claims it has a clear and universal moral. Honestly!" Fanny refolded her arms and kicked a foot impatiently.

"You know," Stevenson continued with a more serious aspect, "a fellow named Vernon did write to me the other day. A clergyman and author. Of religious books, from what he said. He asked me what the story meant. I told him honestly that the writer does the best he can, and then it is for the commentator to decide what it means to him. Or—perhaps if he is a particularly egregious commentator—to decide what it ought to mean for everyone."

"Including the writer?"

Stevenson laughed. "I don't know. If he is a particularly priestly sort, I suppose. When you think of it, hasn't the whole history of Christianity involved particularly learned and persuasive and drably garbed interpreters explaining what the Word of the Heavenly Author really means? As though He hadn't spoken clearly for Himself?"

"Heavens!" exclaimed Fanny. "It's a good thing your father isn't around to hear you say that."

Again Stevenson laughed. "It's a good thing he's not around to hear me say most of the things I say."

For a moment they were silent.

"You know, Louis—what Lang said about all of your heroes being middle-aged professional men? What do you think it means that not a single one of them seems to be married?"

"Do we know that?"

"About Jekyll and Utterson, we do. And there's no evidence any of the others are. There are maids and housekeepers, but no wives."

"Hmm," mused Stevenson. "Perhaps they are married to their work."

"Perhaps."

"Perhaps they were married…but they wore their wives out with their conjugal attentions."

"Not very likely. We women are made of stouter stuff than that."

"American women, it may be," observed Stevenson drily. "But British ladies?"

"You'd be surprised. Maybe their author hates women. Maybe that explains it."

"Curses! You've found me out."

"Will you send a copy to your father?" asked Fanny after a pause. "Will he want to read it?"

"I don't know. On either score."

"I wonder what he'll make of it all?"

"I wonder. At least you made me clean out all the whores."

"What about the dead old men? All the dead old men?"

"All of them?"

"Carew? Lanyon? Jekyll?"

"Father's an old man himself. He'll understand about old men dying. Whether or not he finds it diverting."

"It's interesting, though."

"What is?"

"You take out the whores, and it turns into a story about Hyde killing old men."

13

Jekyll had more than a father's interest; Hyde had more than a son's indifference. To cast in my lot with Jekyll, was to die to those appetites which I had long secretly indulged and had of late begun to pamper. To cast it in with Hyde, was to die to a thousand interests and aspirations, and to become, at a blow and forever, despised and friendless.

—DR. HENRY JEKYLL

LONDON, MARCH 1886

Stevenson strode into his parents' rooms at the Grosvenor with a definite bounce in his step.

"Hello, dear Màthair," he chirped as he whisked across the sitting room, hat in hand, to embrace his mother.

"My," replied the woman, offering him her cheek, "I can feel the chill coming off of you. It must still be very cold."

"It is. Very. And I have run up as fast as my spindly legs would carry me to bring some refreshment into this stuffy room." He peeled off his gloves, tossed them along with his hat onto the nearest chair, and stripped off his heavy overcoat.

"Would you like to hang that up? It looks wet."

"I'm afraid I can't stay long. I've promised to meet Colvin and Mrs. Sitwell at Claridge's."

"I thought we were dining together this evening."

"I am certain I told you that we weren't." Stevenson draped his coat over the back of the chair and took a seat near his mother. "Perhaps we ought to hire a secretary for you and father. To keep track of your engagements."

The look on Margaret Stevenson's face spoke volumes.

"I am sorry, Mother. I was simply trying to be cheerful."

"Perhaps you could find another way."

"I shall." He rubbed his hands together, blowing into them. "Is father napping?"

"He napped earlier. At the moment, I believe he is attending to some needs. Now, your afternoon. Was it successful?"

"I don't know about the afternoon itself, but I did receive some telling news." Stevenson had been to visit his publisher in Paternoster Row, and Charles Longman himself had taken a half-hour to speak with him. Stevenson let his statement hang pregnantly in the overheated room.

"Well," said his mother, after a considerable pause. "What was it? Why must you always tease me?"

Stevenson fingered his moustache puckishly. "I don't wish to bother you with details that would be of no interest."

"Now why on earth would I not be interested in what your publisher tells you?"

"It only concerns money, Mother. Filthy lucre. Far beneath the notice of the Angel in the House."

"If you weren't too old for a thrashing, Louis, I would take you over my knee."

"That was father's business, was it not?"

"Unfortunately. And I fear he failed to exercise the prerogative often enough. Behold the result!"

"I take your point, dear Mama," laughed Stevenson. "And to answer your curiosity, Longman informs me that, ever since the review in the *Times, Jekyll* has exceeded their wildest expectations."

"Oh, Louis," exclaimed his mother with a shiver of delight. "That is wonderful news." She rose from her chair and, shuffling across to him, took his head in her hands and kissed his forehead. The heavy scent of perfumed talc swept him back to another place and age.

"I wish it were a better tale," he said, resisting a boyish urge to brush the kiss away. "But I am happy enough with the results."

"What is all this commotion?" asked a raspy voice from behind the writer. Stevenson looked around to see his father standing in the bedroom door, cane in hand.

"Oh, Thomas," declared his mother. "Louis is just back from Longman's. The report is that the book is selling very well."

"The book? Which book?"

"Jekyll and Hyde," answered Stevenson.

"That one!" The old man let go of the doorjamb and took a stride into the room, stumbling slightly before he steadied himself with his cane.

"May I help you, Father?" Stevenson half-rose.

"I can manage perfectly," snapped Thomas. "It's just that I canna sit for half an hour now without getting up. It is enough to wear any man out. All this bloody *you*-rination."

"Thomas!" exclaimed his wife. "My word!"

For all of his teasing, Stevenson couldn't help but share his mother's shock that his father would broach this particular topic in a forum even this public. It was as though Baxter stood there in disguise, playing at being a doddering father.

"Forgive me, then. I'm not myself lately," sighed the older man, smiling gamely. "So what is this about Longman's?"

"Over three thousand volumes purchased so far," replied his son. "They are certainly going to reprint, and they expect to be into the tens of thousands by the end of the year."

"Well, that's good, I suppose."

"Of course it's good," exclaimed Margaret Stevenson. "In fact, it's wonderful."

"Thank you, Mother," said Stevenson, as he rose to help his father into his chair. The old man dropped down like a sack of potatoes, letting the cane tumble to the carpet.

"Thank you, Smout," he grunted. "And I am happy for you. Is there any news on that *David* thing?"

"Only that it will appear in *Young Folks* very soon."

"Have you added those thoughts on religion? The passages we discussed?" He eyed his son sternly.

"Not yet, Father. It was already in the magazine's hands."

"Surely they could change it."

"They say not."

"For the book edition, then."

"Perhaps."

Thomas Stevenson fixed him again with his best effort at an imperious gaze.

"It was excellent advice you offered me, Father," said Stevenson. "I would be foolish not to consider it."

"You would."

"Do you mind if I smoke?" asked Stevenson, reaching inside his coat for his cigarette case. The craving was sudden and strong.

"Must you?" asked his mother.

"Leave the boy alone!"

"Thank you," said Stevenson. He extracted a cigarette and lit it. "You know, Longman's has just heard from Richard Mansfield."

"Richard Mansfield the actor?" asked his mother.

"The very one."

"I am surprised you have heard of him, Maggie," observed her husband, archly. "You are hardly a theatergoer."

"Nor have I been living under a log, for heaven's sake. I am sure it was Mansfield we saw in *The Mikado.*"

"Did we?"

"I'm certain of it." She turned to her son with a little shake of the head. "What does he want with Longman's?"

"Want with me, in truth. He says he would like to commission a theatrical version of *Jekyll.* There's an American he works with, and they are very keen on doing it. So Longman claims."

"Would it bring any money?" asked his father. "To you, Smout. Not to Longman's."

"To both of us, I would think."

"Oh, Louis. How very exciting!" Margaret Stevenson looked with great satisfaction at her husband, who sat there nodding. "And Mansfield would play Jekyll? *And* Hyde?"

"I can't imagine he would want to play anyone else."

"No. You must tell Fanny. Cable her. How thrilled she will be."

"If it comes to pass," agreed Stevenson. "She will be."

"Fanny," pronounced his father, reaching up vacantly to pull at his ear. "Fanny."

"Yes, dear. Louis's wife."

"Of course. Yes. Fanny will be thrilled."

Nothing in Stevenson's communications with Edinburgh had suggested anything like his father's state of decline. It left him feeling that some significant action was called for. Colvin and Fanny Sitwell, over dinner, suggested Smedley's Hydropathic Establishment in Matlock, declaring it the very best healing spot in all of England—outside of Bath, which the senior Stevenson had written off after an ineffectual visit months back. The old man had initially opposed, tooth and nail, anything other than a direct return to Edinburgh, but he was finally convinced to spend a fortnight in Derbyshire, provided Stevenson himself went along and took the full treatment as well.

"It will either extinguish all the remaining Stevensons," announced his father, "or they shall come away new men."

Stevenson's mother observed that it offered the pair of them an ideal opportunity to spend precious time with each other, and she resolved to wend her way back north on her own. When the old man complained that he would then have no one to share his bed at the spa, Stevenson remarked it was surely not for nothing that his father had been such a longstanding and generous benefactor of Edinburgh's Magdalen mission: perhaps his wife could arrange for one of the erstwhile wayward ladies to come down from Auld Reekie. Perhaps even a pair of them, he added, if this were truly to be a time of paternal and filial sharing. It was an open question whether Margaret Stevenson was more annoyed by her son or embarrassed by her spouse.

The journey up from London was neither long nor particularly arduous in the first-class carriage of the Manchester, Buxton, Matlock, and Midlands Railway. Margaret had provided them with a basket of delicacies from Fortnum and Mason's, and they feasted like giddy youths on an assortment of cheeses, pâtés, biscuits, chocolates, and ginger beer. Engineer that he was, Thomas Stevenson was especially taken by what he deemed the miracles of the Willersley and High Tor tunnels between Cromford and Matlock, 800 and 600 yards long respectively. While Stevenson all but held his breath through each of the dark transits, ready at any moment to be crushed by incalculable tonnes of falling limestone, his father seized the chance to remind him that his life would be far better had he never cast aside his compass and rule for a barrister's wig, let alone for a scribbler's pen and notebook.

"You could have built these very tunnels," he declared. "And better."

Stevenson had managed to hold his tongue. If his father were indeed slipping into a second childhood, he himself was determined not to be dragged back along with him.

They arrived in Matlock in the thick of a rare spring blizzard, with huge clots of wet snow driving down off the peaks into the tight Derwent Valley. They stood for a full ten minutes outside the station awaiting their carriage to Smedley's, stamping their feet in the inch or two of slush that had accumulated on the pavement. Reluctant to drop their bags in the mess, Stevenson held them in his hands, half-relishing the way their weight strained the muscles on the top of his shoulders.

His father suggested in vain that he put them down, then nobly offered to relieve his son of the burden. Stevenson declined. He nonetheless found himself wishing he had a hand free to sweep the flakes away from the old man's blinking eyes as he stood there, enduringly resolute, smiling at his only child.

For days they took the cure, now wrapped from head to toe in wet flannel, now with their feet set soaking in mustard, now with their chests anointed in chili paste while their limbs were rubbed, then rubbed again, with vinegar. Stevenson's skin balked at being seasoned like a goose for the oven, and he developed a full-body itch the likes of which he had never remotely experienced. His father somehow found this amusing, and he excoriated his wife for importing the inherent weakness of the Balfour constitution into the hardy stock of the Stevenson clan.

For his part, Stevenson took to wearing white cotton gloves day and night so as to be deterred from raking his nails into the dreadful crawly tickle. For three nights running, he lay sleepless on his back, hour upon hour, fancying his whole body a giant, en-crimsoned male member, aching for climax. Surely his brownies had never contrived a more thoroughly dehumanizing notion than that. Fortunately, on the third day, after a strict regimen of oatmeal baths, he rose like Lazarus from his affliction to refocus his energies on his father's welfare.

On day twelve, at four in the afternoon, the two Stevensons sat at one of the wicker tables in Smedley's winter garden. The sun had shone brightly through the midday, and the rays passing through the glass of the sizeable conservatory had warmed the air surprisingly. Liberally spaced paraffin heaters maintained a comfortable temperature, at least for the moment, and broad fronds of potted palms arched over the two men's heads, lending to the air a welcome botanical fragrance and a touch of humidity.

"You do seem better, Father," observed Stevenson as he poured the older man another cup of tea. "Would you agree?" Frankly, it was difficult to imagine how mere anointings of the flesh could ever find their way to the real seat of Thomas Stevenson's failing, deep under the steel-gray hair.

His father shrugged. "Maybe. Maybe. I miss Maggie."

"Well, you shall be seeing her again very soon."

His father nodded. "When?"

"In two more days."

"In London?"

"No, Father. Back in Edinburgh."

"Good. Are you feeling better as well, Smout?"

"Like a new man, Father. As you said."

"As I said," nodded the other. "And you'll be going back to London?"

"Only after we go together to Edinburgh. I need to see you safely home."

"Thank you for that." He took his napkin and dabbed lightly under the tip of his nose. "I expect Fanny misses you."

"I expect she does. Would you like another?" He pushed a small tray of teacakes across the table. His father took one and laid it on his plate. His hand trembled noticeably.

"Now, if you must keep writing," proclaimed his father, stressing the *if,* "be mindful always of what I have told you about piety. More than once, as I recall."

Of a sudden, their penultimate day at the spa was bidding to become a Time for Final Words. Stevenson realized with surprise that he was not in the least prepared for it.

"Of course, Father."

"Everything we do in life, we must have final regard for the state of our souls." He looked at Stevenson, who met his gaze but said nothing. A son being launched into life or a son being left behind required, it seemed, exactly the same fatherly tuition.

"Everything you write must have a regard for the same." The old man reached out and turned the teacake slowly on the plate.

"Fanny and I have often spoken of that. She very much agrees."

"Good. And you do as well?"

"I agree with everything Fanny says," laughed Stevenson. "You know that."

"Fanny is a good woman," said his father. "Despite her provincial… her provincial origins." For a moment, his old eyes glinted with merriment. "So, you promised me, did you not, that your young David would take heed of the catechists and finish up as a prime example of a life well and piously lived?"

"I did, Father."

His father smiled and reached again for the cake. He took a small bite and set it back down. "I shall die a fat man."

"No time soon, I hope," said Stevenson, with another twinge.

"I believe I have had a good life," pronounced Thomas Stevenson.

"You have, Father. Long may it continue."

"Perhaps." For a moment the older man sat quietly. "Do you ever wish, Lou, you had done something more with your life?"

"What do you mean?"

"*Done* something. As opposed to writing something."

"Something such as?"

"Well," his father responded with a smile, "you know I'll say like building a lighthouse."

"Or a tunnel?"

"Or a lighthouse. Leaving behind a Skerryvore that you did more than give a name to. One that you conceived of and drew up and labored to bring into tangible being. So everyone could say, 'Look there. That is Lou Stevenson's light!'"

The son laughed. "The Stevensons have already scattered more than their fair share of Pharoses around Scotland, don't you think? There are some who say the coast has grown unsightly as a consequence."

"Perhaps." Again his father grinned. "Of course you could have *done* something with the law as well. Argued cases of great moment. Swayed judgments of note."

"Or spared my special friends a few of the depredations of the tax collector?"

His father chuckled and took another small bite of the teacake. "I confess I can make nothing of this Jekyll book of yours. However, it does seem to have made its mark."

Stevenson's thoughts flashed back to Fanny's wondering what his father might make of the trail of dead old gentlemen strewn in Hyde's wake. He evidently had no focused grievance with that. Perhaps he had not noticed.

"Indeed it has."

"The reviews have been commendatory?"

"Generally."

"And the sales good?"

"Remarkably."

"I suppose you do warn against the perils of self-indulgence."

Stevenson laughed and then told his father the story of the old lady in the Bournemouth bookshop.

"Will you be sending a copy to Cummy?" asked the older man, with a crinkly grin.

"I would be mad to. Wouldn't you agree?"

"I would. It could cost us both our lives."

"I don't believe her displeasure would carry her that far. Do you, father?"

"Ach, laddie. Yui've nae seen the wumman wrought!"

Stevenson returned to Bournemouth to find a slew of letters commenting on *Jekyll*. Most were gratifying, including one from James that remarked, yet again, on the "impertinence" with which Stevenson achieved his most dramatic effects "without the aid of the ladies." As to theme, James assured the writer that, *"there is a genuine feeling for the perpetual moral question, a fresh sense of the difficulty of being good and the brutishness of being bad, but what there is above all is a singular ability in holding the interest."* Thank goodness for that! Reading the missive, scripted in James's fine hand, Stevenson could all but hear, as though spoken aloud and with extreme slowness and clarity, his friend's perpetual equivocation on the business of morality.

There was a long—very long—letter from a fellow named Myers, founder of an organization called the Society for Psychical Research. Aside from a general effusion about the extent to which Stevenson's development of Hyde aligned with Myers's own evolving theories of "a subliminal self" within every man, he was full of very specific observations about how the novel, were it ever to be reissued, might be greatly improved—thereby *"ensuring its position among the masterpieces of literature."* On the matter of Hyde's handwriting, for example, the man observed that "recent psycho-physical discussions" had resolved that, in actual cases of double personality, handwriting cannot be the same in both personalities. Hyde's writing might look like Jekyll's done with the left hand, Myers informed him, or done when partly drunk, or ill. But it would never simply be differently slanted, as the novel had errantly alleged. Stevenson would have loved to loose James on the man in order to expatiate on the virtues of the interesting as opposed to the trivial. He resolved, though, to respond with a humble offering of thanks…but certainly not before he had exhausted every other conceivable option for wasting a quarter of an hour.

Harder to dismiss was a letter from Symonds, postmarked in Davos.

My dear Louis,

At last I have read Dr. Jekyll. *It makes me wonder whether a man has the right so to scrutinize "the abysmal deeps of personality." It is indeed a dreadful book, most dreadful because of a certain moral callousness, a want of sympathy, a shutting out of hope. As a piece of literary work, this seems to me the finest you have done—in all that regards style, invention, psychological analysis, exquisite fitting of parts, and admirable employment of motives to realize the abnormal. But it has left such a deeply painful impression on my heart that I do not know how I am ever to turn to it again.*

The fact is that, viewed as allegory, it touches one too closely. Most of us at some epoch of our lives have been upon the verge of developing a Mr. Hyde.

Physical and biological science on a hundred lines is reducing individual freedom to zero, and weakening the sense of responsibility. I doubt whether the artist should lend his genius to this grim argument. Your Dr. Jekyll seems to me capable of loosening the last threads of self-control in one who should read it while wavering between his better and worse self. It is like the Cave of Despair in the "Faery Queen."

I understand now thoroughly how much a sprite you are. Really there is something not quite human in your genius!

Goodbye. I seem quite to have lost you. But if I come to England I shall try to see you.

Love to your wife.

Ever yours,

J. A. Symonds

Here was tough meat to dig one's teeth into. How perceptive of Symonds to have seen, in an instant, the extent to which *Jekyll* bore on its author's unremitting skepticism over human liberty, not only to choose between good and evil but also, far more taxingly, to move beyond the crippling antinomy of virtue and vice itself—the conceptual "curse of mankind," as Jekyll himself named it. One might indeed argue that our Edenic forebears had brought sin and damnation into the world by their free and untrammeled choice. But, even without raising the boggling question of whether divine omniscience requires a divine foreknowledge that is tantamount to divine predetermination, how was it part of a just plan for Creation that, from the very beginning, humanity should be pressed to survive in bodies that were driven by myriad com-pelling needs—and *then* be told that many of those needs were, at base, completely reprehensible? Where was one to look for freedom of will and, thus, for any notion of individual responsibility—especially, as Symonds had suggested, in this age of Galton and Spencer and Darwin?

Out of this muddle of theological rumination there emerged, how-ever, a more troubling issue. It was one that Stevenson was not sure he had ever adequately confronted, unless it had been in general conversa-tion with his father about things other than writing. Symonds had said that the story threatened to loosen the last threads of self-control in a man who wavered between his better and worse selves. Setting aside the intriguing question of what Symonds's own "worse self" might be, what did this say about the final and consequential impact of the tale on others?

Whatever had driven Stevenson to write *Jekyll and Hyde*, it was never his intention to construct a story that impelled its readers to become worse rather than better men. He had long ago conceded that his original draft was driven far more by James's desire to "interest" than by Fanny's injunction to "improve." Yet even that first version, he firmly supposed, could hardly be read as anything other than a demonstration that evil comes to evildoers—and therefore as an incentive, more or less, to virtue. And now here was Symonds, as acute a reader as he could ever hope to have, saying that Hyde's inventor might as well be Satan whispering at the ear of Eve.

It all put him predictably in mind of Ferrier and what had at first seemed a curious reaction to his pirate story. Stevenson had come to accept that he might write to one end but accomplish another end alto-gether. In that realm of unintended consequences, though, it was one thing to consider the matter of interpretation; it was another entirely to consider instigation. He was far from certain that his alterations of the original tale honored Ferrier and his memory in any significant way, either as a sympathetic examination of the human lot or as a fancifully exaggerated version of the warning Walter might be pleased to see his life underscore. The thought that he might have parlayed a covert tribute to a friend into an actively seductive text chilled him to the bone.

He rose from his chair, walked to the side table, and poured himself a tumbler-full of whisky, reassured by the reserve that remained in the decanter.

"They are perfectly lovely, dear!" exclaimed Fanny, walking back from the mirror that hung between the drawing room windows. "What a sweet man you are!"

She bent to kiss him, then evidently decided she needed to sit in his lap. She slung herself awkwardly across his chair, wrapping her arms around his neck. "Of course, they don't go with this dress at all," she observed, fingering the string of pearls with delight, "but I'm sure I can find something that will set them off just perfectly."

"I hope that 'something' is already in your possession, dearest. The news from Longman's isn't such that we can afford an entirely new wardrobe."

"When have I ever been a spendthrift?" Fanny pouted with a pro-vocative bounce.

"Oww! Consider my frailty, love. I can't make our fortune with a crushed pelvis."

Fanny reached up and pinched his cheek. "You write with your pen, skinny one. Not your pelvis. Besides, the doctor says I have lost pounds and pounds."

"And yet you have just imperiled my midsection so recklessly. I can hardly be certain everything will still be in working order."

"You haven't tried it out lately?"

"Of course not."

Again, Fanny pulled her head back and scanned his face. "Good. I believe I shall take a bath. You'll join me soon…in my boudoir?"

"Wild horses, Pig."

She squealed with excitement and bounded out of his lap. "Look for me to be wearing my lovely new pearls." She looked back over her shoulder from the doorway. "For everything."

"Except the bath, I hope."

"Maybe even the bath."

Once Fanny had charged up the stairs and rung for Millie, Stevenson rose from his chair and walked slowly into his study. Moving to the front of his desk, he hesitated for a moment, turning his ear to the door, and then opened a drawer on the left side, removing a small package wrapped in blue paper and a white ribbon. He stared down at it, turning it slowly in his hands, then he tucked it into his pocket, turned, and left the room.

He paused in the drawing room and, hearing Fanny conversing with Millie as the bath was being drawn, he walked through the dining room and into the kitchen. Valentine sat next to the large worktable in the center of the room, reading a letter. The envelope lay torn open on the tabletop, and she was leaning forward on her forearms, several sheets of paper clasped between her hands. She looked up as he entered and sat up straight, reaching for her hair. Her cap lay discarded next to the envelope.

"Monsieur," she said with the hint of a blush. "I am sorry. I didn't expect to see you again tonight."

Something slid along the floor of the room above them, followed by a sharp footfall or two.

"Tonight's meal was excellent," said Stevenson. "I wanted to thank you especially."

"Thank you, monsieur." Valentine reached for her cap.

"No. Please don't worry."

She regarded him questioningly, and for a moment they were silent. He gestured towards the table.

"A letter from home?"

Valentine nodded.

"All is well there, I hope."

She tipped her head from side to side. *Comme ci, comme ça.*

"Is there anything I can do to help? That *we* can do?"

"No. Truly. It is just…life. Passing as it does." Valentine smiled, turning in her chair to face him. "You are kind to ask."

A thud from above and the sound of voices.

"I have had good news from my publishers," volunteered Stevenson. He stepped towards the table and laid his hand upon it, drumming softly with his fingers. "One of my recent books is selling especially well. And there are hopes of its becoming a play. For the theater."

"That *is* good news!" exclaimed Valentine, with a full and happy smile. Stevenson was unsure he had ever seen her look so unguardedly pleased.

"It is. And I should like to share my good fortune with you, Valentine. In a very small way."

"With me?" She looked genuinely puzzled.

Stevenson nodded, reaching into his pocket for the package. He extended it towards her, well aware that it would be an awkward moment if Millie were to walk in. Even more awkward if Fanny were to barge in, naked and dripping from her bath, with pearls flashing around her neck. He grinned at the thought, grateful to his brownies for lightening the moment.

Valentine smiled and took the package. She looked at it with interest, and then looked back at him.

"Go ahead! Please."

She took a deep breath and pulled at the ribbon, freeing it from the package. Folding back the blue wrapping, she exposed some white tissue and, parting that, uncovered an elegant silver comb, heavy and gleaming, its long teeth carved of the finest tortoise shell.

"Oh, monsieur." This time, it was a full blush. "I don't—"

"Thank you, Valentine. For all that you have done for us. For so many years."

"Oh, monsieur. How can I—?"

"It's nothing, really. *De rien.* You deserve more." This was all taxing enough, but he suddenly felt completely out of his depth. He was certain Millie was about to crash through the door, followed by the local constable and whoever that sermonizing vicar was from St. Peter's. At least Valentine had the good grace not to rise and kiss him. Where that would lead, he had no way of knowing.

"Well," said Valentine, facing the table once again, "I am grateful. You are too kind. You and Madame Stevenson both." She wrapped the comb carefully back in its paper and placed it ceremoniously into her apron pocket. "There. All safe!" Her eyes darted towards the ceiling, then fell back on him. She smiled in her enigmatic way. Was there a French Leonardo, Stevenson wondered?

"Valentine," he said, stepping back from the table and folding his arms. "You should find a man and start a family." It had burst out of him without his having any inkling that it was coming.

She laughed outright and shook her head. "Why do you say that, monsieur?"

"Because you are a fine woman." Stevenson sounded to himself exactly like a schoolmaster, giving a year-end prize to a promising young student. In the back of his head, he could detect his brownies agitating for a more honest response to her question. One that might have something to do with certain thoughts and temptations from which he was now, perhaps, hoping to shake himself free. "And you would make a fine mother. And a fine wife," he added as an afterthought.

"Best to be a wife before a mother." Her eyes twinkled at him. "It is not, is it, that you wish to be rid of me?"

"Heavens, no!" sputtered Stevenson. "Not at all."

"Or madame?"

Good God! thought Stevenson, briefly entertaining the possibility that she meant he might wish to be rid of Fanny.

"No. She values you as greatly as I do. It's simply that you deserve a full life."

She looked up from her hands, her eyebrows rising, one now more cocked than the other. "And what would a full life be like? For me?"

Stevenson found it within himself to chuckle. "I don't know,

Valentine. I am a storyteller. Not a sage."

"Thank you," said Valentine, after a moment or two. "But I am very happy here. With you and Madame Stevenson."

Perhaps an hour later, lying in her bed under the eaves, Valentine could hear the post-bath carryings-on in the Stevensons' room just below. In fact, she thought she could also hear Millie and Agnes tittering in their own chamber next door. At first, she had found it bothersome, listening to her employers taking advantage of their first night together after close to a month apart. Quite soon, though, she allowed herself to imagine what it would be like to lie there naked as one of them stood in her doorway, smiling in at her with those gypsy eyes. She found the thought so arousing that she nearly rushed herself but, with a moderate exertion of self-control, she arrested her pace until, hearing clearly enough the climactic groans from below, she brought herself to the fiery place just as she imagined her willful mistress exploding into flame.

14

This, then, is the last time, short of a miracle, that Henry Jekyll can think his own thoughts or see his own face (now how sadly altered!) in the glass.

—DR. HENRY JEKYLL

BOURNEMOUTH, AUGUST 1888

"So then, Stevenson," said James as he leaned back in his chair and threw an ankle onto his knee. "The theatrical rendition. At long last! Are you quite prepared for a simulacrum of your little study to sail out into the world with another hand altogether at the helm?" He tapped lightly and repeatedly on his stocking, eyeing his host with amusement.

"As long as it provides me with vastly augmented wealth, I do believe that I am."

James opened his mouth to respond, only to be overtaken by a violent sneeze.

"Goodness. Excuse me." He extracted his handkerchief and wiped delicately at his nose and upper lip. "You do realize that this is a liminal moment, do you not? Having one's work dramatized." He hesitated briefly, as though there might be another eruption on the way, but settled back without further issue. "I am somehow reminded, in fact, of that marvelous scene in your original tale when Lanyon is offered Faustian wisdom if he deigns to stay and watch your primitive go through a transformation of an altogether different sort."

Stevenson chuckled, stubbing out the cigarette on which he had been puffing. "'A new province of knowledge…New avenues to fame,' or some such."

"Exactly."

"Are you suggesting, Henry, that I may be on the threshold of cataclysm?"

James smiled drily. "I hesitate to prophesy."

"Well, I managed to survive the depredations of *Puck.*"

James looked confused. "Please?"

"Within a matter of weeks," Stevenson explained, "they came out with their parody. You didn't see it?"

"I don't take *Puck.* Yet I can imagine."

"I believe that I still have it. Would you enjoy a brief selection?"

"Please," replied James, rubbing his hands in anticipation.

Stevenson rose and walked over to the Dutch cupboard. He knelt to peruse a tall stack of papers stored therein and, after a moment, stood with a number in his hands.

"Here it is. February 6th. *'The Strange Case of Dr. T. and Mr. H.'* It is most perceptively subtitled *'Two Single Gentlemen Rolled into One.'"*

James grinned. "Nary a woman to be seen?"

"Nary a one." Stevenson returned to his chair and, flattening the magazine in his lap, addressed James with affected formality. "It begins, of course, with Mr. Stutterson, the lawyer, and several paragraph-long chapters that complicate the plot. Let me jump, however, straight to the revelatory confession, which contains the central conceit. Here. This is Dr. Trekyl."

"Treacle? As in tarts?"

Stevenson shook his head gravely. "As you of all people should know, there being no tarts in the original, there should be none in the parody. That's T-R-E-K-Y-L."

James chuckled, adjusting himself in his chair.

"This is the doctor, then: '*I was very fond of scientific experiments. And I found one day, that I, Trekyl, had a great deal of sugar in my composition. By using powdered acidulated drops I discovered that I could change myself into somebody else. So I divided myself into two, and thought of a number of things. I thought how pleasant it would be to have no conscience, and be a regular bad one, or, as the vulgar call it, bad 'un. I swallowed the acidulated drops, and in a moment I became a little old creature, with an acquired taste for trampling out children's brains, and hacking to death (with an umbrella) midnight Baronets who had lost their way.*'"

"How very quaint," observed James. "The lethal umbrella is a fine touch."

"Rather jaunty, I think. Or would it be abandoned?"

James chuckled once more.

Stevenson smoothed the paper and read on. "'*Well, that acidulated fool, Hidanseek—*'"

"Perfect!"

"'*Hidanseek got into serious trouble, and I wanted to cut him. But I couldn't; when I had divided myself into him one day, I found it impossible to get the right sort of sugar to bring me back again. For the right sort of sugar was adulterated, and adulterated sugar cannot be obtained in London!*'"

"Thanks be to the reformers. And your resolution? *Their* resolution?"

Stevenson laughed. "This: '*And now, after piecing all this together, if you can't see the whole thing at a glance, I am very sorry for you, and can help you no further. The fact is, I have got to the end of my "141 pages for a shilling." I might have made myself into four or five people instead of two—who are quite enough for the money.*'"

"How convenient," laughed James. "I have sometimes wished I could avail myself of such an expedient *fin d'oeuvre*. So tell me, Louis. How was it, bearing the public ridicule? If you can remember that far back."

Laying down the pages, Stevenson reached carelessly for another cigarette. "Quite to the contrary, I am inclined to think Burnand and his crew served me well. I cannot imagine they suppressed in the least the sales of my little shocker. They likely enhanced them."

James tipped his head to acknowledge the plausibility.

"Fanny, as you might expect, was furious." Stevenson struck a light and, bringing it to the tip of the cigarette, drew an appreciative breath. "If she had had access to a bomb, I believe she would at present be taking the cure in Newgate Prison instead of Bath.

"Your violent friend."

"Verily."

"You say Bath, Louis. Is Fanny not well?" James leaned forward with concern, waving an arabesque of smoke away from his face.

"Tolerably." Stevenson switched the cigarette to his other hand. "I believe there's a touch of hypochondria in my beloved helpmeet. I can well understand, though. After all these years caring for me, she might feel in need of some medical attention for herself. She's gone up for a week to take the waters—and to consult with a specialist in women's matters."

"I see." James leaned back once again, placing his hands on the arms of his chair.

"And Alice?"

The American shook his head.

"I am sorry, Henry. It's been a long siege. I know how difficult it must be."

"Thank you. Perhaps we shall talk of it another day."

"Of course."

The better part of a minute had passed before Stevenson jumped in to fill the silence. "You were asking, you know, about my loosing a *Jekyll* other than my own into the world? Steered by another hand?"

"I did," replied James, returning his attention to his host.

"It's curious, but I wonder if I haven't already done as much."

"And by that you mean…?"

"Just that one never knows how the things one writes will be received. I don't mean how they will be appraised, by a reviewer or a purchaser, but how they will be understood. How their impact will be registered."

James reached up to pinch his lower lip between thumb and forefinger. He tilted his head slightly. "You are surprised by that?"

"Not entirely."

"Nor should you be." He clasped his hands tidily on the modest rise of his vest, his fingers interlaced. "I have often given thought to writing a little something in which the understanding of the whole of the piece, even down to the level of deciding what has literally happened, should depend entirely upon a reader's point of view. A reader's assumptions. I simply have yet to find the appropriate vehicle. The trope." He threw his head back and gazed at the ceiling, drumming his fingers on his knuckles as he did. "Some event as witnessed and represented by a young woman with a particularly robust imagination, perhaps. And some irreversible consequences based upon her testimony. Some turn on the ambiguities of *Daisy Miller,* perhaps. But," he said brusquely, lowering his gaze and refocusing on Stevenson, "I take us from your precise point."

"Well—I had a letter from a friend shortly after *Jekyll* was published. And in it the fellow said something that took me rather by surprise. Something that bears on the question of our ultimate control over what we write. Over its final effect."

"And what was it that he said?"

"That *Jekyll* was a dreadful thing, to begin with—and not, I think, because he found it poorly written."

"Of course not."

"Rather that it seemed to him that the book might be capable of eroding a vulnerable reader's self-restraint. 'Loosening the last threads,' I recall his saying, in some poor soul whose better self might be unraveling, giving way to his worse."

"Hmmm. And thus," observed James, "essentially, the book might be capable of eroding the self-restraint of anyone at all. Aren't we all of us teetering on some brink, to a greater or lesser degree?"

"So it sometimes seems."

"And what this fellow said took you by surprise because…?"

"Well, because I would have thought that, if anything, Jekyll's fate would tend to make a reader more cautious about plunging head-long down the path of self-indulgence. Rather than more inclined to do so."

"Well," said James, reaching up to smooth the fringe of hair at the back of his head, "I suppose it doesn't end particularly well for Jekyll, does it?"

"Hardly."

"Then again, it is the shallow reader whose entire reaction to a narrative is determined by the fate of the protagonist."

"And Symonds is anything but a shallow reader."

"Symonds, did you say?"

Stevenson silently rebuked himself for revealing the name. "Yes."

"J. A. Symonds?"

"Yes."

"I know him—I finished his biography of Cellini not long ago. Excellent. Exceptional. And you are perfectly correct. The man can hardly be a shallow reader."

"No."

"But, Louis," James continued as he adjusted himself once again in his chair. "If you are to practice high art, you must pursue the complexities of the human condition—and permit your reader to respond to those complexities in whatever way he chooses."

"And you are certain a reader has that freedom of choice?"

"Of course."

"I wonder what you would say if, for example, your *Princess Casimassima* were determined by a perceptive reader of your own to incline him towards acts of political terrorism?"

"Dear Fanny's bombs and the like?"

"Perhaps."

James looked briefly at the ceiling. "I would think, I expect, that I had succeeded in creating a world in which he were exposed to the very same influences one is likely to encounter in this slightly more tangible world that surrounds us presently."

"Not that you had done something for which you ought to repent?"

"Not in the least. The man would have been free, to begin with, to read my book or not, as he chose. Unless, of course, he were a student at a very progressive school." James chuckled. "In any case, any subsequent actions that reader might take would then be the result of an entirely separate and unencumbered choice. Were he to be at all influenced in any way, it might as likely be by his having ingested a plate of bad fish as by reading anything that I had written."

Stevenson eyed his friend keenly. Whatever else one might say about James, he was a staunch believer in the radical independence of the human will. How might life have been different, he wondered, if it had been someone like this American, and not Cummy, who had presided over the Stevenson nursery? He took a deep breath and settled back in his chair. "As I expected. Dependable old James."

"I am delighted to be of service. So then," declared James, checking his watch. "Before I rush off, do tell me if I should see this play when it opens. Even if the responsible dramaturge is not your own masterful self."

The Strange Case of Dr. Jekyll and Mr. Hyde—The Lyceum—Wellington Street

"The attention of the audience was arrested by the dominant power of the actor. The murder of General Carew will be pronounced the most powerful and horrible thing ever seen on the modern stage."—The Daily Telegraph, *6 August 1888*

"Studies of the horrible are not usually attractive to the public, who, after all, go to the theatre mainly for the purpose of being pleasantly entertained and lifted out of themselves. The truth of this axiom playwrights have more than once found to their cost. Still The Strange Case of Dr. Jekyll and Mr. Hyde *appeals in a certain degree to the love of the occult which is deeply implanted in the human mind, and it may for that reason be able to hold its place in the Lyceum bill."*—The Times, *6 August 1888*

"The town will doubtless flock to see Mr. Mansfield's dual impersonation. Whenever Mr. Mansfield becomes Hyde, his savage chuckles, his devilish gloating over evil, his malignant sarcasms, his fierce energy of hate and revelling in all sinful impulses, awaken strange sensations in the spectator, and the unearthly restless figure of this variation upon Frankenstein's fatal handiwork takes a powerful hold on the imagination. Hyde, in brief, in Mr. Mansfield's hands, is a creation of genius." —The Daily News, *6 August 1888*

Stevenson, Fanny, and Sam had travelled to London to attend the gala opening. They were to have been special guests of the Lyceum's managing principal actor, Henry Irving, who had arranged for a lavish meal to follow the performance at the theater's own Gridiron Room, site of the most storied fêtes of the capital's artistic elite. Mansfield was, naturally, to be there, as was W. S. Gilbert, in whose light operatic productions the actor had dazzled the nation.

When they had arrived at the Grosvenor the night before the performance, however, Stevenson was handed a telegram from Edinburgh bearing the news that his father was failing rapidly. Margaret Stevenson begged her son to hasten north as quickly as he was able. The three of them had boarded the Flying Scotsman the following morning, arriving in Edinburgh just after six.

They'd found his mother in hysterics. She reported in tears that she had scarcely slept in days. Night after night, for over a week, her husband had awakened her time and again to confess to an ever-deepening depression. In the wee hours of the previous morning, the poor man had tugged on her shoulder and informed her, simply but flatly, that the end was near. His wife, begrudgingly admitting to herself that he was right, immediately arranged for the telegram. On the morning of the day their son arrived, Thomas Stevenson had insisted on rising and dressing, but he no longer knew either his wife or the doctor or any of the servants.

Stevenson had found his father sitting in the drawing room, bolt upright, his hands clasped tightly on the arms of his chair, as though a coastal gale were bidding to sweep him away. Directed to look upon his son, the old man had stared in utter blankness at his offspring's frozen features. As often as Stevenson had imagined his father close to death—sometimes, shamefully, with an odious eagerness, but more often in the knowledge that the man had treated him with more patience than he himself might have mustered had their positions been reversed—he had been completely unprepared for this moment. Every feature was unquestionably his father's, but the utter slackness of his gaze could have been the aspect of a spavined nag waiting for the drop of the renderer's hammer.

For a moment, the old fellow's brows had knit tightly above the still-noble bridge of his nose, his eyes first quizzical and then fearful, and then he had turned back to the wall that faced him. It was only a few hours then to the end.

Stevenson arranged for the funeral. It was to be a stately affair, with over one hundred family, friends, and associates borne to the service by a fleet of fifty carriages. Stevenson, Sam, and Cousin Bob greeted guests at Heriot Row, and then the elaborate procession set off across the city to the New Calton Burying Ground. The weather was beastly, unseasonably bitter with a driving rain, and for a week Stevenson had been suffering from a wretched cold. At one point he nearly fainted with the strain of the day, and Fanny, fearing he might soon follow his father to the grave, bundled him summarily back to the house before Thomas's coffin was even lowered into the ground. Bob presided, of necessity, at the interment, grimly aware how his late uncle would have balked at his last public moments being overseen by a young man who, he was certain, had led his son down all the worst paths.

Once it was over, Fanny did her best to reassure Stevenson that it had been a perfectly marvelous send-off, an elegant and fitting farewell from the best in the capital city to one of its most revered citizens. Stevenson, though, fought to stave off the conviction that he had, at the very end, and in an irreversibly significant way, dishonored the hand that had sustained him, for better or worse, all of his days.

Coggie Ferrier had come to the funeral, speaking warmly if briefly with both Stevenson and his mother at Heriot Row. Her own mother, however, had refused to attend—something that Margaret Stevenson found extremely hard to accept. Thomas's passing seemed to put new steel in his widow's backbone, such that it was only with difficulty that Fanny had dissuaded her mother-in-law from calling at 28 Charlotte Square to confront the woman—not only for the slight to Thomas and the family, but most especially to her son. Stevenson, however, resolved to meet with Coggie as soon as it could be arranged, readily accepting that it might have to be under a roof other than her mother's.

In the event, he met her at the George Hotel on a rare sunny afternoon. He arrived before she did, and requested a table by a window. Sitting back to enjoy a cigarette, he scanned the stately room with its huge, round skylight and gilded Corinthian columns. Over half of the tables were occupied by members of Edinburgh's respectable set, even though the time for luncheon had come and gone and it was still early for afternoon tea. He grinned to contemplate what Baxter, Ferrier, Bob, and he would have made of the chance to gather here on a quiet afternoon, scrutinizing this table of prim matrons chatting here, that pair of elderly gentlemen smoking quietly over their papers there. He could almost hear their unruly undergraduate prattle growing louder and louder, drifting towards ever more unsavory topics. He could imagine noisy requests for rough beverages the George had never served—and exclamations of disgust when their requests went unsatisfied. Depending on the day, there might have been a chunk or two of a scone or teacake flung well beyond the bounds of their table, almost certainly a soft chorus of belches, and, especially if Ferrier and Baxter were already into their cups, the physical accosting of a waitress or two and an ostentatious breaking of wind. Now here he sat, conventionally attired and almost conventionally coiffed, owner of a substantial villa on the south English coast and very likely to inherit his father's valet as a butler, of all unimaginable things. That he still recognized himself in the mirror each morning was perhaps a function of superficial physiognomy over anything else.

Coggie arrived a quarter of an hour late, sweeping into the room with profound apologies for the delay. She held Stevenson for a moment longer than he might have expected, her head against his chin, then settled herself elegantly in her chair. How, he wondered, did ladies manage this fashion of the bustle, seemingly more pronounced with every year? As with everything else she did, Coggie moved, sat, and conversed with infatuating grace and ease.

As they waited for their refreshments to arrive, Coggie told Stevenson how moving his father's funeral had been, how splendidly arranged, how deeply honoring to his father and the family. She apologized, finally, for her mother, deftly expressing a loving understanding of her parent while also making it very clear that she found the old woman's accusations utterly unfounded and her recent discourtesy all but unforgiveable. Stevenson, harboring a secret wish that she, rather than Henley, could be his partner in all collaborations rhetorical, thanked her for her great thoughtfulness.

"Well, Louis," said Coggie, after the tea and sweets had arrived. "Your *Jekyll and Hyde* seems to have made quite an impression."

"It has," replied Stevenson, unaccountably sensing the onset of a blush. "It's quite beyond me, why the public has taken to it so. But so they seem to have done."

"There is a play of it now, no? At the Lyceum?"

"There is. Fanny and I were to have attended the opening performance, but we were called north for…" His voice suddenly deserted him and he waved his hand as though to say, *"all this."*

Coggie smiled understandingly. How exceedingly fortunate the man who might awake each morning to find himself the object of that gentle regard!

"I don't suppose you saw the review in the *Times?*" Stevenson asked. "Of the production?"

"No, I didn't. Was it a good one?"

"Not especially," snorted Stevenson. "The best the fellow could say was that it *might* hold its place on the bill."

"Did you have a large part in putting it together, then?"

"Not at all. It was all Mansfield. And a fellow from America named Sullivan."

"So as a consequence," Coggie offered brightly, "if it doesn't 'hold its place,' that will say absolutely nothing about your own work. Which is a wonder!"

"Well, there are some financial ramifications." Stevenson grimaced. "And Jekyll and Hyde are still my children."

"Your Abel and Cain."

Stevenson chuckled. "Abel and Cain, yes. Let us just hope, in passing, that Mansfield's efforts prove to be less damaging to me and mine than Cain's were to his brother."

"Well, if I were the Almighty," offered Coggie gaily, "I should most certainly favor your offering."

"You read my shilling shocker, then."

"Of course I did. As I do everything you write. As I always will."

What to say? *Thank you? What a saintly girl you are? Why didn't I listen to your brother all those years ago?*

"And what did you think of it?" he settled on saying.

Coggie laughed. "It is certainly a gripping tale. I believe I may have lost some sleep over it. Waiting out the midnight hours. Thinking that at any moment a swarthy Mr. Hyde might steal into *my* bedchamber." She shivered histrionically.

"I trust none did," responded Stevenson, surprised by a stab of arousal that she could not have meant to provoke.

"No, thank goodness. Our locks are excellent, mother's and mine."

The moment's titillation was swept away on a wave of pity. Why hadn't this flawless woman found a deserving and loyal husband and gone on to mother a score of red-blooded Scots babies?

"I must say, Louis," Coggie continued, eyeing him closely. "Your Jekyll sometimes reminded me of my own poor brother."

Stevenson winced inwardly. "Oh, Coggie," he exclaimed. "I am so sorry!"

"Why?"

"Well, I don't know," he sputtered. What had he said to Fanny? *This needn't be Ferrier's actual life? In fact it shouldn't be?* "I suppose because I don't think of Jekyll as being a very good man."

"No," said Coggie, thoughtfully. "But he too wrestles with that you might call a 'lunatic brother.'"

"A lunatic brother," echoed Stevenson, groping for an association.

"In the letter you had Charlie Baxter forward to me—that kind letter after Walter died? That is what you called the side of him that he found in the bottle. 'His lunatic brother.'" Coggie smiled at him, with a look suddenly well past pity—serenely wise and enduring.

"I recall," said Stevenson.

"Perhaps," she suggested with a grin, "it was all of the wine you poured into the book."

"I don't know that I am capable of writing about anything without writing about wine." Stevenson blushed again. "At least without thinking about it."

"I suppose one writes about what one knows and loves the best."

"That, or what one knows and fears the most. Not that I wish to take our conversation down too dark a path."

"Of course." She reached for the last piece of her *petit four*. "You described Jekyll's transforming draught as a 'blood-red liquor,' did you not?"

"Compounded with a chemical concoction that Fanny very much wanted me to do away with. But yes. You have a remarkable memory."

She gazed at him for a moment without speaking. "Given what happened to Walter, it would have been difficult not to notice a phrase such as that."

"Again, I am so very sorry, Coggie."

"Not at all. It makes your allegory all the more potent. Universal. We hear constantly these days about the bane of alcohol. Even if we have never seen it devour someone dear to us."

"Perhaps," admitted Stevenson. "But please remember, dear Coggie;

I know Walter to have had a truly good heart. A good soul. Jekyll was at best a hypocrite. At worst…well, you know."

Coggie removed her hand from the teacup and laid it over the back of her other on the white cloth. "Walter was no saint," she said softly.

"I know he wasn't. But neither was he a murderer."

Coggie looked down as though she might be gathering herself for a leap of some sort. "There were things that I don't care to talk about," she continued in a hushed voice. "Not even with you." Her eyes were strained, but they were filled with intimacy and affection. "No matter now," she said bravely. "And I do know that, in the end, while my brother persisted in drinking until the day he died, he truly repented for where his compulsions had taken him. And for the things he had done in pursuing his pleasures. So, if there is a God and if He forgives those who truly repent, I do believe we shall see Walter again. Provided we prove *ourselves* worthy."

Stevenson felt himself as wanting for words as he had been the last time he had seen Coggie's brother. When a hoarse "Amen" tumbled from his lips, he laughed at the power of the hopefulness that tumbled out with it.

Coggie gazed at him with a fixity he was not sure he had ever seen from her. "Think of this, Louis. How happy Walter—your 'good, true Ferrier'—how happy he would be if he knew he had perhaps inspired so well-regarded a tale as the one you have written. And one, moreover, that warns so clearly against the kinds of indulgence that brought him low. Your tale of a weak man makes us all stronger."

She seemed to Stevenson to be completely convinced of what she was saying—and was so very appealing to him in this as well. In the glow of her optimism, and for the rest of a delightful afternoon together, he was able to shut Symonds's letter completely out of his mind.

Part Three

MR. H.

15

I do not suppose that, when a drunkard reasons with himself upon his vice, he is once out of five hundred times affected by the dangers that he runs through his brutish, physical insensibility; neither had I, long as I had considered my position, made enough allowance for the complete moral insensibility and insensate readiness to evil, which were the leading characters of Edward Hyde.

—DR. HENRY JEKYLL

EDINBURGH, AUGUST 1888

Stevenson, Fanny, and Sam headed south after ten days, having confirmed virtually all of the plans for settling Thomas Stevenson's estate. Stevenson's mother would remain in Auld Reekie until the most pressing items had been attended to, and then decamp herself for Bournemouth, where the family could decide exactly what lay in store for them.

Stevenson had received a flattering letter from the editor of New York's *Scribner's Magazine,* offering him a contract for twelve articles to be written over the course of a year at an astounding £60 per article. The magazine was especially interested in travel pieces, which made a return to the United States all the more sensible and appealing. This time, however, Stevenson would be traveling not as an impecunious and unknown foreigner, desperate to claim Fanny from her adulterous husband, but instead as the luminary author of the wildly popular *Jekyll and Hyde*—meaning that all of the household's transportation and accommodation would now be first-class. Fanny, especially, savored the prospect of a triumphal progress across her native continent in the kind of flush circumstances she could only have dreamed of in the past. Sam, too, was keen enough to "go home," and Margaret Stevenson continued to surprise her son with the gameness she brought to her new life as a widow. Stevenson found himself wondering, poignantly, if his mother had not suffered in some of the same ways he had, throughout her years under his father's stern and restrictive eye.

It was not without twinges of profound melancholy that Stevenson bid adieu to the home he had moved to at the age of seven. While Fanny waited with Sam in the library, their luggage already stashed in the family barouche, he undertook a pilgrimage through every room of the house. The most richly charged station of his wistful progress was, not surprisingly, his old nursery on the topmost floor. A few toys remained on the dusty shelves that lined the west wall, some of them the clear originals of this or that prop in the *Child's Garden* poems: a toy drum with a broken head, a pirate's hat and cutlass, a battery of tiny brass cannons. The lingering genius of the place, however, was the spirit of the resolute little Scotswoman who had spent countless long nights with him there, nursing him through fever or fright—Alison Cunningham, to whom he had dedicated his nostalgic collection of verse. *My second mother, my first wife, the angel of my infant life—from the sick child, now well and old, take, nurse, the little book you hold!*

He indulged himself in a lengthy minute at the window, looking across at the long row of houses up against the skyline of Queen Street. It was to this prospect that Cummy had carried him on those frequent nights when sleep refused to come. Pulling back the curtains, she had pointed to whatever windows still shone there high above the dark belt of gardens, wondering if there weren't other sick little boys up there as well, waiting with their nurses for the dawn. Cummy had meant to be there this very day to say farewell. Sadly, a relative had taken ill, such that she could only send a written message to "her boy"—a note that, very much to her customary form, balanced in equal measure deep affection and the sternest admonition about the future.

He entered the drawing room last of all, where the indelible shade of his father hovered in the darkened chamber like the effigy of a vanished king. Of all of the times they had shared the space, it was the very last that had torn from Stevenson words he might have given his soul not to have had cause to write.

> *Once more I saw him. In the lofty room,*
> *Where oft with lights and company his tongue*
> *Was trump to honest laughter, sate attired*
> *A something in his likeness. "Look!" said one,*
> *Unkindly kind, 'look up, it is your boy!'*
> *And the dread changeling gazed on me in vain.*

"Richard seems like a nice boy."

Fanny settled her handbag by her side in their first-class compartment as the Bournemouth train bucked once or twice and eased out of Waterloo Station on the last leg of their return from Edinburgh. They had left Sam in London for a two week stay with a school friend prior to the start of the term. "Don't you think?"

"He does," replied Stevenson, looking up from the *Times*. "They seemed happy to see each other."

Fanny nodded. "I'm worried, though, about his skin."

"Richard's?"

"Sam's, you ninny."

"What precisely are you worried about? That he's growing so fast his skull and feet will pop out his two ends?"

"Honestly, Louis. Your perpetual attempts at humor sometimes try my patience."

"In that event, I shall do my best to be endlessly dour. How is this?"

He pulled his chin down into his chest, arching his lips into a glum scowl. Fanny tittered in spite of herself.

Sam had grown what seemed like three or four inches over the spring and summer, if one judged by the unfashionable rise of his trouser cuffs above his boots. As a result, he fully expected to be moved into the second row of his rugby fifteen. He had also developed an impressive case of acne, something more for Fanny to hold against his birth father, who had suffered the same condition as a youth.

"I myself have always had the skin of a Vestal Virgin," Stevenson declared. "You should have waited to become a mother until you met me. "

"Sometimes I think I did become a mother when I met you. Yours!"

Minutes passed as the train gained pace and London's sooty, brick sprawl yielded to the fields and lanes of Surrey. Fanny reached into her bag for the novel she had been reading: Haggard's *She*. Stevenson had pressed it upon her as both a stirring tale and one, he averred, that boasted a central character with whom she might feel some commonality. Fanny needed to read no more than the title to appreciate his sarcasm. She was nonetheless finding it to be good fun.

"My God! How awful!" exclaimed Stevenson a minute or two later.

"Hmmm. What, dear?"

"*Another murder of the foulest kind,*" he read from his paper, "*in the neighbourhood of Whitechapel. At a quarter to 4 o'clock Police-constable Neill, 97J, when in Buck's-row, Whitechapel, came upon the body of a woman lying on a part of the footway, and on stooping to raise her up in the belief that she was drunk he discovered that her throat was cut almost from ear to ear. She was dead but still warm.*"

Fanny cringed visibly. "Good heavens!"

"*He procured assistance and at once sent to the station and for a doctor. Dr. Llewellyn, of Whitechapel-road, was aroused, and, at the solicitation of a constable, dressed and went at once to the scene. He inspected the body at the place where it was found and pronounced the woman dead. He made a hasty examination and then discovered that, besides the gash across the throat, the woman had terrible wounds in the abdomen."*

Fanny stared at him aghast. "What is this world coming to?"

"It's the third murder of a prostitute in Whitechapel in six months," said Stevenson, shaking his head. "And the second in four weeks."

"Do these women know what they're risking?"

"I have no doubt. But times are hard. And they know they have a market, I suppose. It's a way to stay alive. Or it should be." The thought of Old Town Mary leapt distressingly to mind. Would she and her compeer be reading these accounts as well? Might they just be waiting for a lowland killer to come north in search of new quarry—or for some twisted Edinburgh regular to try his hand at what was now a newsworthy trick?

"One may search the ghastliest efforts of fiction," he read on, *"and fail to find anything to surpass these crimes in diabolical audacity. The mind travels back to the pages of De Quincey for an equal display of scientific delight in the details of butchery; or Edgar Allan Poe's 'Murders in the Rue Morgue' recur in the endeavour to conjure up some parallel for this murderer's brutish savagery. But, so far as we know, nothing in fact or fiction equals these outrages at once in their horrible nature and in the effect which they have produced upon the popular imagination."*

"'Nothing in fact or fiction,'" said Fanny, sighing deeply. "Nothing, at least, they have been allowed to see. Thank God, Louis, you destroyed that first draft of *Jekyll*. A girl trampled in the street, running for the doctor, is a far cry from a bludgeoned whore."

"Amen," said Stevenson.

While it was a considerable relief to be back at Skerryvore after the emotional trials of the journey north, Stevenson struggled to re-establish his routine. Cassell's had finally sent along a contract for a sequel to *Kidnapped*, but David Balfour stubbornly refused to offer any hints about where he hoped to go with his life, and the brownies seemed to have gone into some kind of hibernation. The best the mourning son could do was potter away at a piece tentatively titled, "Thomas

Stevenson, Civil Engineer," thereby parleying his grief and manifold regrets into a lame simulacrum of creative energy. Within a matter of days, however, a letter arrived from Henley in London that put paid even to that meager effort.

It bore the highly unsettling news that, in light of the ongoing series of macabre murders in Spitalfields and Whitechapel, the Lyceum had suspended for an indefinite interval its performances of *The Strange Case of Dr. Jekyll and Mr. Hyde.* The *Times* and other London papers had received dozens of letters declaring how unconscionable it would be for the theater to stay lit while the precise sorts of inhuman violence that were drawing crowds to its seats were also taking the lives of real Londoners in dark alleys mere miles to the east. Not a few editors suggested, in fact, that the brutality represented in the play had effectively inspired the crimes now associated with "Leather Apron." For a brief time, the principal actor, Richard Mansfield, was himself even considered a suspect. It took Henry Irving and some other men of influence to provide him with an unassailable alibi.

Apprised of this shocking development, Fanny stood next to the chair in which Stevenson slouched in despondence, a bottle of whisky by his side.

"There's no reason to think there is any connection," she said softly but assertively. "No reason at all. The first murder—the Smith woman, was it? That happened last April."

Stevenson stared at her blankly.

"*Jekyll* opened in August," she explained.

"And since then, what? Three more women have been butchered."

"One of the killings was the day after the opening. The night after, Louis. Are we supposed to think someone was turned into a monster by three hours at the Lyceum? And then went out the very next night and slit open a prostitute's belly?"

Stevenson looked up at his wife with tortured eyes of the kind she was accustomed to seeing only when he was in the deepest throes of a fever. "It could happen that way," he said. He reached shakily for the whisky and poured himself another measure, spilling a jot on his trousers.

"Louis," said Fanny, pulling a chair up in front of him. She reached out for his left hand and, cradling it in hers, stroked the back of it gently. "If it happened that way…and there's no reason at all to think it did. But *if* it did—even if it did—it would be Mansfield who might feel guilty. It would be his doing, not yours!"

Stevenson peered at her fixedly, pausing before he shook his head. "The story's mine, Fanny. Hyde is mine. I brought him to life. "

"You wrote a book, Louis. What people are talking about is the possible effect of a *play*. The *possible* effect. And it's not even your play."

"I loosed him on the world. And look at what he's done."

"Louis!"

"What a vile, stupid creation he was. Is!"

"Stop it!" cried Fanny, throwing his hand down into his lap. "You're drunk, and you don't know what you're saying. It's total nonsense, for God's sake! There's nothing linking you to anything."

"No? No?"

"None at all!"

What seemed like a cough turned into a deep, gasping chuckle. "There's Symonds, Fanny! No? Symonds's letter. He said it could push a man over the edge, what I wrote. What *I* wrote!"

"Symonds is a madman, Louis. He's unstable. He's a buggerer, for God's sake."

"You don't know that."

"I do. It's written all over him."

He tipped his glass up to his lips. Finding it all but empty, he reached again for the bottle. "Even if he is. And remember the damn… all those reviews."

"I don't remember any stupid reviews. And you're drinking too much. Please stop." Fanny reached for his wrist, but he shook her off and poured himself another measure.

"Remember? The *Times?*" he muttered. "'Horrible things,' wha'd they say? 'not often attracting the public.' But *this* story attracted 'em, didn't it? And something about awakening 'strange sensations?' My God, Fanny!" He threw himself forward in his chair, his head crashing down onto his forearms. His tumbler leapt from his hand and rolled across the carpet past Fanny's feet, leaving a trail of pungent spirits.

"I don't know what else to say." Fanny sat back and folded her arms in a mixture of combativeness and despair.

"Don't you understand?" When Stevenson lifted his head his eyes were flushed and brimming. "Hyde is my creature."

The clock struck midnight. The fire had all but died in the grate, and a chill had taken over the room. Stevenson shivered with the tolling and looked over at the bottle. It lay on its side, empty. No solace there. He rose to his feet and stumbled towards the door, his shoes scraping noisily on the bare floorboards between the carpet and the hallway.

"Shhhhh!" he hissed at himself. "You sound like the fucking cavalry."

He kicked off his shoes and they clattered up against the wall.

"Shhhhh! Shhhhh!" He advanced a few steps in his stocking feet. "Like a mouse. Creep like a wee drunken mousie."

He reached the staircase and, grabbing hold of the newel post, swung himself around it with a momentum that brought him hard up against the inner side of the banister. He struck his face on the handrail, he knew, but it scarcely pained him. Grabbing the rail, he pulled himself up the stairs, one at a time, left foot first, right following. Up. And up.

He reached the top of the flight and spun back towards the front of the house and the door to his room. Was Fanny asleep? Or just lying there waiting? Probably asleep. He stopped at the door and leaned heavily against the frame. Was that her breathing? He snorted to himself and continued down the hall, wondering if the floorboards would creak. No, thank God! On to the next flight. He grasped the rail. Left, and then right. Up. And up.

"Ain't this folly, Thomson?" he giggled under his breath. "Very naughty. Naughtier naughtiest."

He reached the top floor and endeavored to tiptoe down the bare hallway, reaching out with his right hand for support from the wall.

"Am I smudging? Best not smudge."

This was Millie's door, he thought dimly. Millie and Agnes's. He passed quietly by, feeling an excited constriction in his chest. Then this would be Valentine's. *Oh my!* He leaned his shoulder against the doorjamb and reached for the knob, turning it as slowly as he possibly could. Was it turning? Had it moved at all? The latch clicked free of its seat and he almost fell into the room, taking a few quick steps to keep from crashing onto the floor.

There was a brisk rustle of bedclothes. *"Qui va? Qui va là?"*

"C'est moi, Valentine. Ton…mâitre." He closed the door behind himself, pushing it too hard. The latch engaged with a deafening clack. "Shhhh!"

"What are you doing here, monsieur? Is something wrong?" He could hear her sitting up in the bed.

"Yes."

"What is it?" There was the sound of fumbling. She struck a lucifer and lit the candle on her nightstand, staring at him wide-eyed in the mounting chiaroscuro glow.

"Everything's wrong."

"Wait, please. Let me get out of bed. Let me put on my robe."

"No!" hissed Stevenson, again louder than he meant to. "Right there. I want you there. Stay there."

She had thrown her legs over the edge of the bed, uncovering them to rise. She drew them back in, pulling the bedclothes over herself once again. The candle cast her shadow on the wall to Stevenson's left. Huge. Leaning towards him. Perfectly still.

"What do you want?"

"What do I want?"

"Yes."

"What do I want?"

She remained motionless, silent, bracing herself on her hands. Her nightgown was pulled slightly open. He could see the soft swelling of a breast.

"I don't know. Damn me, Valentine, I don't." He did know, though, that he was on the brink of weeping.

"Come," said the woman, sliding to the side. "Come. Sit." She patted the bed next to her. "Look at me."

He did as he was told.

"You do not know what you want?"

His head dropped to his chest and he shook it slowly, side to side.

"I believe I know what you want." Her voice was silken in the chill air. He could smell the warmth of her. "But not this."

"No?" He tried to focus on her face, but the room was swimming in the dancing candlelight.

She reached for a handkerchief on the table and lifted it to wipe a tear from his cheek. He had never seen her do anything so gently, and it unmanned him.

"No," she replied. "Not at all. Now then!" She reached up to gather the bodice of her gown more closely about her. "Tell me why everything is wrong. How it is so."

As best he could in his condition, Stevenson shared his anguish over the dreadful turn he had seen his work take. At times he blubbered, half expecting her to reach out and comfort him, but she sat there calmly, clinically, taking everything in. When he had finished, or thought perhaps that he had, she reached out and, for the briefest moment, pressed his knee.

"Madame Stevenson is right. You know?"

"Right?"

"It is not your fault how someone acts when they read what you write. Unless you tell them this is the way they must act. And even then, it is their choice, yes?"

"I don't know. I don't know."

"Please, monsieur. It is the things we do that matter. Not the stories we tell."

He looked at her blankly. It put him in mind of something. Did it have to do with his father?

"You know the story 'Hansel and Gretel?'"

Stevenson laughed.

"You do?"

He nodded.

"If someone reads 'Hansel and Gretel' and decides to eat children for his supper, has the story made him do that?"

He laughed again.

"It is what you do, monsieur. Your acts. If you had come and forced me this night, that would have been a sin."

His stomach clenched as though he might be ill.

"I wouldn't do that, Valentine. I would never force you. I suppose I thought…I thought you—"

"Shhhh! Shhhh! Let me tell *you* a story." She reached over and slid the candle slightly closer to them on the nightstand, and then adjusted herself in the bed. "One time, years ago—I was thirteen—my brother came to me at night. Very much this way." She nodded gravely. "He was eighteen. He was, how do you say, amorous? He loved the girls. This night, my brother came to me in the middle of the night and he fell on top of me. In my bed. I cried out and he grabbed me by the throat and he told me he would kill me if I was not silent. I was so frightened that I believed he truly would. So I fought him in silence until I could fight no more. He was very strong, you see. And it finally hurt me more, I thought, to fight against him than to let him have his way. And he did."

"God, Valentine," sighed Stevenson. "I am so sorry. I am so sorry."

"You may feel sad at me and my story. Good. Then you feel what a good man should feel. It was also good that, tonight, you did not do something to regret. That would be sinful. It would be unforgiveable."

He could not recall, at that moment, any other utterance that had left him feeling so chastened and penitent.

"Let me tell you this now before you go to bed. Your own bed." She lowered her head and peered at him sternly. "I have been with no man since that night. I was not before and I have not since. I have no taste for these things with men. Do you understand?"

"I do."

Valentine pulled her head back and, surprisingly, laughed softly. "'I do.' This is what you say to the priest, yes? When you marry?"

"It is."

"I do," she repeated, as though trying it on for size. "Now, go to Madame Stevenson."

"Valentine—"

"We will not speak of this. Not with anyone. This is for us alone to know."

He had scarcely closed her door before he began to wonder, in the dim way his condition allowed, how he could have misjudged this woman so utterly, so completely misread her intentions. It was a matter to revisit some time when he felt less likely to vomit.

16

He had an approved tolerance for others; sometimes wondering, almost with envy, at the high pressure of spirits involved in their misdeeds; and in any extremity inclined to help rather than to reprove. "I incline to Cain's heresy," he used to say quaintly: "I let my brother go to the devil in his own way."

—THE NARRATOR, OF MR. UTTERSON

THE TIMES

MONDAY, 10 SEPTEMBER 1888

ANOTHER MURDER AT THE EAST-END.

Whitechapel and the whole of the East of London have again been thrown into a state of intense excitement by the discovery early on Saturday morning of the body of a woman who had been murdered in a similar way to Mary Ann Nichols at Buck's-row on Friday week. In fact the similarity in the two cases is startling, as the victim of the outrage had her head almost severed from her body, and was completely disembowelled. This latest crime, however, even surpasses the others in ferocity. The scene of the murder, which makes the fourth in the same neighbourhood within the past few weeks, is at the back of the house, 29, Hanbury-street, Spitalfields. This street runs from Commercial-street to Baker's-row, the end of which is close to Buck's-row. The house, which is rented by a Mrs. Emilia Richardson, is let out to various lodgers, all of the poorer class. In consequence, the front door is open both day and night, so that no difficulty would be experienced by any one in gaining admission to the back portion of the premises. Shortly before 6 o'clock on Saturday morning John Davis, who lives with his wife at the top portion of No. 29, and is a porter engaged in Spitalfields Market, went down into the back yard, where a horrible sight presented itself to him. Lying close up against the wall, with her head touching the other side wall, was the body of a woman. Davis could see that her throat was severed in a terrible manner, and that she had other wounds of a nature too shocking to be described. The deceased was lying flat on her back, with her clothes disarranged. Without nearer approaching the body, but telling his wife what he had seen, Davis ran to the Commercial-street Police-station, which is only a short distance away, and gave information to Inspector Chandler, H Division, who was in charge of the station at the time. That officer, having dispatched a con-stable for Dr. Baxter Phillips, Spital-square, the divisional surgeon, repaired to the house, accompanied by several other policemen. The body was still in the same position, and there were large clots of blood all round it. It is evident that the murderer thought that he had completely cut the head off, as a handkerchief was found wrapped round the neck, as though to hold it together. There were spots and stains of blood on the wall. One or more rings seem to have been torn from the middle finger of the left hand. After being inspected by Dr. Baxter Phillips and his assistant, the remains were removed, on an ambulance, to the mortuary in Old Montagu-street. By this time the news had quickly spread that another diabolical murder had been committed, and when the police came out of the house with the body, a large crowd, consisting of some hundreds of persons, had assembled. The excitement became very great, and loud were the expressions of terror heard on all sides. At the mortuary the doctors made a more minute examination of the body, after which the clothes were taken off. The deceased was laid in the same shell in which Mary Ann Nichols was placed.

11 September

The Athenaeum Club

Dear Stevenson,

I am sick at heart. I had of course read the English papers in Davos about the terrible string of doings in the East End. It was only when I had returned to London, however, that I heard of the talk that the theatrical piece made from your book may have played a role in bringing about these dreadful events. And now another! I know it is not your play but Mansfield's, yet my heart goes out to you as you live with the people's suspicion that your story may have had a hand in it all. Oh Louis, did I not tell you it was a dreadful thing? I recall saying that all of us had a Hyde lurking within us, struggling to emerge, yet it was never a Hyde of such inhuman brutality that I contemplated. The greatest horror of it all is that I believe I have a notion of who the man may be, yet I am positioned such that I can see no way to play a role in bringing him to justice. Of the many burdens I have struggled under in this life, this now seems the weightiest. I scarce know what to do…or to think of myself.

I stay in London for another fortnight, attending to some matters with my publishers. You may find me at the Athenaeum.

With warm regards to Fanny and to Sam,

Symonds

Stevenson took the third train of the day to London. Fanny had pressed him hard on his reasons for going to the capital so precipitously, but, for reasons that were not entirely clear to him, he had refused to be forthcoming. Perhaps he wanted a free hand in dealing with a matter for which, despite her repeated remonstrations, he felt extreme responsibility and guilt. Perhaps he craved a sort of excitement that he was loath to share. It did feel strangely like those days at Colinton Manse when, as a young boy, he would escape from the house and its grownups to join his cousins out in the fields and alongside the streams, relishing the intoxicating prospect of whatever the day might bring. Only so long could he and they abide being cooped up in the house, despite all its storybooks and toys; there came, infallibly, that irresistible craving for free ranging adventure. The last thing presently on his mind, however, was frivolous recreation.

He withstood Fanny's annoyance and then her outright anger as he packed his Gladstone, assuring her he would return as soon as he had finished with his business. It was only after he had grabbed his things, donned his hat, and slammed the front door behind him that he felt reasonably certain he had dodged the threat of assault.

The train ride was uneventful. The only news in the day's paper was that the previous afternoon, Mr. Wynne E. Baxter, coroner for the South-Eastern Division of Middlesex, had resumed his inquiry at the Vestry Hall, Cable Street, "St. George's-in-the-East," respecting the death of Annie Chapman. Eight citizens had testified.

Stevenson took a hansom from Waterloo to Pall Mall to call at the Athenaeum Club, where he asked for Symonds. Once he had examined the writer's card, the porter allowed that Mr. Symonds was indeed currently in residence but that he was out for the day, expected back, perhaps, in the late afternoon. Stevenson left a message that he would call again at seven, and then walked up to Piccadilly and on to the Savile.

He had vaguely hoped to see Dobbs at the door, but it was another fellow altogether who opened for him. Nonetheless, he was greeted by name at the porter's lodge and assured that there would be a room available for the night—and, should he require it, for the foreseeable future. If Mr. Stevenson would care to leave his bag, it would be taken to his room as soon as one became ready; in the meantime, he might of course avail himself of the morning room, the drawing room, the library, or the bar. Stevenson looked at his watch. 1:30—a bit late for luncheon, and he had no appetite at all. He walked to the bar and ordered himself a whisky.

At seven he was on his way back down Regent Street, approaching the Athenaeum. The august establishment was the first club in London to have installed electric lighting, and as he neared the elegant Neoclassical pile, Stevenson was dazzled by the brightness pouring out the place. He took a moment to look up at the imposing gold statue of Athena herself, atop the massive Doric portico. Dickens, Darwin, Scott, Thackeray, Spencer, Palmerston, Kipling: it was an Olympian lot that frequented this British retreat of the Goddess of Wisdom. Stevenson felt a blend of excitement and dread as he considered just what sort of knowledge one if its members might convey to him this very night.

An elderly porter opened the door to inform him that Mr. Symonds attended him in the South Library. Stevenson followed the man across the marbled entrance hall and through a tall double door into the impressive reading room. All four walls were stacked with books, three tiers of them stretching from the floor to the high ceiling. He spotted his old friend at the top of the stairs to the first mezzanine. Symonds gestured and, after turning to slide a sizeable volume back into its shelf, descended the stairs to greet him. While his expression and handshake were warm and assured, a tentativeness lurked in his eyes.

"My things are just here," he said, pointing to a chair by the door. "Shall we avail ourselves of this fine evening and begin with a stroll around St. James's Park?"

"Perfect."

"I do hope you will join me for dinner. I have a table at Bertolini's. In St. Martin's. Eight o'clock?"

"Excellent. I don't believe I've dined there."

"You'll enjoy it." Symonds retrieved his gloves, stick, and a broad-brimmed, Whitmanesque hat, gesturing towards the door.

The two exchanged nothing beyond pleasantries until they had descended the steps to the Mall and turned west along the upper margins of the park. The air was still and the walkway tolerably well lit, such that they were likely to see or hear well in advance the approach of anyone who might overhear their conversation.

"I am extremely grateful you have come," declared Symonds, once he was sure they were quite alone. "I wasn't certain that you would."

"How could I not?"

"It's a dreadful business, Stevenson."

"It assuredly is. I cannot tell you how shattered I am. I don't know that I ever in my life have felt the way I feel just now."

"I can only imagine."

"That letter of yours came back to mind immediately. Chillingly."

"I am sorry."

"No. There's no need to apologize. It simply confirmed for me that the damned thing might well have some less-than-desirable effects."

"You put it rather mildly." Symond looked at him gravely.

"I am sorry. You're right. It's dreadful of me to express it that way."

"It was not you who wrote the play, however, Louis. Remember that. You neither wrote it nor arranged for the production."

"Small solace, really. Given who conceived of the creature."

Two constables approached them, chatting amiably. Stevenson and Symonds nodded as they passed, keeping silent until the footsteps receded behind them.

"So, Symonds. You can well imagine how curious I am about what you had to say. In your last."

"To be perfectly honest, I half wish I had said nothing."

Stevenson stopped and turned towards his friend. "We can let this drop. This very moment. If that's what you wish."

Symonds looked at him uncertainly and, after a loud sigh, shook his head. "I wish it were that easy."

"How can I help you?"

"First of all, simply by hearing me out."

Stevenson nodded, and they resumed their walk. For two or three minutes the writer waited in vain for his companion to say anything at all. Carriages passed in either direction, one of them bearing a quartet of young men who were evidently swimming in alcohol, even at this early hour. Symonds looked over at Stevenson and grinned.

"Wine, women, and song," joked Stevenson.

"Indeed. Timeless diversions."

Another minute passed before Symonds spoke again, very quietly. "The information I have could be the end of me, Stevenson."

"John!"

"One might almost laugh at how absurdly dramatic that sounds. I assure you, though, that I am scarcely exaggerating. Any feature of what I am about to say might end my career or my life."

"You have long been a true friend," Stevenson managed to declare as they walked on. "You may trust me to keep anything you say in the strictest confidence."

"I count on that. Absolutely."

"I swear."

"Well, let me begin with this." Symonds took a deep breath as he reached up with both hands to adjust the brim of his hat. "You know that I have written a book entitled *A Problem in Greek Ethics?*"

"I do."

"And you know its subject?"

"I believe I do."

"That is my Hyde, Stevenson." Symonds looked sidelong at his friend.

Stevenson felt a bothersome flush spread up across his cheeks, but he nodded reassuringly.

"It has not been…easy."

"No. It wouldn't be, would it? And Janet?"

"I suspect Janet knows. I can't be sure. It is something of which she would never speak."

"Of course." If it were Fanny, thought Stevenson, there was no doubt he would hear about very little else.

"I have spent so much of my time away from her and the girls. Research in Italy. Trips back to London."

Stevenson nodded. As they passed Queen's Walk, the massive façade of Buckingham Palace loomed up in front of them. Its windows, those that were lit, were distinctly less bright than those of the Athenaeum.

"It is here in London, as you might expect, that I stumbled into my current situation." He looked to his companion as though for additional reassurance and, with Stevenson's nod, continued. "There is a certain establishment on Cleveland Street. It's a place where gentlemen such as myself can go and…avail themselves of the various services offered."

"I see," said Stevenson. Where there were appetites, there were purveyors. It was the simplest rule of human economy, and it had no doubt been so from the very beginning.

"There are lads there, you see. As there were lads for the original Athenians. Many of them also work as telegraph boys, as it happens."

Symonds broke off walking and looked doubtfully at Stevenson.

"What should I say?" he continued, clasping his hands behind his back and peering down at the gravel just in front of his feet. "It is nothing I am proud of, Louis. Or remotely at peace with, as you can imagine. But it involves the very essence of me. The very breath. I might, you know, awake the morning after with the deepest sense of shame and self-loathing. Almost always I do. But in the throes of the night, in the midst of drink and gaiety…it is as though I have been clawing up from the depths of the darkest waters, and I finally break the surface and my jaws unclench and I can pull in a huge and reviving breath. It is—" He paused, shaking his head.

"We all swim in those depths, John. In one way or another. Rest assured."

"Thank you, Louis. I know that you know that." Symonds smiled wistfully and walked on. "There are precious few I have shared this with."

"I understand."

"I feel perhaps I can speak with you as I can speak with few others. Perhaps none. I expect it has to do with the things we faced together. At Davos. And face still, no?"

Stevenson nodded. "You do me an honor."

They reached Buckingham Gate and turned back east on Birdcage Walk, passing slowly through the circles of light cast by the gas lamps.

"There is another frequenter of this house on Cleveland Street," Symonds said quietly. "A man of some stature. It happens that he also belongs to the Athenaeum. Which is at the very heart of the matter for me."

"That I can begin to compass," observed Stevenson.

"You can also imagine that, given the nature of the services it offers, this establishment is rather attentive to matters of privacy. The clients rarely see one another, there being a number of entrances to the place. And when they do, the natural supposition is that it is in their mutual self-interest to disclose to no one in the population at large the nature of their custom."

"Of course."

"One evening," Symonds continued, "it chanced that I and this fellow came face-to-face at the door nearest Foley Street—he coming out, I going in. Well, he drew himself up to the full extent of his considerable height and, with a murderous scowl, he looked me dead in the eye and said that if he ever learned that I had breathed a word of this to anyone he would have my balls right off of me, and eat them with my liver."

"My God, Symonds! Are you serious?"

"I hardly find it something to joke about. Those were his very words. It was like something out of a perfect nightmare, considering the whole of it. It nauseates me even now just to think of it."

It took Stevenson a moment to be able to go on. "What else can you tell me about the man?"

"Well, he has considerable money and power, having come into a substantial inheritance. Prior to that, he was a surgeon in the army. He served in the Zulu War."

"A surgeon, you say?"

"I know," answered Symonds. "Gravely injured in the Battle of Kambula, it seems. I don't know how he felt about Africa before he served there. I can tell you, though, that I have never heard a man speak so hatefully of the dark people of that continent. I would blush to repeat the terms that he uses, let alone compass the steps he proposes for pursuing Her Majesty's interests in that portion of the Empire. There has been more than one evening in the Smoking Room when his fulminations have reached a level where one or another of the members has been obliged to ask him to hold his tongue. Or leave the premises."

"Never you, I trust."

"Hardly."

They heard a scuffing of boots ahead and looked up to see a pair of policemen approaching along the walk. It turned out to be the same two they had encountered earlier, circumnavigating the park in the opposite direction.

"We are feeling especially well protected this evening," quipped Stevenson, as the four men recognized each other. "Many thanks."

"All in a night's work," responded the taller of the two, smiling as they passed.

"Well," sighed Stevenson as they moved on, "this fellow of yours does indeed sound like an utter beast. Is there anything particular, though, that leads you to think it is *his* surgical skills that have been on display in the East End?"

"I believe there is."

"And that would be?"

"We have a mutual friend."

"A friend?"

"We share a taste for one of the boys. I would say we share an affection, but affection is something of which I do not believe this man to be capable. A beautiful lad, he is. Handsome. Intelligent. A dear boy.

He…he had been with my man just nights earlier. He is far too intelligent to speak of such things under normal circumstances, but what
he heard alarmed him so that he felt he must speak of it with someone."

"And that someone was you."

"It was. He said that this fellow came in raging drunk and was very
harsh with him. He said that he was sick and tired of the place and of
all of the precautions he had to take to assure that he wasn't forever
ruined for the kind of thing other gentlemen could do with impunity.
When my boy asked him what he meant, he said that a gent with a taste
for ladies could find one any time of day right out in the open streets
and no one would blink an eye. He said the whores and whoremongers
could all go hang, and that the members of Parliament who had passed
the Labouchère Amendment could hang along with them. And then
came the worst of it."

"And what was that?"

"My lad said he didn't know what the Labouchère Amendment was,
and then my gentleman grabbed him by the throat and said something
like, 'It's what requires me to fuck you, you ignorant little cunt. And
not someone with brains.'"

"My God!" gasped Stevenson. If a true, flesh-and-blood Hyde ever
prowled the streets of London!

"And then," said Symonds with a catch in his voice, "and then he
slapped my boy so hard the blood gushed from his nose and he leaned
his face in close to him and said, 'I've a knife to cut it out, you know?
This city's sick heart. As you can well see if you have eyes and ears.'"

They walked on in silence, Stevenson's heart thudding in his chest.
It occurred to him with a guilty sort of relief, however, that if this man
were indeed the killer of whores—and if it were indeed Mansfield's,
or even possibly his own, Hyde who had somehow encouraged his
butchery—he nonetheless had a personal motive that lay well beyond
the scope of *Jekyll and Hyde* in either of its incarnations.

"I hate to say it," said Symonds, after a good minute or two, "but
it is nearly eight. What are you thinking, Stevenson? Can you possibly

bring yourself to put food in your mouth?"

"I don't know. Shall we at least walk to St. Martin's Lane and see?"

Newsboys were still touting the day's papers and their details of the latest Whitechapel investigations as the two friends negotiated Trafalgar Square. They found Bertolini's to be very crowded, but decided at the very least to go in for wine. Stevenson thought at first that Symonds's grim tale had truly done for his appetite, perhaps for some time; but once they were two-thirds of the way through a fine bottle of Barolo, he found himself more than willing to look at the menu.

As he and Symonds were necessarily seated cheek-by-jowl with other diners in the packed establishment, their conversation turned solely on current personal projects and the latest prime-ministerial gaffes. By the time Symonds had settled the reckoning, it was well past nine o'clock.

"What do you propose to do, then?" asked Stevenson, as they crossed over St. Martin's Lane and continued along towards the National Gallery.

"I was rather wanting to ask you what you thought I might do. I feel rather shackled."

"As well you might. The simplest course would be to go to the police. But I'm certain you have thought of that."

"Of course I have. And it has naturally occurred to me that I have no evidence whatsoever of any tangible sort. Nothing beyond the hearsay testimony of a lad whose standing in a court of law would obviously not be strong. Can you imagine his explaining where and how he came by his information?"

"No," allowed the writer.

"In addition, I have no way of knowing where an inquiry in which my young friend participates might ultimately lead. I said earlier that the information I thought to pass on to you might be the end of me."

"You did."

"Imagine if my connection to this place were to emerge in the press. Imagine the impact on Janet. And on my daughters."

"It doesn't bear thinking on," sighed Stevenson.

"What is more, I really do believe that my vicious gentleman knows no restraints. Were he to discover that it was I who put the law on his trail, I would fear for my life."

"And well you should, from what you tell me."

"I am not a coward, Louis," declared Symonds, stopping short to face his friend. "Nor am I a man of no principle. If the only way of stopping him were to take the matter to the law—*and* if I could be reasonably certain of an immediate apprehension, trial, and conviction…" He paused. "Then, I might well have the courage."

"I believe that, Symonds."

"That said, there is my family. And I have no doubt that other parties—men of status and importance, good men at base—might suffer exposure and ruin. I feel I *must* not act either rashly or prematurely."

"Of course not. You are perfectly right in that."

They passed between the great museum and Nelson's Column and turned up Cockspur Street. A busy current of pedestrians and carriages still wove its way down into the huge square.

"So," continued Stevenson, "what to do? It seems beyond denying that this beast has every intention of keeping at it, what with his recurrent butchery thus far."

"It's silly of me, I suppose. I feel a bit like an aspirant for a role in a story by Poe. But it has occurred to me that, if I were to have some tangible evidence of my man's depredations—*if* he is indeed the guilty party—then I would most likely be closer to knowing the appropriate action to take."

"Or *we* would be closer."

"Pardon me?"

"*We* would be, Symonds. I don't mean to leave you alone in this dilemma. Without a staunch companion."

Symonds peered at him with his mouth agape. "You don't mean that."

"I do," replied Stevenson, chuckling as his words resonated in his ears.

From out of the blue, his exchange with Valentine came back to him. *I do*. He was about to wed himself to an extremely dubious proposition, but it felt very much like an act of virtue—perhaps as importantly, like an act of contrition. "I owe it to you. And to the memory of another dear friend. Let us consider it a bold new adventure by Symonds and Stevenson, though. Not Poe." He grinned waggishly, even as his companion sustained his blank stare. "I have been festering in Bournemouth like a weevil in a biscuit, John. Here is the finest summons imaginable to a life of active, as opposed to contemplative, daring. We shall rid London of this plague or die trying."

"You're not serious."

"In my heart and soul, indisputably I am. Let us shake on it."

Symonds looked down uncertainly, then took the hand extended to him.

"Let us both ponder ways we might manage this," said Stevenson as they approached the entrance to the club. "Are you free tomorrow?"

"I am. In the afternoon."

"Let us meet here at two o'clock, then, and consider any options we may have."

"Upon my honour, Stevenson. You are a man of marvels!"

"Too few of them anything other than confabulations, old friend. But here is real meat to bite into. Besides, I am extremely keen on asking this fellow if he is indeed familiar with my tale of London atrocities. At least with any derivative theatricals."

Symonds looked at him with concern. "I had hoped to reassure you on that score, Louis. I regret I ever raised the issue."

"You were merely being a brave and loyal friend, John. I count myself fortunate to have a chance to reciprocate."

He bid Symonds goodnight and began to walk back towards Piccadilly. A shout from behind made him turn, and he saw the night porter racing after a departing cab, waving a top hat in his hand. Someone, most likely someone drunk on hundred-year-old cognac or obscenely costly port, must have left it behind.

For a moment, as the hansom clattered past, Stevenson stood there and gazed at the elegant façade of the club. Given its luminary membership, it was only appropriate that it should blaze in the London night like a caged sun. Yet there was something profligate about it, too. How many women in Whitechapel might still be alive this night if every street corner in the East End boasted similar means of keeping darkness at bay? And if Symonds was right, one of the denizens of this very palace of light might well be the butcher known as "Leather Apron."

Stevenson looked up at the statue standing guard above the entrance. The crown of the goddess's helmet, the tip of her spear, her broad, cloaked shoulders—all of them, backlit by the first-floor windows, glowed against the black London sky. The open hand, though, lay in shadow now, and her features were no longer to be made out.

17

If he be Mr. Hyde …I shall be Mr. Seek.

—GABRIEL JOHN UTTERSON, DR. JEKYLL'S ATTORNEY

The first thing the following morning, Stevenson sent a telegram to Fanny, confirming that something very important was afoot that could keep him in London indefinitely. He considered leaving the message at that—perhaps adding that he was sure she trusted him to honor their welfare as a family in everything he did. When he put himself candidly in her position, however, he realized that, were he to be no more forthcoming than that, she might well be on the next train to the capital with a coil of rope to lynch him.

Instead, he declared that his own abiding welfare and the welfare of many more individuals than he depended on his staying in the city, and he ended with a somewhat coded message: "Impact of play may be amended." She would certainly understand this as referring to something he justifiably felt he must do—but also something more along the lines of conversations with publishers or theater managers than the scheme he was presently contemplating. He reminded her he could be reached at the Savile, refraining from the addendum that he trusted her not to use that information for anything other than posting a letter.

Stevenson spent a pleasant morning visiting with Colvin and Fanny Sitwell, whom he had not seen in a considerable while. Returning to his club for luncheon, he was pleased to be greeted at the door by Dobbs.

"Mr. Stevenson," said the stout fellow as he held the door. "Very good to see you."

"And you, Dobbs. I missed you yesterday."

"I'm very sorry, sir."

"Not at all. You are well? And your family?"

"As well as can be expected, sir. Thank you for asking."

"And how do you find me, Dobbs?" It was all Stevenson could do not to wink.

The man grinned. "That's hardly for me to say, Mr. Stevenson."

"No? I no longer look handsome to you?"

"I'm sure you do, sir. As always."

The writer laughed. "Very good of you to say so."

Stevenson returned to his room to wash up, and then descended to the dining room for a fine luncheon of leek soup, trout, and sherry trifle, all washed down with an excellent hock. As he savored the last swallows of the wine, he looked around at the singular opulence of the room: precious marble columns, ornate Parisian boisseries, mirrored French doors leading to the neighboring ballroom. The task at hand with Symonds was sharply focused—very specific. If somehow their fanciful undertaking were to meet with success and halt this particular abuse of power—power of whatever sort it was—what societal inequities, exploitations, and horrors would remain completely untouched? A man of conscience might despair before the question; alternatively, he might choose to do whatever he could to better the lot of those around him, when and where the opportunity arose, Calvinist determinism be damned.

Stevenson considered his life to this point—what had essentially been an unbroken series of decisions and undertakings in which he had set his own interests above those of others. He might not actually be a bad man, but had his relations with his father or his mother or Fanny or Ferrier or anyone else ever involved his subordinating his own interests to those of another—and then extending himself to actual labor for their benefit?

He sighed deeply, pushing his wine glass away on the pristine tablecloth. Nodding briefly to the gentlemen at the next table, he rose and set off to keep his date with Symonds.

That evening, shortly after eight, a hansom clattered up Orchard Street into Portman Square. As a lamplighter tended to the last few gas lamps surrounding the vast central oval, the cab slowed opposite a row of handsome houses.

"Just here, driver," called Symonds, up through the open hatch. "No further."

"Yes, sir."

"There it is," he said to Stevenson. "Number 43. The one with the bright fanlight above the door."

"We know he is in?"

"We do."

"And there is no other door?"

"There is. Behind. But I have a boy there."

"And he can be trusted?"

"Absolutely."

The horse shifted slightly in the traces, then loosed a torrent of liquid onto the cobbles.

"Sorry, guv'nor," came the word from above.

"Is this a hare-brained scheme, Symonds?"

"Quite possibly." He turned to Stevenson with a doubtful expression. "But it is something."

"Aye, but is it something absurdly fanciful? I confess I have been dwelling upon your suggestive allusion to Poe."

"No doubt a hazard of your occupation," chuckled Symonds.

"True enough. The end result, though, is that I am left wondering if this is something two rational men living in the heart of the most civilized town on the globe should ever entertain as a sane and practical thing to do."

Symonds chuckled again. "Perhaps history will be our judge. Provided it is a story that can ever be told."

"Truly."

Three-quarters of an hour passed without event, the two friends conversing now and again while Stevenson smoked the occasional cigarette.

Symonds ultimately tapped on the hatch, which opened immediately.

"Are you all right, driver?"

"Fine, sir. Ta."

The hatch closed again.

"He should be," growled Symonds. "He is being exceedingly well compensated."

After another long but not uncomfortable silence, it was Stevenson who spoke.

"I don't judge you, you know, Symonds. For who you are."

"Thank you. There are those who do. And would."

"Indeed," sighed Stevenson. "Perhaps fewer of them, though, than would be willing to admit as much in a public forum."

"Do you think?"

"I do. I haven't made a formal study of the matter, but I feel as though I know a thing or two about the effects of respectability and its uneasy cult."

"Indeed," said Symonds. "It is strange," he continued after a moment, "where we come from. Where I have come from, in my wrestling with what is *done* and what is *not to be done*."

"In what way?" Stevenson offered his companion a cigarette. Symonds shook his head and he lit one for himself, waving out the light and tossing it from the cab.

"I first encountered the love of men for men—or of men for youths— at Harrow."

"Not unusual for any school, I suppose," observed Stevenson. He blew smoke out from under the canopy of the cab, and the light breeze carried it away towards the house they were watching.

"Not at all. Although for some—perhaps for most—it is a passing stage of growth. Of maturation. Into, you know, 'conventional manhood.'"

"Of course."

"For others, though, it is the gateway to something unchanging and unending. Paradise and Hell in one."

Stevenson nodded. Nothing particularly apt came to mind to offer.

"I was speaking of respectability, though. And I must say that at school, when it emerged that no less eminent a man than the headmaster was having illicit relations with one of the boys, my initial response was outrage. I don't know precisely if it was the fact that they were doing it—that it was physical. I had formed, you see, some high notions of Platonic affection from *The Symposium* or *Phaedrus*. I can't remember which. So this involvement naturally seemed a squalid and carnal travesty. Or was it that this man was a perfect hypocrite to be practicing behavior that he clearly, and repeatedly, condemned from the dais as a vice? But I would have said then, callow youth that I was, that their affair was a perfect affront to respectability itself. That it was damnable."

"I suppose in many ways it could have been. How old was the boy?"

"Sixteen."

"Past the age of consent, then."

"Then it was twelve, in fact. What I meant to say, though," continued Symonds, "was that my confident embrace of what was respectable began to erode in rather confusing ways."

"How so, John?"

"The man called me to his rooms one evening to tell me how fine a scholar he felt I was. He walked behind the chair I was sitting in and he put his hands on my shoulders and he squeezed them repeatedly. And as he told me that he felt a great fondness for me, as I was doing so well at his school, he ran his hand down my chest and inside my shirt."

"What on earth did you do?"

"I made my apologies and said I wasn't feeling well. I flew out of the room."

"I can well understand."

"As I thought back on it, though, I realized that it was not that a man was touching me. But rather that *this* man was touching me. Who should have been protecting his charges, rather than preying upon us."

"Yes."

Symonds shook his head and then surprised Stevenson with a chuckle. "He was not an attractive man, either. There was nothing the least bit Hellenic about the old coot."

"I see."

"Look," said Symonds, shortly after eleven o'clock. A light had appeared on the first floor. "That is his bedroom."

"You're sure?"

"I am."

They watched carefully for several more minutes, and then the light by the front door dimmed and the windows on the ground floor went dark. Shortly thereafter, a glimmer appeared in a window on the second floor.

"The servants must be retiring," said Stevenson.

"So it would appear."

Stevenson looked at his watch. Ten past eleven. "Can we possibly manage to do this every night, Symonds?"

"I honestly don't know. But to stand idly by, knowing all we already know? With the papers filled, week after week, with…" Symonds shook his head. "If I am ever to be able to live with myself, Louis—"

"I certainly didn't mean to signal any reluctance," interjected Stevenson. "I remain equally committeed. And I continue to think, as we discussed earlier, that it must be we who do this."

"You're perfectly right. The reports of anyone else would be useless."

"There," said Stevenson, pointing towards the house. "The bedroom light has gone out."

"So it has. I expect we should wait a bit longer to make sure he is in for the night?"

"We should."

Symonds tapped again on the hatch. "Driver. Driver?"

A rustle and an odd snort came down from above, as though the man were waking. After a few seconds the hatch opened.

"I think we shall just be a few more moments. For now, stand easy."

"Righty-oh, sir." The hatch clapped shut.

At the same hour the following evening, another cab rolled up next to the wrought iron fence that enclosed the center of the square. It was raining moderately hard, and the cobbles sparkled with lamplight and the splashing drops.

"Night the second," observed Symonds. "What does this evening have in store for us?"

"I wonder." Stevenson peered across at Number 43. The front rooms on both the ground and first floors were brightly lit, and at the upper of the two, a large shadow passed occasionally across the drawn curtains. "It looks as though he may be in his room. He may be preparing to go out."

"Perhaps. We shall see."

"Cigarette?"

"No, thank you."

Stevenson lit one for himself and tossed the match out into the rain.

"Perhaps you haven't noticed that I no longer smoke," said Symonds, looking at his friend with amusement.

"No."

"It is one vice that I have managed to curtail."

"I suppose congratulations are in order."

"I would content myself," Symonds responded with a chuckle, "with your not continuing to tempt me."

"I shall set politeness aside, then, in favor of supporting virtue."

"I should be most grateful. Whisky?" Symonds held up a small silver flask.

"Of course." Stevenson took the container and, untwisting the cap, threw back a generous swallow. The harsh liquid drew a pillar of warmth down through the core of him. "Thank you. Perhaps we should offer some to the coachman. It's a wretched night."

"I trust he has a supply," replied Symonds, taking a long draught himself. "He'd be mad not to."

"Fanny hounds me incessantly to give up tobacco, you know. I don't believe I am able."

"Nor did I think I was. I believe my lungs do feel very much better, though. Save when I am in this smoking chimney of a town."

"Hardly a smoking chimney tonight," observed Stevenson. He waved at the steady precipitation.

"No, not tonight. How is Fanny, then?"

"Fine. Fanny is fine. Happy to be living in a sizeable villa with a staff of three. And a butler, now that my father has died."

"I am sorry, Louis."

"No. His time had come."

Symonds opened his mouth to speak, but remained silent.

"Fanny has no notion what I'm doing here," Stevenson offered after a moment. "I hesitate to think what she would make of all this."

"Understandably."

"Perhaps she would join us. With her pistols." He looked at his companion and laughed.

"Your wife has pistols?"

"Of course she does. She lived in California. There," he said, pointing towards the house, "the bedroom light has gone out."

They had waited eagerly for half an hour more and were just beginning to think the evening would again be inconsequential when a covered black landau pulled up in front of the house. Two oversized carriage lanterns flanked the driver's seat, casting their glow on the withers of two immense chestnut geldings.

"It's his," whispered Symonds. "I've seen it at the Athenaeum." He tapped on the hatch, which sprung open quickly in response. "Steady up there. We'll be following this one. Keep your distance, though."

"I remember, sir."

Two minutes passed and the door to Number 43 opened. A tall and burly figure stood there for a moment, silhouetted against the brightly lit hall. A male servant appeared to offer him an umbrella, but he waved it away and stepped out into the rain in his cape and top hat.

"Our man," whispered Symonds.

They could see the carriage tilt as their subject climbed in; then, with a crack of the coachman's whip, the impressive pair of horses set off at a trot. Their cabman timed it nicely, waiting until the landau was just at the out of the square before he prodded his horse into action. In a matter of fifteen seconds they, too, were into Wigmore Street, heading east at a healthy clip.

"Well, he's not going to Mayfair, in any case," observed Symonds.

"Nor to Buckingham Palace."

"Not if he's looking for streetwalkers. Unless Her Majesty has brought in a new flock of ladies-in-waiting."

They rattled along the thoroughfare, their carriage splashing through the occasional pool of rainwater. Unexpectedly, the landau turned hard right into Cavendish Square, slowed, and came to a halt in front of a brightly lit house. The coachman leapt from his seat and ran up the front steps, knocking loudly at the door. It was opened by a man in livery who let the fellow into the hallway. In a moment, the door reopened and the driver returned to the carriage followed by another gentleman, also dressed in evening clothes.

"What do you make of it?" asked Symonds, looking across at his companion.

"We shall have to see."

The landau dropped down to Oxford Street, where it turned left towards the East End.

Stevenson looked at Symonds and nodded. "A promising point of the compass?"

"It's premature to say."

"Perhaps they're going to the theatre."

"The theatre?"

"The Lyceum. Mansfield is back onstage."

Symonds eyed his companion gravely. "You really must free yourself of that worry, Louis. Besides, they'd be hopelessly late. Even for the second act."

"Point taken."

At Tottenham Court Road, the big carriage veered north, then paused at the head of Bayley Street. It waited for a huge public coach to clear the intersection, then crossed on to Bedford Square, where it came to a halt in front of a stately house on the northern range. Even with the rain drumming on the roof of the cab, Stevenson could hear the strains of a small orchestra coming from within. Through the tall windows, he spied elegantly dressed men and women moving gracefully to the music. As the two gentlemen descended from the carriage, the door of the house swung open to admit them, and the music welled out in concert with the bright chatter of a jovial gathering.

"'Golden Beauty,'" declared Symonds.

"What?"

"The waltz. All the rage."

"Of course."

The door closed, and the landau proceeded around to the east side of the square, where it took its place in a long queue of waiting conveyances.

It was close to one o'clock when the black carriage came back around to the house and picked up its two passengers. At the bottom of Bloomsbury Street, it turned west and returned directly to Cavendish Square, where the second gentleman descended. The door of his house had no sooner opened than the carriage lurched away, heading straight back to Portman Square. Stevenson and Symonds waited vigilantly until the first-floor window had remained dark for a half-hour. With a great sigh, Symonds instructed the cabman to drive back to the Savile Club.

"Well!" said Stevenson. "Next time, we shall have to bring more cigarettes. And whisky."

Symonds laughed. "At least the rain seems to have abated. I am positively exhausted."

They clopped along through the largely empty streets. In Grosvenor Square, they passed two policemen supporting a well-dressed fellow as he stumbled down the pavement. The man bent over to retch, and the constable to his left jumped back to avoid the fouling of his rain cape and trousers.

"I assume *he* had a sufficiency of whisky," quipped Stevenson, taken of a sudden with myriad Edinburgh memories.

"You know, Louis," said Symonds, as they continued on. "I feel I should say something."

"About?"

"Last night. About my decrying the headmaster's ways with the boys of Harrow—and at the same time continuing to indulge in the favors of my sweet telegraph lad."

"It's of no consequence," said Stevenson, feeling far too tired to go into a subject that could be touchy enough to negotiate at the height of his powers.

"Well, it is of consequence. It, too, smacks of hypocrisy. And of exploiting those less fortunate than we."

"It is well to be thoughtful," offered Stevenson, "and, when it is called for, contrite. But none of us always walk the high road."

"Have you used prostitutes, Stevenson?"

The question shocked the writer, less for its directness than for the fact that the answer ought to have been obvious. Had Stevenson been obliged to name a friend who had never resorted to a whore—either as an adolescent or as a grown man—he would have been hard pressed. Perhaps Colvin. But then, what must the man have done for all these years as he waited for his Fanny to be free to wed?

"I have."

"And since you were married?"

"No. Although there have been times of temptation."

"You are fortunate, friend," said Symonds, taking the rare liberty of tapping his companion on the knee. "If I could be married to a person I loved in every way a man can love…if I could live with that person every day of my life…" He shook his head and rode on in silence.

"I would wish that for you," said Stevenson, quietly.

As the cab rattled on through the drizzle, it abruptly occurred to Stevenson that the fellow they were stalking might once have expressed a sentiment very similar to John's. Were his bestial deeds, perhaps, nothing more or less than the cankered fruits of a stymied nature? The depredations of another Hyde, born of another Jekyll's inhibitions? Stevenson felt more than reluctant to afford any sympathy whatsoever to such a blackguard. But what lesson, he wondered, lay in the fact of that reluctance?

~18

Instantly the spirit of hell awoke in me. With a transport of glee, I mauled the unresisting body, tasting delight from every blow; and it was not till weariness had begun to succeed, that I was suddenly, in the top fit of my delirium, struck through the heart by a cold thrill of terror. A mist dispersed; I saw my life to be forfeit; and fled from the scene of these excesses, at once glorying and trembling, my lust of evil gratified and stimulated, my love of life screwed to the topmost peg.

—DR. HENRY JEKYLL

"There is a letter for you, Mr. Stevenson," called the young man from the porter's lodge. "Shall I fetch it?"

"Please do."

Stevenson had just returned to the Savile from a long-overdue luncheon with Henley. His old friend and literary advocate, ever in quest of a quick fortune, had proposed yet another dramatic collaboration. Stevenson had resolutely declined, citing the miserable record of their collaborations to date.

"Thank you," said the writer, glancing quickly at the envelope. It had been posted from Bournemouth and was inscribed with a most familiar hand. He looked up. "I see Dobbs is away again."

"Yes, sir."

"Do you have any notion as to why?"

"I'm afraid his wife has not been well."

"Really? Do you know any particulars?"

"I believe it's cancer, sir. Quite grave, I've heard."

"My goodness," sighed Stevenson. "You would never know it to speak with him."

"Dobbs is a cheerful sort, sir. Never one to complain."

He returned to his room, tossing his things onto the bed and sinking into the chair by the window. He must speak with Dobbs as soon as he had the opportunity. The man deserved a word of kindness and sympathy, perhaps a modest offer of help. With a shake of the head, he ripped open the envelope he had brought from downstairs and pulled out Fanny's letter.

Dear Louis,

I have delayed writing until now so as to spit as little venom onto the paper as I can manage. I'm glad I waited, because I am angry and hurt enough now. If I had sat down any earlier to write, you can be sure that the stationery would have burst into flames from the heat of my pen.

What have I done to deserve so little of your trust? I have been asking myself that question over and over again, and I can honestly come up with no satisfactory answer. If there is anything you feel you need to tell me—if I have any traits or if I have done things that you think are bothersome or insufferable, any grievance or disappointments at all—you have to tell me. I've barely been able to sleep, despite drinking an alarming quantity of laudanum. I seem to be constantly in the kitchen, pestering Valentine for something to take my mind off missing you and not knowing why you've run off the way you have. Fortunately, she has been very sweet, as sweet as I can ever remember. But I've surely packed on several pounds. When you see me, you may not even recognize your dear wife.

Oh, Louis. I hope and pray I am still your Dear Wife, your 'Sweet Pig.' You know how foolish and ignorant those people are who think you and your story had anything to do with these awful murders. If they keep hounding you, just tell me, and I'll come straight up and treat them like the banditos they are.

There. I've gotten it off my chest and I feel so much better. As I'm sure you can feel, this paper is now quite cool to the touch. I do hope to hear more from you soon, to know what you have been doing and who you've been seeing. Most of all to know when you will be coming back to our dear Skerryvore. We won't have many more days here, you know.

Cruikshank is a disaster! I think we'll have to let him go. Valentine found him yesterday going through her things in her room. Can you imagine? I thought he had been a pretty good valet to your father, but life in the south has turned him into a lazy Lothario. I'm quite prepared to live without the services of a butler as long as I have the services of my dear husband, the esteemed author and bony master of my boudoir.

I remain, troubled but patient and so desiring news from you, your dear wife,

Fanny

Stevenson leaned back in his chair, relieved and smiling to himself. How concisely and profoundly Fanny managed to work upon his conscience. Of course she had not deserved the treatment he had accorded her, rushing off to London with hardly a fare-thee-well and following up with nothing more than the briefest of telegrams telling her not to worry. Fortunately, she closed her note in a way that suggested he could readily return to her good graces—provided he sent her some kind of honest communiqué rather soon. And, he supposed, if he were also prepared to cope with a few, perhaps repeated, displays of petulance once he returned to Skerryvore.

He sat down at his desk and penned a letter that sketched in bare outline what he had been up to, strategically allowing her to believe that the London police were playing a significant role as well. As a final sop, he told her that her estimate of Symonds's amorous character had turned out to be far more accurate than his own—but that she had absolutely no reason to worry that her bag-o'-bones lover would ever turn from her transcendent embodiment of female perfection to the questionable enticements of Ganymede. The sum of it, he thought, might keep her safely in Bournemouth and reasonably content.

He was to meet with Symonds again that evening for their eighth consecutive night of surveillance. The regimen was truthfully proving to be exhausting, but Stevenson had throughout been reminded of how delightful and knowledgeable a conversationalist was Symonds. Despite the profound differences in their personal worlds, a great ease had developed between the two of them, far more marked than anything he could remember when they were fellow invalids in Davos. As a result, they seemed comfortable sitting for hours in each other's company without having to fill the cab with idle chatter. At the same time, when they spoke, their conversations were, by turns, searching, profound, and hilarious. There were nights when Stevenson worried that eruptions of laughter from their sequestered cab would betray their presence and spoil the game entirely.

It was therefore almost with more regret than relief that he received word from Symonds that their suspect was leaving London that day by the noon train to Dover and would be away across the channel for a full fortnight. Stevenson replied, saying that he was as determined as ever to complete their work together and that he would be back in London on the 28th. In the mean time, he said, he would return to Bournemouth to see about salvaging his marriage. If Symonds were perchance to hear that he had been shot dead by a .38-calibre handgun—from extremely close range—he should make sure to testify in court on Fanny's behalf, given she had been sorely provoked and was more than justified in doing in her prodigal husband.

Having dispatched word to his old friend, Stevenson resolved to catch a train the next morning. He dined unfashionably early at the Savile and spent a pleasant evening at the Savoy Opera, setting aside his recent aversion for theater in order to take in Gilbert and Sullivan's latest, *Yeomen of the Guard*. While Jessie Bond was superb in the female lead, Stevenson was frankly disappointed at the operetta's lack of trenchant topical satire, and quite unprepared for the seriousness of the ending. The plot, however, focused on a risky intrigue at the Tower of London—which, under the circumstances, struck him as engagingly coincidental.

He arose before dawn to make the 8:54 at Waterloo. He took a light breakfast at the club almost as early as the dining room opened, then hastened back upstairs. As he descended the carpeted stairway to the entrance hall, he spied Dobbs, once again, standing by the door.

"Good morning, Dobbs," he called as he walked across the broad, diamond-tiled floor.

"Good morning, Mr. Stevenson," offered the porter with a bright smile. "Shall I…summon a cab?"

"Please do," the writer replied through a chuckle. "I see you have chosen your words carefully this morning."

"Live and learn, sir. May I take your bag?"

"Please." Stevenson handed him the well-worn Gladstone.

The porter was turning to go when Stevenson spoke again. "By the way, Dobbs."

"Sir?" The man stood there, bag in hand, an open and kindly expression on his face.

"I am told your wife has not been well."

Dobbs glanced quickly towards the door of the porter's lodge, a shade of annoyance flitting across his face.

"Well, sir—"

"You needn't be guarded, Dobbs. Trust in my sincere interest."

The man's eyes widened and he shook his head ever so slightly.

"No, sir. Of course, sir. Thank you for asking."

"I...I am led to believe it may be quite serious."

"Cancer, sir. Of the womb, is what they've seen, anyhow."

"I am so sorry, Dobbs."

"Thank you again, sir." The man's eyes were misting.

"If there is anything I can do to help, I should very much like to."

"You are very kind, sir. Extremely. There is really nothing to be done."

"Oh my!"

Dobbs bobbed his head grimly.

"For your children, then?"

"Oh, sir. They're all long out of the house. Married. With young 'uns of their own."

"So you have a large family, then?"

"I do."

"Good. You're blessed in that."

"I am, sir." The man sniffed twice and adjusted his grip on the bag.

"Well," said Stevenson, thinking it best to leave the conversation there. "I shall be back in a fortnight. I shall look forward to seeing you then."

"Thank you, sir. It's not for me to say, but..." He looked down awkwardly. "You're a kind soul, sir."

As he rode to Waterloo Station, it struck Stevenson how remarkable it was that a man like Dobbs should have his life crumbling around him and still find it in himself to show a cheerful face to the public eye. It was clear that a sense of Duty might hold as powerful a sway over the working classes as respectability held over the more privileged. Was the one a more noble deity, he wondered, than the other? More internal? Substantial? Could duty possibly turn a man against himself—or in the case of some, against humanity at large—in anything like as damaging a way as a consummate regard for appearances? He doubted it. To carry on bravely in the face of trial, burdening no one else with one's anguish, was no hypocrisy in Stevenson's estimation. In this instance, however, it did wall others off from the truth—and denied them the opportunity at the very least to express their sympathy and, perhaps, to help. He deeply wished the man had suggested something he might do.

By September 30th, Stevenson had been back in the capital for two nights, both of them spent in Symonds's company, once again on the watch in Portman Square. On neither occasion had their subject stirred from his house, and they spent the time much as they had done earlier. Symonds expressed delight that Stevenson seemed to have gotten his marriage back on a proper footing, and only once did Stevenson fail to recall that his companion no longer used tobacco.

The evening of the 30th was unseasonably warm and pleasant, but their wait was a long one. Twice, the vigilant pair heard a snore erupt from the coachman above. The waxing moon had long since dropped below the rooftops to the west of the square when a light winked on in the bedroom of Number 43. Within minutes it was extinguished, and shortly afterward the black landau wheeled up in front of the house, its big team snorting and jostling as it waited in the traces. Stevenson cringed as their own horse caught the equine mood and whinnied loudly. The beast had fortunately settled itself by the time the door of the house swung open and the big man bounced down the steps and up into the carriage. With a tap of the coachman's whip, his team burst into motion and clattered down Orchard Street.

The hansom driver waited the requisite moment, then wheeled his horse around in pursuit. They reached Oxford Street in a trice and followed the landau east at a distance of a hundred yards or so. Stevenson checked his watch in the light of the passing streetlamps. It was just past midnight.

They passed at a brisk trot down to High Holbourn and then over the Viaduct. Stevenson's father had often touted the impressive span, close to twenty-years-old now, as a perfect example of engineering's key role in the Triumph of Civilization. Yet while it may have been a cosmetic and olfactory success, thought Stevenson as they raced over the bridge, down beneath the pavement, rank floods of offal still ran their course to the Thames, unseen but hardly eliminated.

As their carriage hastened through Cheapside and Cornhill, Symonds and Stevenson peered at each other now and again with a mixture of excitement and dread. At each measure of eastward progress, it became increasingly clear where the landau was headed—and, given the hour, what its passenger's evening plans would likely entail.

As they left the precincts of the old city, under the gatehouse Geoffrey Chaucer had once called home, Stevenson registered the almost instantaneous degradation of the surroundings. The tall, well-kept stone buildings of Leadenhall gave rapid way to slouching dens of brick, as though the proud constructions of the London town fathers were somehow sinking back into the mire of an ancient Thames-side marsh. The streetlamps were spaced parsimoniously now in this neighborhood of struggling immigrants and down-going Britons, and they burned with a listless flicker, as though they knew too well the hopeless task they faced in checking the encroaching darkness. Here and there, the garish lights of a gin palace blazed like beacons on a dark headland. Despite the lateness of the hour, crowds of shabbily dressed men still raised a glass or roared a song, wooing or winking at this or that equally convivial and ragged woman. Stevenson caught glimpses of low and parted bodices the likes of which had not been seen in western portions of the city since the days of King George. Here and there a skirt, too, was adjusted salaciously, and a raised knee or a smooth thigh invited a purchase as clearly as any gilded shopfront sign. *This was the home of Henry Jekyll's favourite,* Stevenson recited to himself, *like a district of some city in a nightmare.*

The landau's lanterns converged ahead as the carriage turned south towards the river. As their hansom followed around the corner, the two saw with shock that the lane before them lay completely empty. Unless the landau had for some reason broken into a gallop, it could never have covered so quickly the full length of the block. Symonds tapped on the hatch and softly instructed the driver to slow to a walk, but keep going down to the next thoroughfare. As they crossed the head of a tenebrous cul-de-sac on the left side of the lane, a quick glance revealed the landau turning around at the far end.

"That is where he'll wait," whispered Symonds, "or at least take to his feet."

"It's a perfect bolt hole," agreed Stevenson.

"Left ahead," hissed Symonds up to the cabman. "Then pull to the side. Briskly now."

The hansom rounded onto Commercial Road, lurching to a halt just east of the corner.

"I'll jump down," said Symonds. "Wait here, but be ready."

As his companion exited, Stevenson noted that his heart was racing uncomfortably. He took a deep breath, then another, and gripped his heavy stick tightly in both hands. He and Symonds had decided, their first night on vigil, that their job was not to intervene in their man's deeds, but rather to trail him and collect whatever incriminating evidence they could. Stevenson had first proposed that, if they could bring a number of henchmen with them, they might overpower the fellow in the act and perhaps even save his intended quarry; but as sad as Symonds was to admit it, he was reluctant to bring anyone beyond Stevenson into a matter with such potential for compromise. Might they arm themselves, then, such that they could still save a wretched life? Again, Symonds regretted to observe that, were the man apprehended before completing his intended assault, a compelling case could not easily be made against him. And as for their joint capacity, in any case, to subdue him with anything less than lethal force—outright murder not being in their brief—the man's formidable stature and military background left them little hope of success. It was unfortunate, thought Stevenson, that Fanny had not brought her revolvers from California. Their weight in his pockets would have been reassuring.

"Quick," cried Symonds as he ran back around the corner. "He's walking up to Whitechapel Road. You have your stick?"

"I do." Stevenson slapped its heavy head into his gloved palm.

"Driver, wait here. I don't know how long we shall be."

"Yes, sir."

Once Stevenson was down from the carriage, Symonds grabbed his elbow and pulled him strongly towards the corner.

"Quickly. We'll lose him."

As they reentered what turned out to be Union Street, they could just make out a single pedestrian at the far end, barely visible against the glow of a streetlamp across the road at the top of the passage.

"That will be him."

"His coachman may see us," warned Stevenson as they approached the cul-de-sac.

"Shhh!" hissed Symonds, hurrying on. "I can't imagine he's looking out," he added once the side street was behind them. "And there are doubtless enough of our sort out and about. Gentleman anglers."

Their man had turned west on Whitechapel Road, and they halted cautiously at the corner to see how far he had gone on. There he was, crossing the high road towards one of the gin palaces. Stevenson looked back behind them, relieved to see that no one had emerged from the alley where the landau lay waiting.

"We should stay on this side," he whispered. "Walk slowly. If we're seen, we might always be drunkards."

Their man neared a modest crowd that milled outside the drinking place, walking in the road just off the pavement. He held his head at a strange angle—concealing his face, no doubt. The look, though, was precisely that of a mannered villain skulking across a stage. Stevenson again wondered fleetingly if he would ever be able to satisfy himself on that score. It seemed doubtful.

The man continued on past the carousers; then, as he crossed to the other side of a tributary alley, past the pond of light cast by the establishment's big gas lanterns, he stopped, adjusted his cloak, and leaned against the wall of the corner building. A few of the drunken crowd seemed to notice him pausing there. One of them extended an arm in his direction, spilling his drink in the process. A loud "Bugger it!" echoed across the road. A woman raised her voice in what must have been a quip or insult, for a chorus of laughter followed.

Symonds and Stevenson ducked quickly into an opportune recess in the wall to their left. As Stevenson touched the damp brick, he was happy to be wearing gloves. If the vector of consumption could be found thriving on any physical surface, this would be it.

"I suspect he's looking to draw someone out," Stevenson whispered, stepping back from the dark and weeping brick.

"So it would appear."

They could make out that their man was tapping the butt of his stick on the cobbles beside him, although the racket from the drinking place masked the sound. Minutes passed and, at one point, he appeared to check his watch. A man and a woman broke off from the group of drinkers, apparently engaged in an argument of some sort. Finally, with a flourish of what looked like impatience, their mark turned and continued west. He paused at the bottom of Brick Lane, walking several paces up the dark street, then wheeled about and stepped quickly into Whitechapel Road, making to cross.

"Whoa!" came the cry of a cabman, racing in his vehicle up from the High Street.

Their man leaped back, just out of the way of the trotting horse.

"Watch out there!" he yelled, waving his stick. "You miserable cunt!" He watched the cab speed away, then lowered his cane and crossed the broad avenue, making his way down the black defile of the nearest cross street towards Commercial Road.

His two stalkers followed at a safe distance, straining their eyes so as not to lose him.

"He's doubling back towards the carriage," whispered Symonds. "Is this all?"

"We shall see."

They followed along on the north side of Commercial Road, lit only every hundred paces or so by an anemic gaslight. In shops and houses alike, on either side of the avenue, every ground floor was dark, and only in the rare first story was any light to be seen, guttering behind a filthy window or curtain. They passed by a firehouse, its doors firmly closed and its windows shuttered tight. Farther along, the air was suddenly heavy with the scent of yeast. The local brewery was making ale well past midnight, bolstering its stock for another night's carouse. Looking up past the low roofs, Stevenson noticed that a bank of clouds had rolled in from the west, obscuring the better part of the sky. Among the stars still visible he recognized a familiar grouping, and smirked at the aptness of Orion's hanging there above their two unfolding hunts.

Some distance ahead, their man stepped out into the road. He was evidently crossing to approach two women who stood there on the very fringes of a pool of gaslight. Stevenson and Symonds paused in the shadows as he strolled coolly up to them. The women looked at each other, then parted their shawls as though to display their wares. The man's stick tapped twice on the pavement, and he bent slightly towards them. One of the women laughed and shook her head. He turned to the other, who put her arm around her mate and shook her head as well. She pointed down the street towards a lighted door and window on the north side. The man tipped his brim and walked slowly off in that direction. At one point he must have encountered a cat, for he swung his leg with energy and a small, dark form darted away with a yowl.

Stevenson and Symonds waited and watched until he had fully crossed. The big fellow reached the door and stopped. He stood for a moment in the soft wash of emerging light, then stepped inside, ducking his head to clear what was evidently a low portal. His pursuers moved a ways in his direction, only to be spotted by the two women standing under the light.

"Oy, gents," called the taller of the two. "Care for a tumble?"

Again, Stevenson's heart raced at the threat of discovery. He looked at Symonds, who stood there stock-still. The women were crossing the street towards them.

"Watch the door," barked Stevenson. "I'll deal with them."

"As you've rather more experience with their sort," whispered Symonds. He grinned and stepped back closer to the wall.

"Now," said the taller woman, sidling up to Stevenson. "What brings you fine gents 'ere? As if I didn't know." She turned to her companion with a lewd smirk.

Stevenson held out a shilling coin.

"Now that won't buy ya much," cried the shorter one, placing her hands on her hips.

"Will you tell me what that man just said to you?"

"That one?" asked the whore, pointing to the door.

Stevenson nodded.

"Said 'e'd like to take 'is pleasure wiv one of us."

"But only one, 'e said," cackled the other. "Said the two of us myde 'im nervous."

"And you told him...?"

"That we comes as a pair tonight, or we doesn't come at all."

"I see," said Stevenson, smiling despite himself at the *double entendre*.

"Can't be too careful these days," said the taller one. "Not wiv Saucy Jack about."

"You are wise ladies."

"So we sends 'im up there." The shorter one pointed to the door that Symonds was eyeing. "Said we was sarten Molly or Lizzy there would oblige 'im. As Molly an' Lizzy's sommat less partickalar than us." She grinned again at her taller companion. "Now you two gents," she said, swinging her ample hips from side to side. "We'd be 'appy enough to do for you. All big an' happy family like. No? Don't fancy the goods?" She reached into her bodice and pulled out a breast. Stevenson might have preferred it to be a tired and floppy one; it was anything but. "Like what you see?"

"Here," said Stevenson, pulling another shilling from his pocket. "We're detectives following this man."

A look of concern swept over the woman's face.

"No need to worry. Inspector Thomson and I love you ladies. In fact, if you're about later, perhaps we'll take you up on your kind offer. For now, though, there's one of these for each of you." He pressed the coin into her hand.

"Well," said the woman, eyeing him skeptically.

"Shhh!" hissed Symonds, extending a cautionary hand in their direction. "He's coming out."

The four of them froze, looking up towards the door of the tiny beer shop. Their man was emerging, a small woman on his arm. As he placed his hat back on his head, she looked up at him gaily.

"That'll be Lizzy," whispered the tall one, pressing up against Stevenson. She was wearing a cheap scent and smelled heavily of gin. "Told you she'd oblige."

Stevenson silenced them as the couple crossed over Commercial Road and approached the black gulf of a street corner thirty yards down the far side.

"Thank you," he whispered, as the couple disappeared into the darkness.

"Why are we whispering, again?" asked the taller women.

"They're detectives," answered the other. "But 'e says they likes to fuck." She peered up at Stevenson with a toothy wink.

"We do, don't we, Thomson?"

"Like rabbits," replied Symonds.

Leaving the women behind, they crossed the road diagonally, making for the next street.

"Watch the tram tracks," warned Symonds. "They'll be slick."

My God, our boots are noisy, thought Stevenson as they entered what he could just see was Berner Street. He suddenly understood the principle of footpads.

Ahead of them they could barely make out two figures, one of them tall, the other short, walking slowly down the narrow passage. They weaved from side to side, curiously like doting lovers in a lonely country lane. Now and again the sound of laughter drifted back to the stalkers.

"We can't be seen, can we?" whispered Stevenson. He turned his head to be sure they were not silhouetted by anything on the road they were leaving.

"Shhh!" Symonds shook his head.

Close to the end of the street, the couple paused, then disappeared into an opening on the right.

Stealthily, on their toes, Stevenson and Symonds approached the black aperture. It was something like a large, low gateway just to the side of a darkened house. They could tell, almost as much by sound as by sight, that it opened into a large interior court, most likely some sort of carter's yard.

Stevenson felt Symonds's hand on his arm as he moved his head close. "Shoes!" he whispered.

Both of them bent to remove their footwear, at one point stumbling into each other as they tried to keep their balance. Fortunately, neither uttered a sound. Setting their boots against the wall, they inched further through the dark passage. They could indeed see that they were entering a court of some description. The solid black above them yielded, several feet further on, to the slightest hint of dark, clouded sky. From off to the left, it seemed—for it was difficult to tell how sound might bounce around in this place—there came a high giggle, the sound of a woman being touched.

"You like that?" asked a low voice.

"Mmmm. I do," came the answer.

Stevenson clutched his stick more tightly and listened, very much aware of Symonds craning forward in the gloom just to his side.

"Mmmm," came the male voice from out of the shadows, "if you are not just what I require. Here. Let me just slip around behind you."

"Oooh. Like a doggy, then?"

"Woof!"

There was a soft pop of fabric being yanked quickly taut and the beginnings of a woman's cry. It yielded hideously to an unvoiced rush of air and a low gurgle.

"Oooh," came the male voice, grimly low and soothing. "And again?"

Another soft sound followed, impossible to interpret, and then the distinct suggestion of something heavy slumping to the ground.

Stevenson's straining eyes could make nothing out. He turned his head, as though to screw his hearing to the next notch, but he could detect no sound save the rush of blood in his own temples. He could feel that the hand holding his stick was shaking, and he realized that the rest of him was shaking as well. He felt Symonds's grip on his arm, surely to steady him, but its effect was nil. He felt himself crouching like an ape, and the muscles of his face tightened into a scowl. He felt fear, yes, but something else too that drew his hands into cramped knots. Was he about to vomit? Or explode with rage? Why ever had they decided not to intervene?

A sudden glint of light gave dim shape to the court. The man must have had a dark lantern, and he was opening the aperture ever so slightly. Stevenson inched forward, looking to his left. Up against a wall, in the slight glow of the lantern, he could just make out what looked like the woman's outstretched body. Looming over it, with his back turned, was her assailant.

"Now, let's see," came the low voice once again. "Where is it that we begin?"

On the instant and without a thought, Stevenson burst in his stocking feet out into the courtyard, screaming like a Highland chieftain. "We've got you, you murderous bastard!"

"Louis!" shouted Symonds behind him, "for God's sake!"

Springing up, the man kicked the lantern to the side, casting them instantly back into darkness. Stevenson raised a hand to his brow, as though it might sharpen his vision. He heard the harsh scuff of leather soles in front of him, and then he was cast onto his back as the juggernaut slammed into him and hurtled past. There was a muffled thud behind him and a deep moan, then the sound of boots running out through the low portal and into the street beyond.

For a moment, Stevenson lay there dazed. His left shoulder throbbed mightily, and he reached up to feel that his coat had been swept clear back off of it. He ran his fingers along his clavicle, half expecting to feel a ragged break there under his shirt, but the bone seemed sound. He sat up and realized, confusedly, that he was hatless.

"My God!" came a voice from behind, then what must have been the sound of Symond's stick scraping on the cobbles. "Stevenson. Are you there?"

"Barely," replied Stevenson. "And you?"

"I believe I'm fine. I'm frightened out of my wits."

"Do you have a light?"

"You're the smoker," answered Symonds. "My God. What do we do?"

By now Stevenson was standing. He reached into his coat pocket and extracted a box of lights. He struck one and turned slightly to see his stick lying there, three feet off to the side. His hat lay just behind where he had fallen. Symonds, hatless too, stood between him and the gateway in an unsteady crouch.

"Over there," he said, pointing to his left.

Stevenson turned, extending the light in that direction. He had just registered again the dark form lying there when the match burned down to the bottom.

"Damn!"

He struck another lucifer and padded across towards the rough brick wall. Lying there on her back was the obliging whore. She'd had a name. What was it? He bent closer. Her eyes were open but they were rolled back into her head, the whites glinting like boiled eggs. Her chin was raised, and, in the shadow of her shawl, two wide, dark lines stretched across the whole span of her throat. Just before he waved out the match, he spied as well a shimmering puddle of black flowing out from her neck.

"Light another," barked Symonds. "His lantern's over here. There," he said, handing the thing to Stevenson once they'd lit it. "Is she dead?"

Stevenson turned the beam on the woman in mute confirmation. She looked to be close to forty, somewhat younger than Fanny but clearly worn by hard years. Her lips were full and painted, but her brow was high and surprisingly refined. One hand was cast back over her head, but the other lay open by her side, holding a wet mass of something. Stevenson bent to look more closely. Grapes.

"We must hurry," whispered Symonds from behind him. "Before someone comes."

"We must check for evidence."

"We have the lantern."

"Is there anything else?" Stevenson stood and swept the narrow beam from side to side.

"There!" exclaimed Symonds. He pointed just to the right of the body.

Stevenson redirected the light and saw a long and slender shape gleaming moistly in the beam. He stooped to pick it up. A knife—not of a tradesman's or a hunter's sort. A surgeon's? He stood, and once again swept the light widely.

"We should go," said Symonds.

Stevenson nodded, padding back to his stick and hat and shining the lantern to help his friend.

"What on earth came over you?" Symonds whispered harshly as they found their boots in the passageway and stooped to put them on.

"I don't know. Honestly."

"I thought you'd gone mad. Thank God we escaped with our lives."

"Aye," replied Stevenson. "But so did he."

They made their way to the top of the street just as a single fellow driving a rough cart rattled around the corner. Hurrying westward, hoping that their hansom still waited for them, they left the carter to find his own dark way down to the bottom of Berner Street.

19

O my poor old Harry Jekyll, if ever I read Satan's signature upon a face, it is on that of your new friend.

—GABRIEL JOHN UTTERSON

THE TIMES

MONDAY, 1 OCTOBER 1888

Two more murders must now be added to the black list of similar crimes of which the East-end of London has very lately been the scene. The circumstances of both of them bear a close resemblance to those of the former atrocities. The victim in both has been a woman. In neither can robbery have been the motive, nor can the deed be set down as the outcome of an ordinary street brawl. Both have unquestionably been murders deliberately planned, and carried out by the hand of some one who has been no novice to the work. It was early yesterday morning that the bodies of the two women were discovered, at places within a quarter of an hour's walk of one another, and at intervals of somewhat less than an hour. The first body was found lying in a yard in Berner-street, a low thoroughfare running out of the Commercial-road. The discovery was made about 1 o'clock in the early morning by a carter, who was entering the yard to put up his cart. The body was that of a woman with a deep gash on the throat, running almost from ear to ear. She was quite dead, but the corpse was still warm, and in the opinion of the medical experts, who were promptly summoned to the place, the deed of blood must have been done not many minutes before. The probability seems to be that the murderer was interrupted by the arrival of the carter, and that he made his escape unobserved, under the shelter of the darkness, which was almost total at the spot. The body has been identified as that of ELIZABETH STRIDE, a widow according to one account, according to another a woman living apart from her husband, and by all accounts belonging to the "unfortunate" class. Her movements have been traced up to a certain point. She left her house in Dean-street, Spitalfields, between 6 and 7 o'clock on Saturday evening, saying that she was not going to meet any one in particular. From that hour there is nothing certainly known about her up to the time at which her body was found, lifeless indeed, but not otherwise mutilated than by the gash in the throat, which had severed the jugular vein and must have caused instantaneous death.

Not so the corpse of the second victim. In this case the purpose of the murderer had been fulfilled, and a mutilation inflicted of the same nature as that upon the body of ANNIE CHAPMAN. It was in the south-western corner of Mitre-square, in Aldgate, that the second body was found. It was again the body of a woman, and again had death resulted from a deep wound across the throat. But in this instance, the face had also been so slashed as to render it hard for the remains to be identified, and the abdomen had been ripped up, and a portion of the intestines had been dragged out and left lying about the neck.

Stevenson's gorge began to rise as soon as he saw the headline: a second new murder overnight in the East End!

It was the detail regarding the intestines lying on the Chapman woman's throat—like a garland of bloody sausages, as his brownies rendered the detail to his mind's eye—that sent him dashing from his wing chair in the morning room. He barely reached the cloakroom, shouldering an elderly member out of the way as he dove into the water closet and vomited his breakfast into the porcelain bowl. "For the love of God!" he gasped as he left the stall and staggered over to the washstand to scoop cold water up onto his face.

He made a supreme effort to gather himself, then walked out into the hallway. Dobbs stood there waiting for him, a look of profound concern on his face. The young man from the desk in the porter's lodge was there by his side.

"Mr. Stevenson," said Dobbs, stepping forward. "We were told you'd taken ill."

"I'm fine," answered the writer. "Just a little indigestion, I think. Thank you, Dobbs. I shall be just fine."

The man stood there motionless, fidgeting with his hands.

"Truly. I shall."

"Well, sir. If you say so."

"I do. Many thanks for your solicitude. I am fine."

Back in his room, Stevenson brushed his teeth to scour the vile taste from his mouth. He took a moment to collect himself, then looked at his watch. A quarter past nine. He had arranged to meet Symonds at noon to discuss their obligations and options. He dearly wished it could be sooner.

As their hansom clattered once again through Aldgate, barely twelve hours after their last passage, Stevenson shuddered despite the unseasonable warmth of the day. The weather was brilliant: bright sun with a few puffy clouds sailing down the Thames on a gentle westerly. Still, he fought back a chill as they rolled closer to the theater of last night's butchery. Symonds noted his companion's unease and looked across at him sympathetically, his own lips a taut line.

Their cabman bellowed from above, and they looked forward to see a tiny street urchin scuttling out of their way. The lad gestured obscenely as they rumbled past.

"They learn young here," joked Symonds.

"And hide little."

They were surprised to find that their destination sat like a flatiron right in the angle of Commercial and Whitechapel Roads. Last night, in hot pursuit of their quarry, they had somehow managed to ride right along the north wall of the precinct's police station, never noticing its commanding presence. More shocking, perhaps, was the realization that the killer himself had strolled boldly down Church Street just a few steps to the east. Given his obvious familiarity with the area, he must have known he was giving a narrow miss to a warren of law enforcers. It was remarkable hubris.

The cab bore right onto Commercial Road and pulled up in front of an impressive arched entrance, disgorging its two well-dressed passengers into a modest throng of the far less well attired. Just beyond the station door, an organ grinder cranked away on his instrument. A delicate monkey, decked out in a garish vest and cap, perched on the man's shoulder, eyeing the passersby with rapt curiosity. Stevenson and Symonds climbed several stone steps to the ground floor of the station, nodding at two constables who stood aside to make way as they entered. The reception hall was spacious and modern, lined with benches on which a variety of bedraggled men and women sat in postures of anxiety, annoyance, or dejection. The pair walked up to a tall central desk rather like a judge's bench, behind which a uniformed officer sat bareheaded, attending to paperwork.

"Good morning, Constable." Symonds raised a gloved hand and laid it on the front edge of the desk. His fingers drummed nervously.

The policeman looked up with scant enthusiasm. "Yes, sir?" he drawled. Stevenson could well imagine how the accumulating days, months, and years spent laboring in such a precinct might wear a man down to a jaded and cynical nub.

"I wonder if Detective Inspector Abberline might be available to speak with us."

The man surveyed the two of them with a vaguely lupine air. He took in a breath, exhaled slowly through flared nostrils, and set his pen down on his papers with exaggerated care.

"And what might your business with the Inspector be? If you would." His head tipped back and he peered at them down his long nose.

Symonds glanced at Stevenson, then again faced the man.

"It is in regard to the murder of Elizabeth Stride." He extracted a small leather case from his coat and pulled out his card, laying it on the desk with a soft snap.

The man paused to examine the credential, blinking quickly as he pulled himself into a more erect posture.

"I'll just see if the Inspector is available, Mr. Symonds. Nicks!" he called, turning to another policeman who sat in a chair behind him, the morning paper on his knee. "I'm just stepping away for a moment."

Constable Nicks folded his reading matter and walked slowly to the desk, taking his seat with weary resignation.

"If you'll wait here," said the first man, "I'll see about Inspector Abberline." He pointed to one of the benches. A reasonable span of clear wood stretched between an older woman, who held a sleeping infant against her chest, and a disheveled graybeard who appeared to be as dead to the world as the child was.

Stevenson walked across the tiled floor and, with a quick nod to the woman, seated himself on the hard bench. She smelled distinctly of coal-smoke and something else; perhaps bacon. He looked about the room, recalling heady times in Edinburgh when he, Baxter, and Ferrier had spent more than a late-night hour or two in a similar setting—always, however, to be quickly released back to their careless ways through a simple recitation of their family names. The usual occupants of these particular benches would seldom enjoy such freedom from consequence.

The old fellow to their left started, and then belched in his sleep—then belched again more loudly. Symonds slid six inches closer to Stevenson, shaking his head with a snort.

Footsteps sounded in the corridor across the way, and they looked up to see an officer and a middle-aged man in a tattered wool jacket walking towards them. The latter progressed with some difficulty, pulling his left leg stiffly along, the toe of his boot scraping over the floor. He must have been the victim of an early stroke, or some sort of military injury or factory accident.

"Thank you, Mr. Diemschutz," said the constable, as he escorted the man over to the exit.

"Aye." The fellow glanced towards Stevenson's bench as he exited, inexplicably nodding his head. The woman next to Stevenson disencumbered an arm from her child and nudged him softly.

"That's the bloke what found one of 'em last night," she whispered, pulling a long face.

"Indeed. And how would you know that?"

"I lives above Dutfield's Yard is how. That's Diemschutz, the carter. They say 'es the one what run in on Saucy Jack. Stopped 'im dead in 'is business."

"Really!" exclaimed Stevenson. "A sad thing to witness."

"Wors'an sad, sir. Beastly!" The child stirred in her arms, squeezing out a tired whimper, and she bent again to soothe him. The policeman from the charge desk emerged from the corridor opposite, ah-hemming loudly as he approached.

"If you'll follow me," he said, and extended his hand back the way he had come.

The three of them walked briskly past a series of closed doors, their footsteps echoing harshly in the tiled hallway. In one of those offices someone must have been smoking a cigar. Stevenson sniffed enviously at the sharp aroma. He had forgotten to bring cigarettes.

"You are lucky to find Inspector Abberline here," volunteered the constable, turning to them as he led the way. "He's had a busy day."

"I expect he has," said Symonds.

The man wheeled around at the far side of an open door and tossed his head towards the entrance.

"Thank you," said Symonds as he led Stevenson into the room.

Standing behind a cluttered desk was a tallish man with a receding hairline and impressive black muttonchops. His fingertips were poised on the edge of the desk, as though he were a sprinter taking his mark for a race.

"Mr. Symonds?" he asked in a voice livelier than anything they had yet encountered in the morose building.

Symonds nodded, raising his hand partway to his shoulder. It could have been the gesture of a diffident schoolboy, thought Stevenson, and this man was an internationally renowned scholar.

The inspector stepped around the desk and reached out for Symonds's hand. "I am Detective Inspector Abberline. Of the Metropolitan Police."

"Inspector," replied Symonds, shaking his hand. "And this is Mr. Stevenson."

"Mr. Stevenson." Abberline's grip was unexpectedly limp, very much at odds with his energetic manner. He motioned the men to two chairs flanking the near side of the desk, then returned to his own seat. Once settled, he leaned forward with his elbows on the desk. "Constable Briggs informs me that you would like to speak with me about Elizabeth Stride." He joined his fingertips into stars just under his nose and stared at his visitors with preternaturally wide-open eyes. He was most likely operating on very little sleep.

"We would," replied Symonds, with a glance at Stevenson.

"A dreadful incident," said the inspector. "One of two last night, as I expect you know."

Symonds nodded. He removed his gloves and laid them neatly on his knee. Reaching down for the small satchel he had been carrying, he opened it and carefully extracted the dark lantern, laying it on the desk. "We recovered this item early this morning. In what we now know to be Dutfield's Yard."

Abberline craned forward with an expression of incredulity. "You what?"

"And this as well." Symonds removed a handkerchief blotched with dark brown stains. He laid it softly alongside the lantern on the inspector's desk. "Please. Look inside."

Abberline reached out and picked up the grim parcel, unwrapping the stiffened cloth with a hint of apprehension. Did one ever get fully used to the horrors that were to be encountered in this line of work? Stevenson wondered. Perhaps it was a little like writing—or dreaming: never knowing what might pop out of the darkness into full and chilling view.

"I believe you will find that to be the Stride murder weapon," offered Stevenson, once Abberline had completed the unsavory task of unwrapping it. "If you care to examine it against the slashes on the poor woman's neck."

The inspector's head jerked up and he stared piercingly at the writer. "*Slashes*, you say. You know, then, that there was more than one wound."

Stevenson nodded. It had struck him as curious that the *Times* account had mentioned only "the gash." Perhaps it had something to do with the verification of possible witnesses.

The inspector took a deep breath and set the knife down very carefully. He wiped his hands distractedly against the sides of his trousers, then leaned sharply forward.

"Would you gentleman care to tell me how you came to be in possession of these objects?"

Their initial conversation went very much as Stevenson and Symonds had expected it might. Abberline listened to their account of the Portman Square surveillance, first with disbelief, and then with increasing agitation. Their recounting of the previous night in Whitechapel was met with even greater alarm. The man did his best to maintain his composure, but the veins standing out along the sides of his high brow testified to his great discomfiture. Had they perhaps not realized what danger they had put themselves into? Were they not aware that, by removing the lantern and the knife from the murder scene, they were tampering with critical Crown evidence and jeopardizing what was likely one of the most significant criminal investigations in the nation's history?

When Stevenson countered by saying that the evidence would never have remained to be found in Dutfield's Yard if they had not been there to interrupt the murderer in his task, Abberline blustered that such a conjecture could never be definitively proven. He rose impatiently from the desk and strutted over to the window, staring out into the street with his hands clasped behind his back. His fingers worked nervously, like wrestling crabs. Stevenson could just hear the street organ below, grinding away in its numbingly uniform tempo.

"Well," said Abberline at last, turning back towards the two of them with a look of resolve. "I very much think that this is a matter for Scotland Yard."

"But we understood," declared Stevenson, "that you yourself were with Scotland Yard, no?"

"I am indeed," Abberline replied, reseating himself. "But I have been seconded to Whitechapel for the duration of this particular investigation."

"I see," said Symonds. He looked uncertainly at Stevenson.

"What do you suggest we do, then, Inspector?" asked the writer.

"I will notify Chief Inspector Swanson that you two gentlemen will be coming in to speak with him."

"And when should that be?" asked Symonds.

"As soon as tomorrow, I should think. The chief inspector will be extremely eager to hear what you have to say. I can assure you of that."

Symonds nodded. "And as for the identity of our man—I assume I had best disclose that to you now?" Stevenson could hear a quaver in his friend's voice.

"Please, no!" exclaimed Abberline, holding up his palms. "That is something for you to convey directly to the chief inspector."

Symonds looked vaguely mystified. "But, given that it is you who are in charge of the investigation—"

"Again, any specific name is for the chief inspector's ears. I assure you, we are working under a very strict protocol with this case, as I expect you will understand." He looked back and forth between the two of them. "Now, is there anything else?" Meeting with no response, Abberline clapped his hands together lightly and stood to signal the end of the interview.

It was curious, mused Stevenson as they walked down the echoing corridor towards the exit. Abberline had seemed far and away the most energetic and genial officer at the Whitechapel station, yet the look in his eyes as they left had bordered on relief. He must have been truly exhausted.

"I quite understand how Abberline felt," remarked Symonds, as their hansom struck out for the West End. "What we have done is unlikely to be a daily occurrence in these climes. Most definitely the stuff of one of your own fanciful narratives."

Stevenson chuckled. "And, I allow, most definitely prosecutable. Tampering with criminal evidence!"

"Ought we to worry about that, do you think? Prosecution?" The strains of the recent weeks showed on Symonds's face: there was darkness under his eyes and an unrelenting tenseness in his brow.

"Not at all, I expect. Especially if the evidence we give leads to an arrest and a conviction."

"And what if it emerges in court that it wasn't the authorities who collected the lantern and the knife? Might that not eliminate the items from consideration?"

"That won't happen," replied Stevenson. "Not unless they don't want to catch our murderer. Nor unless his barrister was there in Dutfield's Yard, taking notes."

They rode on in silence, the clip-clopping of their horse's hooves bouncing off the tall facades of Leadenhall Street. The fine weather of early afternoon had yielded to low cloud, and a few tentative drops of rain blew in under the roof of the cab.

"Why do you suppose Abberline refused to let you name the fellow?" asked Stevenson, shaking his head in puzzlement as he adjusted his knees for a little more shelter. "I fully understand the importance of the case;

the world is watching. But, if I were Abberline—and truly in charge of the entire investigation in this precinct—I might be tempted to let my curiosity override my sense of procedure."

"Perhaps that too has something to do with your being a writer," responded Symonds with a weary grin.

"Perhaps," Stevenson agreed. "By the way, did you notice the change in the constable's demeanor when he saw your card?"

"No."

"Your scholarly reputation seems to have preceded you. Even in these unenlightened latitudes."

"I find that quite unlikely," snorted Symonds.

The hansom jostled on in a freshening shower. Despite the lingering warmth of the day, Stevenson threw the worn lap robe over their legs.

"You know, there is still the matter of your own future, John," he volunteered after another considerable pause. "We have yet to take the final step. Once you name the man to Swanson, you will have set a sizeable stone to rolling. Lord knows where it will come to rest."

"And if I don't name him, Louis, Swanson and the others *will* most certainly have me up on charges," Symonds replied. "But worse than that, my silence would amount to a capital crime in the court of self-opinion. And the court of self-opinion, as you very well know, is for me the most fearsome jurisdiction of all."

"As for me, Symonds. Upon my word, as for me."

At two o'clock the following afternoon, Stevenson and Symonds sat at 4 Whitehall Place in the office of Chief Inspector Donald Swanson, the senior officer named by the commissioner to head the East End murder investigation.

The chief inspector was a Scotsman—from Thurso, Stevenson discovered, after inquiring about the fellow's birthplace as soon as he heard his accent. His voice and cadence were not altogether unlike Stevenson's, a fact rendered all the more striking given that the officer's moustache was a virtual twin to the writer's own. As he sat there across from the man, Stevenson took the strange notion that he could be staring into a distorting glass on Bournemouth's amusement pier, glimpsing the way he might look if he had any real flesh on his bones. A non-skeletal Louis—as Cummy, Margaret, and Fanny might have liked to see him. If Swanson could have been a more portly twin, however, his manner was not particularly brotherly. After reviewing what he had read in Detective Inspector Abberline's report and asking the two of them to confirm—point-by-point—the veracity of the account, he leaned back in his chair and crossed his sizeable arms. The impression was that of a combative walrus.

"You must forgive me for saying so, gentlemen," he said, "but this taking of matters of the law into a regular citizen's hands smacks of vigilantism." He waited, weighing the impact of his words before he proceeded. "It is frankly the kind of thing we might expect to encounter in the Wild American West."

Stevenson was obliged to smile at the analogy. He could just imagine Fanny patrolling the East End on horseback, chaps on her legs, spurs on her heels, and a Winchester repeating rifle holstered on her saddle.

"Do you find that amusing, Mr. Stevenson?"

Something in the man's tone and demeanor brought up the writer's blood. Perhaps it was an echo of Mr. Henderson, "Auld Hendie," the loathed and brutal schoolmaster of his early Edinburgh days.

"Forgive me, Chief Inspector," Stevenson replied. "But I believe I heard that a man named Lusk—an Englishman in fact—has recently founded something called the Whitechapel *Vigilance* Committee. To aid the Metropolitan Police, I am told, in their now rather lengthy and still unavailing efforts to end these frightful murders."

Swanson bristled satisfyingly. "I assure you, the Metropolitan Police are in no need of any such assistance."

Stevenson watched as the man reddened a trifle more, then indulged himself in the skeptical arching of an eyebrow. The impudent gesture earned him an admonitory scowl from Symonds. In truth, there was nothing to be gained from angering this man, and potentially a good deal to be lost, especially for Symonds. He resolved to be civil.

For the better part of a minute Swanson drummed his biceps arhythmically with his fingers. It was evidently his way of settling himself. "Remonstrations and second-guessings are all very well and good," he crooned presently with exaggerated calm. "We are, however, precisely where we find ourselves. Now, you say you were present in Dutfield's Yard when the deed was done?"

"We were," answered Symonds. "God help us."

"And you clearly saw the man cut the victim's throat?"

"No. Not exactly. It was, as we told Inspector Abberline, utterly dark there."

"I see. How very unfortunate."

Symonds looked at Stevenson in modest bewilderment. "There can be no doubt," he declared, "that it was he that did the murder. We followed him from his house. He was never out of our sight."

"Except, one presumes, for certain portions of the carriage ride."

"That can hardly be of significance," exclaimed Stevenson. "The landau was moving at a brisk trot the entire time."

"But you are certain that the man you then followed on foot was your man?"

"We are," replied Symonds.

"And you are certain the man who rushed from Dutfield's Yard was him."

"As certain as a mortal can be."

"I see," said Swanson. "And the man's name? Are you now prepared to name him? This gentleman from Portman Square?"

"We are," replied Symonds, with a confirming glance at Stevenson.

Swanson eyed them intently, but remained settled back in his chair. "And his name is…?"

"His name is Thomas Hallett."

Swanson sat there impassively for several seconds, then his right hand rose slowly to his face and he stroked his moustache with studied calm.

"Thomas Hallett. Of the shipping family?"

"And of Portman Square," confirmed Symonds.

"I see. And you are absolutely certain it was he? In the landau, stalking the streets, and in Dutfield's Yard?"

"Again, as certain as a mortal can be."

"There is no need to be metaphysical, Mr. Symonds. This is a matter of some gravity."

"I am well aware of its gravity, Chief Inspector," responded Symonds with a more than a hint of pique.

"I presume you have told no one else of this?" asked Swanson. "No one beyond myself...and Mr. Stevenson?"

"I have not."

"Very good. That's very good. Well, Mr. Symonds," said Swanson, rising from his chair. "I cannot approve of your methods, as I am sure you will understand. But you have nonetheless done your Queen and her people a very great service. I, particularly, am extremely grateful. Is there anything else you wish to say to me?"

Symonds gazed at Stevenson, then shook his head. "No. I believe that is the sum of it."

"Thank you then. And thank you as well, Mr. Stevenson." He smiled in a markedly officious manner. "As it happens, I am a great admirer of your work. My son is as well. *Treasure Island* is one of his favorites."

"It pleases me to know that," replied the writer. "I am flattered."

"Will there be anything more for now?" asked Symonds.

"Not presently, thank you," said the man. "We will of course proceed immediately with this new aspect of our investigation. Posthaste." He nodded for emphasis. "If we have any need of further information, from either of you, we will of course be in touch. I believe we have information regarding where you may both be reached?"

"You do," replied Symonds. "It was all taken down by the constable in the Back Hall."

"Very good," said Swanson. "As it should have been. Well, gentlemen. Good day. And let me again offer the most profound thanks for your indispensable information. You may count on our pursuing it with the utmost vigor."

The strength of his parting handshake suggested that the man was indeed capable of great vigor, if he so chose.

"Well," sighed Symonds as they walked up Whitehall towards Trafalgar Square. "The stone you persist in mentioning is most certainly on the roll now."

"It is in truth. The die is cast."

"I am extremely glad that you and I have done this," Symonds added, turning to his friend with a warm smile. "I might say I *think* I am glad, but that would simply be the voice of anxiety speaking."

"You do look relieved. And it was essential for us to do. Let us now hope that your bold sally has the full results that we aspire to. And nothing more or other."

"Would you join me in raising a glass to that hope?" Symonds gestured towards a public house, one much favored by members of Parliament, that they were just passing.

"With all my heart."

20

Time ran on; thousands of pounds were offered in reward, for the death of Sir Danvers was resented as a public injury; but Mr. Hyde had disappeared out of the ken of the police as though he had never existed.

—THE NARRATOR, JEKYLL AND HYDE

Stevenson caught the 11:35 to Bournemouth the following morning. He had dined with Symonds at the Savoy his last evening in the capital, pledging to rush back if his services or company were required before his old friend returned to Switzerland. They consumed a good deal of wine, finishing with as good a *Trockenbeerenauslese* as either of them had ever tasted. It brought back rich memories of frigid postprandial strolls in Davos, when the snow squeaked underfoot and the stars paraded their vast and lustrous regiments high above the sentinel pines. The alcohol and the day's exhausting events had left Symonds extraordinarily unguarded, and as they said farewell, tears had run unfettered down his cheeks.

The train journey was uneventful, save that Stevenson shared a compartment with a pair of young solicitors and a charming old bespectacled matron whose King Charles spaniel passed gas with criminal frequency. There was a supremely awkward initial moment, shortly after the train left Waterloo, when the offensive miasma rose and noses twitched and eyes roamed in a subtle effort to detect the source. The human occupants quickly fell into whichever postures best suggested that they were not themselves to blame. The two attorneys seemed well enough acquainted to reassure each other in short order, and they looked over at Stevenson in accusatory tandem. Stevenson cocked an eyebrow in a way calculated to signal modest annoyance and noisily opened his copy of the *Times*. The spaniel, with its muzzle resting on the plush seat, raised its eyes and peered about as though it were following the flight of a bluebottle around the ceiling of the tight space. The woman looked at her dog and shook her head. The odor eventually subsided, only to be replaced by another of greater magnitude.

Stevenson was fighting the urge to leap up and throw the window open when the woman lowered her book with an exasperated sigh. "I am afraid it is my dog, gentlemen. I am ever so sorry. Please do open the window, if you wish. Or take a seat elsewhere. We shall not be offended."

The three men laughed, exchanging looks of relief and amusement. What an extraordinary old woman to give voice to the unspeakable! Stevenson stood and opened the window a good six inches, relishing the surge of untainted air.

"I'm sure I don't know what it is," said the lady, looking around at the men with a bemused twinkle, "but there is no use pretending little Minzy isn't something of a social menace."

As he approached the door at Skerryvore, Stevenson was again not altogether certain which Fanny might be waiting there to greet him. His homecoming after the initial surveillances of Portman Square had been tempestuous, exacerbated by the fact that his wife had felt compelled to give Cruikshank his walking papers even before the master of the house returned from his "selfish adventures." The man had gone beyond incursions into Valentine's room, and had actually accosted her in the garden shed. Although Fanny insisted that it naturally fell to the head of the household to attend to all such unpleasant transactions, said head of the household's unconscionable truancy had obliged her to act in his stead. His return would likely have been even more tumultuous had he not thought to scribble a letter to her each day he'd been away—and to bring back as a peace offering an obscenely expensive Japanese kimono and an elegant parasol for his "wee geisha." Still, he had little doubt that when Fanny learned he had been close enough to the Stride woman's murder to be bowled over by the fleeing killer—a scene he felt honor-bound at least to sketch for her in broad strokes—he would be the target of some powerful spousal invective.

In the event, he was perfectly right. She greeted him warmly at the door, pattering up in her slipper-feet and hugging him with the power of an amorous little she-bear. As soon as they had retreated to the parlor for a pre-tea glass of sherry, the interrogation began. She managed to draw out a sufficient number of particulars regarding the night of September 30th that her effervescence suffered a precipitous decline. London paid a huge force of policemen to enforce the law, she observed with indignation, so why would the sole breadwinner of her family hazard his life in this very uncertain endeavor? Once Stevenson assured her, however, that the affair had now been left completely in the hands of Scotland Yard, her affect improved markedly. With the second glass of sherry and the dramatic deployment of the gift parasol, Fanny was again as buoyant and flirtatious as she had been when he'd first ventured across the threshold.

Valentine prepared an excellent meal that evening—beef stewed in wine along with potatoes Lyonaise and some sautéed green beans she had somehow managed to scare up despite the lateness of the season. Capped by a sinfully rich chocolate torte, it was a feast that Stevenson thought either equaled or surpassed the previous night's fare at the Savoy. When he sought Valentine out to tell her so, she smiled a coy smile and allowed that Mrs. Stevenson had wanted him to feel especially welcome. Fretting a mite under the suggestion that her gesture had been more for his wife than for him, Stevenson bid Valentine goodnight and retired upstairs to his bedroom.

He found Fanny sitting in her robe at her dressing table, removing a pair of rather extravagant hooped earrings—the ones, he sometimes said, that made her look like the bride of Long John Silver. She turned towards him with a tentative smile.

"Can I ask you something, Louis?"

"Of course."

"I was taking a bath several nights ago and, as I was drying and powdering, I thought I might have found something."

"Something?"

"Something in my breast. A lump."

"Goodness!" Something tightened in his own chest, as it invariably did with a health scare in the family. Fanny's crises came so regularly nowadays, though, that he was not unduly alarmed. "Have you seen a doctor?"

"Not yet."

"Do you think you should?"

"I don't know, Louis," she exclaimed with a great sigh. She looked up at him in the mirror. "Could you feel it?"

"Of course."

"Here," she said, opening her robe. She reached up and grabbed his hand, guiding it to the lower outside of her left breast. "Oooh, your hand is freezing."

"I'm sorry, Pig. I didn't know I was going to be doing this."

She pressed his hand into her flesh, sliding it around under her own. "Do you feel something?"

"I feel your breast."

She slapped his hand and moved it about some more. "Anything?" Her eyes were riveted on his reflection.

He shook his head.

Letting go of his fingers, she raised her breast with her left hand and felt with the other. "Right here," she said. "Tiny, but it feels like a lump. Here." She grabbed his hand again and pressed it to the spot.

"Do you feel anything?"

"Nothing unusual. At all. Are you sure you're not just desperate to have me fondle you?"

"Louis!"

"I'm sorry, Pig. I honestly didn't feel anything. If you are concerned, you can always go to see Doctor Barrett."

Fanny pursed her lips into a thoughtful moue. "Perhaps I'll just wait and see if it gets any bigger."

"A sensible course of action, I would say."

Fanny nodded. "But you didn't feel anything?"

Stevenson shook his head. "I am sure, though, that you could always get Valentine to check. I expect she has a more experienced touch."

Fanny threw his hand off her shoulder and quickly covered up, belting her robe snugly. "I don't know why I put up with you," she declared. "You can't take anything seriously."

When Stevenson returned from the water closet, Fanny was propped up against a raft of pillows in the middle of their bed, the counterpane pulled up under her chin.

"I've missed you these last several days," she said, in a lilting voice. "I always miss you."

"And I have missed you as well." Stevenson slipped out of his jacket and untied his cravat. "It has been an insanely trying string of days."

"I wish I had been there with you."

"I doubt you would have wanted to be, love. Not for a great deal of it." He unbuttoned his shirt. Peeling it off, he reached for his nightshirt.

"What's that!" exclaimed Fanny, leaning forward over her knees. She pointed to his shoulder.

Stevenson looked down to discover an ugly bruise that ran from the end of his left clavicle well down into his meager bicep. He looked up at her sheepishly. It seemed best to be candid. "That's where the fellow bowled into me."

"You poor dear," she crooned, leaning back and pushing the covers down on his side of the bed. He could see as she did so that she was wearing no nightclothes. "Come here and let Fanny make you feel better."

He made to climb in next to her and she giggled. "Do you want to take those off?"

He looked down and noticed he was still in his trousers. He went to pull them off, nearly falling over when he caught a foot partway through the process.

Another giggle. "And those, too."

He removed his drawers, climbing onto the mattress and lying there with his head resting on two pillows.

"Was it just horrid?" asked Fanny, nestling up against him.

"'Horrid' hardly does it justice."

"Well, you're safe now. Here with me."

"Yes. Yes I am."

He felt her hand slide across his stomach and then pull slightly back so that her middle finger settled into his navel. She sighed contentedly then moved her hand towards his injured shoulder. Barely touching his skin, it hovered there with the weight of a feather.

"Does that hurt you, love?"

"Not really."

"You are far stronger than you look."

Stevenson laughed. "It's good of you to say so."

"It's true."

She inched closer and moved her hand stealthily down the mid-line of his stomach, past his navel to the hair of his groin, where she twirled her finger playfully.

"So manly," she whispered in his ear. "Me braw laddie."

Encouraged by a definite if preliminary response to her touch, he rose onto his left elbow to kiss her and felt a sudden stab in his shoulder.

"Owww!"

"That hurts you?"

"I'm fine."

He bent to kiss her and, as their lips met, he reached up to cup her right breast. The nipple was hard, and she arched her chest up into his caress.

"Get on top of me," she whispered in his ear.

Her legs parted and he rolled over between them, propping his elbows on the mattress so as not to be too heavy. He could feel himself grating against the roughness of her hair, unsure whether she was ready for him. He was about to reach down when the image of Lizzy Stride leapt unbidden to mind. She'd lain there supine, like Fanny, but with her eyes rolled back into her head and her life's blood flowing out onto the filthy cobbles.

"What is it?" asked Fanny. "What's wrong?"

"Oh, God," replied Stevenson as he rolled over onto his back.

"What is it, Louis? Have I done something wrong?"

She lay there largely uncovered. An instinct as strong as the one that had driven him to accost Lizzy's killer made him pull the counterpane up over his wife's nakedness. As it happened, a substantial fold in the sheet fell just at her neck, and it was all he could do to banish the hideous specter of the Eddowes' woman lying butchered with her glistening viscera yanked up just so.

"I've dampened your ardor, haven't I? With my worries about a lump?"

He shook his head.

"Then you're thinking about those poor women."

Stevenson had no sooner nodded than he began to sob.

"Here. Sit up, love. Let me just hold you."

He did as Fanny instructed, and he wept there in her arms.

"It was awful, Pig," he managed between sobs. "I should have stopped it. The poor—"

"I know, love. I know."

Somehow, the force of her words and the warmth of her embrace had their intended effect and he managed to control first his shaking and then his tears.

"There, there," crooned Fanny. "There, there. I think you're better now."

He nodded like a child, as though this were only a nightmare he had awoken from in his Edinburgh nursery and Cummy were soothing nothing but illusory fears.

"There's something I need to be sure of," whispered Fanny.

Stevenson looked at her curiously.

"Symonds hasn't won you over, has he?"

"Pardon?"

"To his sort of love? Is that why you're really having trouble?"

Fortunately the candle was still lit and he could see the mischief in her eyes. Stevenson seized hold of the whimsical spirit as though it were a lifeline.

"He *has* won me over. Entirely."

Fanny eyed him with budding concern, and then it was his turn to grin.

"Because I don't believe I have ever met a man more courageous than Symonds." He felt the prickle of more tears beginning to flow. "Nor am I sure I could ever have written one."

"Let's just hope this all comes to a good end," said Fanny, lying back down and turning onto her side to face him.

"Amen." He turned himself just as she had done and slipped back against her like a stacked spoon.

Throughout his long days in London, Stevenson had struggled to write anything other than letters. During the most recent interval in Bournemouth, though, he had managed to begin a dark tale about two Scottish brothers, one of them a more-or-less sensible but rather boring fellow dedicated to maintaining the ancient family estate, the other a devilish rover given to immediate pleasures and the endless allure of adventure. There were obvious parallels to *Jekyll and Hyde*—as to virtually everything else Stevenson had ever written—but it occurred to him throughout many hours when he sat with pen in hand, framing the initial chapters, that it could have been a portrait of his own current selves: the hardworking, "biscuit-bound" husband of Bournemouth and the free-ranging, self-indulgent invigilator of dark London streets. In any case, with his latest return to Skerryvore, he took up his budding Highland tale with renewed vigor. He was pleased to find that it came with some ease and considerable promise of ultimate weightiness.

The other project of these Bournemouth days, of course, was the family's future. Stevenson continued to correspond with *Scribner's,* and it seemed increasingly likely that an American sojourn would be not only practicable but also exceedingly lucrative. A good friend of the magazine's editor had invited them for a substantial stay with his family in Newport. Fanny had managed to secure a description of Charles Fairchild's "cottage," quipping that the quaint term might apply if one compared the place to Versailles, but that it yielded little to Buckingham Palace in sheer bulk and architectural ambitiousness. She was, she said, very eager to be a guest, and she resolved to enjoy a bath in every one of its multiple marble tubs. Margaret Stevenson was also making ready to leave Edinburgh, having seen to the rental of Heriot Row.

Stevenson had just received what would likely be his mother's final letter from Auld Reekie when another epistle arrived from Symonds.

4 November 1888

Dear Louis,

I hope this finds you and Fanny well, and that you are having good fortune developing the little "winter's tale" we spoke of. Simply remember to keep your sentences shorter than James's. A reader can age decades in the toils of that man's syntax. (You do know, of course, how much I admire his work!)

As you will shrewdly observe from the postmark, I am still in London, or was at least when I wrote this. There is still some difficulty with my printers, and there are also a few other projects upon which I have been at work that I will not bore you by describing.

I had heard absolutely nothing from Chief Inspector Swanson since you and I spoke with him—is it a full month ago now? In any case, I took the liberty of calling on him several days ago to see if there had been any progress in our little undertaking. I find that, most of the time, I am quite at ease with my decision and so very grateful that you helped me summon up the fortitude to put it into practice. There are nights, however, when I awake in the small hours and imagine certain possibilities that I would much prefer not to entertain. Swanson, in any event, was quite pleasant—rather more so than before, I should say—and assured me that the investigation was proceeding satisfactorily. When I pressed him for details, which you will understand I felt compelled to do, he naturally told me that he was unable to provide me with any particulars. "The affair is well in hand" is what he must have said four or five times. We shall see. At least there have been no further murders.

Life in London is invariably entertaining, as hard as you may find that to believe!!! I have been to the theater several times, including to an indifferent Ibsen called "The Lady from the Sea"—very much below his usual standard. I don't believe there was a single stuffy gentleman or lady in attendance who stormed out in moral outrage, at least none that I saw. I have mostly dined in, returning once to Bertolini's but not nearly as pleasantly as when you and I were there. Our strapping fellow has been into the Athenaeum once or twice, and you can imagine how challenging it has been for me to maintain a civil and settled demeanor, however much depends upon that.

I wished to express, once again, my profound gratitude for the staunch friendship you have offered me these last weeks—and indeed for the whole span of our acquaintance. My debt to you is incalculable and my affection boundless.

I remain, as ever, your greatest admirer and most devoted servant,

J. A. Symonds

The weeks had passed quickly, but it was troubling to hear from Symonds that Scotland Yard's investigation was still only "progressing"—and, more than that, that Hallett was still at large. Stevenson knew from first-hand experience how slowly the wheels of justice could turn, particularly with a suspect as well placed as this one. Swanson, Abberline, and the others would be excruciatingly careful about their pace and exactitude. It was certainly to be hoped, however, that the case would be resolved in the reasonably near future, as it was difficult to imagine that the information Symonds and he had provided could not, in the end, be exploited in a conclusive way.

Ever since he had received Fanny's letter documenting Cruikshank's indiscretions, Stevenson had looked to apologize to Valentine for having brought the fellow into the household. No opportunity had presented itself during his previous stay in Bournemouth, so he was all the more eager to find the right moment now that he was back.

It came one afternoon when Fanny had gone into town to see about acquiring steamer trunks for their upcoming relocation. Stevenson was in his study writing letters when he spied Valentine passing the window with a small bunch of Michaelmas daisies. She looked in as she went by, catching his eye and smiling. He heard a door open and close and, laying down his pen, he rose and walked through to the kitchen. She stood by the worktable, scissors in hand, trimming the stems and placing the delicate purple blooms into a cut glass vase.

"Those are lovely," said Stevenson as she turned to acknowledge him. "Aren't they?"

"The last flowers of the year?"

"I believe, yes."

He suddenly found himself at a complete loss for what to say or how to stand. "How quickly the year is passing!"

She nodded, inserting the last of the flowers into the vase and arranging them with a speed and deftness that left him grinning. Were all women born with an ability to toss found objects into patterns of beauty with such effortless aplomb? Did they always tilt their heads just that way, weighing their success in an instant, before they flitted off to their next task with serene assurance?

"We shall be leaving soon for America."

"Yes."

"We are so pleased that you will be coming with us, Valentine. Madame Stevenson and I. And of course Sam."

"I am content," she replied. She rinsed her hands in the basin and dried them on a checkered towel. "And I am excited to go," she said, turning towards him and leaning back against the bench. "It will be a great adventure. For all of us." She smiled with reassuring warmth.

"Valentine," he said, looking down for a moment at his feet. "I have been meaning to apologize for Cruikshank."

"It is nothing."

"No, it is not nothing. He did things he should not have done. And I feel responsible for having put you in a position that you should never have had to suffer."

She looked at him with a resigned smile. "These things were not of your making. These things are in the nature of men and women. They are old as time, no?"

"That may be. But they were not at all acceptable, the things he did."

"Others have done worse."

Stevenson burned under her level gaze.

"And we survive, do we not? You are very kind, Monsieur Stevenson. But the people who truly need the protection of good men like you are the poor women of London. Women like that poor soul again yesterday."

"Like whom?"

"You have not heard the news?"

"No." His stomach knotted.

"Another poor woman killed. Butchered. By this fellow they are calling Jack the Ripper. There, monsieur, is something that goes beyond our common nature."

Stevenson flew out of the house with neither overcoat nor hat. He all but ran into town, breaking into a copious sweat despite the coolness of the day. He stumbled from the newsagent's, reading in disbelief, nearly trampling in the process a pair of ladies who were strolling by.

There had indeed been another murder, of a woman named Mary Ann Kelly, in Dorset Street, Spitalfields. *"This is the seventh,"* read the *Times, "which has occurred in this immediate neighborhood, and the character of the mutilations leaves very little doubt that the murderer in this instance is the same person who has committed the previous ones, with which the public are fully acquainted."*

The woman had been found in her bed, Stevenson read, on her back, entirely naked. Her throat was again slashed from ear to ear, "right down to the spinal column." This time, however, the ears and nose had also been cut clean off. As for her torso, both breasts had been sliced away and placed on the bedside table. The abdomen below was laid completely open, with the kidneys and heart removed and left on the table next to the breasts. The liver had been excised and lay atop her right thigh, and as for the uterus, it was cut out and "appeared to be missing."

For the first time since he was an undergraduate, as far as Stevenson could recall, he became ill in a public place.

"Of course it is horrid, Louis," allowed Fanny, throwing herself into James's chair in the parlor and slouching there with her arms tightly crossed. "But you've already taken completely unconscionable risks."

"Do you feel no sympathy for the women who have died?"

"They chose their fates. They didn't have to walk the streets."

"Do you really believe that, Fanny? That a woman chooses to be a prostitute because it is an amusing way to earn a pound?"

"Of course not." Her eyes glowed like hot rivets. "But you are our pound-earner, Louis. Sam's and mine. How are we going to survive if you go off and do something gallant and foolish and something happens to you? And it's not even gallant. These are whores he's cutting up."

Stevenson shook his head in exasperation. "You talk of Sam's needs?"

"Of course I do. You should think about Sam, even if you don't give a damn about me."

"And what would Sam think of me if I failed to do something? If I just sat here and watched the slaughter go on? What would that say about how a man ought to live?"

"Tell him nothing," Fanny suggested. "Or offer him the example of going to the police. You already have."

"And to what avail?" asked Stevenson. He wheeled around and strode over to the fire. Throwing his arm onto the mantle, he lowered his forehead down onto it with an audible groan.

"They're investigating, aren't they? Symonds said so. Give it time, Louis. I beg you! Let the police do their jobs."

"They do nothing. I don't know why, but they do nothing. Or they do it so slowly that these poor women go on dying." He thought back on the interviews with Swanson and Abberline and the curious impressions he had taken of their demeanor. He turned again to face her, his aspect melding anger with supplication. "And do you care nothing for how *I* feel?"

She looked genuinely puzzled. "What do you mean?"

"There's the small matter of the play."

Her look was pure exasperation. "We have been over this so many goddamned times, Louis. I'm sick of it. What makes you think your damn stories are so powerful they make people act a certain way? Who are you? God Almighty? This is all completely insane! It's just, just… complete shit!" She began to weep.

He stood there for a matter of minutes, then walked slowly over and put his hand on her shoulder.

"I am sure Symonds and I will undertake no lunacy. We simply need to do something to answer our consciences. We need to do something any moral soul should feel bound to do."

Fanny looked up with reddened eyes and tear-slicked cheeks. "Look what happened before. Your shoulder was almost crushed. You could have been stabbed."

"I know. It won't happen again."

"How do you know it won't?"

"We won't put ourselves in the same position again. Symonds and I will formulate a plan that involves no risks. It may be that we can simply prod the police along in their investigation. That would be the best way of progressing, by far."

"Are you telling me the truth?" It bordered on heartbreaking, her look.

"Of course I am."

"Can I come along?"

"To London?"

She wiped at her tears with a knuckle and nodded. "To London."

"We couldn't stay at the Savile. No ladies," he smiled.

"We could stay at the Grosvenor. Like we always do." Suddenly she was a child, begging for a sweet.

"We could," Stevenson agreed, bending to kiss her head.

21

My devil had been long caged, he came out roaring.

—DR. HENRY JEKYLL

LONDON, NOVEMBER 1888

"So, John, you've heard nothing more from Swanson? Nothing at all?"

Stevenson, Fanny, and Symonds sat in an elegant suite in the Grosvenor Hotel, sipping their mid-afternoon tea. Rain beat on the tall windows, and the casements rattled now and again in the strong westerly. It was still early November, but the gas fire was lit and they had gathered their chairs closely around it for warmth.

"Not a word."

"How long do such things usually take?" asked Fanny. "Do we know?"

"I expect every case is different. Would you agree, Louis?"

Stevenson nodded and reached for a cigarette. He lit it and drew in deeply. "What is your feeling, John? Could there be something irregular happening here?"

"I don't know. Honestly. But I am loath to sit idly by while Hallett continues to run rampant."

"Shall I tell you what I have been thinking?" asked Stevenson. "Thoughts that may speak to the lethargic pace of the investigation?" He blew a slim jet of smoke up towards the chandelier.

"Please do."

"Bear in mind that I earn my living making things up. Fabricating patterns." He gazed at his wife with a lively grin.

"Then I shall be sure to listen with the greatest possible skepticism," chuckled Symonds.

"I always do." Fanny reached over and slid the ashtray closer to her husband.

Stevenson glowered at his wife in mock reproach. "You'll also do well to recall that I am a duly-sworn member of the Scottish bar. So you might accord me a modicum of credibility as well." He went on, affecting now the voice of a haughty barrister. "We have, then, an array of facts before us. And we are now looking for a narrative thread that binds them all together. First," and he raised a slender forefinger to one side of his moustache, "no evident action has yet been taken by Scotland Yard. This despite their having in hand, for over a month now, some extremely useful information about the man whom we know to be the killer. Had they been only as vigilant as we have been, rank amateurs that we are, they would most certainly have tracked and apprehended him after this last murder."

His companions nodded.

"Second. It was my distinct impression that, despite anything he may have said explicitly, Chief Inspector Swanson seemed as vexed as he was pleased that we were approaching him with said information. Would you agree, Symonds?"

"I believe I would. So he seemed."

"I would also say that, when Swanson asked Symonds to name the killer, he looked less interested than a donkey at the opera. Now, moving backwards in time, we have Detective Inspector Abberline. His manner was far more welcoming and professional than Swanson's, but he showed a curious reluctance to hear Hallett's name as well."

"How so?" queried Fanny.

"He insisted that all particulars of that sort were meant solely for the ears of higher-ups," Symonds explained. "It was indeed curious."

"It suggested to me that this is an investigation on which the reins are being held very tightly," Stevenson went on. "I can certainly see the point of keeping sensitive information away from the average, patrolling constable; but for the inspector in charge of the entire Whitechapel endeavor to balk at hearing the perpetrator named, within his own precinct house? That strikes me as very odd indeed."

"It does," agreed Fanny, leaning forward in her chair.

"Finally," said Stevenson, carefully stubbing out his cigarette, "there was the remarkable business of Hallett walking within forty yards of the Whitechapel police station, with no apparent qualms at all. He clearly knows the neighborhood."

"So either the man was drunk," offered Fanny, "or he was emboldened by some other factor. He was effectively fearless."

"My thought exactly. So," Stevenson concluded, turning to their companion, "can you, dear Symonds, conjure up a plausible scenario to account for the Metropolitan Police seeming to take only a fitful interest in our man—and also for our man's apparent disregard for the threat of the Metropolitan Police?" He steepled his hands in front of his nose expectantly.

"How could I not?" Symonds replied. "I have been thinking of little else for the past week."

"And your theory?"

"Quite the obvious one, I should think." Symonds looked at them both with an eyebrow raised. "That the police are for some reason wary about what Hallett might divulge if he is called to account."

"And why would the police be wary?" asked Fanny. "Hallett isn't one of them, correct?"

"Not at all," answered Stevenson. "But the police answer to people more powerful than they."

"Indeed." Symonds turned guardedly towards Fanny. "Perhaps Louis has told you about the house in Cleveland Street?"

Fanny looked to her husband before she nodded.

"I took the liberty," allowed the writer. "I hope you will forgive me."

"Of course." Symonds blushed slightly but went on. "This establishment, as you can imagine, makes every effort to mask the identity of its clients. At the same time, one occasionally comes to learn something about one or another of them. And some, I fear, are very highly placed."

"Oh my!" exclaimed Fanny. "And Hallett himself is well connected too, isn't he?"

"He is," Symonds replied. "An heir to thousands. But I also know that hardly a week passes at the place without a visit from another fellow who is an equerry to the Prince of Wales."

"And an equerry is what? I don't think we have equerries in America."

"An equerry is a kind of aide-de-camp to a member of the royal family," Symonds explained. "They once looked after the nobility's horses. But their responsibilities in this day and age are considerable. This man of whom I speak is himself a lord."

"Well, there it is," exclaimed Stevenson, slapping his leg.

Fanny looked at her husband and nodded slowly. "So Hallett might be arrested…but unless the charges are dropped and the affair is hushed, he would go to the *Times* with information about this male brothel and its highly-placed clients. Provided he knows about this equerry person."

"He is extremely likely to know," replied Symonds. "Hallett makes it his business to know everything. If Somerset's involvement were somehow a secret to—" His hand rushed to his mouth. "Oh my. What have I said?"

Stevenson's look of surprise gave way to a grin. "Nothing I can even begin to remember. Can you, Fanny?"

"Can I what?" she said, grinning as well.

Symonds snorted in amusement. "Thank you. Both. I was saying that there are other men of prominence and power who use the place. There are rumors—although rumors only, mind you—that a certain young member of the royal family itself, someone rather high in the line of succession, has been a patron."

"These are plausible rumors?" asked Stevenson.

"Very."

"Well," declared the writer as he leaned back in his chair. "There's our plot. If it's not the truth, it's such a damn convincing fiction that it ought to be."

Fanny clapped her hands in satisfaction. "I think it's completely convincing!" Her expression sobered abruptly. "Although we're not just discussing the fates of paper characters, are we?"

"Hardly," affirmed Stevenson.

"So what's to be done?" she asked. "What do we do?"

The afternoon gave way to evening, and the rain moderated its assault on the glazing. The three of them entertained a number of plans, all of them based on the assumption that Scotland Yard would ultimately fail to pursue the case against Hallett. If Swanson were to surprise them, they agreed, and hauled the man in during the next twenty-four to forty-eight hours, they need do nothing more. They assumed otherwise.

Their hope was that Hallett could somehow be dissuaded from further butchery. He evidently had no fear of the police, so there was no use in threatening to do in the future what they had already fruitlessly done in the past. Somewhat more promising was the threat to go to the press with the story of Lizzy Stride; but, as Stevenson pointed out, there was no knowing if the papers would be any more willing than the police to risk turning a sizeable stone—which might then turn another even more sizeable one—under which a member of the royal family might be sequestered. Perhaps the best strategy, they concluded, was to threaten Hallett with the public exposure—by whatever means—of his own sexual inclinations and practices. Once that story was out, with whatever further revelations and consequences it yielded, the police themselves would be all the more likely to move on him. Symonds, of course, was all but certain to go down in the fray. Nevertheless, he bravely reiterated his earlier promise to take that devastating chance if all other steps failed.

They ordered supper brought up: thick beefsteaks with two bottles of fine cabernet. As they dined, Stevenson, with a wineglass in his hand and the vivid example of Walter Ferrier very much in his thoughts, commented on what could be the insuperable strength of Hallett's addiction. Even if this man could somehow be intimidated into standing down from his dreadful compulsion, who was to say that he would not resume it in the months or years to come—or simply carry it across the Channel the very next week? When Fanny insisted they must nonetheless take some definitive action or count themselves morally bankrupt, Stevenson felt there was really nothing holding them back.

"If we are resolved to proceed, then," he said, setting down his glass and pouring himself a cup of coffee, "what is our plan?"

"Well, to begin with," observed Symonds, "the confrontation must be in a private setting."

"Agreed," replied Stevenson. "Despite the potential danger of dealing with Hallett in an isolated spot."

"Surely we can enlist some others to be there," suggested Fanny. "And there are already three of us. And just one of him."

Stevenson turned to his wife with concern. "I would suggest, love, that it would be extremely unwise for the both of us to be involved."

"And why is that? Because I'm a woman?"

"Because you are Sam's mother. If something untoward were to happen, we would risk leaving him alone in the world."

"That means you think there's likely to be trouble?"

"I would certainly hope not. But it's difficult to predict."

"Well," said Fanny, "we'll see."

"Yet Fanny is right," said Symonds. "We can surely enlist some aid."

Stevenson tugged thoughtfully at his ear. "I hesitate to bring too many others into the affair. As you yourself felt earlier, no? Some compromising information is bound to be bruited about." He looked sympathetically at Symonds.

"I don't agree at all," countered Fanny. "I'd think a show of force might cow the man. Make him more inclined to go along."

Symonds frowned. "I am not at all certain that Hallett is a man to be cowed. Still, I agree it would be best for there to be four or five of us present. And perhaps some men of physical stature." He looked apologetically at Stevenson, then spread his hands to his sides as though to acknowledge his own unimposing physique.

Stevenson nodded matter-of-factly. "And location? A private room at the Athenaeum will hardly do," he noted with a smirk, "and Portman Square is out of the question. He will have a substantial household."

"You have no home in London, John?" asked Fanny.

"No longer. And, aside from that, I cannot imagine Hallett being prevailed upon to pay me a visit in any case. He has a rather low regard for me, I fear."

"That is probably to your credit," said Fanny with a gracious smile. She lit a cigarette. "So what would lure him out? What is this particular wolf's goose?"

"We certainly know what draws him to the East End," mused Stevenson. "But that seems to be very much on his own timetable. And this is not a conversation for a public thoroughfare, no matter how crepuscular."

"The establishment on Cleveland Street?" suggested Fanny.

Symonds shook his head. "I think, though, that you've likely hit on your goose."

"A boy," exclaimed Stevenson. "New boys."

Symonds nodded.

"Where?" asked the writer.

"I don't know. But we can certainly find a place."

"And how do we get him there?" asked Stevenson.

"I expect my telegraph lad might be the means," Symonds offered. "He could tell Hallett that he has learned about a new den of pleasures. Perhaps with some exotic fare. Lads from Bombay? Mormon youths from Utah?"

"There are 'special offerings' like that?" Fanny asked. "And that would attract him?"

"Yes on both scores. You can be sure."

"This would require quite a deception on the part of your young friend," observed Stevenson. "Is he up to it, do you think?"

"My boy Matthew has...a certain dramatic flair." The shade of another blush rose on Symonds's face. "One day he might well leave the telegraph office for the stage."

Stevenson looked over at Fanny, who sat there ruminating, her cigarette held up next to her face. She raised a brow, and then nodded.

"Well, then," said Stevenson, sliding to the front of his chair. "It sounds as though we have our plan. One thing remains. Or two."

"And they arc?" asked Symonds.

"Finding a location—"

"I will make that my business," declared Symonds. "Together with finding a pair or three of good men. And then?"

"And then a means of getting Hallett there."

"That's for my lad, didn't we say?"

"No. I mean a conveyance. We can't have Hallett riding there in his landau. We don't want a carriage man or his men involved."

"A hansom, then," suggested Fanny. "Engaged by John's young friend and stopping at Portman Square to pick Hallett up. Wouldn't he spring at the chance to travel anonymously in a new situation like this?"

"Brilliant," exclaimed Stevenson. He turned to Symonds. "Do you see, John? Here is the true genius of the Stevenson clan. Odysseus in a dress, conjuring up a Trojan whore."

Four days later, the details had all been attended to. The uncle of Symonds' telegraph boy was a builder, just finishing a pair of terraced houses in West Hampstead. They were not quite ready for occupancy, but one of them could easily be made to look inhabited from the outside. The street was quiet and isolated, perched on a steep rise above Shoot-Up Hill and very close to the railway. Symonds had also had luck recruiting a pair of men to augment their numbers. George Lusk's

Whitechapel Vigilance Committee met every evening at nine at The Crown in the East End. It had been a simple matter to secure the services of a couple of its members who, Symonds felt, could be counted upon to believe strongly in their cause. He had offered them a significant advanced payment, and assured their discretion as best he could through a promise of more, were they to keep their endeavor completely *sub rosa*.

That evening at ten, Stevenson and Symonds were riding in a hansom cab up Edgware Road. Each of them carried a substantial stick. Symonds's, in fact, concealed in its shaft a narrow sword.

"Here's hoping I shan't have to resort to it," he confessed, drawing the blade halfway out to show his companion.

"Are you at all practiced in its use?"

"Not particularly," shrugged Symonds. "I was rather counting on being inspired in the moment. Should the need arise." He smiled sheepishly.

"I shall trust to this." Stevenson slapped the heavy head of his cane into his gloved hand. "Although I dearly hope, as you do, that words will suffice. You are certain of your men?"

Symonds nodded. "They should be there when we arrive."

"And of your boy?"

"Matthew will not fail me."

They soon reached Shoot-Up Hill, where they turned east through a thickening fog. Gas lamps along the way glowed inside balls of gauzy vapor, the sum of them strung out like burning pearls on a long black wire. St. Elmo Mansions sat a hundred yards up the first road of the left, just short of a streetlight, its name readily legible in the backlit fanlight over the door. The bow windows on the first floor were illuminated as well. While there were no plantings as yet in the narrow front garden, the place could well pass for occupied. Stevenson nodded approval to his companion as they stepped down from the cab.

"Thank you," said Symonds to the driver. "If you could attend us around the corner there, we should be finished close to half past eleven. Let us come to you, though."

"Yes, sir," said the man, and the horse clopped off.

The two of them stepped through the gate and up to the front door.

"It should be unlocked," said Symonds. He tested the handle and the door swung inwards into an illuminated atrium. Another door, half glass, led to the tiled inner hall, where two men stood leaning against the wall.

"Batchelor. Laughton. Thank you for coming," said Symonds, walking up to them. "This is Mr. Stevenson."

The two men nodded. While it was certainly good to have the numbers, neither of them looked to be much more imposing than the average man. Batchelor was almost the writer's height and certainly of a stouter build, but there was something halting about his manner, a man to be led but not to lead. Laughton was short and markedly overweight, with the red face of a drinker and a cheery manner to match.

"Shall we go upstairs?" asked Symonds. "I see from the window that the flat is already lit."

"We done that, sir," affirmed Laughton. "We brung lamps and lucifers, just like you said."

"Excellent." He looked at his watch. "10:25. We may expect our visitors at eleven. Has either of you two gentlemen thought to bring a deck of playing cards?"

The time passed quickly enough. Stevenson stood near the window, listening for the sound of a carriage and struggling, now and again, to hide the strange yawns that came with his overwrought nerves. Symonds and Laughton, seated next to the rough table, engaged in small talk over the lantern that rested there. Batchelor meanwhile leaned against the mantle on which the other lantern glowed brightly, inspecting, then nibbling, each of his fingernails in turn.

Eleven o'clock. 11:05. 11:10. No sounds rose from the street. Stevenson looked uneasily at Symonds.

"They will be here," the latter declared with assurance. "Matthew can be trusted."

Just short of 11:15 a hollow clop of hooves echoed up the street, growing steadily louder. It had to be them. Stevenson longed to look out the window, but Symonds peered at him sternly, motioning him back against the wall.

The hansom stopped just below, its horse dancing nervously for a moment before it settled and stood still. They could hear the iron gate open and close and, a moment later, the front door. The faint sound of voices swelled to audible conversation as the inner door opened.

"It's just up the stairs, sir," said a high tenor voice graced with an affected lilt. "The first-floor flat."

"It sounds awfully damn quiet to me," growled a much deeper voice. Stevenson flinched as he recognized it. He stared over at Symonds, who had risen from his chair and grasped his stick in both hands.

"What? Is everyone asleep?" the voice went on. "Tucked up all tidy in their beds, are they?" The low laugh made Stevenson want to retch.

Footsteps echoed up the first flight of stairs to the landing and then back around.

"They're a quiet lot," said the lighter voice. "They does their work in silence. Not knowing English and all."

"No English! Now, that should be amusing."

They arrived on the first-floor and approached the door.

"It should be that for you, sir. Very amusing."

The knob turned and the door swung open. The first to enter was Symonds's friend, still wearing a telegraph company uniform under his heavy overcoat. He was small and fair with what looked to be blue eyes and features of a girlish delicacy. In the second he entered, he caught Symonds's eye and stepped quickly off to the side, making way for his companion.

Stevenson was prepared for Hallett to be a large man, but the figure that followed Matthew into the room made the door look as though it had been scaled for a lesser race. He was well over six feet tall, with massive shoulders the muscling of which was evident even beneath his heavy cloak.

"What mischief is this?" he scowled, looking around the room.

"There are no boys here." It was an exceedingly handsome face: high brow with a long, narrow nose and prominent cheekbones. The moustache was neatly trimmed, but the man's expression was the essence of arrogant cruelty. He wheeled around as Batchelor pushed the door shut and retreated a full two steps, his diffidence growing more apparent by the second. Hallett raised his stick in threat, and the man stumbled back almost to Stevenson. Hallett wheeled again, leveling his gaze at Symonds.

"You!" he hissed. "You sniveling bitch. I thought I had put you on notice to stay clear of me."

Symonds pulled his shoulders back and faced up to the man, his stick still gripped tightly in his hands.

"Well?" snarled Hallett, taking a step closer. "What exactly is afoot, then? Why are we all here?" He scanned the room with a mocking sneer. "We merry gentlemen. And then these…others." He stared with disdain at Laughton, who met his gaze with ruddy determination.

"We know who you are," said Symonds, just managing to find his voice. "And what you have been doing."

"What I have been doing? Do you mean this?" He pointed his stick at the youth. "What you have been doing as well, no? Buggering the blond boy? Fucking his lily-white arse?"

"We followed you to Whitechapel, Hallett. We saw what you did on Berner Street." Symonds pointed to Stevenson, who felt his blood chill as the man's gaze turned on him. If a serpent could have arms and legs, he thought, and wear a top hat, this would be he.

"You did, did you?" said the man, slipping into a matter-of-fact voice that was somehow more appalling than his growl. "Saw me wiv me knife an' all." He turned to broad Cockney. "Doin', who was it? Eddowes? Stride? It is *sooo* hard to remember." He turned back to Stevenson and, quite unbelievably, winked.

"You have a choice, Hallett," said Symonds, again bracing himself.

"I do? Oh, good. Do tell."

"You can stop what you've been doing. Swear on your honor to stop what you've been doing—"

"Wait, wait, wait," interrupted the man, fluttering his fingers like a pantomime fool. "Honor? You speak to me of honor?"

"I do," replied Symonds. "Do you have any?" Stevenson could hear anger mounting in his friend's voice. It didn't bode well.

"Well," replied Hallett, spreading his feet to the width of his shoulders and leaning his hands on his stick in front of him. "We shall see. Perhaps I do. And what's my other choice, then?"

"Failing your stopping, you can resign yourself to our telling the *Times* everything about you."

"They'd never print it," sneered Hallett. "I know certain *thingsssss*." He drew the word out like a whispering asp. "And they knows I knows 'em." He gazed smugly at Stevenson. "Besides," he added after a pause, "it's only whores I've been seeing to. Who cares in the least about whores?" He glanced hatefully at Matthew. The youth's lip trembled as he looked on.

"In truth," continued Symonds, "I was rather thinking of telling the *Times* about Cleveland Street. About you and me and Matthew and everyone else at Cleveland Street."

"You'd ruin yourself for this?" scowled the man, peering at Symonds in disbelief. "For a handful of common sluts?"

"I would."

"No," said the man, with a violent shake of his head. "They won't publish. They wouldn't dare."

"Then I shall go to other papers," cried Symonds. "Less hide-bound papers. And to the Church. And to Parliament. And I shall shout the news in the street myself until your family hangs its head in utter shame!"

With the rising wail of a beast, the man leapt at Symonds, ramming his hand up under his throat and dashing him back against the wall. Laughton rushed forward, grabbing the attacker by the right arm. "Batchelor!" he screamed. "Batchelor!"

As Laughton's companion approached, Hallett tossed the smaller man back and, whirling with his cane, caught him just above the eye. There was a distinct crunch and the little fellow collapsed to the floor, blood gushing from his forehead. Batchelor took one step back, then two, and then he grasped the doorknob and rushed from the room.

Symonds crouched unsteadily against the wall, his hands raised to his throat, his eyes bulging from their sockets.

Hallett turned back towards him. "Now, you art-fancying little cunt. Shall we end this little farce?" He grabbed Symonds's throat once again and, dropping his stick, concentrated all of his prodigious might on the other's neck.

Stevenson looked on, inexplicably petrified. Symonds's eyes were rolling back into his head. "Stop that!" he called out at last, shocking himself with his imperious tone. "Stop that, you fucking scunner!"

Hallett looked back over his shoulder. Sizing the writer up with an infuriating coolness, he laughed obscenely and turned again to Symonds.

It was enough. Stevenson ran the last steps to the wall and, raising his stick in both hands, he brought it down with all his might. He swung so hard that he felt his boots lift off the floor as the blow whipped down towards the neat part in the fellow's hair. The stick might well have broken, but it held fast. The crack that pulsed up through the shaft was in Hallett's head, and Stevenson was powerfully inclined to feel it again. A bitterness flooded his mouth, like a fiery draught of the strongest whisky he could imagine. Fire and spirit. Spirit and fire. He felt his tongue broach the slippery wall of his teeth. Hallett almost managed to turn again after the first blow, almost managed to see Stevenson's face contort as he struck, but he did not quite get it done before the heavy cane fell again.

The second blow was like a bellows to the first, and the flame inside Stevenson roared larger. There at its incandescent core, writhing in the scalding vapor, he fancied a tiny simulacrum of himself, half boy, half ancient man, crouched and then rising, straining, stretching out arms and legs and neck until his smoldering skin split at the extremities and a far larger, brighter, more shimmering version of himself burst forth. He scarcely had the strength or will for another blow—but there. And there again. And then it was Matthew's voice calling out behind him.

"Mr. Stevenson, sir! You've done for him. Sir! You can stop now."

Symonds was still on his feet when Stevenson thought to look back at him. His breath came in harsh pulls, but it was coming.

"John," cried Stevenson, dropping his stick on the floor. "My God! Here. Sit! Matthew. Find some water."

Matthew also found Batchelor, out in the foggy street, cowering against a low shed opposite the house. When they were back in the room, Stevenson handed the poor man a five-pound note and told him to hurry his companion in the hansom below down to the South Hampstead Police Station, there to secure medical attention. The little fellow was bleeding profusely, but he answered to his name and managed, with some assistance, to stumble down the stairs and into the cab.

Stevenson sent Matthew for the carriage waiting around the corner at the top of the street. Together with Symonds, he dragged Hallett's limp body out of the flat and down the stairs, the feet thudding down every riser. A boot snagged on one step and was pulled straight off, but the two left it lying there as they manhandled the massive body through the door and gate and onto the damp pavement. While they waited for the cab, Stevenson held his fingers against the man's neck. The pulse was strong enough and regular, but his breathing was extremely shallow. Once the hansom clattered up, they managed with Matthew's help to heave the unconscious man up onto the floor and prop him against the seat, with his knees jammed up close to his shoulders. They would have to ride with the half-doors open; but with a lap robe thrown over Hallett's head, it was unlikely anyone would notice the cab's unusual fare. Matthew assured them he could find his way safely home, and, with a curiously shy farewell, the young man made his way towards West End Lane.

They arrived at Portman Square just short of midnight. A lamp still burned outside the door of Number 43, and the ground floor windows were illuminated, so it was well that they stopped several houses short of their destination so as not to be noticed in arriving. With the driver's assistance, they pulled Hallett from the cab and dragged him along the pavement to the foot of the steps that rose to his front door. As the driver turned the hansom as quietly as he could manage, they leaned Hallett against the rail and placed his hat and stick in his lap, folding his gloved hands over top of them.

While Symonds pinned a note to his cloak, Stevenson once again checked the man's pulse. No change, despite the blood he was obviously losing. He tiptoed up to the door, half expecting it to fly open and flood the scene with light. The house remained perfectly still. Turning to be sure that Symonds was on his way back to the carriage, he reached up for the unusual knocker. It was the face of Medusa, hinged on a heavy plate of coiling serpents. Gripping it firmly, he brought it down three times, hard, despite the alarming din, then turned and raced for the cab.

Stevenson struggled hard to catch his breath as they trotted towards St. James. If he had ever felt this wrought, the memory escaped him entirely. He asked repeatedly if Symonds needed medical attention, only to be assured by his friend that he would be just fine. Stevenson resolved, still, to see him all the way to his room at the Athenaeum.

As they turned on Piccadilly, he thought of the note he and Symonds had quickly penned to leave for Hallett's discoverers. *We are returning your master,* it read. *He received no more than he deserved. It might be best to summon a doctor. Tell anyone who asks that Jack has met with Justice.*

"God in Heaven, Louis! Have you killed him?"

Fanny sat up ramrod-straight in her bed at the Grosvenor, staring aghast at her husband. Twice she had asked him to sit while he rendered his grim account of the evening. Stevenson protested that he was still far too agitated. He had managed to stop pacing the thick carpet, but he continued to sway on his feet as though the opulent suite were a square-rigger pounding through an antipodean gale.

"I doubt it. His pulse was strong enough when we left him. If his people fetched a doctor, I expect he can be saved."

"Not that he should be, the beast."

"No. No. Where are the cigarettes?"

"In the sitting room."

Stevenson disappeared for a moment, then returned to resume his pacing, a cigarette pinched between his thumb and first two fingers.

"I can't tell you how restless I feel," he said. He blew a great jet of smoke up towards the electric light fixture. "Wild." The memory of the pummeling possessed him, both the horror of it and, more strongly, the confounding elation he had felt. Somehow, it felt like an infidelity.

"Won't you please sit down?" Fanny abjured him. "Take off your overcoat at least."

He stopped his shuffling and looked down. Nodding dumbly, he slipped out of the heavy garment and tossed it on a chair.

"And Symonds?"

"Symonds will be fine. He's had a dreadful scare. He assured me, though, he's fine."

"And now?" Fanny adjusted herself against the pillows. "Will Hallett's people go to the police?"

"I don't know. If they do, I honestly don't know what they could pass along. I am quite certain we weren't seen."

"You're positive?"

"How could I be? But they wouldn't be in the habit of waiting up for him, would they? Given the hours he keeps." He walked over to the bedside table, tapped off his ashes, and resumed his perambulations. "Or *kept.*"

"God, Louis!" Fanny sighed. "Do you think they have any notion of what he's been up to? This 'gentleman' they work for?"

"Hard to say. But if they didn't before, they may well now."

"Why? How so?"

"Symonds and I left a note. To let it be known this wasn't a random thrashing. We said that Jack had come to justice. Something along that line. Any of them who knew, as his coachman must to some degree have known, are likely just to say the jig is up. Can you imagine their running off to Scotland Yard? Asking Inspector Swanson to avenge their kind employer, Jack the Ripper? Anyone smarter than a bedpost will simply let it out that their master has taken deathly ill."

"And if he'd somehow managed to keep it all a secret?"

"Our mentioning Jack might set them to thinking. And, besides, I really can't imagine they have any notion at all of who did for the bastard."

"So you say." Fanny threw off her covers and slid out of bed to don her robe. "What if Hallett recovers?"

"Which, I suppose, he may. I'm afraid I don't have much experience cracking heads."

"Thank the Lord for that. But couldn't *he* go to Scotland Yard?" Fanny adjusted her robe and slipped back into bed. "And charge you with assault? You no longer have any evidence in hand against him."

"I wouldn't if I were he."

"Because?"

Stevenson stopped again and gazed at her intently. "The police may have overlooked his depredations until now. Owing to certain political pressures. I seriously doubt, though, that they would actually take his side in an ensuing legal case." Fanny appeared to agree. "What's more, he's now substantially added to his own ledger. Criminal assault against a gentleman? There are five of us who could attest to that. Provided Laughton recovers."

"And he should?"

Stevenson nodded.

"All right," continued Fanny as she reached back to adjust her pillows. "That's reassuring." She sat there for a moment, looking about the room. "Of course, Hallett could still come after us, no? Directly. If he recovers." The anxiety in her voice was patent.

"I have thought of that. But I don't see how he could possibly know who I am. Moreover, we'll soon be in America. I worry far more about Symonds."

"Honestly," agreed Fanny. "But I suppose Hallett could find out from the police that you went to them with John."

Stevenson shook his head. "I don't think so. Again, though, their laying off the wretch to this point is a far cry from collaborating with him going forward. To assist a murderer in his revenge?" He shook his head once more. "I can't imagine Abberline or Swanson revealing my name."

"Let's hope you're right."

Stevenson stubbed out his cigarette and looked about vacantly, as though he might fetch another.

"Won't you please sit down? You're making me impossibly nervous. As if I weren't nervous enough already." Fanny slid to the side and patted the mattress next to her. "Here. Sit!"

Stevenson sighed and sat down by her pillows. He turned and leaned back against the headboard, swinging his feet up onto the counterpane. "Damn it! My boots." He grimaced at a dark smear of mud on the cream-colored fabric.

"It will wash out," said Fanny, patting his arm.

Stevenson chuckled.

"What?"

"'Out, damned spot!'" He smiled at her. "I'm just another murderous Scotsman now. Or the next best thing."

"And I suppose you think your wicked wife put you up to it?"

"No," he grinned. "You were just a co-conspirator."

"I can live with that." She slid closer. Grasping his arm in both her hands, she laid her head on his shoulder. "Are you feeling more calm?"

"No. This is likely the most exciting night I shall ever spend. Aside, of course, from my first night with you." He smiled at her again, a trifle distantly. "And, for all intents and purposes, it is a night that can never have happened."

Fanny looked at him with her eyebrows raised.

"We've entrapped a man. And then I have beaten him nearly to death."

"There is that!"

For a moment they sat in silence.

"My boots."

"What about them?"

"I really must take them off."

Fanny stared at him in amusement. "The damage is already done."

"Truly I must." He swung his legs to the floor and untied his shoes, placing them side-by-side next to the bedside table. He swung his stockinged feet back onto the soiled counterpane. "Do you think I shall ever have a biographer?" he asked after a long minute.

"Now there's a change of topic."

"Not really."

Fanny snorted dryly. "Colvin's offered to take care of your immortality. Hasn't he?"

"Colvin is a wee bit older than I."

"True."

"Healthier, though. Perhaps he'll outlast me."

Fanny squeezed his arm again, more sharply. "I don't want to hear that, Louis. Especially not on a night like this."

"A night like this." He turned towards her and kissed the top of her head. "It is truly ironic, Fanny. As I've said to Symonds, I've amused myself for weeks now thinking this whole affair was very much like something I was conjuring up in a book. With myself as the hero. And you, of course, as the heroine." He leaned over and kissed her again. "And, once more, it's a tale that can never be told."

"Well, I don't know."

"What do you mean?"

"Set it in New York City," suggested Fanny. "Call it 'The Vigilantes.'"

22

Here then, as I lay down the pen and proceed to seal up my confession, I bring the life of that unhappy Henry Jekyll to an end.

—HENRY JEKYLL

BOURNEMOUTH, NOVEMBER, 1888

On the 20th of the month, a letter arrived at Skerryvore from Symonds. It read:

My dear Stevenson,

I expect you have been following in the Times, *even back in Bournemouth, but since my last, Charles Warren has resigned as Commissioner of the Metropolitan Police after being informed by the Home Secretary that he could make no public statements without Home Office approval. I frankly do not know exactly what this means or where it might lead. It is apparent to me, however, that there is considerable alarm at the highest levels over the Whitechapel affair—more particularly, over the way the relevant hypotheses and facts are released to the collective nation. I imagine you and I are among the least surprised in all of Creation to learn this.*

It also happens that Thomas Bond, the police surgeon who is head of the CID, has further detailed the similarities between the murders of Nichols, Chapman, Stride, Eddowes, and Kelly, and has concluded that all five were, as he says, "no doubt committed by the same hand." Again, how distressing and how satisfying it is, all at once, to be so much in the know.

Word has finally been released at my club that our man has, "tragically," suffered a "massive stroke" and is now unable either to walk or to speak. The prognosis, we are told, is not sanguine, and we have been invited to include the poor chap and his extended family in our thoughts and prayers!!! You can imagine how I felt upon receiving the word in an official notice. I of course have no way of knowing if his abilities to communicate and perambulate are, indeed, so severely affected. I am hardly planning a visit to his residence in order to verify.

I hope and trust, dear Louis, that you are at peace with our actions. I myself most certainly am. We must not, as you said, be mere bystanders in life, even when our prospects for influencing the course of things may seem slight. I worry, of course, in those dark hours before dawn that our fellow will recover; and that he will find some way of exacting some terrible kind of vengeance against his assailants. But, in the bright light of day, I truly believe, as strongly as I hope, that this demonic scourge has been brought to an end. There has been no further depredation in Whitechapel and Spitalfields, and until that heartening lack of news is supplanted by something more dire, I choose to think that we are well and finally rid of our Mr. H.! I have taken the precaution, however, of engaging my dear Matthew as a valet and amanuensis, feeling that he will inevitably be safer with me in Davos and Venice than here in London. How Janet will treat this news, I fear I cannot predict, but do this I must.

Again, I can well believe you are following the papers with the same anxious eyes as I. I will, however, be in immediate touch if anything comes to me by other channels. For the nonce, may you rest easily in the confidence that, in serving this city and country as bravely and admirably as you have done, you have also served

Your most affectionate and appreciative friend,

J. A. Symonds

"What *will* Janet say, I wonder?" asked Fanny as she set the letter down and resumed her handiwork. For days she had been knitting mufflers for the upcoming Atlantic crossing. She had just finished Sam's, in his old school colors, and was starting Stevenson's—in solid burgundy, in case, she teased him, a rough crossing led him to dribble more wine than usual.

"That likely depends on what Symonds tells her," Stevenson replied, "and how he and Matthew behave in her company. Perhaps also on how much she wants—or is prepared—to know."

"It's hard for me to believe she has no inkling. Living with him all these years."

"They are so often apart," observed Stevenson. "Symonds travels constantly. I expect he is away from their home as often as he's there."

"Still, don't you suppose they sleep together? Don't you suppose she could tell if his heart wasn't in it?"

"I don't know. Perhaps you should write to her and ask."

Fanny seemed to cast about for an arch retort, but she held her tongue. Moments passed, her needles clicking rhythmically away, before she spoke again.

"You don't have any dark secrets, do you, Louis? Like Symonds's? Things I don't already know about?"

Stevenson's gut lifted a trifle and he glanced over at his wife. Fanny looked at him with a measure of concern.

"It seems late in our marriage to be asking such a trenchant question," he responded with a grin. "Besides, aren't you underestimating your formidable intuition? Surely, my weird woman knows and sees all."

She paused in her knitting. "But you're so endlessly inventive, Louis. I never know one day to the next what new passions or depravities you might be coming up with."

"New passions and depravities, you say?"

"Yes."

"Well, Pig. I think I can honestly say there are none."

"You *think* you can?"

"There are none. Which is not to say that my various passions and depravities of long standing don't remain hale and hearty."

"Your addictions to the grape and tobacco leaf foremost among them," she observed with a droll squint.

"I haven't had a glass of claret since last evening—and not a single cigarette for the last half-hour. Moreover, rather than addictions, I much prefer to call these things intense and consuming tastes."

"Consuming tastes," she repeated thoughtfully. "Of course." Fanny returned to her knitting for some time before she looked up again.

"Tell me this, Louis," she said. "Honestly. How consuming a taste do you think you have for the transport of rage?"

The baldness of the question disarmed him. Stevenson felt his pulse quicken. "And this," he said with an uneasy grin, "from someone of your temper?"

Fanny smiled fleetingly, then sobered once more. "I can't stop thinking about what you did to Hallett." She dropped her hands into her lap. "And Symonds's little friend having to tell you to stop. Lord knows I've often enough seen you angry. But I'd never known you to club a man unconscious with a walking stick."

"No." Stevenson drew a deep breath. "No more than I. Generally I curse and throw things, do I not?"

Fanny stared hard, clearly determined to stay on the scent. "Please don't take my questions as a criticism, dearest. There was hardly an option. He was strangling Symonds, for God's sake. And he'd almost killed that other poor man." She paused.

"But?"

"But nothing. I suppose I'm just curious how it feels to have done what you did. How it felt doing it. Maybe how it feels now."

"Do you think that is something a wife ought to know?"

"Do you think it's something a wife shouldn't know?"

Stevenson paused for a moment, then shrugged in weary resignation. How uncannily could Fanny, time and again, bear in on a worry or a raw nerve.

"No," he responded at last. "Fair questions." He took in another great breath and let it out slowly. "To be honest, Pig, it was horrid. Frightening as well, bashing in another man's head the way I seem to have done. Even a man like Hallett. I can still feel it in my hand. Fortunately, he didn't bleed like Laughton. I must say, though, I felt completely justified thrashing the bastard. And it wasn't anything Cummy ever taught me about, you know. Or father. The codes of law and respectability have wretched little to say about how much head-bashing a man is entitled to do on his own righteous initiative. Perhaps *obliged* to do. I had to find my own way up there."

"You say righteous initiative." Fanny's brow arched inquisitorily. "There's a certain pleasure to be had in righteousness, no?"

"So…?"

"Was there pleasure to be had in clubbing the man, Louis?" Fanny's gaze pierced him.

"Not exactly pleasure." Was that completely honest? Perhaps it was. The fire of his arousal had been of an entirely different sort than lust or luxury, more something he imagined William Wallace might have felt at Stirling Bridge. "But just cause and a chance to enact it did make for a heady brew."

"You make it sound intoxicating."

"Is there any surprise there? Given my predilections?" He grinned uneasily, adjusting himself in his chair. "Your phrase was apt, though. 'The transport of rage.'"

Fanny's brow knit with obvious concern. "It's as though you turned into Hyde. Bludgeoning old Carew. How did you say it? 'Tasting delight…?'"

"'From every blow.' I know. I can scarcely believe that I knew how to write that scene at the time I did. Before I joined the ranks of dedicated head-bashers."

"But you did write it."

"I did."

"So it must always have been in you, mustn't it?"

Stevenson rose and walked over to her. He bent and kissed her gently on the part of her hair. "I believe I might have said it to you back then. When my ill-fated draft was still burning on the grate. 'We write what we know.'" Or had he said that to Coggie?

Fanny looked up at him, eyes wide. "Thank you, Louis."

"What for?"

"For your candor."

"I admit it's only what any husband owes to his wife. Nothing less."

Fanny nodded quietly. "Well," she said after a moment. "I suppose this all leads us to an interesting realization."

"That being?"

"That for all of our talk about your taking inspiration from Ferrier, Jekyll is far less a version of Ferrier than he is of you." She peered at her husband for his reaction.

"Walter was a sot, bless his tortured soul," volunteered Stevenson after a moment. "But he was one of the gentlest souls I ever met."

Fanny's squint returned. "And you?"

"You have me, Pig. Taken and bound. I may have figured Hyde as a raging young man when, in actual fact, he is the perfect embodiment of Old Man Virulent." He looked at her squarely. "I'm almost surprised you've never charged me with that."

"It may have occurred to me," she admitted with a sigh. "But we had to get on."

"We did. And we do."

"And you feel you're getting on with yourself."

"I do. As I said."

Fanny nodded slowly, her expression an amalgam of confirmation and lingering concern. How striking it was, thought Stevenson, that she had managed to convince him there was no place in respectable fiction for the side of his nature that had led him to Valentine's bedside—yet that, as a consequence, Hyde had become the avatar of another part of himself, equally unregenerate but, for him at least, considerably more unsettling for him to recognize. *Of course I can stop,* he recalled thinking as he stood over Hallett's body with Matthew's gentle entreaty still echoing in his ears and his bloody stick still firmly in hand. *Of course.*

"Well, Louis. What now?"

"What now?" Stevenson reached out to squeeze her knee. "Don't worry, Pig. I like to think it was all just a useful boiling up of my ancient Highland blood. Rob Roy come back to life in a moment of desperate need. Symonds is alive, no? If I had just stood there—"

"I know. I do."

"And I'm unlikely ever again to be in a similar fix."

"Of course."

"And if we are ever again served, perchance, a corked bottle of wine…I swear I won't club the poor sommelier to death."

"I sincerely hope not. That would truly make us social pariahs. Even in America."

With a look of tolerable satisfaction, Fanny returned to her knitting—leaving Stevenson to ponder, once again, what he hoped were the unmistakable differences between Hallett and himself when it came to the pleasures of brutality.

In the weeks that followed, Fanny paid a visit to the doctor, convinced that the lump in her breast had increased in size. Doctor Barrett, who kept a surgery just their side of the town center, was an older man with a reputation for brilliant diagnoses, a reassuring bedside manner, and an unmatched taste for French vintages. Stevenson had in fact first met him in the shop of Bournemouth's preeminent wine merchants, where they had engaged in a pleasant and informed conversation about the relative virtues of Pauillac and Margaux. After palpating Fanny's lump, the doctor declared that it was almost certainly nothing but a small cyst. He cheerfully assembled a rather imposing hypodermic and, after asking Fanny to look the other way and relax as much as possible, skillfully jabbed the long needle right into the center of the thing. Fanny let out a deafening yowl, thereby pitching Stevenson, who was sitting anxiously just outside the door of the examination room, into a fit of sickening recollection. The fluid that the doctor aspirated, though, was consistent with his initial diagnosis, and the lump itself was scarcely detectable afterward. By the time Fanny had dressed and rejoined her husband in the waiting room, another imposing cloud had lifted from the family spirits.

Unfortunately, that very night, the brownies obliged the dreaming Stevenson to stand powerlessly by as the doctor sliced off both of Fanny's breasts, laying them out on the table precisely the way he imagined the Kelly woman's to have been. True, the managers of his midnight theater had never been in the habit of constructing moral fables, but Stevenson could not help but conclude that they were trying their hand at something simple but edifying, concerning how quickly she and others he loved might any day be taken from him.

In any case, he awoke to discover with profound relief that his feisty little American helpmeet lay there in bed beside him, very much alive, snoring, and whole.

Stevenson's mother finally made her way to Bournemouth at the end of the month. After her first meal at Skerryvore, she announced that she had seldom dined more deliciously. When Margaret subsequently offered to pay for their travel to America provided Valentine accompied them, Fanny immediately booked passage for the entire household on the *Ludgate Hill,* a new steamer of 4,000 tonnes that offered surprisingly favorable rates on its next crossing—probably, Fanny surmised, because it was scheduled to sail for New York on Christmas Morning.

Sam was able to leave school a day earlier than expected, and he hoped to spend the night with a friend in London before traveling down to Bournemouth. Stevenson and Fanny seized the chance to travel up to the capital to say their farewells to Colvin and Fanny Sitwell, who would be out of town the week they sailed. The four of them shared a fine meal at Verey's, with Stevenson and Colvin sparring comically for the honor of paying the bill. The latter, claiming seniority, eventually prevailed; Stevenson promised, in return, that he would do his best to lead an especially exciting life across the waters, so as to make Colvin's proposed biography all the more gripping and profitable for its scribe. Fanny promised in turn to contribute to the adventures in any way she could, although she observed, with a wink at her husband, that the things a writer might actually *do* in life could surely never measure up to the things he might conjure up in his fiction.

At eleven the following morning, the couple stood waiting in the huge concourse of Waterloo Station. Fanny stared anxiously at the clock suspended over the platforms.

"We're planning on the 11:20, aren't we?" she asked, fiddling with the buttons on her overcoat.

"We are."

"Where do you suppose he is? Why is he late?"

"Don't fuss, Pig. I am certain he'll be here. And if he's delayed, we can always catch the next."

"I suppose." She peered nervously into her handbag and extracted a handkerchief. She was about to blow her nose when she spied her son coming through the main entrance, two huge bags in hand. "There he is!" she cried, scuttling towards him in a frenzy of anticipation. Stevenson bent to pick up her handkerchief and followed her over to the strapping young man, whom she held crushed in a prolonged embrace. He was blushing, but his complexion looked considerably improved.

"Goodness, Sam," exclaimed Stevenson, wincing at the strength of the young man's handgrip. "You've grown even more. I suppose we must now prepare to be eaten out of house and home."

"I shall be perfectly happy with a side of beef a day," Sam replied with a grin. "For breakfast. And, Louis," he added, looking his stepfather straight in the eye with an assertiveness that was new to him. "I'd like to be called Lloyd from now on. If you would."

"Lloyd!" replied Stevenson, trying it on for size. "Well—of course. Lloyd you shall be."

"Samuel Osbourne's the name of some fellow or other in America."

Stevenson laughed uncertainly. "But we're going to America."

"True enough," said the lad. "But I'm not going back there as his son, Lou. I'm going back as yours."

"So, was it hard leaving school?" asked Fanny, once they had settled themselves on the train. There were only the three of them in the first-class compartment. Lloyd sat across from them, flanked by his over-stuffed bags.

"Not especially. I'll miss Richard. And some of the others on my rugby side."

"Of course," said his mother. "Sports bring people together, don't they? At least people who get to play sports. Men, that is." She leered at the two of them in affected resentment.

"They do. I suppose it's like Lou and me playing at war all those times." He looked warmly at his stepfather.

"Sport and war," observed Stevenson, suddenly wistful. "Purposeful violence. They say there's nothing like sport and war for forging bands of brothers. 'For he today that sheds his blood with me shall be my brother.'"

"We read that in school!" Lloyd exclaimed. "That's Henry V speaking to his men before Agincourt. That speech gives me chills."

Stevenson nodded. "It's one of the best. A speech one might sell one's soul to have written. My kingdom for lines such as those!"

"You males of the species," scowled Fanny. "I swear you love each other more than you love us."

"Some of the boys at school, anyway," declared Lloyd with a snigger.

"Oh?" replied Fanny.

"You know. The prissy ones. The tennis players. The faggers. I surely won't miss them at all."

"Did they ever bother you?" asked Stevenson.

"What do you mean? Did any of them ever send me notes or something like that? Or poems?" He laughed again, but less comfortably.

"Well, I don't know," replied Stevenson. "I suppose I just wondered if any of them ever did anything to make you feel uneasy."

"Aside from just being the way they are?"

"I suppose."

"Well, no. Not that they'd dare."

"I see," said Stevenson.

For a few moments they sat there quietly, jostled softly from side to side by the undulations of the rails.

"Why did you ask me that, Lou?" said Lloyd at last. "Weren't there boys like that at your schools?"

"Most definitely," Stevenson replied. "Not that it was always easy to know."

"No. It's not," agreed Lloyd. "There was a chap on our rugby side, in fact, who turned out to have a crush on Richard. A bloody big bloke, too. One of the props."

"Did Richard know it?" Fanny leapt in to ask.

"He did. The fellow sent him a poem."

"What did Richard do?" asked his mother.

Lloyd laughed.

"What?" Fanny persisted.

"He talked to him one day out on the pitch after practice. He said it was an excellent poem but that he had a girlfriend back in London. Then the fellow claimed, of course, that Richard had misunderstood everything. But he hadn't."

"Goodness," exclaimed Fanny.

"I know. I couldn't believe Richard told him it was a good poem. I probably would have bloodied the fellow's nose, if I'd even let myself be alone with him."

"Really?" asked Stevenson.

"Well, wouldn't you? I know you're not exactly a pugilist," the boy added with a restive grin, "but still."

"I suppose many young men would feel the way you did, Sam," conceded Stevenson. "Excuse me! Lloyd!" He smiled apologetically. "Perhaps I would have as well. At your age."

"Would have? Would you feel any differently now?"

"Quite differently, I think. Although it has been years since I had a *tête-à-tête* of any sort out on a rugby pitch."

"Good old Lou," laughed Lloyd. "How I've missed your wit."

"Well, I'm afraid you're in for several months of it now."

"I'm more than ready."

"We are in for such a lively time," declared Fanny, relaxing visibly.

Stevenson leaned his head back against the upholstered bench, staring up at the ceiling of the compartment. "You mentioned our old war games a moment ago. Do you remember how you always insisted that they turn out in line with the historical facts?"

"Of course I do."

"Would you still feel that way?"

"I suppose."

Stevenson eyed him warmly.

"Do you think I shouldn't?" asked the boy.

"I have had an experience or two lately," Stevenson offered in response, "that have led me to believe that we can sometimes influence the way significant matters unfold far more consequentially than we ever thought we could."

"In what way?"

"It's actually part and parcel with what I was just saying about how one's thoughts evolve as one moves through life. I don't know that this is just the right time to go into particulars." He looked over at Fanny, who nodded. "Suffice it to say that there are times to stand back and accept things. Established attitudes or situations we are not particularly able to change. I nonetheless believe there are other times when we have to summon up a little more boldness and faith. Shape our collective destinies."

"You remind me of Valentine," chuckled Lloyd.

"How so?"

"She used to say it might be pleasant to change history. Don't you remember?"

"Well," said Stevenson. "Valentine turns out to be quite a wise woman."

"My, but we're getting philosophical," observed Fanny. She stared out the window and then wiped with her handkerchief at the border of an expansive patch of frost. "Look," she said, pointing to the shape. "It's a pistol!"

Newport, R.I., U.S.A. 20 January, 1889

My dear Symonds,

So, long it went excellent well, and I have had a time I am glad to have had. Ere we cast ourselves upon the waters, my erstwhile Edinburgh nursemaid, dear old Cummy, braved the Despicable City to bid her boy farewell. She came down with Ferrier's saintly sister, Elizabeth, and James even surprised us on the quay at Tilbury, with a case of champagne in tow. Medicinal comforts for the voyage, he proclaimed. Our first port of call was Le Havre, where we took on the most unlikely consignment of apes, cows, and over one hundred horses! Fanny, as you can imagine, was apoplectic; Lloyd (as Sam now calls himself) was consummately charmed. Small wonder the rates The Dear One had been able to obtain were so very reasonable!

O it was lovely on our stable-ship, chock full of stallions; she rolled heartily, rolled some of the fittings out of our stateroom, and I think a more dangerous cruise it would be hard to imagine. But we enjoyed it to the mast head, all but Fanny; and even she perhaps a little. When we got in, we had run out of beer, stout, curaçao, soda-water, water, fresh meat and (almost) of biscuit. But it was a thousandfold pleasanter than a great big Birmingham liner like a new hotel; and we liked the officers, and made friends with the quartermasters, and I (at least) made a friend of a baboon whose embraces have pretty near cost me a coat.

Really enjoying my life, in sum. There is nothing like being at sea, after all. And O why have I allowed myself to rot so long on land? My reception here was idiotic to the last degree; if Jesus Christ came, they would make less fuss. The pilot who took us into New York Harbor somehow heard I was on board, and refused to leave the ship until he had met the man who had inspired the play that has somehow taken Broadway by storm. It is very silly and not pleasant, except where humor enters; and I confess the poor interviewer lads pleased me.

As you can imagine, I have continued to give much thought to our past adventures and was reassured to find in the American press no fresh news of our man. It has been hellish difficult accepting that I shall likely never know if my shilling shocker played any role in inspiring the late depravities. I sometimes dream of stealing into the blighter's house to look for a certain theatre receipt, that or a certain slender volume in soft covers. Had our discourse been more civil that wild night in West Hampstead, perhaps I might have asked him directly. Yet my dilemma nicely captures, does it not?, the difference between the cask-of-all-answers that is fiction's to tap and the damned ambiguities of life itself. (Though bless ambiguities, really, in the end!) While I continue to regret having loosed my wretched Hyde upon the world, you and I have at least mopped up some of his loathsome offal.

I will be sure to let you know how we get on in Newport, curious specimens that we are in the peripatetic little ménage I call Family.

Love to Janet and my kindest regards to your brave young friend.

Yours ever,

R. L. S.

Author's Note

The strict historicist in Lloyd Osbourne (as we must now call him) might be pleased with a good portion of what you have just finished reading. It is very much in line with what we know of Stevenson's life—as reflected, for example, in the very different (but each of them very useful) biographies of Ian Bell, Frank McLynn, and Claire Harman. Anyone interested in the writer will count it a great blessing that he left behind, along with a number of personal sketches and memoirs, eight volumes' worth of letters, wonderfully presented in the Yale edition of Bradford Booth and Ernest Mehew. While I have necessarily taken great liberties putting spoken words into the mouth of one of Victorian Britain's most lively conversationalists, many of the letters included here are direct or slightly edited transcripts of Stevenson's actual correspondence—as is Symonds's first letter to the author regarding *Jekyll and Hyde*. It seems only fair to have let these people speak for themselves where their doing so felt reasonable and appropriate. Experienced readers of Stevenson will also notice, beyond the selections from *Strange Case of Dr. Jekyll and Mr. Hyde* that head each chapter, numerous images and phrases are borrowed from his writings. All of the poems cited here, as well, are from Stevenson's pen; most may be found amongst the timelessly charming pages of *A Child's Garden of Verses*. Finally, the account of Stevenson's unpublishable Oedipal reverie is a close transcription of one portion of his remarkable "Chapter on Dreams."

This fiction, to the extent that it is a fiction, grew out of a scholarly project I undertook a dozen or so years back, tracing the social and biographical origins of Stevenson's little shilling shocker. The account I was able to render there, I felt, did not do justice to a profound literary-historical irony: that a story written in part as an act of moral contrition should, after one permutation, have been blamed for inspiring one of the most horrific series of crimes in European history. It is that singular misalignment between an author's intentions and his possible impact that has driven this effort.

I have, of course, taken some liberties with the historical record. Stevenson was in actual fact already in the United States by the time the Ripper began his macabre program. As you are now well aware, my fictional Stevenson delays his family's emigration to America and remains in England in order to see the Symonds/Hallett affair through to the end. If he seems in this a cousin to Sherlock Holmes—or perhaps, at those specific times when Symonds is taking the initiative, more to Dr. Watson—my apologies. My own *fin de siècle*-loving brownies seem to have taken me irresistibly in that direction.

I should say that when Stevenson resolves in these pages to move beyond writing about life to actually *doing* things that make a tangible difference, he is mirroring a pattern that became well established towards the end of the real author's days. The most notable of many examples found Stevenson, during his last years, becoming what we would now call a political activist, boldly advocating for the native residents of Samoa, the island on which he spent the last four years of his life. Those Europeans who loved his writing found this real world involvement to be a damaging distraction. Most famously, Oscar Wilde declared, "I see that romantic surroundings are the worst surroundings possible for a romantic writer. In Gower Street Stevenson could have written a new *Trois Mousquetaires*. In Samoa he wrote letters to the *Times* about Germans."

Stevenson did not, however, abandon his fiction in Samoa, and one of the most compelling narratives that he wrote there—*The Beach of*

Falesá—offers a striking model of a bystander to evil who ultimately risks everything to bring it to an end. The novella's protagonist, Wiltshire, is a Cockney trader rather than a Scotsman of letters, but his ultimate confrontation with the "gentleman villain," Case, shows Stevenson exploring in a fable the heroic virtue of setting aside quotidian business and literally coming to grips with a darkness. My brownies are thoroughly acquainted with Case and *The Beach*, since I have taught the book multiple times, and I strongly suspect that this had something to do both with my invention of Hallett and with our heroes' subduing of the man. As for the possible creative influence of Wiltshire, I hope Stevenson would be pleased to be shown in these pages displaying some of the pluck and commitment of one of his more complex and under-appreciated protagonists. We know he loved to *play,* at least, at war.

So, in a bid to make the long and involved history of *Jekyll and Hyde* even more interesting, I have sometimes taken real liberties with fact—albeit (I hope) in ways that reflect some well-established patterns in Stevenson's later life and writings. Virtually everything you have read here up through Stevenson's dismay at the charges brought against the play (in other words, Parts One and Two) is in line with broadly documented fact. All of the details of Saucy Jack's crimes, as well, are historical, with the newspaper accounts drawn directly from the *Times* of London.

While Stevenson and Symonds were indeed longtime friends, their meetings in London and their interventions in the Ripper investigations are complete fabrications. My hope, though, is that they are both compelling and plausible enough that I may be forgiven for distorting the true record.

Finally, I believe it is already abundantly clear that Thomas Hallett is invented out of whole cloth, as is the shipping family of which he was the heir. Unfortunately—or perhaps fortunately—the historical figure for whom he stands in is now no more substantial than last week's nightmare. We can only hope that, in some no-longer-documentable pattern of history, he was nonetheless held rigorously accountable for his crimes.

Acknowledgments

Thanks are due, above all, to my family, who patiently endured my decades-long obsession with Stevenson and his most riveting tale, offering support and encouragement when both were sorely needed. My wife Dottie, daughter Abby, and son Dan were with me all the way, from that endless 2002 slog up a sodden Samoan mountainside to stand by Stevenson's grave, through a memorable fireside evening a dozen years later when I read them a draft of the Lizzie Stride chapter and they smiled approval over glasses of mulled wine, to their indispensable last-minute advice on the shape and tone of the whole. Thanks, too, to Dickinson College, for affording me the time to work on the first iteration of the book. Among my colleagues there, Susan Perabo helped me more than she probably knows. Her extraordinariness as a writer is matched only by her ability to inspire and improve the writing of others.

Among the world's avid preservers of the Stevenson legacy, John Macfie of Edinburgh's Stevenson Club deserves special thanks for his vital help in securing permissions for this volume. With his wife Felicitas, he also hosted the Reeds several years back at 17 Heriot Row, where he shared some his vast knowledge of the writer's city, family, and boyhood home over serial glasses of Prosecco that RLS himself would have relished.

To Eric Kampmann at Beaufort Books I owe profound thanks for boldly and generously taking on a project that, as so often happens, was peddled at many doors before anyone really deigned to open up and chat. Megan Trank has been wonderful to work with as Beaufort's Managing Editor—prompt, judicious, and efficient—and I could not have found a better reader than James Carpenter to help me kill the many darlings that, diverting as they were to explore, were definitely sidetracks off the mainline that the narrative needed to take.

Finally, boundless thanks to my mother, Betsy Mook Reed. My father and sister were the other academics in the family, but it was she whose lifelong love of classic tales of adventure first introduced me to *Treasure Island*. I can still hear her bedtime readings in all of the requisite voices—boy, peg-legged cook, and parrot. The echoes, here, of other Stevensonian voices are undoubtedly owing to her.